Nobody's princess

Also by Sarah Hegger

Nobody's Fool

Nobody's Angel

Published by Kensington Publishing Corporation

Nobody's princess

SARAH HEGGER

ZEBRA BOOKS
KENSINGTON PUBLISHING CORP.
http://www.kensingtonbooks.com

ZEBRA BOOKS are published by

Kensington Publishing Corp.
119 West 40th Street
New York, NY 10018

All Kensington titles, imprints, and distributed lines are available at special quantity discounts for bulk purchases for sales
promotion, premiums, fund-raising, educational, or institu-
tional use.

Special book excerpts or customized printings can also be
created to fit specific needs. For details, write or phone the
office of the Kensington Sales Manager: Attn.: Sales Department. Kensington Publishing Corp., 119 West 40th Street,
New York, NY 10018. Phone: 1-800-221-2647.

Zebra and the Z logo Reg. U.S. Pat. & TM Off.

First Printing: March 2016
ISBN-13: 978-1-4201-3743-9
ISBN-10: 1-4201-3743-3

eISBN-13: 978-1-4201-3744-6
eISBN-10: 1-4201-3744-1

10 9 8 7 6 5 4 3 2 1

Printed in the United States of America

To Kim Handysides,
for all the friendship,
support,
and love you give so freely.

ACKNOWLEDGMENTS

This book took a lot of effort by a few very special people. Thanks to Rhenna Morgan for keeping the spirit of Penny alive. To my long-suffering editor, Esi Sogah, for not yelling at me when I so clearly deserved it. And to the team at Kensington, who work so hard to bring my words to readers. Also, to the members of the Sarah Hegger Collective—you guys are why I keep writing.

Chapter One

Tiffany needed a man, about six-two with blond hair and a tan. Right now, or life as she knew it was over. *Teeny* exaggeration, but she was desperate for one white male, twentysomething, handsome, light eyed, and ripped and cut like every girl's dirty dream.

In Chicago, a city of a shade over 2.7 million people, 48 percent of them male, and 31 percent of them white, how hard could that be? Of course, to accurately calculate the chances she'd need to break that down into how many of the male residents were white and between the ages of twenty-five and thirty-five. If she could get five seconds to write this all down in her book, she could do it.

"Did you get hold of the casting agent?" Piers fussed with his camera, his face already the telltale pink prefacing a meltdown. Dear God, not that. Piers could throw a time-chewing tantrum to rival a toddler. Time was not her friend today.

"No." Tiffany snapped her book shut and hit Redial. She kept Piers in her peripheral vision. *Please, let the woman be there.* Piers was going to go nuclear any second now. If Piers lost it, the shoot would run over. Her new life started in a little under three hours and she couldn't be late for that.

"Hi, you've reached the voice mail o—"

"Shit." Tiffany ended the call. She refused to let this stop her. If necessary, she'd march outside and drag the next blond man in here, but she was going on her date. Tonight. "I'll keep trying." She smiled apologetically at Piers. As if that would stop a meltdown. *Not.* "Okay, let's get the rest of you ready."

It was so unfair, she had all the other models—Asian, black, Hispanic, Indian, and Franco, who was Italian, but apparently had the bone structure and sleek, long hair to pass for Native American. Tiffany wasn't sure his real name was Franco. Maybe he wasn't even Italian.

"Tiffany?" Piers tapped his foot impatiently.

She spun toward the cluster of hotness lounging about, looking effortlessly gorgeous. Except that much perfect took serious work. The fresh bagels she'd fetched that morning lay untouched—two hundred and fifty calories per bagel, another fifty for the cream cheese. She moved the bagel plate to the other side of a dish of strawberries. One dish aligned to the right of the cream cheese, another to the left. She snatched up a strawberry and popped it in her mouth. Four calories. You had to love numbers.

The models shifted to their feet in a tidal wave of undulating muscle. Pumped up, made up, and ready to shoot. Six-two, six-four, six-one—no, the order didn't work for her. Tallest to shortest or the other way around would be better. Maybe even tallest in the middle and descending in height order on either side. If Piers ever asked her opinion, she would tell him so. This was not her job, however. Her job was gofer, as in go for this and go for that. Shut your mouth, do as you're told, and show up looking fabulous. She took a deep breath. Two hours and fifty-five minutes to the launch of New Tiffany.

"Give me beautiful, darlings." Piers glanced up from his

camera. "Get me that casting agent," he yelled at her. "And for Christ's sake get them oiled down." Piers winked at the models. Flirting with the "meat" was his sole prerogative. "I need muscle. Big, shiny, I want to lick it muscle."

Didn't they all. Tiffany patted the side pocket of her Dolce & Gabbana tote, reassuring herself that her book was safe and waiting for her.

She hit Redial with one hand and grabbed the bottle of body oil with the other. God, she'd stroked more abs than any girl could fantasize about. Pretty much her only job perk. Six models, each with a six-pack, did that make thirty-six abs or eighteen? It would depend on whether you considered one ridge of muscle as consisting of two separate . . .

"Lower," Franco purred in her ear.

"Oh, puh-lease." Tyrone grabbed the bottle from her and oiled himself. "There's nothing down there, sister." He rolled his eyes at Tiffany dramatically. "And believe me, I've looked. Now, if you really want to—"

She slapped a handful of oil onto the nearest corrugated stomach. Her gaze drifted to the hot pink corner of her book peeking over the edge of the tote, the abs calculation forming in her head. She needed to write it down before she forgot. A tiny moment of sanity hovered, right there between those special pages. Later.

"Time?" Piers shouted.

Tiffany checked her phone. *Shit.* "Two forty," she called back and braced for impact.

"Christ on a stick, Tiffany." Piers started his meltdown. Tiffany counted slowly backward. *Five, four, three, two, one, and*—"Fucking twenty to fucking two. Shit. Fuck. Bum. Bugger. Willy. Dick."

The models suppressed a snicker or two. They couldn't help it. With his British accent, it never sounded that bad when Piers swore. It sounded sort of cute. The cuteness wore off fast, and after seven years of working for Piers it wasn't even mildly amusing.

"Get that silly cunt from casting on the motherfucking phone and ask her where my fucking white boy is. Tell her to get his pale arse down here or he will never work in this motherfucking cesspit of a fucking fuck-nose shitting town again."

"Impressive," one of the models murmured beneath his breath. This must be his first Piers shoot.

"He's just getting started." Tiffany grabbed the oil and smeared. The waves of rage emanating from Piers almost made her hands shake. She tried the casting agent again. Shit, she had only booked the studio for another two hours and fifty minutes. Her schedule was sliding straight into the toilet.

"Adjust the package on . . ." Piers clicked his fingers as he came up blank on the name. "Um . . . number two."

"Tyrone," number two helpfully supplied.

Heat crawled over Tiffany's face. Her gaze dropped to the bulge of Tyrone's crotch. Tyrone spread his arms out and grinned. "Go ahead."

Sinfully beautiful, and Tyrone knew it. She couldn't resist grinning right back. Such a pity he was gay. And she was in a steady relationship with the most wonderful man. In. The. World. Everybody said so. Ryan was perfect. Maybe not exciting, but she'd had exciting, and look how that had ended up? Disaster. No, Ryan was the one for her. No more wild, crazy rides. Her phone buzzed in her hand.

"Is that the casting agent?" Piers demanded.

"No." Tiffany glared as Lola's name lit up her screen. The woman's timing couldn't suck more. As much as she needed to speak to Lola—and she really, really needed to speak to her—she didn't want to answer the call now. Five days she'd waited for Lola to call back. Lola pretty much ignored every call she didn't feel like taking. Conversely, when Lola wanted to speak to you, she wanted it now and would blow up your phone until she got hold of you.

She hit Ignore and slipped the phone into her pocket. Why today of all days? It must be some kind of cosmic joke. Could you calculate coincidence? You must be able to. Nearly everything broke down to numbers in the end. Her gaze strayed toward the tote again. Her book seemed to shimmer and pulse for attention. Perhaps she could just quickly . . .

"Hi, I'm looking for Tiffany?" A deep voice spoke from behind her.

Tiffany whirled on her four-inch heels and looked up. And up some more. *Oh, thank you, sweet Jesus.* Her white boy was here and he was gorgeous. His blond hair was cropped close to his scalp. It brought all your attention straight to that face. And what a face. You could break rocks on that jawline. The straight blade of his nose rescued him from pretty, but the mouth beneath it curved full and etched, made for nibbling on.

Tiffany did a quick, happy two-step. He even had beautiful blue eyes. He might be a shade on the tall side, but they could fake that a bit. Not as young as she'd first thought, but makeup would fix that. Two vertical lines between his eyebrows gave off a sort of *don't mess with me* vibe. She beamed at him. "You're perfect."

He raised an eyebrow, and returned her smile cautiously.

Oh, yes, yes, yes. He had one of those smiles, all innocent on the outside until you looked into those bad-boy eyes. Scrap the Botox, those laugh lines were smoking hot. She did a quick body scan. *Nice. Very nice.* If he looked as good out of that tight T-shirt as he did in it. Seriously, where had this boy been hiding himself?

Tiffany patted the sort of forearm that could be best friends with a jackhammer, and mentally forgave the casting agent. "Okay." She stretched her fingers to capacity to grip his arm. Wow! And this from a girl who worked with wow every day. "We are going to have to hurry. Strip and let's get you all pumped up."

"Where the hell have you been?" Piers snarled. "Your call time was one thirty."

Blondie opened his mouth to reply. Tiffany spun him toward makeup. No good arguing with Piers when he was on a tear. A waste of time they didn't have. Things were turning around. The white boy was here, and he was gorgeous. The shoot would finish on time, and then she could deal with Lola. And still have time to prepare herself for *the night*.

Blondie stood there giving the other models a thorough eye scan. Gay. What a shame. She shook her head at herself. What did it matter? She was practically an engaged woman.

Blondie hovered at her side.

Clichés sucked, but some of these boys had no brain beneath all that brawn. Hooking her hands beneath the hem of his T-shirt, she tugged. "You have to take this off for makeup."

"Are you taking my clothes off?" Blondie folded his huge paws around hers and stopped her. He had a great voice, like hot chocolate laced with rum. The sort of voice that would do great bedtime stories.

She hauled back on her thought path. "You have to strip."

He looked right at her. Not past her or around her, but right at her as if he wanted to see straight into the center of her.

"Strip?" Up went one eyebrow.

Something she didn't want to name crackled through

the space between them. Sweat prickled her palms. Her hands were still fisted around his shirt, exposing about two inches of stomach. He had a garden path trail of hair disappearing below the low-slung waist of his jeans. That would have to go. Pity. Tiffany dragged her stare off his navel and focused on the writing on the front of his T-shirt: *Never trust an atom—they make up everything.*

Cool shirt. She and Blondie were probably the only two people in the world who thought it was funny. "Yes, strip."

She pulled at the shirt and his hands tightened over hers. Tiffany glared up at him. Following up on late with an attack of modesty? Unbelievable. Did he think he would be modeling undershirts and long johns? "You have to take it all off."

"Normally I get dinner first." Those bad-boy eyes danced at her, inviting her to share the joke. For a second, she badly wanted to.

"Tiffany, sweetie." Tyrone appeared beside her. "That's not your model."

"What?" Tiffany stared at Blondie. Of course he was her model, because otherwise she was stripping . . . A whimper caught in her throat.

He looked back at her.

Tyrone took her by the shoulders and spun her around. "That's your model."

He pointed to a beautiful Rocky (as in the Picture Show, not Sly) look-alike talking earnestly to Piers. Piers lapped it up, waving one hand through the air and patting the pretty blond boy on the arm.

"I . . ." Tiffany peered over her shoulder. Please let the last two minutes be a figment of her imagination. Her figment grinned at her and tucked his hands into his back pockets.

"Tiffany," Piers bellowed. "Get Mark into makeup.

And get him a cup of coffee. The poor boy has had a horrible day."

"I'm so sorry I'm late." Mark approached her, his big blue eyes awash with apology. "I'm new in town and I got lost."

"Sister," Tyrone cut across him, "save it for the preacher and get your ass all prettied up. We are not getting any younger over here."

"Yes, of course." Mark scurried over to makeup, leaving Tiffany standing with Blondie.

"Well." She hoped she wasn't blushing as much as she thought she was. "I thought you were one of the models."

"Thank you, I think." His voice held enough of a laugh for Tiffany to see the funny side. The corners of her mouth tilted up.

"Tiffany," Piers demanded from across the room. He waved his hand over a pair of briefs and frowned. "Do we like the color of these?"

And just when things were looking up. Thank God she'd had the foresight to pack different colors. "You don't like them?"

"It's just . . ." Piers plucked at his bottom lip, thrust one hip out, and stared down at the model's skimpy underwear. "He has this lovely skin and I don't think these do anything for it."

Tiffany clenched her belly in protest. Piers looked ready to take one of his stands. This would throw her whole schedule off. There wasn't enough of those briefs for anyone to give a shit about the color. And the model wearing them had an honest-to-God eight-pack, all carved out of his deep chocolate skin. She went with the tried-and-true response, guaranteed to win the argument. "That's the color the client wanted."

Tiffany held her breath as Piers glared at the yellow briefs. *Take the shot, Piers. Please, please, please, take the shot.*

"I don't know why I must always work with people who have such fetid taste." Piers stalked over to his camera.

Tiffany let her breath out.

"I wouldn't wear yellow underpants if you paid me." Blondie's heavy baritone stroked her eardrums. His voice sent goose bumps frog-marching up and down her spine.

"Well, we're paying him." She turned to frown at him. "If you're not a model, then what are you doing here?"

"Looking for you."

Goddamn it. Her phone slipped out of her hand. Blondie caught it in one paw.

"Do I know you?" Tiffany snatched her phone back.

"Nope." He shook his head slowly. "We've never met. But I know *of* you. I'm a friend of your husband. Lola told me where to find you."

"What?"

"I'm a friend of Luke's. Your husband?"

That's what she thought he said. Her heart skipped a beat. "Fuck!"

Chapter Two

The studio tilted around Tiffany.

"Is there somewhere we can talk?" Blondie glanced at Piers and back at her.

"Luke?" She forced the name past her stiff lips. "You want to talk about Luke?"

Threes, trouble always came in threes. Someone must have proven that. What were the odds? She needed to work out the odds. First *the date*, then Lola, returning her call today of all days. Now this guy showing up out of nowhere. Her fingers twitched to write this down, try to find the connection. The pink book beckoned from her tote bag.

"Yes." Blondie smiled down at her. "His stepmother—Lola, is it? She told me where to find you."

Son of a bitch! She should never have contacted Lola. That was her first mistake. Nothing good ever came of contacting Luke's family. Only, with the proposal looming and the way things stood, she hadn't really seen an option. She couldn't very well accept the proposal of one man while she was still married to another. "I don't have time to talk about Luke." *Ever.* "And ex. He's my ex-husband."

Up went Blondie's eyebrow. "Um, not according to—"

"He's my ex because I say he is." Her breath sawed through her mouth. She forced it to slow down. Nobody but Lola knew she and Luke were still married.

"O-kay." Blondie held up his hands in surrender. "Whatever, but I still need to talk to you about Luke."

"Well, hello." Piers slithered up beside her. His gaze fixed over her head. "And who might you be?"

This was all she needed, Piers asking questions.

"Thomas." He held out his hand to Piers. "Thomas Hunter." The name suited him, direct and no-nonsense.

Piers slid his fingers into Blondie's—Thomas's—and leered over his slow hand squeeze. "Are you a model?"

"No." Thomas gave a rumble of laughter. "I'm an engineer."

"A real man, then?" Piers sidled a bit closer. "You should consider modeling. You have fabulous bone structure."

"My mother will be pleased to hear it." Thomas slid his hands into the back pockets of his jeans and smiled down easily at Piers. "Actually, I just needed Tiffany."

The way he said that made her belly tighten. Her phone pinged. And right on time, Lola crashed the party. At least she'd given up calling and was sending texts. Tiffany had a thing or two to say to Lola about sending hot blond men to her place of work. Men who knew Luke and knew he was still her husband.

"We all need Tiffany." Piers put his arm around her shoulders and tugged her closer. Tiffany almost lost her balance. "I need her now and you can have her later."

"Um, no." Tiffany wriggled out from beneath Piers's arm. God, she could smack him. His little display of affection was only to impress on Thomas that he wasn't really a screaming bitch. But then, she only had a few more hours to put up with him. "I can't see him later. I have a date."

Piers threw her a look that said he didn't give a shit.

"Why don't I take your number and I can call you later," Thomas said.

"Look." She needed to shake him off before he screwed up everything. "I—"

"Here." Piers grabbed the phone out of Thomas's hand. His fingers flew across the touchpad. "This is Tiffany's cell and I put mine in there as well. Just in case. You can call me anytime for anything."

"Um, thanks." Thomas peered down at his phone.

Tiffany twitched to snatch it and start deleting. Piers really shouldn't be handing out her number to anyone, particularly not Luke's friends. Luke was out of her life, gone, over, except for the car. And the divorce.

"I'll call you later," Thomas said.

"Don't." Tiffany stepped away from him. "I have nothing to say about Luke."

"Yeah." He pulled a rueful face. "That's not going to work for me. I can see you're busy, so I'll call you later."

He turned and strolled his very fine ass away from her.

Tiffany smirked at his broad back. *Not if I see you first.*

Tiffany barely stopped herself from running as she crossed the parking lot to her car. As it was she did a quick scan to check that no big blonds lurked in the shadows waiting to spill her secrets to the world. That exit line of his had a bit of a threat hanging off the end of it.

Thank God, the shoot was over. Piers had grown steadily more toxic as the afternoon progressed. A last-minute idea change from the client had turned him feral. She hated her job. Correction, she hated working for Piers, but her options weren't exactly overwhelming with no qualifications and a high school diploma Daddy had fixed for her. Still, her job had paid for the repairs to her girl.

And there she was. Her girl. Sitting in the middle of the nearly empty parking lot, reducing the cars around her to rolling tin cans. The Lamborghini Miura, with its *come fuck me* lines and parking-lot hustle. *Mee-you-ra:* even the sound of it made her tingle.

Except the Miura wasn't really hers. First, she'd belonged to Luke. The three of them had been twined together—her, Luke, and the Miura—in a fast, wild ride that took your breath away. God, they had laughed and laughed as Luke opened the Miura up and let her eat the highways. Young, beautiful, carefree, and in love. A pang shot through her chest. She wasn't that Tiffany anymore. She was this Tiffany, the one who was going to do the right thing, marry the perfect man, and love the life she should have lived all along.

Tiffany had started the repairs with the idea of giving her back to Luke. She'd broken the Miura, another victim in the wreckage she and Luke left behind. It seemed right to fix it. That had been the plan, anyway. So why, when the car was all fixed and beautiful again, did she still have it? Daddy asked her that all the time. Even Ryan wanted to know.

Sweat broke out over her skin. Lola, Luke, and that Thomas guy all converging on her and threatening to topple her stack of lies. *Oh, God*, she had to keep this from Daddy and Ryan. She needed to calm down. It was bad, but not quite hopeless. Yet. What she needed was a plan.

The weight of her book in her tote hung reassuringly heavy against her shoulder. If she got home fast enough, she would have ten minutes before she got ready. Some girls did chocolate, others took long bubble baths, but she had her pink book filled with wonderful numbers. From panic to poised in a few neat calculations.

Nothing could get in the way of her marrying Ryan. She'd been ready for this since the day they met. Ready to settle down and help Ryan grow his career. Raise a few children together, throw fabulous parties for beautiful people, and live the life she was born for.

Tiffany slid the key into the lock and turned. The door rose to stand, as designed, like the horns of a bull. She didn't want to think about that time in her life. Mostly, she didn't want to think about Luke. Her secret was still safe. She had kept it for seven years. This was just a minor hiccup, a bump in the road. Well, she would flatten it. A quick call to Lola, and her plan was in motion.

Tonight was going to be one of the biggest nights of her life. She was getting engaged, for real this time. Not two kids, crazy in love with each other and not thinking past what they had in their pants. With Ryan, she had the real thing: a mature relationship, based on mutual respect and friendship. And the sex was comfortable, satisfying, and frequent enough for both of them to feel good about it.

Okay, Ryan didn't turn her hormones inside out, but that was good. She wasn't twenty anymore, but staring down the barrel of her thirtieth birthday. At this point in her life, sex wasn't a two-backed beast that gobbled up everything in its path. It was supposed to be an extension of her intimate and caring bond with her partner. That was how Ryan put it.

The Miura crackled and popped into life beneath her. It licked along her nerve endings like the rasp of a cat's tongue. Almost four hundred pounds of torque in a decadent V-12 engine, and it was all hers. At least for now.

Light traffic saw her home quickly, and it was still early

as she let herself into her Gold Coast condo. Her cleaning lady had been there and left the huge shutters open.

Tiffany poured a glass of a crisp Sauvignon Blanc and stepped out onto the enclosed deck. Fold-down glass shutters ran the length of the room, open to admit the evening breeze. A gentle Latin beat floated in from her neighbors' apartment. She'd never met them, but she liked their music. Not so much the couple on the other side of her. They liked to party and they liked to fight, and they did all of this loudly.

She looked around the airy, sleek lines of her home. It had been a gift from Daddy after she'd split from Luke. Cool hardwood eased the ache of her bare feet as she carried her shoes into her bedroom. The other bedroom stayed empty for the most part. All dressed up and ready for a guest. But she didn't have guests here much. Most of her friends were married, some of them even on their second and third marriages. Which brought her right back to Luke.

On her deck, she eased onto the daybed and sipped her wine. Her book sat on her lap. Pink so hot it made you blink with tiny rhinestones swirling and dancing across the cover. She cracked it open and found a blank page. The familiar weight of the glittering pen rested in her hands as she wrote. Numbers. Neat, precise, ordered. No guesswork and no room for error. From the first moment she had learned to count, numbers had been her friends. Of course, Daddy didn't think much of her interest in numbers, so she kept it to herself.

"Everybody has a gift, Princess. Your gift is to be beautiful."

And she was, on the outside, but inside she hugged her numbers to her until she got the chance to write them down in her book. If you looked for them, every day was full of small calculations and examples of numbers in action. Carefully she recalled all those instances throughout the day when she'd wanted to reach for her book. When the world swirled into chaos, numbers were the way out. Simple calculations, more complex concepts, they all broke down to the basic relationship between one number and the other. Addition, subtraction, division, and multiplication; predictable, constant, reliable.

She let the numbers work their magic. The panic subsided and peace moved in. This was all doable. First, the special dinner Ryan had called and reminded her about that morning. Tomorrow, she would call Lola and find out where Luke was hiding. Lola had to know where he was. Then she would track down Luke and get her divorce.

Tiffany tossed back the last of her wine. She debated pouring another one. What the hell, she deserved it after the shock she'd had. Her phone blinked with a missed call from an out-of-town number. She listened briefly to the message. Then had to listen again because she'd paid more attention to the voice than the words. Thomas had called. He said it was urgent. It all sounded a bit dirty in that killer voice of his. He wanted to set up a time to see her.

Delete.

She got to her feet and padded through to her open-plan kitchen that faced Lake Michigan. Everything in the condo faced that incredible view. She found the wine and topped off her glass. The last she'd heard from Luke, he was working in an ashram in India. Luke in an ashram! She'd pay good money to see Luke getting up with the sun and meditating. Or even better, Luke doing communal chores like cleaning toilets. She could have had the papers served to him there, but decided against it. Actually, she'd been deciding against it for the past seven and a half years.

The Tiffany who married Luke wriggled and squirmed,

not ready to be tucked away forever. Tough shit. Wild Tiffany had run out of time. She took a huge gulp of her wine. It went down the wrong way and she came up for air coughing and spluttering. The problem with her divorce—other than she didn't have one—was that nobody else knew. Daddy, Ryan, and all her friends assumed she was divorced. Most of the time she thought of *herself* as divorced. They could all go right on thinking she was divorced, because she sure as hell wasn't going to tell them.

Why hadn't she filed for divorce? She didn't really know, or want to know. Maybe it had something to do with that piece of her that questioned if marrying Ryan really was the right thing for her. She didn't trust that part, though, because that was the part that ended up married to Luke.

But she missed her sometimes. At times it felt like she had two Tiffanys wrestling for space inside her. One Tiffany knew Daddy was right, her future lay with Ryan. The other one craved the speed of the Miura, top down, wind whipping through her hair, and screaming her defiance at the top of her lungs.

The whole thing made her head hurt. Perhaps if she charted it all out on a graph, she would see it more clearly. She almost opened her book again.

Her phone rang. Thomas. She hit Ignore and checked the time.

Time to get beautiful.

Chapter Three

Tiffany rocked her Versace halter stretch dress that cleaved to her like they were conjoined. Opaque from above her cleavage to well above her knee, it provided enough peek-a-boo leg to smoke a pair of silver Jimmy Choo sandals.

A quick spritz of the Joy Daddy gave her every birthday and she was unstoppable. The subtle perfume lingered in the air, and Tiffany breathed it in. It was the same perfume her mother had worn, one of Tiffany's few memories of her. It was like having a tiny part of her mother with her tonight.

The doorbell interrupted her last-minute check. Ryan must have sent the car early, eager to get their evening under way. She checked her reflection one more time. Everything as it should be for a perfect daughter, soon to be perfect wife.

Are you ready for this? Ready to be this Tiffany?

The doorbell pealed again. Of course she was ready. Lingering tendrils of her crappy day were upsetting her balance. Taking one more sniff of Joy for good luck, she opened the door.

Lola barreled through like a small force of nature, swathed in white fox despite the heat of June and hiding behind a large pair of bejeweled sunglasses.

Tiffany gaped at her, frozen in place for a minute. She hadn't seen Lola in years. The woman looked good. Great, actually.

"Precious." Lola dropped the fur over the kitchen counter and tossed her dark, gleaming hair over her shoulder. "I have been trying to get you *forever*."

"Yes." Tiffany lifted the fur out of a small ring of condensation left by her wineglass. Lola here, now, was definitely not in the plan. The car was due any minute. A wave of panic threatened as her past and her future headed toward each other at warp speed. "I was working today."

"All day?" Lola gaped. She wore a figure-clenching scarlet bandage dress that stopped just short of her crotch. Perfectly toned, tanned legs ended in a towering pair of Manolos.

"Since about one thirty."

"Precious." Lola's voice quivered. "They could not pay you enough for that." Her hands flashed scarlet polish and diamonds as she whipped off her sunglasses. "Is that the new Versace line?" Her brown eyes homed in like a scalpel on Tiffany's dress. "It's simply divine. What are you now? An eight? Did you see it in a smaller size?"

She needed to get Lola out of there. Now. "I was going to call you in the morning."

"I saved you the trouble." Lola tossed a red-gloss-and-white-teeth smile at her. "Did you get my present today?"

Present? Tiffany didn't like the sound of that.

Lola shimmied her skin glittered cleavage. "I sent a big, blond hunk of muscle your way."

Thomas Hunter. "Yes, I wanted to speak to you about that—"

"*Muy guapo, sí*. And so manly." Lola growled the last word.

Spanish, seriously? How much Spanish could Lola have picked up when she was still Debbie Wilson from Iowa? Tiffany shook her head and concentrated on the main part of her gripe. "You shouldn't have told him where to find me."

"Really?" Lola blinked at her. "I thought you'd love him."

"He's a stranger and you told him where I worked." Tiffany stared at Lola. How could she not be getting the point here? "And you told him about Luke."

Lola waved her hand in a nose-searing draft of Poison. "He already knew about that. Apparently Luke told him."

That rocked Tiffany back a bit. Her secret was turning out to be not so secret after all. "Anyway, I can't help him. I don't know where Luke is. That's why I was calling you."

"That's what I thought." Lola raised a hand to her head and pressed her forefingers into the skin between her brows. Not a line marred her forehead. She flung a hand toward the door. "And I have solved the problem for everyone."

Tiffany turned to look behind her. And stopped.

A figure, possibly male, dressed in unrelenting black broken by the pasty white of skin for a face and hands.

"Dakota?" Tiffany took a step closer. Her last memory of Luke's half brother was as a cute ten-year-old, all gap-toothed grins and tousled hair.

Dakota peered at her from beneath the inky swath of his hair. His face stayed in a rigid mask of teen scorn.

"You don't know where Luke is. Hot man doesn't know

where Luke is, but he does." Diamonds flashed as Lola jabbed her finger at her son.

"Weren't you away at school?" Lola shuffled the poor kid from one boarding school to another. At least when she and Luke had been married, that had stopped for a while. If she was still married to Luke, did that still make her Dakota's guardian? She should have sent him a birthday gift every year, a card at the very least. He'd been such a sweet kid. With Lola for a mother, God help him.

Dakota blinked at her. Light played over the row of piercings that went from mid-brow to the end.

"He is expelled." Lola tottered into the kitchen. Wrenching open the fridge, she grabbed the bottle of wine Tiffany had opened earlier. Lola hauled open cupboards until she found the wineglasses and grabbed one.

"Expelled?" *Make yourself at home.* Tiffany shrugged off the thought. That was Lola for you. Why take a hand when she could grab the whole arm.

"God, I needed this." Lola took a slug of her wine. "Which brings me to how we can help each other."

Tiffany struggled to align this dark, brooding ghost with the bouncing ten-year-old she'd last seen. *Shit.* He must be seventeen by now.

"This is the sixth school, and I can't deal with it anymore," Lola said from the inside of her wineglass. "Then you called and it all became clear."

It took a while for Lola's words to penetrate. Tiffany whirled about. "What?" This had all kinds of trouble scrawled all over it. The Lola she remembered had no problem making her needs other people's problem. And Lola had a lot of needs. Calling Lola had been a huge mistake. Time to end this. "I'm not sure I can help you. I'll call you in the morning and we can talk then. Right now, I have a date."

Like hell she'd call in the morning. In fact, she would change her cell number in the morning. It would be a pain in the ass, but getting rid of Lola had shifted to the top of her priority list. After getting to her date. She checked the time. *Shit.*

"A date?" Lola's eyes narrowed speculatively. Tiffany knew she was close to mid-forties, but she looked not a day over thirty. "Are you still seeing that man your father set you up with? Roland? Ronald? Randy?"

"Ryan," Tiffany said. *Show no fear.* Where the hell was Lola getting her information?

Lola's eyes glittered as she made thousands of minute calculations. "Things must be getting serious?"

"Yup." Lola needed to go. Tiffany picked up Lola's fur and held it out. "And the car is due here"—she checked her phone for the time—"now."

Lola chugged the remainder of the wine. "Does your father know about, you know?" Lola leaned forward. "Our missing friend?"

"No." *Damn.* Strategic error, because now Lola looked smug.

"And we will keep it that way." Lola winked at her. She jerked her shiny head at her son. "Get in here."

Dakota shambled a couple of steps forward.

"Lola, I have to go out." Tiffany shook the fur in encouragement.

"I know, Precious." That wink again that made Tiffany grind her teeth. "I know everything, and this is your show. I will not interfere." She put the glass down on the counter with a loud click. "This works out nicely for everyone. *Si?*"

Tiffany concealed her wince as the other woman slid obediently into her coat. "I'll call you in the morning."

"You can't." Lola replaced her sunglasses. "I'm going away in the morning."

Something about the way she said *away* made Tiffany itch to ask.

The intercom from the lobby chimed. Her car waited downstairs.

"Okay." Tiffany grabbed her purse. "Then you call me when you get back. Nice to see you, Dakota. Take care."

A disquieting glitter played across Lola's face. She clicked her fingers at her son. He shoved his hands in his pockets and stepped into the kitchen.

"Don't fuck up." Lola opened the front door and sailed toward the elevator. Her heels clacked against the marble corridor outside Tiffany's condo.

Tiffany's mouth dropped open. *Wow!* As far as parental advice went, just, wow.

Dakota blinked.

The elevator pinged from the hallway. Lola was walking away. And Dakota wasn't going with her. He stood in her entrance hall like the walking dead with a middle-distance stare fixed on the view.

It was difficult to run in five-inch sandals, but Tiffany managed to catch up with Lola as the other woman stepped into the elevator. "Where are you going?"

"Away." Lola pursed her lips as she jabbed at the buttons on the elevator panel. "I told you that."

"Yes, but what about Dakota?"

The teen stood exactly where she'd left him. He kind of curved over like a bold-print exclamation mark. "Come on." Tiffany waved her hands at him. "Your mother is leaving."

The elevator doors slid shut. The soft whir of mechanics carried Lola away.

"No." Tiffany hit the down button. "No, no, no." This wasn't happening to her. This. Was. Not. Happening. The illuminated numbers above the door crawled up to her penthouse and she leaped inside. "Hurry." She begged the descending floor numbers to go faster.

The elevator opened onto the lobby and Tiffany skidded across the slick marble floor to the entrance, her vision locked on the flash of scarlet on the sidewalk. Lola was not leaving Dakota with her.

"Miss Desjardins?" The doorman jumped into step behind her. "Is everything all right?"

"No!" Tiffany hit the street outside in time to see Lola leap into a cab and slam the door.

"Drive." Lola smacked the driver's seat with her fist.

The cab moved away from the curb.

"You are not leaving him here." Tiffany banged on the roof to stop the cab.

Lola closed the window, leaving only enough of a gap for Tiffany to hear. She pressed her finger to her lips and winked. "You be good to me, Precious, and I'll be good to you."

Blackmail? Seriously? Tiffany ran as the cab crawled forward. "Stop."

"Miss Desjardins?" The doorman hopped off the curb and back on again. His face creased in a frown. "Did you need a cab?"

Lola made frantic go motions at the driver. Her jewelry flashed in the dim cab interior.

"You can't leave him here." Tiffany tottered after the accelerating cab. Her heel caught on a manhole cover and she almost went ass over teakettle. "Don't you dare leave him here with me. Where the hell are you going?"

The cab pulled into the traffic. A horn blared and Tiffany leaped back out of the path of a Jeep full of cruising kids. "Get out of the fucking road, lady."

No goddamn way was this happening to her. The town car driver stood beside his car, not even pretending not to enjoy the show. She streaked past the frozen doorman to her building and leaped into the elevator. "You are so not doing this to me." She glued her glare to the climbing numbers above the door. Her fingers tapped against her thigh, willing it to go faster.

Dakota stood exactly where she'd left him as she scrabbled through her purse for her phone. He hadn't even flinched. She jabbed her fingers at the keypad.

"Hello?" A male voice answered. Thomas Hunter.

"Shit! Fuck!" Tiffany hung up quickly. She'd hit the wrong buttons. She took a deep breath and dialed Lola's number.

"This is Lola. I will be away until the eighteenth. You know what to do, darling."

"Lola," Tiffany bellowed at the voice mail. "Answer your phone. You're not leaving your son here with me."

She hung up and dialed again.

"This is Lola. I will be away until the eighteenth. You know what to do, darling."

"She won't pick up." Dakota spoke from behind her.

"What?" *Holy shit.* When had his voice gotten so deep? Tiffany blinked at him stupidly.

He shrugged, done with talking for now.

"Do you know where she's gone?"

Nothing. Tiffany charged over to him. With a start, she realized they were now eyeball to eyeball. Dakota wasn't a little boy anymore. "Could you answer my question?"

The contempt in his expression almost made her flinch. "She's gone on a snip and safari."

Tiffany shook her head to clear her hearing. "A what?"

"A snip and safari." Dakota drew out each word painstakingly as if she were brain dead.

Tiffany dragged in a deep breath. Hysteria bubbled up

her throat. Her voice rose like a banshee. "What the hell is that?"

"You go to South Africa, get a face-lift, and go to a private game reserve to recover."

Tiffany blinked at Dakota. That was even a thing? She shook her head. Not the most pressing question right now.

"Miss?" The town car driver stood in the open doorway of her condo. "Am I still driving you to dinner?"

Dakota looked at her. The driver looked at her. Tiffany wanted to scream and melt into a puddle all over her shining hardwood floors. Ryan. Ryan was waiting for her. Ready to start the night that would launch her new life, while her past life was stuck in her condo. *Fuck*, how had things gotten so out of control? Her book sat on the kitchen counter and she looked at it. There wasn't time.

"Go." Dakota jerked his head toward the driver. "Because she sure as shit isn't coming back."

"Miss?"

"Just a minute." Tiffany glared at the driver. "Could you wait in the car?"

He sighed and strolled back to the elevator.

"Don't you have a friend you can stay with?" It was the best she could manage. She wanted to yell at the teen that he couldn't stay here, but it didn't seem fair. His mother had just dumped him, and none of this was his fault.

Dakota shook his head.

Tiffany fumed at his back as he slunk over to the deck. What the hell was she going to do now? She dialed Lola again. And got voice mail. With a growing sense of futility, she left another message. "I have a date," she said to Dakota's back. "I can't miss it."

He didn't seem to hear her. She could call Ryan and cancel, but he'd want to know why. Panic whipped the wine in her stomach into acid. This was Luke's brother. Luke, who she was still married to. Luke, who Ryan thought was a part of her past. Dakota had bits of metal stuck to the back of his T-shirt. What if Ryan found out about Luke? *Breathe.* God, she was going to throw up. *Breathe in and breathe out.*

Simple. Ryan couldn't find out. She would have to get rid of Dakota somehow. There had to be someone else who could take him. He could stay here for the night. Then in the morning, she would find the solution. "I have to go out."

Dakota examined the furnishings of the deck, his hands jammed in his pockets.

"I have a date." It sounded so lame. "A very important date that I can't miss. We can sort this out when I get back."

"So, go." Dakota sniffed and threw himself onto her daybed. The legs screeched across her beautiful hardwood floors.

She grabbed her purse, strode for the door, stopped, and came back. It didn't seem right to leave him here. She briefly imagined taking him to dinner with her. Oh, God, that would go down so well. He was too old for a baby-sitter. Tiffany clutched her purse to her middle. "Will you be okay, on your own?"

Horrible things happened to teens when they were left on their own. Her mind cycled. Odds. What were the odds of something happening to Dakota? She factored in his age, the area, crime statistics. She stopped. There were too many variables to be reliable.

"Go." He put his head back and shut his eyes. "You have an important date, remember?"

"It is important." God, she wished she knew her neighbors, she could ask one of them to watch him. Watch him? He was seventeen, not seven. She reached for her book.

"Miss?" The driver stood with his arms folded by the

elevator. "I don't wish to concern you, but we're running late and I was given explicit instructions."

"I know." Ryan always gave explicit instructions. She pulled her hand back from the book and a touch of sanity. "Give me your cell number," she said to Dakota.

He must have one. All teens had one. If she had his cell number she could sneak off to the bathroom during dinner and check on him. Her proposal dinner! Damn, when she got her hands on Lola . . .

"Why?"

"So I can check you're all right."

"Fuck." He cut his hostile gaze in her direction. "I'm not in fucking day care."

She swallowed, hard. All the black definitely worked to make him more intimidating. But he was seventeen. She was the adult in charge. *In charge?* She almost started laughing hysterically. "Cell number."

Dakota snorted and fired off his number as rapidly as his mouth could move.

Tiffany opened her contacts and entered them, number for number. She hit Dial. Dakota's pocket rang and she ended the call. *Okay, what next?* "Have you eaten?"

Up and down went his shoulders.

"Well, there's food in the fridge." Tiffany waved in the direction of her hulking Sub-Zero. "There's some salad, some yogurt, fruit." It didn't sound all that appealing when she said it out loud. "Eat what you like." She clutched her purse tighter. He wouldn't want any of that. "Or you could order pizza?" She found her wallet, grabbed a handful of twenties, and held the money out to Dakota. "Here."

He kept his eyes shut.

Tiffany contemplated marching over there and stuffing the money into the pocket of his baggy pants. She slapped the notes on the counter instead. "Order yourself a pizza if you get hungry."

He yawned in a wide flash of teeth.

"I won't be late." Not anymore, anyway. *Shit*, Ryan might want to come up after dinner. *One problem at a time, Tiffany.* First dinner and then . . . whatever. "Okay, I'm going now."

Nothing.

Chapter Four

Thomas shook his head. He'd become an honest-to-God stalker. Sitting in his car outside Tiffany Desjardins's swanky condo building—address courtesy of Luke's stepmother—enjoying the soap opera going on for the last ten minutes. Glamorous women running out of expensive condo buildings in heels and yelling at each other wasn't a thing you got to see every day. Something big was going on, and his gut was telling him it had to do with Luke.

His gaze tracked Tiffany's tight ass as it sashayed back into the building. Damn, she was fine. He'd expected as much from what Luke had told him, but the reality exceeded even that. He'd almost swallowed his tongue that morning when she'd started stripping him in the studio. Under different circumstances he would have been up for it. But he was knee-deep in a pile of shit, and Tiffany was the branch to pull him out.

Screw Luke, anyway. He should have left the son of a bitch to sweat out his malaria on his own. Probably would have if he hadn't recognized Luke as a hometown acquaintance when he'd stumbled on him in the middle of Zambia. He'd done what any right-minded person would have done and helped him. He liked the guy—Luke was funny as all hell and, it turned out, they knew a few of the same people from college days. *Bosbefok!* That's what the South Africans on his exploration team called it—fucked in the head by the African bush.

The doors swung open and Tiffany strutted out wearing a scrap of blue material that made his eyes pop out of his head. Those shoes were the stuff of wet dreams. She couldn't be wearing a whole hell of a lot under that dress. She slithered into the black town car, her face locked in a *don't even think about it* scowl. Tough shit. She had to talk to him and tell him where her bastard of a husband was hiding. He'd turned over every other rock he could find, and the son of a bitch was still MIA.

The town car holding his last shot at finding Luke drove away. Maybe he should follow? *Nah.* Dressed like that, she was off on a date. And she wouldn't want him butting into her date any more than she liked him showing up at her work. Thomas laughed softly to himself. *Date?* That girl should not be dating, not with the mess she had on her plate. He couldn't believe she and Luke were still legally married. The Luke he'd met had spoken about Tiffany as if she were a nasty piece of his past, best left way, way behind.

A hot mess—his brother Josh's specialty. Not him, though. He didn't like hassle in any area of his life, which brought him right back to sitting there like a stalker waiting for her to get back so he could talk to her. The clock in his head went right on ticking. He eased his neck, but the tension crept back up his muscles.

He liked his life ordered. Compartmentalized. Neatly stacked into bundles that he could deal with one at a time. Girls like Tiffany were a whole lot of scattered mayhem. If one of his bundles wasn't threatening to topple over and crush everything, he wouldn't even be here. He made a creaking, falling sound effect in his head and realized he'd made it out loud. You could take the boy out of *Star Wars* . . .

Except this wasn't about taking over the world or defeating the Death Star. This wasn't even about gold or diamonds. It was all about rare earth, seventeen little chemical elements that were so hard to find and wanted by just about everybody. Only a geologist could get excited about rare earth, or maybe a geek like him.

Still, he'd found a rich deposit and Luke, the miserable son of a bitch, had the proof. They needed those results, or one of the big mining and mineral boys would be in there making a deal with the Zambian government before a small player could catch a whiff. The small player, in this case, being him and his partners.

Thomas rammed the heel of his hand against the steering wheel in frustration. Dammit, what had Luke been thinking? Actually, he had a fair guess what Luke had been thinking. Luke, the self-proclaimed eco-warrior, was determined not to let anyone mine that little portion of Africa. *Too late*, Thomas wanted to yell at him. The deal would be made. Nobody was going to walk away from a deposit like that, and no African government was going to turn its back on that kind of revenue. Except Luke wasn't there to be yelled at. He'd disappeared as effectively as smoke.

Thomas had tracked him back to Chicago, and his stepmother. She'd handed over Tiffany on a platter. One of these women had to know where Luke was. Luke loved his kid brother, he must have let his family know how to reach him. And Thomas was gonna stay right on their heels until they handed him over. He needed those results and he needed them now. His fledgling company stood poised and ready to make this happen. They also stood poised on the edge of going under if it didn't.

A car pulled up with a pizza delivery logo along the side.

His stomach growled in envy. How much money would it take to get the delivery guy to sell him the pizza instead? He leaned forward and peered up at the glass-and-metal tower of the condo building. He didn't have that kind of money.

Why had he thought he was so clever in keeping those results as secret as he could? Why hadn't he made another copy? Because another copy would only increase the risk of those results finding their way into other hands. Christ, he should have made a copy. Basic stuff, computing 101.

The pizza delivery guy got out and strolled through the double glass doors. Not even the super rich turned their noses up at pizza.

Thomas checked his watch. Tiffany wouldn't be back any time soon. She showed up looking like that on a date with him, he wouldn't let her go home in a hurry. Point being, he had time to get himself something to eat. His stomach growled its agreement. He hadn't eaten since lunch. He'd picked up one of those bagels from the table at the studio. The low-fat cream cheese had done next to nothing to meet his craving for protein. He started his truck. He'd spotted a small Mexican place down the road.

The doors opened and Luke's kid brother came out. The kid had the pizza with him.

Thomas locked on the pizza box. Surely the kid couldn't have scarfed the entire thing already? Digestive power like that would be nothing short of legendary. Something about the kid's manner made him wait.

The kid stopped and grabbed a slice out of the box. He

folded it in half and took a bite. Saliva flooded the inside of Thomas's mouth.

The kid had a backpack over one shoulder as he headed off down Oak Avenue, threading his way through the late shoppers. He lifted the set of Beats from around his neck and put them to his ears. Those must have set Hot Mommy back a few hundred. But then, according to Luke, Mommy could afford it just fine.

The kid flipped through his cell before slipping it back in his pocket.

Thomas slid out of his parking spot. He would keep an eye on the kid, at least as far as the Mexican restaurant. The boy looked to be about eighteen, all legs and arms without the muscle to give them a reason for being. The kid was oblivious, his fingers flying across his phone as he texted.

Thomas rolled down the window. "Hey."

The kid's head bopped up and down to the music no doubt blaring through that killer set of headphones. Just his luck, they would be the noise-canceling type. Thomas looked for somewhere to park. Both sides of the street were crammed bumper to bumper.

What was the name Luke had said? He kept thinking airplanes for some reasons. Nobody was going to call their kid Boeing, however screwed up.

The kid crossed an alley and kept walking.

Two guys came out of the alley and fell into step behind the kid. Thomas wouldn't have noticed them, except they seemed to be walking really close to the boy. They were both older and bigger, too. Thomas's Spidey sense tingled.

One of them grabbed the kid by the arm. The pizza box sailed through the air, flipped open in mid-flight, and dropped warm, gooey pizza all over the sidewalk.

Ah, hell no. He squeezed the front end of the truck into the alley and jumped out. A horn blared behind him. Thomas gave it the finger over his shoulder.

The kid's face had gone even paler as he spoke rapidly to the two men.

The men crowded the kid toward the alley.

The kid glanced over to Thomas, a brief flash of raw fear before he masked it again.

A slow burn simmered in the pit of Thomas's gut. He hated wasted food, particularly when he was ready to chew his arm off from hunger and the pizza lay scattered across the sidewalk in a cheesy smear.

But most of all, he hated a fucking bully.

Chapter Five

Tiffany hit the restaurant at a dead run. Ryan hated tardiness. She steadied her breathing as she sedately trailed the maître d' to her table. Ryan would be quick to pick up anything wrong. God, she'd sucked at acting as a kid.

"Hello, Princess." Her father rose from the seat beside Ryan to kiss her on the cheek. Tiffany gaped at him. Her mouth moved and she made some reply.

Ryan rose next and gave her a slightly warmer kiss before holding a chair out for her.

They seated themselves, and both men smiled across the table at her. They were in a hot new restaurant, all burgundy, silver, and crystal. A hip new take on an old-style ladies' lounge. Tables were set far enough apart to guarantee privacy. Amber light flickered from the small cluster of votive candles nestled between orchid blossoms. The place screamed romance.

Until she looked across the table at her father. Her head spun. If she'd got it all wrong and this wasn't a proposal, then she had a reprieve on the Luke front. Right? She dug her nails into her palms. But if she'd got it all wrong, it meant Ryan wasn't going to propose. No proposal, no New Tiffany. Damned if she knew whether that bubble in her belly meant disappointed or relieved. Confused came closest to what she was feeling.

"I suppose you're wondering what I'm doing here?" Her father's chiseled, handsome face relaxed into a smile.

Tiffany forced herself to focus. "It's always nice to see you, Daddy." And it was. Her father had the same classic good looks and impeccable sense of style as Cary Grant. His dark hair had elegantly and graciously changed gleaming pewter as he'd aged.

The waiter hovered with the wine bottle and she gave him a nod.

"I'll let Ryan explain," her father said after the waiter moved away. "As you were late, we ordered for you."

"I'm sorry, I got caught up at work." She flinched and waited for the lecture about her job.

Her father took a sip of his wine, rolling it around his mouth before swallowing. He beamed at Ryan in approval. "Perfect."

Perfect was a big thing with Daddy. Something was up. Her belly tightened. Daddy always had something cutting to say about her working for Piers.

Ryan smiled at her and she clung to that lifeline. He wore the suit they'd picked out together at Hugo Boss; charcoal gray with a starched white shirt and a red tie. Ryan was handsome in the same style as her father, the lines of his face carved in bold, masculine sweeps that invited you to drop your troubles on his broad shoulders. His dark hair was impeccably, but conservatively cut. "You look beautiful." Ryan winked at her. "But then, you always look beautiful."

"Watch yourself, son." Her father chuckled. "Don't get too carried away with her father right here."

Ryan slid him a look and chuckled back.

Dear God, they were tag-teaming each other. Tiffany

curled her mouth up into a smile and grabbed her wine. She barely stopped herself from chugging the glass. With the two glasses from the condo, she was dangerously close to sloppy impulse control territory. Her silverware didn't balance. Two knives and a spoon on one side of her plate, two forks on the other. She took away one knife and placed it on her bread plate, bisecting the circle through the center.

"Your father and I are celebrating." Ryan leaned forward as he spoke. His cuff links gleamed as they peeked out from beneath the sleeves of his jacket. Simple, square and gold. Conservative, understated, classy. She bet her father had a pair exactly like them.

She looked from one to the other. She'd seen her father and Ryan together hundreds of times. Her father had introduced her to Ryan. Maybe it was her day making her super aware, but she'd never really noticed the similarities between them before. "Okay."

"Ryan has accepted a partnership in our firm." Her father leaned his arms on the table, just like Ryan. She was right about the cuff links.

"That's great." It was great. They both looked really happy about it. It was just . . . not the reason she thought she was there. She hid her confusion behind a smile as they talked a bit more about their partnership.

This was a dinner to celebrate *their* new partnership. A lump lodged in her breastbone. She'd had such high hopes for tonight. All through this nuts day, she'd clung to the hope that if she could get through it, her pot of gold was waiting for her.

The waiter arrived. He put a green salad, no dressing, in front of each of them. She picked up her fork. Her stomach clenched so tight she wouldn't get a thing down, but she needed something to do with her hands. She'd told everybody she was getting engaged. She wasn't getting engaged at all. Her father was getting a new partner.

"Tell her the rest," her father said.

Tiffany stopped pushing arugula around her plate and looked at Ryan. *God, please let the rest be better.*

"Tiffany." He placed his knife and fork side by side on his plate. "You and I have been seeing each other for two years now."

"It's our anniversary." Part of the reason she'd been so sure this was a proposal. Ryan had been dropping hints all week. *Damn it*, her father had been dropping hints right along with him. Leading her on for no reason would be cruel.

"Didn't I tell you she would know that?" Her father dabbed the corners of his mouth.

"You were right, Carter." Ryan dabbed. "Tiffany, your father and I, we want to cement our relationship."

What about cementing our *relationship instead?* Daddy had pushed her and Ryan together, told her nothing would make him happier. Even gone so far as to say that her mother would have loved Ryan. Since Luke, she'd made sure to get Daddy's approval before she took any of her dates seriously. Had her father pimped her out for a new partner? No, not possible, she was his Princess. He always said so. She forced a sweet smile and nodded for Ryan to continue.

"And it's no secret that you and I have been heading in a certain direction for a while now."

A small bubble of hope pushed through the gloom. Tiffany's gaze flickered to her father. This was sounding more like a proposal. With her father sitting right there. The hope bubble popped. She didn't care which way her father sliced this, there was nothing romantic going on here tonight.

"What Ryan is saying, Princess," her father took over when Ryan went silent, "is that he has asked me for your hand in marriage."

Her mouth dropped open and she snapped it shut again. It *was* a proposal. Her father was proposing for Ryan. Her mind blanked. Her crazy day had spiraled into the most crackpot night ever. She saw herself years from now telling her children how their father proposed. *Well, sweeties, your father proposed by getting your grandfather to ask.* Laughter boiled in her stomach, except her brain wasn't finding this funny at all.

"Of course, I said yes." Her father gave her a pleased smile. "Nothing would make me happier than to see you settled with a good man like Ryan."

The two men exchanged a warm glance. Neither of them seemed to find any of this odd.

"He hasn't asked me." The words came out of her mouth and she sounded all of five years old.

"Sweetheart." Ryan touched her hand. "You don't have to worry about that. Of course I'm going to ask you, and not with your father sitting right here. This is more of a *pre*-proposal."

"What?" Only half of that made sense. Her brain latched onto the proposal part.

"Except we have some concerns." Her father rearranged his knife to line up perfectly with the fork.

Tiffany glanced at her father and then at Ryan. She was so lost here. "Concerns?"

Her salad was whipped away and replaced with a fillet of sole accompanied by lightly sautéed vegetables. Tiffany nearly turned her nose up at it. Fish and veggies weren't going to cut it at all. Another waiter went past their table with a dessert trolley. Chocolate cake! Hot damn! A piece of chocolate cake with chocolate frosting, and sauce all over it. There were times when a girl needed carbs and sugar, and this was one of them.

"Ryan feels, and I agree with him . . ." Her father took up the line of crazy again. "We feel that you are not ready for such a large step."

Her pulse marked triple time. She speared her fork into her fish. It hit the plate and screeched.

Her father reached over and covered her hand. The one Ryan had touched. "Don't be angry, Princess. We love you, this is for your own good."

She dropped her fork onto the plate with a clatter. The couple at the next table whipped their heads in her direction. *Go ahead and stare. I can lay money this is the first time you've seen this.*

Her father and Ryan stared at her, wearing matching *caring* expressions.

Shit! This was one of those things. One of those things where people got together and told the screwed-up one just how wacko they were. An intervention. That was the word. This was a fucking intervention. She grabbed her wine-glass and chugged the remnants. Let the calories roll. Was that the seams of the Versace she heard groaning? She'd come here dressed for a proposal and got an intervention instead. What did one wear to an intervention? Perhaps Chanel would have been more the thing. The insane urge to laugh once again roared through her.

"We feel, your father and I," Ryan continued in his *everything will be all right* voice, "that you're still harboring an unhealthy attachment to your ex-husband."

And then she did laugh. Luke. This was about Luke. That made it four in one day. Trouble wasn't supposed to come in fours. Threes. That was the rule. Everybody knew that. "I'm over Luke."

They stared at her. Ryan winced a tiny bit. Her father's eyes filled with pity.

"I am." A horrible thought snapped her mouth shut. Did they know? They couldn't know. Her hands shook so badly she dropped them into her lap.

"We don't believe you are." The corners of her father's mouth tilted down. "I have been waiting for you to do something about that car since your divorce."

He said *divorce*. Sweet relief almost brought tears to her eyes. They didn't know.

"I want us to have a future together, darling." Ryan oozed sincerity with his dark gaze. "For us to go forward together, we need to be free of the past. I know I'm ready, but you, my darling, have some unfinished business."

The votive candles flickered cheerfully in the center of the table. Her brain stuck on the play of light on the crystal facets of the bowl. Familiar lies churned in her gut. "Ryan, I—"

"I know." He squeezed her dead fish hand. "I know your first marriage was painful for you. I know you have strong feelings for your ex-husband. Feelings of anger and resentment."

"My ex-husband." She tried the phrase out, daring to peer up at Ryan. Her heart was pounding so hard it threatened to bust right out of her chest. They didn't know the worst part.

"Yes, Luke." Ryan placed her hand carefully on the table. There should be a ring, right there, third finger. Ryan covered it with his. "You're stuck in the past and it isn't healthy."

"You need to make peace with your past." Her father pushed his plate away. They must have gotten together and practiced their earnest expressions. "You need to resolve whatever it is that lies between you and Luke. For us. For our future."

Tiffany dragged her gaze up to his. "Daddy, Luke is out of my life."

In all ways, other than a legal technicality.

"Princess. The car?" Her father weighted the words like an 18-wheeler struggling uphill with its abnormal load of disappointment. He had her there, but as long as he didn't know the full truth there was still hope. So she'd sell the car. Tiffany opened her mouth to reassure them. She couldn't do it. Selling the car would be like ripping a limb off. Her nails dug into her thighs, probably ruining the Versace. If she didn't watch it she could lose everything. "You know why I had to fix the car."

"Yes, we do." Ryan tipped her chin up so she had to meet his gaze again. "You wanted to atone for the past, but that doesn't explain why you still have it."

"I'm going to give it back."

Her father sighed, setting the candle flames dancing amongst the orchids. "When, Tiffany? When are you going to give Luke his car?"

"When I find him." She took a huge sip of her wine. "He's always traveling somewhere. Tibet or Tokyo and I don't know where the hell else. It isn't as if I can just shove it in an envelope and mail it to him."

"I understand that." Ryan's expression softened, his tone endlessly patient; it pressed on her shoulders heavier than her father's disappointment. "But I don't think you are being entirely honest with either of us. Do you want to know what we think?"

No, she wanted to snap at him. *I want my fucking proposal.* Of course, she didn't say that. They were good-cop, bad-copping her, and she had to take it because she was guilty as hell.

"I think the car is a symbol for you. It's a reminder, a memento, of your youth and your past," Ryan said.

"I don't want a memento of my marriage, it was bad enough living through it the first time." Except it hadn't been all bad. Not really. Sure, the end had been brutal, but there had been times at the beginning . . . great times. Tears pricked her eyelids and she blinked them away. Shit, could her father and Ryan be right? Was she hanging on to the past? To Luke?

Ryan leaned forward in his seat. "I love you, Tiffany."

"We both do," her father chimed in.

"I want to spend the rest of my life with you," Ryan said.

"Nothing would make me happier," her father said. "You've chosen the perfect man in Ryan."

"Do this for us."

"It's time, Princess."

The candlelight cast loving shadows across their handsome faces. Their expressions were identical, part concern, part affection.

"This wasn't how I was expecting tonight to go." *Not even fucking close*. "I was expecting a proposal."

Ryan looked down.

Her father met her look. "Tiffany, are you ready for that?"

"I thought I was," she said in a wooden voice. "I made a mistake. Luke was a mistake. It's in the past."

"Then prove it," her father said. "Start by getting rid of that ridiculous car." Her father watched her, candlelight playing across his features.

Tiffany dropped her gaze. The thing was, he was right. Some part of her was hanging on to the past. Actually, considering her non-divorce, her father was more right than he thought. Her fingers curled into tight fists in her lap. The fight in her vanished under a tsunami of tired. "I want to go home."

"Don't be petulant, Princess." Her father's lips tightened. He sat back, folded his hands on the tabletop, and waited for her to simmer down.

"I'm sorry." She wrestled her temper under control. It upset Daddy when she got too emotional. Her mother had never yelled, always handled every situation like a perfect lady. "This has all taken me by surprise."

"Of course it has." Ryan smiled at her. "Now, let's all have a nice dinner and talk about the future. Our future."

"Which reminds me." Daddy tapped the edge of the table. "I'm going to need to see your divorce settlement so we can draw up a little pre-nup between you and Ryan."

Her lies closed around her like a trap making it difficult to breathe. "Sure, Daddy."

"Eat your fish, Tiffany." Ryan pushed her plate closer. "Can't have you wasting away on me before our big day."

Tiffany picked up her knife and fork. Dinner was fucking awful. She dredged up a few smiles, managed some light chatter, and made her escape as soon as it was polite to do so. Ryan didn't press to come home with her—*thank you, Jesus*. He stood beside her father as they put her into a cab. She didn't turn around as she drove away.

She dropped her head against the back of the seat. "What a mess."

"Did you say something, miss?" The driver glanced in the rearview mirror.

"No, nothing." In twenty-four hours her life had gone apeshit. She'd gotten herself into this mess. If they ever found out the full truth, life would be over. Bang would go her proposal and any chance of her future with Ryan. God, her father would never get over it. Her mind whirled so badly she thought she might puke. She dug around in her clutch. Lipstick, compact, spare tampon. She tapped the back of the driver's seat. "Do you have a piece of paper and a pen?"

The driver scrabbled around a bit and handed her a pen and an old sales receipt. "Is this okay?"

"Perfect." All she needed was room to think, to put the world into order again. She jotted down a formula, any formula would do: $y = x^3 - x^2$. Random numbers flashed past the cab—a street sign, a car registration, anything. She filled them into her formula and solved for y. Every equation had a solution, it had to, and you began by assigning values to the variables. The churning inside her stilled as the numbers obediently conformed.

The idea hit her halfway through her second equation, and it was so beautiful in its simplicity, she laughed out loud. Sitting in her condo, right that minute, was the way to make x plus y equal marriage to Ryan.

Chapter Six

Tiffany wriggled her toes to relieve some of the pressure on the balls of her feet. Her scarlet peep-toes looked incredible, but Jimmy Choo didn't make shoes for standing by the side of the road in Nowheresville, Utah, facing down the attitude of a sulky teen.

Daddy was wrong about the shoes, but right about her ability to plan. *"Let me handle that for you, Princess."* How many times had she heard that? She shuddered, despite the blistering heat. Letting Daddy handle this one for her was so out of the question, it didn't bear thinking about.

"I told you this was a dumb idea." Dakota shoved his Beats back around his ears and fished his iPhone out of his pocket. Yes, he'd told her. And told her. But a determined woman did what she had to do.

The plan had seemed so perfect. She had Dakota, for the next four to six weeks as it turned out. Her head gave a sympathetic throb. On the plus side, having Dakota meant knowing Luke's whereabouts. After her dinner with Ryan and Daddy, she knew she needed to find Luke and find him fast. Daddy expected a divorce settlement, and she aimed to get him one. Sure, he would notice the date was wrong, but once it was done, she could get to work on earning his forgiveness. A wedding to Ryan would do the trick nicely.

Dakota could take her to Luke. Even better, she had the means to sweet-talk Luke into coming back to Willow Park with her and filing a joint petition. A large gesture of atonement that would get Luke back to Willow Park and grease the wheels to a speedy divorce. The Miura—Luke's girl—all repaired and pretty again. Luke would do anything for that car. It would hurt like hell to hand her over, but a girl had to do . . . and all that. Add everything together, toss in a nice bunch of symbolism, and it meant loading the toxic teen into a 1972 Lamborghini Miura and driving from Chicago to Canyons, Utah.

It had taken some fancy persuading to get Dakota to give up Luke's address. However, turned out Dakota would rather spend the next few weeks with his brother than her. Suited Tiffany down to the ground, and gave her enough leverage to get Dakota in the car at a ridiculously early hour the morning after her intervention dinner. He had still only given her the town name, but it was enough to see her on her way.

She eased a small pebble out from under her toe and stared down the strip of black tarmac that stretched endlessly in both directions. So much for her tidy equation, and she was fresh out of new ones. On the side of the road, desert scrub lurked and waited to take over again, choked with bugs and crawling things.

List of lessons, so far. One—never take a road trip in Jimmy Choos. Two—if you do take a road trip, don't do it in a vintage sports car. She turned back to the hissing Miura, willing it to suddenly spring to life. She'd been forced to leave three pieces of luggage behind because the Miura had no storage room. Not having the time to unpack them, she'd left them in her entrance hall with a note for her cleaning lady. Pray God she had enough in the bags she brought to see her through, because it looked like her journey had gotten a lot longer.

Lesson three—heat and vintage sports cars don't mix. Why did Utah have to be so damn hot? Even now, sun damage crawled all over her skin. She growled her frustration at the unresponsive car. And things had been going so well. They cleared Illinois easily, hit Iowa and passed more corn than any person could want. Sailed straight through Nebraska, more corn and some cows adding variety. They'd even found a nice hotel where she'd grabbed a few hours sleep, and even better, a few Dakota-free hours.

It was all Colorado's fault. She'd thought it might be prettier. And it had been a beautiful drive. Should have gone with Wyoming. *Dumb, dumb, dumb*. She'd pushed through Denver, nearly screaming from the incessant buzz leaking from Dakota's headphones and his attitude stinking up the car. Dakota hated her. How had they gone from her reading him *Diary of a Wimpy Kid* to this? She had to admit it was at least partly her fault. Never mind not sending birthday and Christmas gifts, a phone call every now and again wouldn't have killed her. Especially since she'd seen, firsthand, Lola's maternal skills.

So she'd sucked up the attitude and stuck with her driving. Roadwork had been her downfall. Between the dark, the flashing orange lights, and bossy men waving flags at her, she'd managed to head south instead of west.

Another little snag on classic cars. No navigation system and no direction thingies that lit up on your rearview mirror. It wasn't until she saw her first sign to Albuquerque that she got that sinking feeling. Even she knew Albuquerque wasn't in Utah.

No problem. She'd stopped at a gas station, consulted

the GPS on her phone, and bought a map to be sure and got them heading west again. Pioneer woman at her finest and looking fabulous while she did it.

And then, Utah struck! Everyone she knew flew straight into Salt Lake City for the killer skiing. Skiing meant snow, not sun broiling the top of your head. About an hour ago, her bright red Italian diva started to do this strange jerking thing. Tiffany had steered the juddering car off the highway and turned off the ignition. The Miura had coughed, once or twice, and then belched smoke from under the hood.

"Now what?" Dakota yelled at her over the sound exploding from his Beats directly into his eardrums. "Got a plan, Barbie?"

Not a clue. Dakota had taken to calling her Barbie, which pissed her off no end, but then most people took one look at her and assumed she was dumb anyway. Even Daddy and Ryan tended to do her thinking for her.

Maybe they had something there, because she'd managed to land herself in a whole heap of trouble. Her spirits sank even lower.

A puff of smoke drifted over from the Miura, and Tiffany eyed the car's hood nervously. The older Miuras had a nasty trick of spitting oil onto the carburetor and exploding. Had they ironed out that little hitch in this model? She wasn't going anywhere near that smoking hood. And she for sure wasn't going to start the steaming diva up again.

She dug around in her Kate Spade and came up with her cell. At least they had reception. Great. She could call, but call who? Phoning home for a rescue was out of the question. They had no idea she was even out there, let alone having a clue as to why. She was going to have to get herself out of this. The hopelessness of the situation pressed down on her.

Heat haze shimmered against the horizon. Dirty green scrub eked out a determined existence in the parched soil between her and the distant mountains where they rose up to have their ends abruptly truncated by the endless blue arc of the sky. Southern Utah, according to the map app on her phone. Nothing to worry about, other than the sister-wife thing, and those people seemed nice enough. You wouldn't want to marry one, though.

She thumbed the GPS up on her phone. Okay. There they were; a red dot right in the middle of a yellow streak for the road.

"Hey," Dakota yelled.

Tiffany turned her back. She really didn't feel up to another version of how dumb her plan was. She kind of got that by now. The red dot moved as she shifted the map in the direction they were taking. There had to be a town here somewhere. There had to be. Even sister wives had to shop.

"Tiffany?" Dakota's boots crunched loose sand and gravel.

At least he hadn't called her Barbie this time. They were on a highway, at least, which meant someone should be along at some point. Woman and boy, alone on a deserted road. Shit, it had all the makings of a horror movie. She swallowed the lump of fear growing in her throat. Letting her imagination run away with her wasn't going to help. A trickle of sweat slithered between her shoulder blades and slid into the waistband of her jeans.

"Hey, Barbie."

If she even looked at him right now, she'd take her Jimmy Choo and smack him around the head with it. *He's a teenager*, she reminded herself harshly. And before that, he'd been a cute kid who used to hang around with her a lot. He was also the only one who knew where to find Luke. A new layer of perspiration slid down her sides. She tugged her silk camisole away from her clammy chest.

"Hey!" Dakota waved his twiggy arms at her.

Two and a half days and only a handful of words, and now he was Chatty Cathy. Luke was in for a shock when he clapped eyes on his "baby" brother. Dakota, it appeared, was in a black phase, from his limp, dyed hair all the way down to his knee-high Doc Martens. He was so pale, he could've wandered straight off the set of *The Walking Dead.* And the piercings were so last year. His T-shirt looked like a whole lot of small mammals were being group slaughtered across his skinny chest. She turned back to her phone. She should have known this would end badly. Everything to do with Luke anywhere near her life ended in a big pile of crap.

"For fuck's sake, *Tiffany.*" Dakota dragged the syllables of her name out deliberately.

She consented to meet his glare. "What?"

"Car." He jerked his head to indicate the road behind him.

"It's broken down."

"Not that one, Barbie." He curled his lip at her. "That one."

And for the first time in seventy-two hours, Tiffany actually felt like smiling. Because the heat shimmer had coalesced into the outline of a vehicle moving their way. They were saved. And she hadn't even had to call Daddy to come and get her. "Hey." She leaped for the shoulder of the road and waved her hands. "Help me," she threw at Dakota.

He lumbered up next to her.

Then again, maybe she should ask him to stand back. The driver might take one look at him, panic, and drive on.

"They can see you without you going all spaz."

"But they might not stop." Tiffany pinwheeled her arms in the air.

The vehicle took shape into one of those big trucks like her contractor drove. The sun glinted off the chrome detailing on its fender and obscured her view of the driver. An old movie flashed into her mind, the one with the truck and the car where the truck kept trying to kill the car. She stopped waving. This could be very stupid. Horror movies always started with some girl doing something dumb, like flagging down an unknown truck. She'd be better off calling AAA. She changed the motion of her hands to indicate the driver should carry on.

"What are you doing?" Dakota frowned.

"There could be a psycho in there."

He gave her that teen look of total scorn. "There are two of us."

Oh, she felt so much better now. There might be two of them, but her workouts were mainly Pilates. Lots of tone, not a lot of punching-type muscle. And Dakota might be all decked out in black and chains, but he'd be about as effective as a fart against a thunderstorm if the driver of that truck was anywhere near as large as his vehicle.

The truck slowed.

Too late, he'd seen them. He might be a she. Women drove those trucks, too, and it might be a woman in the cab. A really big woman with bulldog tattoos who called herself Bubba's bitch.

The right flicker blinked and the truck pulled to the side of the road.

Did serial killers signal? Her heart pounded in her ears, and more sweat coated her skin. "He's stopping."

"Really?" Dakota dished out the death look.

A small cloud of dust swirled around the large wheels

of the truck. The door opened. A boot hit the ground. Not a cowboy boot, but sort of a workman type boot and way, way too big to belong to any woman. Jeans covered the top of the boots as a second leg joined the first.

The Terminator wore boots like that in the first movie. Her mouth dried.

The driver cleared his door. The baking sun hit the blond lights in his hair. He was tall. Very tall, and filling out his tee to the point where the seams protested. "Well, hello again."

Chapter Seven

Tiffany's belly bottomed out. "What the hell are you doing here?"

"Well, now, let me think. I know—it looks like I'm rescuing you," said the second to last man on earth Tiffany wanted to see again.

"I told her not to drive that stupid thing." Dakota deigned to lower the Beats.

Thomas slammed the door of the truck. "I thought you were going to call me."

"I never said I would call." Her lame comeback deserved the glare of scorn he tossed her way. His broad shoulders casting her in shadow, he strode toward her, a mountain of angry man.

"I told her it was a stupid idea." Dakota jammed his hands in his pockets.

She glared at Dakota.

Thomas's sunglasses concealed his eyes, but the set of his mouth was grim enough to tell he wasn't pleased. "I've been following you for days." His head jerked in the direction of the Miura. "I never thought anyone would be dumb enough to drive a vintage sports car all the way from Chicago."

Dumb. The word clattered through her brain. Her vision went hazy, her breath sawed through her lungs. People gave her that *what a pretty moron* face all the time, but he'd come right out and said it. To her face. "I'm. Not. Stupid."

Both males turned to stare at her.

"No, just marooned in the desert." Thomas crossed his arms over his chest.

True enough.

He stepped toward the car and reached for the hood.

"Don't." It would be an awful waste of all that lovely flesh. Not that she gave a shit about him. She was more concerned she might get hit by flying mechanical bits. "What are you doing?"

His shades blocked the look he threw her as he touched the hood. "Testing how hot it is."

"I could've told you that."

He snorted. "Why would I believe anything you said?"

He arrived, out of the blue, asking questions about Luke and then called her a liar. And wait a damned minute here. "You followed me?"

"Yup." He straightened from the hood and made his way around to the passenger side of the Miura. Thomas bent a long way down to peer in at the dash.

Dakota growled and gave her a sort of *you're too stupid to live* look.

"He followed me." Tiffany tried to get her head around that. "All the way from Chicago. Who does that?"

"Who cares?" Dakota stuck his chin out. "Did you happen to notice we're stuck in the desert?"

Thomas popped his head up. "Actually, I followed Dakota."

"You know each other?" She was forced to ask Dakota as Thomas disappeared into the car again.

"Duh." He rolled his eyes.

Dakota had no appreciation for their dilemma. They were stuck in some—whatever its name was—desert with a very angry stalker. She bet Dakota didn't know which desert either. You actually had to spend time in school to learn anything. Something neither she nor Dakota had managed to do. Poor kid. Of course, it was hard to feel any sympathy for him when he dished out all the attitude, but she tried anyway.

"It looks like it overheated." Her stalker straightened from the cockpit of the car.

"You think?" Jeez, the car redlined, then almost blew up. She didn't need him to tell her that. In fact, she didn't need him at all. She Googled the number for AAA.

Her finger paused over the Call icon. Her father paid for her membership. She'd brought lots of cash and no credit cards to keep him in the dark. That was what all the movies did when a person wanted to disappear. She'd been rather proud of herself for thinking of it. And her bank account was still connected to Daddy. Yes, she should have opened her own by now, but there hadn't really seemed a need, and every time she brought it up, Daddy laughed it off. Why go to all that extra trouble and pay extra bank charges when you didn't have to? Calling AAA might just blow this whole thing open. Would they call and tell Daddy his daughter was stuck in the middle of whichever desert with her ex-husband's car and her ex-husband's younger brother? And a big, blond stalker. *Let's not forget the stalker.*

Still, as rescuers went, at least she'd met Thomas Hunter before. Other than looking seriously mad, he didn't seem all that dangerous. You never could tell, though. "Are you planning to follow me all the way through Utah?"

"Is that where we're heading?"

"Yes." Damn, she'd walked right into that, and now he knew where they were going.

"Via New Mexico?"

There was that, but still. She kept her squirming on the inside. "I never actually got as far as New Mexico, and it's not my fault. I got turned around in Denver."

Dakota snorted.

Fat lot of help he'd been, sleeping most of the way. Giving her crap the rest of the time and making it even harder to concentrate. "I must have missed the signs in that roadwork."

"Okay, but what about all the other signs along the way?"

"It was dark!" Enough with the interrogation, he had some explaining of his own to do. "You've been following me all this time?"

He shrugged one shoulder, as if people did this sort of thing every day.

"That's illegal." Not to mention creepy and annoying as hell.

"No." He didn't seem to give it a moment's thought. "What's illegal is what your husband did. I need to find Luke, and you are my best chance of doing that."

"Ex-husband."

"Not according to the law." He folded his arms over his chest. Muscle bulged beneath his tan skin. The sort of arms a girl wanted to gnaw on. *Focus, Tiffany!*

It all felt like too much, and she wanted to sit down. She looked around for a likely rock and found nothing. Her feet gave a sympathetic throb. This was getting totally out of hand. How the hell had she ended up as this girl? The one who needed rescuing by a virtual stranger.

By lying, that was how. By not getting her divorce because some part of her couldn't let it go. Now she just wanted to get on with her life. The one she wanted, not the one she was living right now. Was that too much to ask?

God, she felt tired. Tired enough to crawl into a ball and sleep.

Thomas stared at her.

Dakota stood beside him, looking pissed.

No change there, then. She dragged her gaze away from them. When had she managed to collect all these men in her life? All of them, currently or potentially, mad at her. "Now what?"

"It looks like you have a problem." Thomas jerked his head at the Miura.

"Don't worry about it." She hauled up some bravado from somewhere. God knew she didn't have a whole lot of it to spare right now. "I'll sort it out."

Thomas grunted and shook his head. "How?"

"The usual way." She waved an airy hand. Her heart sunk right into her murderous Jimmy Choos. She was going to have to call AAA and risk them getting hold of Daddy. The gig was up. She really should have known better than to try to pull something like this off, by herself. Unless . . .

It wasn't much, but it was worth a shot. She had to face facts, and she wasn't swimming in options right now.

"You're right." Her voice stroked the air, soft and husky. She widened her eyes and blinked at him, a slow lowering of lashes. *Ergh!* Doing this made her skin crawl. She hadn't put Delilah on in years. But if Delilah could pull her out of the fire this one time, it was worth a shot.

His brows rose above his sunglasses.

She slunk toward him, her hips slipping into a swaying rhythm as easily as if they did this all the time.

Fraud, yelled her conscience.

Shut up. Tiffany stamped on it. *We do this like Delilah or we call Daddy.*

Her conscience slithered away, grumbling.

One top strap slipped down her shoulder and she left it there. When she was close enough to touch, she stopped and peered up at him. "I'm so silly." *Perfect.* A shade apologetic, and a whole lot bedroom. "I should never have taken the Miura." A teardrop misted on her lashes and she blinked it away.

He bent his neck to look down at her.

Tiffany peered up at him, resting her hand below the swell of his pectoral muscle. Warm, hard flesh pressed against her palm through the softness of his T-shirt. "It's just . . ." Biting her lip, she gave a little shrug. The strap slid another inch down, exposing the top swell of her breast. "I don't know that much about cars. I was desperate and I didn't think."

His expression was unreadable through his glasses. Was he buying this crap? He opened his mouth and shut it again.

"I don't know what to do." She pressed a bit closer. Her belly cramped, ready to heave at her own bullshit. He smelled great, like warm skin with a touch of spice. "Do you think you can help me? I'd be very grateful."

"I'm not going to leave you here." He cleared his throat.

"You're not?"

"No, I would never do that."

Apparently, men really did have only enough blood to work one head at a time. "You'll help me? Really?"

"Jesus." Dakota's eyes bugged out of his head. "She's totally playing you."

Thomas's head snapped over to the boy and back at her.

So close. A few more seconds and he would've offered to carry her all the way through Utah.

"For real?" Thomas frowned down at her.

A split-second decision was called for. She dropped Delilah back in her box. "I'm desperate."

"Damn." His chest expanded on a huge in-breath. "You're scary good at that."

She shrugged one shoulder. "It has its uses."

"Did you see that?" Thomas turned to look at Dakota. "She totally had me going."

Dakota rolled his eyes.

Tiffany tried to get a read on Thomas. "I need to find Luke and find him fast."

"Why?" His head snapped back to her. "Why would you need to find Luke so badly you'd do something like this?"

Like hell she was telling him that. He already knew too much about her.

"Because her daddy doesn't know she's not divorced," Dakota said.

All the breath left her in a rush. Dakota had thrown her under the bus. She turned to glare at him. They didn't even know this man, and Dakota handed out her life like it was for public consumption.

"What?" Thomas whipped off his glasses.

The direct glare of his blue eyes made her want to crawl away. She could only imagine what he was making of all of this. If it hadn't been her life in such a mess, she might have even seen the craziness herself.

"Her father thinks she's divorced." Dakota put another nail in her coffin.

Thomas looked from her to Dakota and back again. "I don't get it. Why not tell him you're not divorced and fly down to Utah like a normal person?"

God, it bugged her how reasonable that question was. "Are you going to help me or not?"

For a long, tense moment, he stared at her with his arms crossed over his chest.

Tiffany met his gaze. Tension prickled down her nape and snapped her spine straight.

He shook his head and stepped away from her. Grabbing his phone out of his back pocket, he thumbed through it. "Yes, good morning. I'm gonna need a tow truck. My car has broken down . . ."

Yes!

"You almost blew it." Dakota glared at her.

"Bullshit." She kept her voice low and her gaze on Thomas. "And what the hell are you doing? You had no right to tell him all that about me."

Dakota snorted. "I did you a favor before he figured out you were playing him. We need his help, Barbie. Even you can figure that out."

He's just a kid. He's just a kid. If she said it often enough and loud enough, she might stop in time before she wrung his scrawny neck.

"It shouldn't take too long," Thomas said. "We are less than thirty miles from the nearest town and they have a tow truck available."

"Great." It would be safe to estimate a tow truck traveled at the speed limit. So, sixty-five miles per hour, supposing the driver was already on his way, meant he would be here in 27.7 minutes. Unless the driver was not in town but on another tow. Assuming he worked on an average radius of thirty miles from the town . . . Tiffany dug in her bag and grabbed her book. Thomas's gaze swung her way and she slipped it deeper into the bag again. Later.

The sun pounded on the empty road.

Dakota huffed a loud breath and wiped the sweat off his forehead.

"Can I ask you something?" Thomas broke the silence.

"Can I stop you?"

He flashed her an appreciative grin. "What made you drive the Miura?"

Dakota made a rude noise and gave her a smug look. She wanted to stick her tongue out at him. The answer to Thomas's question was not something she was prepared to get into, so she shrugged. "It's a car, isn't it?"

Thomas gave a huff of laughter. "Yes, but it's a vintage sports car. They're not generally used to drive across the country."

"Apparently not." She glared at the Miura. Still, when a girl needed a divorce settlement yesterday, there was very little she wouldn't do.

"So, why?" Looking like he was enjoying a tailgate party, he leaned his hips against the fender of his truck.

Stalker or not, that truck had air-conditioning. Another little refinement vintage sports cars didn't have. The truck had air-conditioning and seats. Getting off her killer shoes for a bit sounded like salvation. With her makeup melting down her face, her smile didn't quite make it. God help all of them if she ended up with wrinkles from sun exposure. "Can I sit in your truck?"

"Sure." He strolled to the side of the truck and opened the passenger door.

Taking that as an open invitation, Dakota dove into the back.

Tiffany limped the few feet to the truck like she was walking over splintered glass. Thomas cupped her elbow, and as much as she would like to have been too proud to lean on him, her feet hurt too much and she let him guide her into the truck. The hand under her elbow had a warm, strong grip. She toed off her shoes. Heaven. Sweet Mother of God, it made her tear up.

Thomas climbed in the driver's side and turned on the air.

She put her face in front of the vent. The kiss of cold air against her face was better than a skin-rejuvenating facial. She totally got why dogs did this. "It's a symbolic gesture." She was so pathetically grateful to be off her feet and out of the heat and she didn't have to tell him more than the bare bones. "The car."

"Don't tell me that is *the* Miura?" His gaze sharpened and he looked from her to the Miura and back again. A knowing grin split his face.

Tiffany's heart sank. Obviously he and Luke really had been friends. The thought of how much Luke had told him had her squirming in her seat. There was not a lot to be proud of in her Luke years. Despite the cold air blowing on them, her cheeks heated.

Thomas whistled beneath his teeth. "Yeah, that would be some kind of symbolic gesture. You had her repaired?"

"Yes." The humiliation of that time, so angry and betrayed by Luke, still burned inside her. Now Thomas Hunter knew about her mammoth tantrum. Tiffany hunched her shoulders and stared out her window. Thank God, he went silent. Desert stared back at her. She really wished she knew what to call the dry, shimmering expanse. The thready beat of drums from Dakota's Beats whispered from the back of the truck.

"That must have taken some money."

"It did." Tears burned the back of her lids, and she had to get out of that truck before she made more of a fool of herself. "I'm going to check on the car."

"I thought you were hot."

She slid her feet into her shoes again. Even the sheer torture of four-inch heels in the desert was better than staying here and talking about the Miura.

He made a motion to go with her.

Even if it was hotter than a sauna out there, she needed some breathing room. "Don't."

Thomas whistled beneath his teeth as she strutted over to the Miura. His brief look into the cockpit had told him the car had been lovingly put back together. No expense spared to restore her beauty. "That is one beautiful machine."

"Sounds like crap, though." Dakota decided to join the conversation.

"No, that's twelve cylinders of awesome making sure you're paying attention." Thomas didn't need his Spidey sense to know a whole lot was going on here. Watching her drive away from the condo the other morning, he'd made a snap decision to follow her. He'd tracked her across three states, becoming more and more convinced with each passing mile that he'd done the right thing. He'd lost them and wasted time trying to pick up the trail in Denver.

Fortunately, Dakota liked to keep the world up to date via Instagram, and he'd picked up the trail again. Standing by the side of the road, she'd looked about as lost and help-less as a girl could look. Some screwed-up sense of chivalry had him buckling into his armor and ready to come to her rescue. He needed some answers here because she said she didn't know where Luke was. He wasn't sure what to believe at this stage. Maybe Dakota had some answers for him.

He turned in his seat to face the kid. "You're looking at the sexiest car ever made. And this one is an SV, top of the range, last off the line." Thomas itched to get that hood open, but he'd better wait until she cooled down—Tiffany and the Miura.

"So, what makes it so special?"

"For its time, it was revolutionary." The kid's expression

stayed flat and dull, but at least he was talking. Just what kind of shit was Dakota into? Another question for another day. Those two toughs in Chicago had melted away before Thomas could get close to them. All Dakota had said was yes to pepperoni and no to olives. "The shape." Thomas traced the lines of the car with his hands. "Everything else was still boxy and solid and then they unveiled this baby. You see how it echoes the shape of an airplane wing?"

"No."

"Try harder."

"Uh . . . okay, sort of."

"Right, so it blew all the competition out the water. It's still rated by car lovers as one of the most beautiful cars ever made. At the time, Lamborghini was still new. They were an upstart tractor manufacturer and they were gunning for Ferrari." Thomas shook his head and smiled. "Ferrari must have been so pissed to see this little beauty hit the road."

"So, it's a cool shape. Lame." Dakota sniffed.

"No, man." Thomas could feel himself getting into his subject. He had to watch for people's eyes glazing over when he found his zone. "The engine. They mounted it transversely behind the cab to make sure they could fit a long V-12 onto a short wheelbase. It's got two massive Weber carburetors on it, twelve pistons, four camshafts, and twenty-four valves. All that and the timing chain, and they're right by your head when you drive. That's before you get on the road and let those twin exhausts purr at you."

"Huh." Eyeing the car, Dakota shrugged. "You like this stuff?"

"Sure. It's sexy, makes a lot of noise, and goes fast. What's not to like?"

Outside, Tiffany touched the hood and snatched her hand back quickly.

"No, I mean like science and stuff?" Dakota indicated his tee. It was one of his favorites: *Come to the nerd side, we have pi.*

"Yeah."

Tiffany tucked her hand into her armpit and crossed the other arm over it.

"So, you're like a geek."

"Not like a geek." Thomas laughed. "I'm total geek."

"Then what's with all the—" Dakota made a vague hand motion to encompass his chest.

Thomas looked down at himself. No grease stains, yet, but if he got that hood up, no promises. "What?"

"The muscles and shit."

"These?" He raised his arm and popped his bicep. "Dude, these are strictly for the ladies."

Dakota gaped at him, mouth open. It took the kid a moment to catch on that Thomas was kidding around, and then, the tiniest of smiles tilted one corner of his mouth. "Seriously?"

Tiffany stomped to the edge of the road. It took some kind of balance in those sky-high heels. They turned her walk into one long, undulating torment for any straight man watching it. Thomas also wasn't sure it was within the laws of physics to move in a pair of jeans that tight. Not that he was complaining. That was one fine ass she had there. He was also nearly certain she wasn't wearing a bra under that tiny little top.

Thomas shifted in his seat and shut the door on his way-ward thoughts. "Okay, seriously. I have two older brothers. Both of them are crazy overachievers. I wasn't going to get left behind in any way, shape, or form. They got fit. I got fitter. They bulked up. I bulked up more. Sibling rivalry."

"That's so fucked up."

Man, the kid had a mouth on him. "Not at all. It would

only be unhealthy if I did it without knowing why. As a kid, I wanted to be as good as, if not better than them. Now I work all over the world. In the sort of places it pays to be in shape."

"Like where?" Dakota curled his lip back.

"Zambia, most recently. Before that I spent some time in Cameroon. That's a tough place, you have to be fit to survive it."

Dakota sniffed and stared out the window at Tiffany. She paced alongside the edge of the road, stopped, and raised her hand to stare into the distance.

"So, what's her story?" Thomas kept the question casual.

Dakota swung his gaze back at him and raked him over with dark eyes. "Why don't you ask her?"

Damn, the kid clammed up same as he had the other night. Thomas feigned a casual shrug. "She's not really into sharing with me."

"Dude." Dakota sneered. "You followed her from Chicago."

Yeah, there was that.

Tiffany slunk back to the truck. Ignoring the helping hand he offered, she settled into the front seat with a soft sigh. She frowned at the front of his shirt and rolled her eyes.

He could hear the gears in her head turning, and it made him smile. "What? You don't like pie?"

"I don't eat pie."

She smelled great. The lady didn't want to play nice, though. Tough shit. He wasn't above a little bribery. "I picked up your extra luggage."

Her chin jerked up and she eyed him through narrowed slits. "You did what?"

"When I saw you leave your condo, I waited for a bit, and when you didn't come back, I had a chat with the doorman and he let me up. Your housekeeper was there. She thought you left your luggage behind, so I brought it."

"And she told you where I was?" Those blazing green eyes of hers could burn holes in his head.

Best he not get into the how of persuading her housekeeper and her doorman into letting him into her apartment. Tiffany already had him on *America's Most Wanted*. "I told you, I need to find Luke." And he wasn't above doling out some flattery and charm to the housekeeper to get it. "It's urgent."

"So you followed us?" She gave a soft growl and shook her head.

Okay, it didn't look good when viewed from her angle. "I'm not weird or anything. I just really need to find Luke, and you're my best shot at that. I got lucky, too. Dakota put your whole journey on Instagram. I just followed the pictures."

Tiffany shot Dakota a filthy look.

"You're welcome." Dakota glowered at her.

What was up with these two?

Turning back to him, her eyes narrowed to grim lines of suspicion. "Why do you need to find Luke so badly?"

"Why doesn't your dad know you're not divorced?"

Her lips tightened and she turned to look out the window.

Tiffany glared at the desert. As much as she wanted to know what the hell Thomas Hunter's deal was, she didn't want to answer his questions in return. For now, they were stuck together and she was a tiny bit grateful he was there. When the tow truck came, they could go their separate ways again. Unless he decided to keep following her all the way to Luke.

"Is there more in the car?"

"What?" She turned back to him.

"More luggage." He smiled the sort of smile that must go over really big with the girls in Geekville.

"Yes." Bits of her teetered on the edge of melting. Picking up her luggage had been a nice thing to do, even if he'd used it as a way to get information out of her housekeeper. "I'll get it."

"No, I'll get it." He already had the door open and swung back to Dakota. "You got everything?"

Dakota jerked his chin at the backpack sagging against the seat beside him.

Muscle bunched and coiled beneath his tee as Thomas strode over to the Miura and leaned in. He straightened and she dragged her stare away from that supreme ass. With her bag in one hand, he turned back to the truck.

The slogan on his shirt almost made her laugh out loud. Pi, one of those glorious mystery numbers that she should know all about. Except the once or twice she'd asked someone, they'd given her the *pretty moron* look that made her want to squirm and howl. Apparently, it was one of those hundreds of things she should've learned in school. After you got that look enough times, you learned not to ask. God, she just knew pi would be something worth knowing about, a number that could unlock a whole world of other stuff. The bits she picked up on the Internet had her salivating for more. She wanted to know about the infinite series, how the rate of conversion worked. Things she'd read and not understood. With nobody to ask, she had learned to keep her questions to herself.

Thomas was still outside, so she reached over and grabbed her book. Working quickly, she thumbed open the lock and made a quick note of the slogan. It really was funny.

"Is that her luggage?" Leaning over the backseat, Dakota faced the open hatch at the rear.

"Yup." Thomas loaded her remaining bag into the covered cab of his truck.

"She's such a girl."

Tiffany tucked her book back into her bag. "*She's* sitting right here."

Dakota pursed his lips together in a sullen snarl. They had gone to bed the night before and got up that morning without exchanging so much as a grunt. Ninety-six hours, she'd thought, ninety-six hours and then she was free to become Mrs. Ryan Cooper. This was going to put a real wrinkle in her timing. By her calculation, the tow truck should be another fifteen minutes, unless she'd miscalculated and the tow truck worked a wider radius. Then again, they were in Utah. Utah? For the love of God, what could Luke be doing in Utah?

Thomas climbed back into the truck.

"Thanks," she said. "For getting my luggage."

"It shouldn't be much longer until the tow truck gets here." He checked his watch.

She nodded that she understood. All the driving was catching up with her. That and the heat. She hadn't slept well because of the coming meeting with Luke. The last conversation they'd had face-to-face hadn't gone well. Tiffany hunched her shoulders. It had been a disaster with both of them yelling and screaming, her crying, him looking like putting his fist through a door. The look on Luke's face when he'd seen what she'd done to the Miura was burned in the back of her brain.

At some point around three that morning, she'd made a decision. She wasn't that girl anymore. Ryan and Daddy were right. She needed to put Wild Tiffany away and get on with her life. There was no reason for the conversation with

Luke to go badly. With the Miura as her ace in the hole, all she had to remember was she was not the same girl. Luke wasn't going to make her angry because she wasn't going to allow him that sort of control over her emotions. She would logically point out how neither of them could get on with their lives while they were still married, give him the car, and then it was back to Willow Park and a quick divorce. Maybe she would even manage an apology for what she'd done to the car, but that might be pushing her maturity too far. If she could, she vowed, she would.

"How long is this going to take?" Dakota threw himself around in his seat.

God, his shirt was awful. Did people actually make things that ugly? And who bought them? Dakota, obviously, but who else had that little taste? What was it with these two and their shirts? She gestured toward the disturbing logo. It looked kind of evil. "What is that?"

Dakota shoved his Beats back over his ears. Another slap in a whole series of them from Dakota. Maybe she'd grow immune to them by the time they found Luke.

"Anaal Nathrakh." Thomas answered her.

Tiffany stared, no closer to knowing.

"Grindcore metal band," Thomas said.

"You know them?" Dakota's eyes narrowed as he studied Thomas.

Was Dakota wearing eyeliner? *Note to self: keep makeup case locked.* She didn't want him in there messing with her Clarins. The memory of what he could do with nail polish nearly made her laugh. Lola's ridiculous dog with streaks of Summer Sizzle Red all over his fur.

"Sure." Thomas grinned at Dakota. He really did have a nice smile. It crinkled up the corners of his eyes and made furrows down either side of his tanned cheeks. "I saw them when I was last in Germany. Incredible concert."

Dakota actually sat forward, his eyes sparkling with interest. "Really? Did they do 'Between Shit and Piss We Are Born'?"

Tiffany groaned beneath her breath. This was going to be one long nightmare.

Chapter Eight

The scenery outside Tiffany's window had stopped being interesting forever ago. Thirty minutes past her estimated arrival time and no sign of the tow truck. She needed to kill time and her book was out of the question. People always asked what she was writing and then she had to make something up. They never quite believed that a girl like her could have such a passionate interest in numbers. They asked, she answered, and then came the *pretty moron* look.

Maybe she should leave Ryan a message. Then again, it might do him good to sweat a bit.

Annoying buzz from Dakota's headphones blended into the hum of the truck engine. At full volume, that crap must be an eardrum assault. She flipped through the offerings on her iPad. There had to be something on here worth burning time.

The clear sky outside the window outlined Thomas's profile. He wasn't model good-looking. It must've been the stress of Piers approaching meltdown causing her to mistake him for a model. Anybody trying to make a career in modeling would've had his nose fixed and gotten some Botox for those smile lines around his eyes. *Tap tap-tap*

tap tap-tap-tap went his long forefinger against the steering wheel in time to the beat leaking out of Dakota's headphones.

"What are you reading?" His sudden question made her jump.

"Emma." Ryan had said she would enjoy it.

"Really?" He glanced at her. His eyes were a clear cloudless blue, ringed with dark lashes. Men always had the best lashes. It didn't seem fair. They aged better and got those giraffe lashes. "So you like Jane Austen?"

"Yeah." As soon as she got around to reading Jane Austen, she probably would. "Doesn't everyone?"

Thomas gave a quick bark of laughter. "If you're into love stories."

That perked her right up and she tapped the icon to open *Emma.* She'd gotten halfway through that one about the Russian brothers and had to give up. Everybody was fighting all the time in the stupid thing. If she wanted family drama, all she had to do was visit Daddy for half an hour. But a love story, that sounded quite good.

Emma Woodhouse, handsome, clever, and rich, with a comfortable home and happy disposition, seemed to unite some of the best blessings of existence; and had lived nearly twenty-one years in the world with very little to distress or vex her.

Tiffany heaved a sigh. It was one of *those* books. She should've known. Still, it was about a girl and she was clever and rich and things seemed to be going right for her.

"Have you read *Pride and Prejudice*?"

So, they were going back to Mr. Chatty. "No." Her concentration wavered off the page. Hadn't even seen the movie. "Have you?"

"Sure. I had to hide it from my brothers, though." He gave her a quirky little smile.

The sort that hit her in hot waves. "Is it dirty?"

"What?" He looked at her strangely.

Tiffany's stomach dipped. Damn, she'd said something dumb. This was what happened when you could count on one hand the number of English classes you attended in a year. Maybe she would have been better off with her book after all.

"You don't really like Jane Austen, do you?"

Busted. She could go with a lie and see where that led, but she already knew Thomas didn't give up easily. "I've never read any Jane Austen."

"Then why read it now?"

Tiffany gaped at him. Was he kidding her? Ryan had put the book on her iPad because he said it would help improve her mind. Confessing that sounded pathetic. "Why did you read it?"

"Because I love books." His gaze drifted over and met hers. "I read anything and everything."

That sounded like a challenge to her. "Have you read"— she scanned her iPad—"*Of Mice and Men*?" Stupid title, like some sort of Disney movie.

"Steinbeck, sure." He nodded. "Great story, but totally depressing."

Great. Stuck in a car with a hot brainiac. She searched her bookshelves again. *"The Painted Bird?"*

"Kosinsky."

"Yeah."

"I've read it."

"Lolita?"

"Yup."

"1984?"

"Yes."

"The Great Gatsby?"

"For sure."

"Middlemarch?"

"Uh . . . maybe . . . yes."

"Ulysses?"

"Yup."

"Madame Bo . . ."

"Bovary and yes."

"The Portrait of a Lady?"

"No."

"Aha." Tiffany did a happy little wiggle in her chair.

"Have you read *Portrait of a Lady?*" He chuckled like it wasn't such a bad thing if she hadn't.

"No," she said. "But I'm going to."

He pointed toward her iPad. "When you get through all those others on there."

"Yes." She pretended to read, but her attention kept straying to Thomas. He smelled good, too. Not like expensive aftershave or cologne, but woodsy and manly and warm.

"Can I ask you something?"

If she said no would it stop him? Probably not. "What?"

"Why do you have that list of books on there and you haven't read any of them?"

"I never said I hadn't read any of them."

"Have you?"

"No."

"Why not?"

"I don't have the time."

He raised an eyebrow at her. His brow had a language all of its own, and right now it sneered, "Oh, yeah?"

"I have a job, a life and friends and things. I don't have time to sit and read, read, read all day. Not like some people." She glared at his profile.

He kept his attention on the road for all of five minutes. "You know what I think?"

"Why do people always ask that? Because they don't really care if you say yes or no, they're going to tell you anyway." The guy must be ADD or something. Why couldn't he look at the scenery and be happy doing that?

"I don't think you want to read any of those books on there."

"Of course I do." He hadn't even known her for one full day and he thought he was going to tell her what she did and didn't like.

"Did you choose them?"

"No."

"Who did?"

"Ryan."

"Ryan?"

"My . . . Ryan." What was Ryan to her anyway? Not still a boyfriend, but not a fiancé either. She must be the only girl alive who was sort of engaged.

"Aha." He made a noise like he'd stumbled onto the secret of life and then clammed up.

Not likely. "Aha, what?"

"Nothing."

It didn't look like nothing from where she sat. She so wanted to ask, but that meant carrying on the stupid conversation. She pointedly returned to her reading.

"If you could choose what you wanted to read, what would you read?"

Tiffany growled her exasperation and peeked at Thomas. "I can choose whatever I want to read."

"Okay. If I took you to a bookstore right now and said pick any book, what would you pick?" Up went the chatty eyebrow in challenge.

Tiffany squirmed in her seat. There was no way she was answering that. She'd had this conversation one too many times to be fooled. He might seem interested now, but she'd tell him and then he'd get the *pretty moron* look on his face. Then, he might laugh or make some comment and she would know he was thinking *what the fuck.*

"Not going to answer?" He didn't seem to get that she was ignoring him. Or maybe he didn't care.

"What's it to you?"

He held her gaze for a moment before going back to the road. "Because reading is something to enjoy, and if you're not going to enjoy it, then you might as well not do it."

Okay, that was a new one. Ryan said reading improved the mind. He said well-read people were cultured and interesting people. She'd been to enough dinner parties with Ryan's friends to know that was true. Finally, she'd gotten tired of sitting in the corner with nothing to talk about. And every time she did open her mouth, their faces went all carefully blank. She wasn't well read. She wasn't read at all. Daddy didn't read and he didn't think it was important that she read. "Reading improves the mind."

"For sure it does." He nodded. "But it's not supposed to be a punishment. I don't think any of those authors on your iPad wrote their book to torture someone."

"Huh." Tiffany made a mental note to remember that for Ryan next time they had this conversation. "I'm not much of a reader, that's why Ryan made this list of books for me. So I could learn stuff."

"What sort of stuff?" A smile curved his lips up, but she didn't think he was laughing at her.

"Well, these books for a start."

"Lots of people don't read. It's no big deal. But I think you might be missing out by not reading."

It made sense the way he said it. Still, she didn't trust this whole *live and let live* thing he had going on. Smart people were arrogant, like they knew how much you didn't know and that made them special. And he was smart. She recognized the type. "And, okay, your T-shirt. I don't understand what it means."

He looked taken aback. "Come to the nerd side, we have pi." He read the slogan like saying it out loud was going to make her understand. "It's a play on words, pie and pi."

Tiffany dug her nails into her palms. She knew that much. "I meant I don't understand pi."

He frowned a little and Tiffany braced for the tone.

"Pi is a number," he said. "Actually, it's a letter of the Greek alphabet, but in mathematics, it has a numerical value." He glanced at her. "Did you do trigonometry or geometry at school?"

"Yes." When she was there, which was not often. Daddy rated pageants over grades.

"Then you would have used pi."

"Huh. I guess I forgot." When she was younger, she'd told her father how much she liked numbers. Daddy had laughed and said it was a shame to mess with a pretty head like hers by putting numbers in it. She peeped over at Thomas. He watched the road. He didn't seem to think there was anything wrong with the fact that she didn't get his tee. "It's the sixteenth letter," she said. "Pi is the sixteenth letter of the Greek alphabet."

"I didn't know that."

"It represents the ratio of the diameter of a circle to its circumference." It came out in a breathy rush.

He raised both eyebrows. "So you do know about pi, then?"

"A little." She feigned a casual shrug. This was the point when most people were already looking at her like she'd grown horns. Thomas, though, cocked his head and watched her as if he really wanted to talk to her some more. Digging her nails into her palms, she took the leap. "Do you know anything else about pi?"

"Do I know about pi?" he scoffed. "I'm wearing the T-shirt."

She hauled up a bit more courage. She'd smack him if he laughed. "Could you tell me?"

Instead he looked at her as if she'd handed him the moon. "Okay, stop me when I lose you, because I could go on all day."

"Okay." Maybe he was a bit crazy, but in a nice way.

"Speaking of pie, I'm getting hungry. Once we get the car towed somewhere, we'll get something to eat."

"Sure."

He glanced over at Dakota, who texted and bopped his head to the crashing noise in his ears. "He'll be sure to be hungry. I was always hungry at that age."

Tiffany sat still and waited. She wondered if she should mention she had very specific dietary needs, but she was enjoying the moment too much to screw it up. Daddy hated it when she started with what he called her "picking and fussing."

"Now, pi is an irrational number with an approximate value of 3.141596—"

"Stop." Tiffany held up her hand. Lovely numbers floated around in her head. She almost purred. "Pretend I don't know anything and start at the beginning."

His face lit up like Christmas. "That I can do."

Chapter Nine

Tiffany had never met someone who liked numbers as much as she did. And he never once gave her the look. He kept talking decimals, irrational numbers, circles, tangents—delicious terms that wrapped around her like fluffy clouds of awesome. She itched to write this all down. The more he spoke, the more questions she had. They bubbled up in her brain until she almost blurted them out. At some point, he'd even grabbed an old flyer from the glove compartment and shown her some calculations. Too bad the tow truck's arrival brought his mathematical lecture to a halt.

Thomas hopped out of the truck and opened her door.

She liked that he had manners. When he extended his hand to help her down from the cab, she let him. His hand closed around hers in a warm clasp. A tingle of awareness caught her totally off guard and shot straight up her arm in a bolt of sensation. Her gaze jerked to his.

His eyes widened as if he got it, too.

Uh-oh. Being attracted to Thomas Hunter, not on the agenda.

"This your car?" The tow truck driver strolled toward them. If he drove like he walked, Tiffany got why it had taken him so long to get there.

"Yes." Tiffany pulled her hand away from Thomas with a stern lecture to her nerve endings to calm the hell down.

The driver's glance took a slow meander from her toes to the top of her head, stopping in between at the interesting parts. His mouth split into a grin as he pushed his ball cap back on his head. "She's a beauty."

Thomas stiffened beside her.

Men had given her that look since she hit puberty. According to Daddy, it was her gift, the thing that made her special. More importantly, it was the part that made Daddy smile because it reminded him of her mother. So she worked hard to be good at it. Wild Tiffany didn't give a shit, she ate pizza and went out without brushing her hair or putting on makeup. When she'd been with Luke, Wild Tiffany had been firmly at the wheel. "I think she's overheated," Tiffany said.

"Do you now?" The driver gave her a kindly smile. He might as well have patted her on the head and called her "little lady." "Well, we'll just take her someplace where they can have a look at her and see. A sweet, young thing like you doesn't need to go messing around with cars and stuff."

There, that was what people saw when they looked at her. As if she really needed the reminder.

The trucker grabbed a filthy rag from his back pocket and wiped his hands. "Sure is a hot one today. Cars breaking down up and down the highway."

Tiffany threw Thomas a triumphant glance. Other people's cars broke down, too.

"Of course, nothing like this little baby." The driver made as if to pat the hood and then snatched his hand back. "Wouldn't want to get her all dirty. Would we, baby?" He circled the car on his way to his truck. "You sure are a pretty little lady."

It took Tiffany a moment to realize he was talking to the car.

"I almost feel like I should get territorial," Thomas said in her ear.

It made her want to laugh. The warm brush of his breath teased the hair on the back of her neck. She crossed her arms over her tightening nipples.

Thomas followed the tow guy to lower the hydraulic lift. Chains clanked and she winced as they brought them close to the Miura. She needn't have worried. The trucker was in love. He wiped his hands before he went anywhere near her girl. The chains had never been so lovingly fitted beneath the front chassis of a car. With a whine the hydraulics pulled her girl up onto the back of the truck.

Not her girl for much longer. The sadness pressed in, tears pricked behind her lids. She blinked them away and glanced around for a distraction.

The chain looked strong. How strong? She checked out the hydraulic motor. How much force to lift the Miura? Of course, that would depend on the weight of the car, but would anything else factor into it? All her mental notes fought for space in her brain, beating back the sadness. Later, she'd write them in her book and try to find the right calculation.

The lift stopped with a metallic *kachunk* and the trucker clamped the wheels. The Miura perched like an empress on the bed of the truck. Handing her over to Luke would hurt like a bitch. So much time and effort, not to mention money, had gone into restoring her beauty. Tiffany had almost convinced herself the car was hers.

Thomas handled everything. He filled in forms, handed over registration documents, and signed things. All the while, she couldn't look away from the car. "Now what?"

Thomas strode back toward her. "Now we follow him

into the nearest town and see what we can do to get her back on the road."

"You're coming with us?" It beat climbing into the tow truck, but still . . .

Staring at her as if she'd lost her mind, Thomas said, "I can't leave you on the side of the road. What sort of guy do you think I am?"

"I don't know what sort of guy you are." Other than a fellow numbers geek and someone who read what seemed like all the time.

"Why don't I tell you while we follow the truck?"

It sounded fair enough to her. The tow truck eased back onto the highway, carrying her girl on the back.

"I should never have driven her," Tiffany said as he opened his truck door for her.

"Yeah, but who could resist?" His smile took any sting out of his agreement. He shut her door and strode around to the driver's side. He moved like he meant business. It was more than the size of him, he had a way of looking like he knew where he was going and nobody would stop him from getting there. Getting back into the truck he said, "Ready?"

Dakota fidgeted in the backseat. "Thank fuck."

"Do you kiss your mother with that mouth?" Thomas glared at him.

"Sure." Dakota's face went hard as flint. "It wouldn't bug you if you'd met Debbie."

Thomas raised his eyebrows. "Debbie?"

"Lola's real name." Lola, aka Debbie, had her own set of rules. "Lola does things her way." Meaning, she did things for herself and only for herself. Tiffany's heart hurt a little for Dakota.

"Damn," Thomas said so softly only she could hear him. "Luke told me about her." Thomas eased the truck onto the road. Dakota's Beats buzzed, but he kept his voice low. "I thought he was exaggerating."

"No." Tiffany shook her head. Luke and Thomas must have gotten into some deep stuff. Luke reserved his Lola stories for people he really liked. "Luke seems to have told you lots of things."

"We were friends." Thomas grimaced a bit. "Right before he screwed me over."

Welcome to the world of Luke Holt. Been there, done that. "How did you meet him?"

"He was mountain biking across Africa, tangled with the wrong mosquito and ended up with malaria. We found him and made sure he was taken care of."

"Wow." Classic Luke, screw the world and everyone else in it. "How did he screw you over?"

Thomas glanced at her and then back at the road. "Look." A muscle twitched in the side of his jaw. "It seems we're stuck together for a while. We might want to share a bit of information."

"How much information?" He was likeable, but trust? She wasn't sure about that.

"Why don't we tell each other why we need Luke so much?"

"You first."

His mouth split into a wide grin. "You're tough."

"I don't know if I can trust you."

"Fair enough." Thomas chuckled. "Like I said, I met Luke when he was biking through Africa. He got really sick. Some local villagers near the site brought him to us. We had the meds he needed and we kept him there until we could arrange a way to get him to South Africa and the hospitals there. It took a few days, and Luke and I got to talking. We hit it off." Pausing, he took a deep breath. "We talked about a lot of shit. You, his dad." Thomas jerked his chin toward Dakota. "Him. And we argued about what my company was doing there."

"What were you doing there?"

He quirked a brow at her. "Let's stick to Luke for now. Anyway, when he left, Luke was so opposed to our project he stole my survey results. I need them back." The quiet way he said that prickled along her nape. Thomas Hunter was a man on a mission. "Your turn."

"That was a total dick move," she said, playing for time while she sorted how much to say. "Even for Luke."

"To be fair, he thinks he's saving Africa from some big first-world corporate rape," he said.

"Is he?"

"Nope." Thomas shook his head. "It's only a matter of time before that resource is found, and at least with my company, we'll try to make sure we get to it as responsibly as we can." He took a breath. "The misery of being exploited by capitalists is nothing compared to the misery of not being exploited at all."

"Huh?"

He threw her a smile. "It's a quote from a British economist back in the sixties."

Economist. Crunching the numbers on how the world went around. She'd always been fascinated by the idea. Talking to Thomas was nice. He didn't talk down to her or lecture her. "Going to tell me what this mysterious resource is? In our newfound spirit of trust."

He gave a bark of laughter. The lines around his eyes crinkled when he laughed. It was awesome and she looked away quickly. "Gonna tell me what you need Luke for?"

Her turn had rolled around. "I need him to divorce me. If he comes back to Illinois with me, we can get it done fast."

"The divorce your father doesn't know about?"

As he knew that much already, she nodded.

"So, why now? Why not before?"

"What's the mineral?"

Shaking his head, he chuckled. "Okay, the mineral is called rare earth."

"What?"

"Don't worry, Barbie, you can't wear it around your neck." Dakota's venom oozed over from the backseat. So much for hearing nothing through that noise coming from his Beats. She really, really hated that name.

Thomas stared at Dakota through the rearview mirror. "You've got to stop that, dude." He spoke quietly, but his tone radiated the sort of authority Tiffany would never even attempt. "You don't speak to anyone like that and especially not a lady."

"She's not—"

"Think carefully before you finish that sentence." Thomas's jaw locked tight.

Dakota dropped his gaze first and thumbed up the volume on his music.

He didn't have to defend her, but he'd done it anyway. A little more of the tension inside her uncoiled.

Thomas jerked his head at the backseat. "He doesn't like you much."

"He blames me because of what happened with Luke. Luke left to get away from us . . . me." And Dakota had some right to his anger. After their last fight, Luke had left and not been back to Willow Park since.

"Now you?" Thomas said.

As much as she wriggled inside, he'd kind of earned a bit of her trust. "I'm sort of engaged." She said it quickly before she changed her mind. "But I can't get engaged until I get a divorce."

The look of surprise on his face almost had her regretting her moment of honesty. "How can you be sort of engaged?"

The question caught her off guard. She'd had him going

in a different direction entirely. "Ryan and my father think I am still holding on to the past. They want me to get rid of the car to prove I'm not. So I'm taking the car to Luke and getting him to agree to the divorce at the same time."

"Ryan?" He pursed his lips. "The guy who got you the books. Is that your sort of fiancé? Does he know you're still married?"

Tiffany studied his face carefully for signs of mockery. "All you need to know is that I need to find Luke and get my divorce."

"I gave you more than that," he said.

"You followed me across three states." It was a deflection and the look on his face said he knew it, too. Tiffany hissed a long breath of relief as he nodded and went back to driving. Being treated as a person and not a pretty face warmed her inside. It wouldn't last long, and the story of how she got there would only hurry along its death. For some reason, which she didn't want to examine, she needed to hold on to the way Thomas treated her.

The town nestled between a range of low hills, obscured by the ridges of rock from the road.

Dakota leaned forward and braced his arms on the back of her seat. "Jesus."

Jesus had nothing to do with this town. And *town* was a rather optimistic description. A motley collection of buildings lined the street, barely holding their own against the steady incursion of red earth.

"I imagine it was a lot busier. At some point in its history. Maybe." Thomas peered through the windshield as he drove. "They have a diner."

And a garage.

They followed the tow truck into the dusty parking area of a small auto repair shop. Through the open doors, the dim hulks of cars sat suspended on two lifts. A man lumbered out of the sun dappled interior and over to the tow truck.

Thomas parked and Tiffany climbed out of the car with him.

Dakota put his head back again and closed his eyes. Probably for the best. One look at Dakota and this town would break out the pitchforks.

The mechanic's coveralls were pushed down around his waist to rest under the curve of his rotund belly. He stuck his fists on his hips and stared at the Miura. "That yours?" he asked Thomas.

Thomas looked at her quickly and Tiffany shrugged. Ryan never asked her opinion before he took charge. Then again, she always sat back and let Ryan take charge.

"Yes," Thomas said. "She overheated."

The mechanic took a step closer to the tow truck and peered at the car. "She's a fancy piece, all right." Grunting, he jerked his head. "Bring her in and I'll put her up on the rack and take a look."

Tiffany eyed the repair bay with misgiving. An older-than-dirt pickup shared the space with an even older VW bus. Tools and oil littered the ground beneath the cars. A transistor radio sat on a workbench playing a classic rock ballad. The aerial was taped to the window with a peeling piece of duct tape. She had trouble imagining the Miura in there. "Do you think he knows what he's doing?" she whispered to Thomas.

The mechanic and tow truck driver were busy unloading her girl and couldn't hear her over the whine of the hydraulics.

"Sure as hell hope so," he said out the corner of his mouth. "How soon can you let us know the problem?" he called to the mechanic.

The man glanced up. He jerked his thumb over his shoulder at the two relics up on his maintenance lifts. "Got an oil change and a busted clutch in there." He jammed his fists on his hips again and dropped his head to stare at the ground. "Let me think."

Tiffany stared at him. Thomas stared at him. Even the tow truck driver stilled and stared at him. In the stretched silence, a pair of magpies yakked at each other in a nearby mesquite bush. Tiffany thought she might even be able to hear the grass growing.

"Morning." He spoke so suddenly she jumped.

Her heart sank. She couldn't stay in this horrible little town overnight. She was sure they didn't have a hotel.

"Can't you put her up now and have a look?" Thomas asked.

The mechanic stuck his stubbly chin out. "In the morning."

Tiffany opened her mouth to argue.

A gentle squeeze of the arm from Thomas stopped her. "Is there anyplace we can stay overnight?"

Jesus, take me now.

"Sure." The tow truck driver grinned at them cheerfully. "There's the A1 motel just the other side of town." Misgiving slid across his blunt features as he peered at Tiffany. "Of course, it isn't fancy or anything, but it's clean and Val will serve you breakfast if you ask her nicely."

"Then we'll be sure to ask her nicely." Thomas smiled.

"You're staying?" Tiffany was almost afraid to ask the question. Of course she'd be fine without him, but it would be nice if he stayed.

"If you ask me nicely." He grinned at her. She liked his smile. It reached inside and dragged an answering one out of her. He strolled back to the truck and opened the passenger door. "Only a total dick would leave you here, alone, to deal with this. Lucky for you, I'm a nice guy."

Chapter Ten

Tiffany followed Thomas and Dakota into a cheerful-looking diner in the center of town. As one, the occupants turned to stare as the three of them wove through the crowd to an empty table. Tiffany raised her chin. She'd never let them see her fidget.

Thomas called a greeting to the room.

A few muttered replies and people got back to their conversations.

Near the back of the restaurant, Thomas found them a booth. The Formica tabletop gleamed, clean and scrubbed. Signs of wear showed on the bench but, thankfully, no food stains or leftover grime.

Dakota took his headphones off. "I'll have a burger with everything."

"That's one thousand seven hundred and seventy calories in one meal, before you order a drink," Tiffany said.

Dakota and Thomas blinked at her.

"Who cares?" Dakota's face twisted into a sneer as he put his headphones back on.

"You just worked that out?" Thomas raised a brow.

"Yes." Tiffany hesitated, and rechecked her addition. Five hundred and forty calories for a large order of fries, four hundred and ninety for the onion rings with the double cheeseburger topping it off at seven hundred and forty, give or take a few calories.

Thomas went back to his menu. "I don't see the calories written on the menu."

"They're not." Tiffany's mouth watered at the picture of the burger. She couldn't remember the last time she'd eaten one. "What are you having?" She'd lay money on something sinful and delicious.

Thomas had a strange look on his face. "You keep all those numbers in your head?"

"Yes," Tiffany said. "You need to know what you're eating."

"But you've never been here before."

"I know that." The number thing had slipped out and now she was stuck with the explanation. She kept all sorts of numbers in her head, and thanks to their conversation in the car, she had pi in there now, too. "But most burgers work out at around about the same, so I averaged them."

Thomas lifted his brow. "You averaged them?"

"Yes."

"So, by implication, you have a running tally of the calorie count of most burgers in your head."

"I suppose so." Tiffany squirmed in her seat. It infuriated her father when she did the number thing out loud. It was easier to just pretend it was all about calories.

"I think I'd prefer not to know. But what the hell." Thomas grinned. "I think I'll join him. You?"

"I'll have the garden salad." Pursing her thin mouth, the waitress jotted it down on her notepad. "With no dressing and no croutons."

"How many calories?" Thomas leaned his elbows on the table. Challenge gleamed in his eyes. He thought he had her beat, but he'd have to do a whole lot better than that.

"Twelve per cup, so around thirty-three for the bowl. It would've been eleven calories per cup, but this one has carrots and tomatoes in it."

"Right." He shook his head.

She wished she could work out what he was thinking. "What?"

"You know the calorie count of everything you eat?"

"Sure." Tiffany shrugged. She also knew the diner had 30 four-seater tables and 3 six-seaters tucked in the three available corners. The last corner led to the bathroom. Of the possible 138 diners, the diner was currently at about 78 percent capacity.

"And you can add them up, just like that?"

"Yes."

He grunted and crossed his hands on the table in front of them. It brought him right onto her half of the table. It didn't seem to bother him that he was in her space. It bothered her, though. There was too much of him. She hadn't missed the way the waitress had eyed him up as if he were an ice cream cone, either.

"So you look at menus and count the calories?"

Tiffany rolled her eyes. And there you had it. He might have spent all that time in the truck talking about pi, but at the end of the day he was the same as everyone else. It was her fault for thinking he might possibly be different. See something different in her. But if he wanted to talk about calories with the pretty moron, so be it. "Listen, buddy." She did some leaning of her own. "You don't think I fit into these skinny jeans by eating a burger and fries, do you? Because I have news for you, if you think girls slip into a size two with no effort, then you're not as smart as you think you are."

"Really." The devil danced in his blue eyes as he brought his face closer to hers.

Tiffany almost backed off, but didn't want to give up that much ground.

"If you think men care as much about how you get into those jeans as how to get you out of them, then you're not as smart as you think you are."

Tiffany snapped back into her seat and glared at him. "You're a pig."

"No, I'm honest." He smirked.

Her irritation seemed to bounce right off him as he looked around the diner with interest. "I don't get you."

He jerked his head back. "There's really not that much to get." He spread his arms out. "What you see is what you get. WYSIWYG."

"You're such a geek." But it made her smile.

"I could deny it, but why bother." He sat back in the booth and folded his arms over his chest. "But that wasn't what I was getting at before. I was thinking it's pretty amazing that you manage to remember all those numbers and add them up like that. That's impressive."

"Anyone can add up numbers." This subject made her uncomfortable. The number thing was her secret.

"Not that fast." He seemed sincere with blue eyes staring back at her, clear and readable.

She looked a little closer. Maybe he was for real. "I bet you can."

"No." He shook his head. "I'm the shit when it comes to math, but I can't total a whole bunch of numbers in my head that quickly. I don't think I could remember all those calories, either."

Tiffany pursed her lips. He didn't seem to be packing any sort of hidden meaning. "For real?"

"Yeah. And I made the dean's list for math at college."
He gave her one of his grins.

Those lips needed a permit for concealed weapons.
Even now, her answering smile wanted to break free. She
didn't quite know what to say. All her life people had told
her she was pretty. A childhood of modeling and beauty
pageants had made sure she knew that. This was better,
though. Being smart was something nobody, not even
Ryan, said about her.

The waitress brought their cutlery and set it down in a
wire tray of condiments. Ketchup, mustard, fry sauce, salt
and pepper. Ketchup in the wrong place.

Thomas leaned over and swapped the mustard and
ketchup bottles so the bottles ranged neatly from tallest to
shortest. Looked like she wasn't the only person who liked
things to be organized correctly. The condiments looked so
much better this way.

"I was thinking," he said, unwrapping his cutlery and
placing the fork on one side of his plastic place mat and the
knife on the other. "We should team up."

"Team up?"

"As in we both have a common purpose, which is to
find Luke."

She got where he was headed with this, but needed to
hear him spell out the details. Riding with Thomas might
solve most of her problems. "Okay."

"Driving the Miura doesn't seem to be the best plan,
given what's happened." He didn't know how far she still
had to go. Still, she was listening and she nodded for him
to continue. "You gotta admit, you'll be far more comfortable in my truck."

His easy smile didn't fool her. Tension radiated from the
stiff line of his shoulders. He had nearly as much invested
in finding Luke as she did. Teaming up made sense, and

she hadn't given much thought to what she would do when the Miura was repaired. This breakdown had already cut into her schedule. Another mishap and Thomas Hunter might not be there to rescue her. It seemed a logical solution. Except, and this was a kicker, he was a stranger.

"Look"—he leaned forward on his forearms—"I know you don't know me, and the following thing looked bad. I told you I had to find Luke, and I do. My company is going under without that survey. I've put my heart and soul, not to mention my life savings, into my company succeeding. You know where Luke is, or at least Dakota does, and I have the means to get you there."

She aligned the condiment tray in the center of the table as she chewed it over. He seemed a straight-up sort of guy, and only God and the mechanic knew how long she'd be stuck there waiting for the car. "I have to wait for the Miura to be repaired."

"Then I'll wait with you," he said. "I'm sure I can rent a trailer from somewhere. I spotted one behind the repair shop. We load the Miura on the trailer and tow it to wherever it is we're going."

"Okay." That did sound reasonable. She had a much better chance of delivering the Miura in mint condition if they towed it. A small voice whispered that maybe spending so much time with Thomas Hunter wasn't the best idea. Already, she was starting to like him a bit too much. Add the niceness of him, the way he made her feel comfortable around him, and the hot geek thing together, and you might have trouble. "But no weird shit."

"Like?" Up went an eyebrow.

Heat crawled up her cheeks.

"You mean like hitting on you?" His eyes twinkled at her. "I—"

Straightening in his seat, he locked his gaze on something behind her.

"What is it?" Tiffany peered through the lettering of the daily special on the window into the street. A woman marched a lagging set of children behind her and disappeared into the pharmacy.

Thomas nodded to a little way down on the opposite side of the street. "Over there."

It looked like a dress shop to her. Not the sort of dress shop she was going to spend any time in. Two men stood in front of the dress shop. Just two guys dressed in jeans and tees like everybody else. One of them smoked while the other thumbed a smartphone. "What am I looking at?"

"Those two guys." Thomas frowned and stared harder. "Do you know them?"

"Those two?" They looked the same as any of the other people who milled around the town. "What about them?"

"Nothing." Thomas shrugged. "I need those one thousand six hundred and sixty calories."

"One thousand seven hundred and seventy," Tiffany said, still looking out the window. All she saw was two men hanging out.

"Do we have a deal?" One huge hand stretched across the table toward her. "Until we find Luke, and then you never have to see me again. Unless you want to."

Tiffany slid her hand into his, hoping like hell she was doing the right thing. She had that niggling feeling that she was agreeing to a whole lot more. "Deal."

Chapter Eleven

The tired signpost to the A1 motel didn't exactly fill Tiffany with confidence. Neither did the fact that it took at least another three signposts before they pulled into a massive parking lot. The size of the parking lot, far too large for the two-story block of rooms, was explained by four large rigs at the far end. Sun glared off the huge, silent cabs. Great, a trucker motel.

On the plus side, Thomas went into the reception and came out again a few minutes later looking triumphant. He tossed a key over at Dakota. The teen snatched it out of the air, grabbed his backpack, and disappeared through a blue door marked 2E.

Tiffany waited for her key. A shower sounded like the closest thing to heaven right now. About three inches of road dust coated her skin.

Thomas sauntered over to where she stood beside his truck. He came a little closer and then some more. The gleam in his eyes put her on high alert.

Tiffany didn't realize she'd backed up until the car warmed the back of her shirt.

Thomas kept coming until the heat from him skittered over her skin and tightened low in her belly. She dropped her head back to maintain eye contact. Her knees got a bit iffy and she leaned into the solid truck.

He caged her between his hands on either side of her shoulders. His voice, husky with naughty promises, stroked across her skin. "Are you ready?"

"Ready for what?" Her voice shook slightly. She should shove him off her. Her brain sent the message, but it got lost in translation and melted in the slow burn coiling up from inside.

His clear blue gaze, suddenly smoky and sexy, sent an unmistakable message.

Yes, please! Her nipples leaped to instant attention. She wanted to cross her arms over her breasts, but he was too close.

"I have our key." Dangling from his large finger was a key attached to a card with the lettering 2F.

Spit dried in her mouth. "What?"

"You, me, a motel room." He waggled his eyebrows.

Fuck. See, this was what happened when you found yourself in the middle of nowhere with a strange man. All that nice had gotten her to lower her guard. It took her a moment to realize he'd pulled away from her. A huge, shit-eating grin split his face. She glared up at him and tried to get her breath under control. Her heart still leaped around her chest. "What the hell was that?"

He laughed even harder. "You should have seen your face."

Her knee twitched, ready to make a painful point in a sucker shot, straight to the source of the problem.

He held out the key and dropped it. "Payback."

"For what?" Tiffany scrambled and snatched it out of the air. Embarrassment made her cheeks flame hot. He'd got her good. And her libido had been so totally on board with the idea. Damn, where was a hole to crawl into when you needed one?

Raising his voice to falsetto, he batted his lashes at her. "I'm so desperate. Please help little ole me." The grin took over again. "Unless, of course, you were feeling grateful enough for the rescue . . ."

"In your dreams." She swiveled and marched over to her own blue door.

"You have no idea." He sauntered around to the back of the truck, flipped open the hatch, and grabbed her bags. "Do you need all of these?"

"Of course." She smiled sweetly at him. Let him haul those heavy bags around. A small lesson in what happened when you messed with Tiffany. "All four of them."

Except her petty revenge didn't work out so well, as he effortlessly brought them into her room and stacked them inside the door in a mouth-drying flex and bunch of muscle under his tee. The door shut behind him.

Tiffany sat on the edge of one of the two double beds and toed off her shoes. Blue and green floral comforters that must have been pretty cheerful back in the eighties covered both beds. A television perched in front of the mirror atop a scarred dresser. The room smelled slightly of lemon detergent. She wriggled her tired, swollen feet in relief on the rough carpet. At least it looked clean.

She dragged her purse onto the bed beside her and pulled out her book. All the stuff Thomas had told her had opened up a whole world of things to explore. First things first, though. Checking her phone, she saw three missed calls from her father. Nothing from Ryan. What the hell? Would one phone call after the way they'd left things the other night be too much to ask? Except maybe Ryan didn't see anything wrong with how they'd left things. She could break and call him. Nope. If he wanted to talk to her, he could call her. Daddy was a different problem. She hit the Call Back icon.

"Princess?" His hot chocolate voice greeted her.

"Hey, Daddy, I see you called."

"Where are you, Princess? I was expecting a call from you first thing this morning."

"I left a message." Lying to him felt wrong, disloyal, but she'd been working on her story since she left Chicago. "I needed to get away for a day or two."

"Really?" His voice jumped to attention. "You're upset."

She wriggled her toes into the carpet and tried to find the right words. "You took me by surprise at dinner. It wasn't what I was expecting."

There was a momentary pause. "Ryan and I realize that, Princess, but it had to be said."

Did it? Through the sheers on the window she could see the outline of Thomas's truck. Maybe it did. It had taken that much to get her to take the car back. Still, the words wouldn't come to agree with him.

"Princess," her father said when she didn't respond.

Her heart dropped to the waistband of her jeans. She knew that voice. Daddy was about to tell her something she didn't want to hear.

"Now, I know you're not going to want to hear this." Was she a genius or what? "But Ryan spoke to me about this before we set up that dinner. He has a point, otherwise I would never have agreed to it. The repairs to that ridiculous car are merely a symptom of a bigger problem. I haven't said anything before because I thought there would come a point when you would sell the car and move on. But it's been seven years, Princess. Don't you think that's enough time?"

Guilt writhed inside her. Daddy had no idea what she was hiding from him. And he would be so upset. Her mind skewed into the past.

> *Her lying in her bed, staring at the ceiling. Her little legs only reaching halfway down her big, big bed. And that sound. The soft rise and fall of someone crying. A man crying. Crying as if he would never feel whole again. Daddy.*
> *"My Princess, it's only you and I now."*

"Now, I realize you're probably disappointed." Tiffany shut the image out and concentrated on her father's voice. "In time, you'll come to see Ryan and I are right about this. Marriage is a lifelong commitment, and it's hard to make it work at the best of times. You both need to go into it without reservations and dragging baggage from the past."

"I know, Daddy," she said, because he expected it. Daddy was right most of the time. "I just need a little time to think things over."

"Princess." His bedtime-story voice smoothed and settled deep, deep inside her. "There's nothing to think about. Put this behind you so you can move on."

"Okay." She knew when she was beat.

"Promise me, Princess."

"I promise." Her voice clogged in her throat. She'd been his princess since her mother died. He'd been so alone in those first months, so desperately sad, and the only thing that broke through the unbearable sadness was his princess. Sometimes, though, the princess felt like it had her by the throat, slowly choking the life out of her.

"That's my girl." She heard the smile in his voice. "If you need a bit of time, take it. I know you'll come to see all of this the right way. Ryan is a good man. He cares about you and your future. He will make you a great husband."

The mirror behind the television reflected her face back at her. She looked a mess. Her hair hung limp and her makeup was nearly all gone. She stared at herself as the steady drone of Daddy listing Ryan's fine points barely registered. It was weird—she knew everything he said was right, but the girl staring back at her didn't look so certain. Tiffany dropped her stare.

Of course she was sure. God, the sole reason she was sitting in a trucker's motel in Utah was because she'd ignored her father's advice. If she'd listened when he'd told her Luke was no good for her, she wouldn't be there right now. Lying to her father.

"You're right, Daddy," she said when he stopped talking. "I'll take a day or two to relax and then we can celebrate."

"Good girl." His tone warmed the small, cold place inside her.

"I have to go," she said. "I have a yoga class now."

"Don't stay away too long." Her father chuckled. "You know I miss my princess when she's not around."

"Bye, Daddy."

"Bye, Princess. I love you."

"I love you more."

"Impossible."

She ended the call and put her phone down. Time to put the girl in the mirror to rights. A shower, a nourishing face-mask, styled hair, and the right Tiffany reappeared. Slipping into a pair of lounging pants and a camisole, she grabbed her iPad and her book.

"Tiffany." Thomas tapped on the door. "Dakota and I are going to have a look around and then get something to eat. Do you want to come?"

She stared at the door in amazement. They just ate a

couple of hours ago. "No, thank you," she called back. "I think I'll get an early night."

The lock on her book slid open and she found a blank page. This was almost the best moment, a blank page filled with endless possibilities. She slid the pen free of its holder. Where to start? *3.14159265359*, she wrote. *Pi. Twenty-two over seven*, she jotted down beside it. Next, she carefully drew a circle. Then she went to her iPad and read a bit further than she had before. Thomas had talked about this, and it made sense. *Constant.* She wrote the word in her book just outside her circle and then—best of all—a formula: $C = \pi \cdot d = 2\pi \cdot r$

Back to the iPad and she read some more. So, if she rotated the line about its center, it would sweep out a circle whose area was . . . she looked at her formula . . . π. . . . what?

Numbers, order, it flowed into her like good whisky, sliding down your windpipe and settling in your stomach with a delicious burn.

Chapter Twelve

Tiffany peeked at Thomas's chest across the table.

Dear Algebra, said his tee, *Stop asking us to find your X—she's not coming back.*

She'd never wear it, but she wanted that T-shirt. Her morning had rocked along nicely so far. She'd slept well, and the diner made her an egg white omelet with vegetables. It had taken some time to rouse Dakota out of bed and get him to come to breakfast. Fortunately the lure of food got him up and running.

Dakota and Thomas tucked into the All-American: two eggs, bacon, sausage, pancakes, and hash browns. Didn't they care what they put into their bodies? Then again, by the look of them, they didn't have to. She bit into a piece of dry toast and chased it with black coffee.

Dakota had forgone the makeup that morning, and it was much easier to see his resemblance to Luke without the thick black lines around his eyes. After breakfast, they took a walk to the repair shop.

The sun warmed her legs exposed by her crisp linen shorts. Pairing them with a cool, floaty tank because of the heat, she'd lathered on the sunblock. Shorts and heels, a total no-no, so she'd sacrificed the heels for a pair of Ralph Lauren ballet flats.

Families, out and about, transformed the town into a lively bustle. It was like she'd wandered onto the set of a forties sitcom. People actually nodded and greeted them.

And Thomas greeted them all back. He even stopped once or twice to chat. God, where did he keep all this good cheer?

The mechanic looked exactly the same as he had the day before. Down to the same coveralls pushed under his belly and, Tiffany swore, the exact same stains on his forearms. Something country crackled out of the radio. The Miura sat on the lift looking very vulnerable and alone. The VW bus seemed to have gone home.

"Morning," Thomas greeted him.

"Clogged radiator." The man sniffed and came out from behind the pick up. "Could flush her out, but your best bet is to get a new one."

Poof. Tiffany's good mood disappeared.

"How long?" Thomas rubbed the back of his neck.

"Got to find the right part, order it, wait for it to get here, three days labor. I would say two weeks."

Forget good mood disappearing, now she was plain pissed.

Thomas dragged in a deep breath. He wanted to pick the mechanic up by his scruff and shake him. Two fucking weeks. He didn't have anywhere close to two weeks. He'd spoken to his partners last night. They had the appointment with the Zambian minister next week. It had taken them months to find the right man to talk to, and now they had him. News was out and the big players were already sniffing around. He had to find Luke, get those survey results, and get them to Zambia. The other two were relying on him, killing time in a hotel in Lusaka.

Three weeks he'd been stateside already, and the itch to get back to site chafed at him. It was what he did, out on site, sometimes with days separating him and the rest of the world. He liked it that way. Being back in the States choked him, made him restless.

Beside him, Tiffany muttered beneath her breath. She might as well mutter. He had a word or two for her. Why had the stubborn woman insisted on getting in that pretty piece of a racing machine and gone screaming across the country? He could go on without her. *No, I can't.* A deal was a deal, and leaving her there would be a dickhead thing to do. God, his conscience always sounded like his mother. "What should we do?" Way to go on keeping his temper out of his voice.

"I don't know what you're going to do." Her green eyes sparkled. "But I'm not waiting here for two weeks."

"You want to leave the car?"

She tossed her head. "Are you nuts?"

Thomas braced for whatever was coming. The brain of Tiffany seemed to be a dark and mysterious place. Every time he tried to get a bead on her, she shifted out of range. In their first meeting, he'd pinned her as Barbie, just like Dakota. He wasn't so sure anymore. Barbie had sharp teeth and a look in her eyes that made him think again. Right now, she had her phone in her hand thumbing through her contacts. Looked like Barbie also had a plan.

Hitting a contact, she put her phone to her ear. "Chuck, babe," she said into the phone.

Thomas had to roll his tongue back into his head. She stood right there and yet, he would swear another woman had materialized in front of him.

"You'll never guess who this is?" she said, her voice smooth like the stroke of velvet on naked skin.

It was beyond freaky. Suddenly, she seemed to shimmer and sparkle and ooze fuckability. She'd caught him unawares yesterday in the desert. Watching it now, he felt a bit better about having fallen for it like a trout on a worm. Man, she was scary good at this shit.

"Oh, babe, you're too good to me." Her giggle burned with naughty, sweaty sex, and pictures exploded behind Thomas's eyes.

Even Dakota watched her with mild curiosity.

Chuck, whoever the hell he was, must be panting by now. At the same time, Thomas wanted to beat the shit out of Chuck for even thinking that way.

The mechanic looked like he'd died and gone to heaven. The guy needed his jaw punched shut.

Her legs went on forever in those teeny-tiny shorts. Thomas let his gaze roam up to the pert swell of her breasts. No bra straps over the smooth curve of her shoulders. He should look away, but then she started talking again.

"I'm going to have to ask you to do something for me, babe." Chuck got it with both barrels. A flutter of those dark lashes, and a pout that Chuck couldn't see, but could certainly hear. "You're a bad boy, Chuck."

Thomas could imagine what Chuck wanted her to do for him. He wanted to do much the same.

"No, babe, I need a radiator for my sweet girl." A pause while she listened. Her voice, when she spoke, rasped across the nape of his neck. "Really? Four days? Is that the best you can do?"

She nodded as Chuck spoke.

"Two?" She gave a little squeal. What would a man have to do to get her to make that noise again? Thomas shook his head. He must've wandered into a freaky parallel dimension.

The mechanic took a few dazed steps closer to her. Pulled like metal to a magnet.

"Oh, Chuck." She made his name into a moan. "If you could do that for me, I'd be your slave for life." A throaty giggle. "You're so bad."

Another of those breathy giggles that shot straight to his dick. His only consolation was that the mechanic was catching flies with his mouth open. Thomas checked to make sure his own mouth was shut.

"And you can send it to me here?" The words said one thing, but the voice said something entirely different. "Where? Just a minute." She pulled the phone away from her ear and turned to the starstruck mechanic. "Where are we?"

"Youngtown, Utah," he said.

She repeated the address into the phone. "Two days would be wonderful, Chuck, but tomorrow would make me your girl for life! I know you will." She did a little purr thing and hung up. "Chuck says he'll try to get the radiator here by tomorrow afternoon."

Thomas gave his head a quick shake. "I'm sure he did."

She turned back to the mechanic. "Will that be good?"

"Sure." The mechanic swallowed. "I'll put her right up and get her done."

"You would?" Had she been possessed by the spirit of Marilyn Monroe? "That would be wonderful."

The mechanic sucked in his gut and pushed the flab into his chest. "No need to thank me, ma'am. Keeping my customers happy is my number one priority."

"I can see that." She put her slim hand on the mechanic's forearm.

The man puffed up like he'd just single-handedly won World War Three.

"Right." Tiffany turned, and triumph sparkled in those incredible eyes. "What shall we do with the rest of the day?"

A reluctant smile threatened his face. He tugged it back down. She had an honest-to-God super power going on there. "Not all men fall for that shit."

She tossed her glossy black hair with a smile that made him want to sit up and beg. "Wanna bet?"

He grunted. Because, no, he did not want to bet on that.

Dakota sucked a breath between his teeth. "Fucking freaky."

"Ever seen the Grand Canyon?" Thomas looked up from the map in his hand. Her map, the one that was supposed to get her all the way to Canyons. Tiffany stared at him. Was this a trick question? "No."

She peered over her shoulder at Dakota, who shrugged.

"Wanna go?"

"To the Grand Canyon?"

"Yeah." Thomas waved the map around, all perky and excited. It was kind of infectious. "It's about three hours' drive from here. Well, the North Rim is. I've never seen it, you've never seen it, and I'll bet Dakota hasn't either."

Dakota jammed his Beats over his head. "I don't do nature."

Thomas pushed them off his ears. "You don't want to come?"

"No." Dakota's expression dissolved into open scorn.

The frown on Thomas's face looked as if such a thing fell beyond the limit of possible.

"Hang on, Sparky." Tiffany needed to get her vote in here and fast before Thomas had them abseiling off the side of a mountain. "I never said I wanted to go either."

His shoulders drooped. "Why not?"

Tiffany opened her mouth to tell him and then shut it again. She really didn't have a reason why not. They'd pretty much seen all there was to see of Youngtown, and there was only so long she could spend in her motel room. It was the kind of day that seemed to be made for a trip somewhere. "Okay, then." She shrugged. "Let's go and see the North Rim of the Grand Canyon."

And just like that the sun came out over Thomas's face again.

"Count me out," Dakota said.

"But you can't stay here." Tiffany tried to picture leaving Dakota on the God-fearing streets of Youngtown and failed.

"Why not?"

"We can't leave you on your own in a motel room." If Dakota even stayed put.

"I'm seventeen." He sneered. "I don't need a babysitter."

"He's right." Thomas engulfed Dakota's shoulder in a meaty paw. "You won't be too bored? The Grand Canyon is one of the natural wonders of the world."

Dakota shrugged as if it were a matter of complete indifference to him.

Leaving him all by himself didn't sit right with Tiffany. "You sure you don't want to come?"

Dakota turned his shoulder. A second later his Beats leaked the heavy bass throb of his music.

"Do you think we should?" Tiffany studied Dakota's back as he slouched away.

"He's seventeen," Thomas said. "He can take care of himself for a few hours. Besides, look around you. Just how much trouble can anyone get into here?"

It was an excellent point.

"But I don't hike." Ground rules needed establishing

here. "And I don't go down gorges and things like that. We go, we look at the view, maybe take a few pictures, and come back."

The Grand Canyon was spectacular. An awe-inspiring miracle of nature not in the least ruined by the throngs of people. Tiffany had a great day, as it turned out. Thomas's infectious excitement swept everything along in its path. She called Dakota a couple of times to check up on him. He ignored the calls, but at least he responded to her three text messages.

They drove back in the descending twilight, both of them dusty, tired, and relaxed. She didn't even mind the layer of crud on her ballet flats. Her bag held a precious collection of pamphlets full of facts and figures. Thomas hadn't questioned her need to have them, he'd collected her a whole bunch more.

Tonight, she would enter them into her book, cross-check and investigate, play around with the numbers and see what happened. The perfect end to a great day, and most of that due to the man silently driving the truck. Thomas was so open in his reactions to everything, her guard slipped constantly. In the end, it became easier to go with his flow. Mostly. She'd barely stopped Thomas from signing them up for a white-water river trip.

He took everything in, sucking up huge greedy gulps of the world around him. She'd never met anyone like him. If she'd been with Ryan or one of her friends from Chicago, it would've been a much more muted sort of day. Ryan didn't get excited and, if he did, he certainly didn't show it. Also, Ryan did Rome, Paris, London, and Venice. He did not do the Grand Canyon. And why not?

The silky swish of the truck wheels on the road lulled her into a sort of meditation. Outside the window, parched desert flew past. Long shadows made grotesque shapes of the straggly trees in the ochre sand.

Come to think of it, why hadn't her father taken her to the Grand Canyon? There had been hundreds of families milling about. Little kids being toted along on their fathers' shoulders or holding tight to their hands. Her heart gave a weird, little twinge. Daddy had taken her shopping in New York, to the theatre in London, even the opera in Rome—trips for a princess to her mother's favorite cities. He'd never spent a day in the hot sun, eating ice cream and enjoying the simple awe of seeing something so incredible. She'd even let Thomas talk her into eating ice cream. It had seemed right somehow.

"Can I ask you something?" Thomas broke into her thoughts.

"Can I stop you?"

The corner of his mouth tilted up. "That thing you did earlier, at the repair shop, it was the same thing you pulled on me by the side of the road. It was like it was you, but not you. Then today, you were completely different."

A bit of honesty couldn't hurt. "Luke used to call her Delilah."

Thomas flashed a grin, but kept silent, waiting for her to go on.

"I did a lot of beauty pageants when I was younger." It sounded a little strange as she listened to her own words. "Delilah is sort of like a skin I can slip into. Every woman has an inner Delilah."

"Yeah." Thomas laughed softly. "But yours is like a super power."

He said it as a joke. It wasn't meant to hurt. She knew

that, but a weight pressed against her chest and she wanted to cry. Just like that. Without really knowing why.

"Hey." He slid his gaze from the road to look at her. His voice, gentle and caring, slipped past her defenses.

"I didn't like the pageants." She couldn't hold his gaze any longer and she stared out the window. Vibrant bolts of orange and scarlet shot through the darkening sky.

"Why?"

She shrugged. The weight in her chest made breathing uncomfortable. She shifted in her seat. "I was a doll." Her mouth kept moving, as if it had been waiting for the opportunity to get this out. "Like those ones you see in the plastic boxes. Their faces all painted and their hair all carefully curled and stuck a certain way. My father used to tell me stories when I was little. They were stories about a princess. Princess Pearly Perfect. And she was me." She pressed her hot forehead to the cool glass of the window. "When we would go to the pageants and I would start acting out or being a little shit about something, he would say to me, 'Let me see Princess Pearly Perfect.' When she grew up, she became Delilah."

"Huh."

"Can we turn the AC down?" She rubbed her palms against her arms to dispel the goose bumps. She felt cold, exposed by her confession, and she wished he'd say something.

He leaned forward, adjusted the dial, and went straight back to watching the road as he drove, one hand on the wheel, the other resting lightly on his thigh. He looked relaxed, easy, like he was listening and not coming to any conclusions. His deep voice rumbled through the cab. "I had Spider-Man underpants."

Tiffany burst out laughing.

"I did." He turned to her and grinned. "My mother had

to buy me about eight pairs because she could never get me to take them off."

"Do you still have Spider-Man underpants?"

"I don't wear underpants."

The atmosphere in the truck shifted. Her gaze drifted down to his crotch, even as she cursed herself for asking the stupid question in the first place. Disturbing visuals ran in a show reel behind her eyes. The blatant eroticism of them left her shocked, and hot. Her mouth dropped open in surprise. She crossed her legs and turned to stare out of the window. The idea of what he wasn't wearing beneath those jeans was doing things to her girl parts that it had no business doing. Okay, this was not good.

Ryan. She stubbornly forced a picture of Ryan to the front of her mind. The naked shots of Thomas kept right on coming. Ryan. Her boyfriend. She had enough man mess on her plate without tossing in a dollop of lust for Thomas Hunter—going commando. *Oh, my.*

"So why did you do them?" Thomas said.

"Huh?" Damn, she'd missed the question.

"The pageants. Why'd you do them if you hated them?"

Because Daddy wanted me to. A pathetic answer, even in her own mind. She clamped her lips shut in case they decided to toss it out there anyway. She shrugged and kept staring out the window. "How much longer?"

She needed to get out of that truck and get a good breath of fresh air. Being enclosed in this small space with him, the fading light, the conversation—not a good idea.

"Almost there." He snapped on the radio.

A raucous blast of pop music hit the air.

Thomas would've gladly kicked his own ass if he could. What had he gone and said the underpants thing for? He'd only wanted to make her laugh.

She'd been sitting there looking so forlorn he wanted to reach over and scoop her into his arms. That was off the cards, so he'd tried to make her laugh. And ended up making himself horny.

The crap blasting out of the radio provided a bit of relief. It had been brewing inside him all day, this inconvenient awareness of her. That Delilah thing she did was a kick in the balls. He could get his head around that. Every male with a pulse got that. He struggled with the other thing.

Sure, up until that point, he'd thought she was hot, but kind of like you looked at a Van Gogh and thought it was beautiful. You admired, you appreciated, but there was no way it was ever going to be yours, and you knew that. Then she'd unleashed all kinds of sweet throughout the day.

He'd never expected the fun in her or how easy it was to spend time with her. Except for those itsy-bitsy shorts. Too often, he dropped behind to watch those long, long legs and that incredible ass walk away from him. He shifted in his seat and tapped one finger to the music.

This was not the direction his thoughts should be going. His gaze strayed to the length of skin and muscle resting beside him on the seat. Damn, she had amazing legs. He snapped his gaze back to the road. And kept them there for the rest of the drive back to Youngtown.

Chapter Thirteen

Tiffany climbed out of the truck and stretched her cramped legs.

The door to Dakota's room flew open. He beamed at them as he trotted up to the truck. "Hey, guys. How was the Grand Canyon?"

Tiffany nearly looked behind her to see who he was talking to. It was the first time Tiffany had seen him smile since Lola dropped him off. His big goofy smile took her back to that sweet kid years ago.

"Great."

"Impressive."

Their responses crashed into each other. Tiffany risked a quick peek at Thomas.

His jaw clenched tight enough to endanger his teeth.

"Whoa." Dakota threw out his hands as if to ward them off. "Did you guys like have a fight or something?"

"No," they both said at once.

"We're just tired." Thomas stared at Dakota with a slight frown. "It was hot."

Dakota seemed to have had a personality transplant. "So, like, do you guys want to do something tonight?"

Swinging his head from one to the other, Dakota bounced on his toes like a toddler.

No, she didn't want to do anything. She wanted to disappear into her room and wash some of the dust off and with it, any lingering thoughts about Thomas. Then she would carefully copy all the information from her pamphlets into her book, move the numbers around, and things would make sense again. But Dakota just about wagged his invisible tail and she didn't want to squash his enthusiasm. He could be reaching out to her.

"Like what?" A small frown wrinkled the skin between Thomas's eyes.

What the hell, she could cut the kid some slack. He'd probably spent the day going out of his mind with boredom.

"Maybe we could, like, go and get a burger or something?" Dakota squirmed in his sneakers. "I was reading there's an old drive-in on the edge of town. We could grab some burgers and go and check it out. The lady at the front desk said they would be open. Come on." He grinned. "It'll be fun. I've never been to a drive-in movie. It's like a relic from a past age. I could post it on Instagram."

"You didn't want to see the Grand Canyon, but now you want to go and see a movie at a drive-in?" Thomas raised an eyebrow.

"Sure." Nodding and shifting his weight from one foot to the other, Dakota's energy almost burst out of the seams.

Thomas shook his head and turned to her. "You game?"

"Sure." *Stupid.* "Give me about thirty minutes." She looked at the fine layer of dust on her legs. "Make that an hour."

"But—" Dakota screwed up his face.

"You got it," Thomas said.

* * *

Movies were one of Thomas's greatest loves. This, however, was sheer hell. He'd backed the truck into place so they could open the tailgate and stretch out. All of them propped against the back of the seats with him wedged between Tiffany and Dakota. Another thing he hadn't really thought through clearly. Because now Dakota had retreated into a zoned-out silence and Tiffany slept. How could anyone, especially a woman, sleep through Chris Hemsworth saving the world? The sleeping wasn't so much the problem as where she was sleeping. On him. Dakota had his Beats on and his own movie soundtrack going in his head.

Tiffany had lasted all of fifteen minutes before she slumped against his side. So, what did he do? He rested his arms on the back of the seat to give them all more space. Another stupid move, because now she cuddled into him like a sleepy kitten. A kitten? He wished. There was nothing cute about the way she pressed into his side.

Her breath huffed warm and moist against the skin of his neck and her hand lay across his abs, resting on his belt buckle. She smelled like warm vanilla and a bit flowery, and he got a whiff of her every time he breathed. Keeping his arm on the back of the seat was a battle because his arm kept wanting to curl around her and press her closer.

Dakota laughed out loud and Thomas tore his attention away from Tiffany.

The kid's stare was stuck on the screen while his head bopped up and down to his Beats. Something with that kid was so off tonight he could feel it crawling over his skin like bugs. Dakota's eyes glittered and he was way too talkative. Yet another thing he didn't have time to sort.

He needed to get his survey results and get back to Willow Park. It was taking him far too long to find Luke. Time he hadn't banked on. He also hadn't planned on his little party of three and their road trip. The plan had been to spend some time at home before leaving for Zambia. This jaunt cut into his family time, but his mother would understand. She'd kick his ass if he even thought about leaving Tiffany and Dakota. He'd kick his own ass, come to that.

Still, he needed to get home. His older brother Richard was expecting another baby any day now and he'd been in Zambia for the birth of his first child. He was determined to be there to welcome the newest member of the family into the world. He liked the excitement and the constantly changing environment of his job, but the downside was the loss of connection to the people that mattered most to him. He hadn't had a serious relationship, well, ever. Not since he'd decided at fourteen that Dominique Frazer was the love of his life. She'd, unfortunately, decided his other brother, Josh, was the love of hers.

Sure, he'd had relationships, but they were always temporary. His lifestyle gave him a good out whenever he needed it. He didn't screw around. When he was with a girl, he was with that girl, but he never promised or intended to stay forever.

Tiffany shifted against him.

He drew in a careful breath. His libido strummed through his blood on a low-level hum of appreciation. It helped to be sandwiched beside a moody teen on the other side.

"Whoa." Dakota's yell made him jump. "Did you see that?"

Thomas nodded. He hadn't seen a damn thing.

Tiffany stirred and raised her head. "Sorry." She stiffened as she pulled away from him. The warmth faded from his side as she pushed herself into a sitting position. "I think I drooled on your shirt."

"No worries." Jesus, he must be losing his mind, because he even thought that was kind of cute.

She pushed at her hair to get it out of her face. It streamed down her back in a long, silken fall of inkiness.

He gritted his teeth until they ached. He had no business thinking about wrapping her hair around his fist. And where things would go from there.

They sat through the rest of the movie in silence. When it was done, he drove them back to the motel. As Tiffany disappeared into her room, he let out a deep breath. Her friend, Chuck, had better produce that radiator, and fast.

Tiffany already had too many men in her life.

Chapter Fourteen

Tiffany woke with the sheets tangled in her legs and sweat coating her torso. A night weaving through one erotic fantasy after another left her hot and aching. Even in her dreams, she had no business whoring it up with Thomas Hunter. Maybe a run would scratch the itch clawing under her skin. It'd been days since her last workout. The cellulite must be multiplying as she lay there.

She pulled on a pair of workout pants and a crop top. The top ended well above her belly button and left her stomach bare. Her pants didn't help, cut low across the hips. They were fine for a session of hot yoga in a Chicago gym, but she hadn't anticipated slogging down the road in rural Utah. There was nothing for it. Even her book wasn't relieving her itchiness. She needed to work off some of her excess energy. Quietly, she let herself out into the still morning. She checked the time on her phone and winced. Only the very brave and very stupid got up at this time. The mountains blurred in an early morning haze draped over the land. Dew sparkled in lacy cobweb festoons between the trees and threw a blanket of bling over the grass.

After a few stretches, she set out. Her footsteps pounded

a dull tramp in the still morning. Selecting her running playlist, she slipped in her ear buds. The higher elevation jammed in her chest almost immediately and she slowed her pace. It really was rather beautiful with the mountains providing a dramatic counterpoint to the brush.

A car passed her and the driver raised her hand and waved. Tiffany smiled. It was the sort of courtesy you forgot about until you saw it happen. It was nice. She kept the run short. God knew where she could end up if she strayed too far from the motel. Still, by the time she turned, her mood had lifted. Her breathing adjusted to the altitude and she'd worked up a decent sweat. The sun gained some height, and with it, the last of the morning cool vanished. She calculated calories burned by her run. That would go some way to dealing with the hot dog she'd eaten last night at the drive-in. She hadn't had a hot dog since she'd gone to a kid's birthday party when she was five. Daddy had almost hopped out of his skin. It was very lucky he wasn't there to see her now. Ice cream and a hot dog, all in one day. He might have a coronary.

The careful eating habits from her pageant days were ingrained. It had made Daddy so happy when she won. Maybe because her mother had been a model, and Daddy tried to mold her into a perfect replica of the original. She didn't remember much of her mother: the scent of Joy, eyes the same color as hers, and a laugh that made everyone around her smile. Things might have been different if her mother had lived.

The motel pool water sparkled and beckoned her from across the parking lot. She pulled her phone out of the pouch sewn into her pants and turned off her music. A short swim would be great, but she hadn't thought to pack a swimsuit. Of course, she hadn't planned on being

stranded in Youngtown, Utah, for however many days it
took Chuck to produce a radiator.

There was nobody at the pool. She could be in and out
before anyone noticed. Her running top would work for
one half of her. There was one pair of shorts in her bags
that might do the trick. She headed for her room.

And plowed straight into a warm wall of muscle. Thomas,
hot and male, and smelling like heaven. Her hands made
contact with his hard pecs. Reflexively, her fingers curled
into the warm muscle. The skin on her belly slid against
his, washing her in a wave of heat that spread from the
point of contact to murmur temptation low in her belly.
She opened her mouth, but no sound came out.

Holy shit. Thomas was an eye feast. Big, hard, and cut
in all the right places. His large hands burned through the
fabric at her hips.

"Hi." Her voice came out in a stupid tween fangirl
squeak.

Rough and hoarse, his voice stroked her spine. "Hi."

"Um, sorry, I didn't see you there." Her face must be all
red and sweaty, and she had zero makeup on. Her knees
did a weird collapse thing and she had to tighten her
muscles to keep herself upright.

He was naked from the waist upward. The scent of soap
clung to him. Naked skin pressed against hers in a slow,
steady burn. "Have you been for a run?"

Her mind blanked. She didn't trust her voice, so she
nodded at his chest.

Dark brown nipples stood out against the tan of his
chest with a very light dusting of hair in the center. Sweet
Mother of God, but he had those sort of washboard abs
that made her head go fuzzy. And carved laterals disappearing into the waistband of his board shorts.

"You're going for a swim?" A rush, more breath than

vocal. She spent her working life around seriously cut men wearing a lot less. She'd run oil all over bodies like this one only a few days ago and her breathing had been fine. Her fingers spread across his muscle, anticipating rubbing oil all over him. If she leaned forward an inch, she could press her mouth to the curve of his throat.

A distinct rasp made her look up. "Tiffany?"

"Yes." Right there in that lazy, hot blue gaze was the burn telling her he felt it, too. She melted under his unwavering stare, hypnotized.

"It seems we have a bit of a problem."

No problem, yelled her hormones.

"This thing between us—"

"No." It came out more like yes, and she cleared her throat. "No," she said and tried to mean it. "I can't." She pried her fingers away from his smooth muscle and stepped back. "It's not going to be a problem, because I'm not going to let it be."

His hands dropped from her hips immediately. She missed the warmth.

His lips twitched. "If you say so."

"I do." She nodded so hard, her ponytail jerked up and down. Ryan was waiting for her at home. Ahead of her was Luke and the messed-up issue of her divorce. There was no space in her life for another man, however good he smelled or however much she wanted to wrap herself around him. "I can't."

He stared down at her, his face unreadable. For a moment, she wanted him to argue with her, sweet-talk her out of her decision. He shrugged and stepped away. "Okay."

She felt cheated, and she had no right to. Dredging up a smile, she said, "Enjoy your swim."

He spun and strolled toward the pool, leaving a gaping, man-sized hole where he'd stood.

She opened her door and slipped inside. Then she risked a peek around the doorjamb. Damn, but he had a great body. His faded board shorts hung indecently low on his hips, but curved around his ass lovingly. She rubbed her hands together vigorously to get rid of the imprint of his chest. Her decision had to be final. With another nod she shut the door to her motel room. It hit the latch with a determined click. Okay, time to stop screwing around. She was attracted to Thomas Hunter, but that didn't mean anything. There were lots of attractive men in the world. This wouldn't be the last time she looked at another man and tingled in all the right places. They were animals. Sexual attraction was part of the drive to reproduce. And there were some mighty fine animals prowling around on two legs. She didn't need to freak out every time her ovaries recognized a good sperm donor.

Her phone vibrated and she looked down.

Let's talk, Ryan texted.

She smiled at her phone. Thomas Hunter was hot, but Ryan was the man for her. She dialed his number.

He answered almost immediately. "Hey, there. Are we fighting?"

"Not anymore." She laughed, relief making her almost giddy. "Are you calling because you miss me?"

"Always." That was sweet. She had no business being mad at Ryan. He'd told her the truth. She was the lying dirtbag here. Guilt could be messing with her head. Getting her all hot and bothered over Thomas. With things back to normal with Ryan, her girl parts would behave again.

"Where are you?" Ryan asked.

"Sulking." Back to normal with Ryan meant getting this Luke thing squared away.

"You know that is only self-defeating, right?"

"I know." She loved how grown up Ryan was. "I'll be home in a day or two. Now, tell me what you've been up to."

Ryan took the invitation at a gallop.

She made the appropriate noises into the phone as he told her about an up-and-coming real estate deal he was involved in, something to do with warehouses and an office complex. She only really heard the numbers. Testing her theory, she peered through the blinds on the window facing the parking lot and the pool beyond.

Thomas stood there, water streaming down the planes of his chest.

A girl could lick—she snapped the blind shut. Too soon. She wrapped up the conversation with Ryan and made sure to say good-bye nicely.

In the shower, she made a decision. This was a boundary thing. Hers blurred around Thomas. They were merely strangers traveling the same path for a short time. When each of them got what they wanted from Luke, this would be over. When Dakota was settled with his brother, they would part ways. Thomas would go back to whatever it was an engineer did in Africa, and she would start planning the most perfect wedding day.

She dug through her suitcases and found an Alexander Wang tank dress and paired it with a pair of high-heeled sandals. Now she felt like the real Tiffany. A visit to the Miura was next on her list. An entire day in rural southern Utah was a challenge to fill. But there would be no more outings alone with Thomas. From now on, they went everywhere as a threesome or not at all.

"Good plan, girl." She gave herself a firm nod in the mirror. The dress clung to her in all the right places. After she'd seen the car, she'd use the rest of the day to get a jump on wedding planning. She would need to see what was trending in wedding dresses. There was also the venue to be considered, flowers, the right caterer, all that stuff.

Of course, Ryan and his mother would want a say. His mother was a lady of strong opinions, which she liked to share. And Daddy would want to be consulted about everything. His princess was getting married. It was a big day for him. A big day for her, she meant. Her big day. Mrs. Ryan Cooper. Her heartbeat accelerated uncomfortably and a fine sweat broke over her skin. She wanted to be Tiffany Cooper, most of the time.

She grabbed her purse. Stepping out of the room, she surprised a middle-aged man dressed in overalls.

He took a step back when he saw her and uttered a hasty "Ma'am."

Tiffany nodded to the man and stalked down the corridor to the room next door. She rapped sharply on the door. "I'm going to take a walk to the repair shop," she called through the closed door.

"Like that?" Dakota spoke from almost directly behind her.

Tiffany jumped and spun around.

Hands jammed in his pockets, Dakota raked his gaze over her. "You're wearing that to a repair shop?"

She refused to be intimidated by a seventeen-year-old. Tiffany raised her chin and stared back. Yes, she didn't blend in with the locals, but she wasn't a local, so there really was no problem.

The door to Thomas's room opened behind her. His presence hit her in a warm wave. "Why don't we drive?"

Tiffany looked down at her heels. That was probably for the best. She gave a vague nod in his direction, careful not to make eye contact, and moved toward the truck. Her nape prickled a warning that his gaze was on her. He opened her door and she smiled her thanks at his shoulder. The smell of soap on warm skin teased her as he climbed into the truck beside her.

Outside her car window, the day began in Youngtown. A young couple with a stroller and their dog raised their hands and waved. She sensed Thomas looking over at her once or twice, but she kept to her view. The whisper of sound from Dakota's music was the only break in the silence.

The repair shop was hosting a town meeting as they drove up. About twenty men milled around the parking lot, chatting to the mechanic. The star of the show? The Miura. The car must've been washed because she sat there gleaming like a visiting queen, all the men clucking around her.

Tiffany opened her door and jumped down before Thomas could do the honors.

As one, the men turned to look at her. Tiffany pushed her shoulders back and glided over. "Good morning," she greeted the gathering at large.

A bass rumble responded.

The mechanic, who had a fresh pair of overalls on for the occasion, materialized from the crowd. A shiny name tag announced his name as Corey. "The boys came on over to admire your little lady." His gaze drifted between her and the car.

Behind him the men bobbed their heads in agreement.

"It ain't often we see something like her in these parts."

Again, she really hoped he was talking about the car.

More rumbling and nodding from the fan club.

Corey sidled closer. "Your man, Chuck, gave me a bell this morning. Said that radiator was on her way. He dug one up in Salt Lake, so he's sending her on down. Should get here before I finish my lunch."

Tiffany got an eye-watering waft of cologne. She greeted the news with a big smile and an inward wave of relief.

"That's great. Do you know how long it will take you to get it installed?"

"Shouldn't take me long. If we get no problems from her, she'll be done by this evening." Corey winked at her, flashing a dazzling white smile. "Got me some help to make it go a bit faster."

"I knew I could rely on you, Corey." She touched his arm. A little positive reinforcement never hurt. And she was out of Youngtown that evening. Hell, yes.

Thomas whistled something beneath his teeth. It sounded a lot like Tom Jones's "Delilah." Smart-ass. But nothing could get her down right now. Corey would get the radiator that afternoon. She would be on the road again by tomorrow morning.

"I took a bit of a liberty this morning." Corey sidled closer. "Seeing as she don't like to be driven all that much. I asked Hank, over there"—a heavyset man with a handlebar moustache nodded in her direction—"if you could use his trailer. Hank's a bit of a collector and he has one of them fancy trailers you can put this little beauty up on."

"It would be my honor," said Hank, his voice surprisingly high for his walrus appearance.

"Of course, we'll rent it from you," Thomas said. "I can drop it back when we head back to Chicago. Once we get the car to where she's going."

A shocked silence descended on the parking area. "You aren't keeping her?"

Tiffany could have kicked Thomas as all the men turned to look at her with varying degrees of horror. "Unfortunately, she's not mine." Her chest tightened as she said the words. Long, fast rides down quiet roads were a thing of the past. "I've only been able to look after her for a short while."

Corey looked at her mournfully.

"I'm really going to miss her." Tiffany's throat clogged. Seven years of love and money into making the Miura beautiful again. After what Tiffany had done to the beautiful old car, it seemed only fair.

"I'm sure you will." Corey patted her shoulder awkwardly. "She sure is a thing of beauty."

"Thank you." She cleared her throat. Stupid getting sentimental over something that wasn't even yours. "You've been great."

Corey went all shades of red and actually looked a little misty eyed.

Thomas whistled again.

Corey shot him a frown. "That feller of yours all right?"

"He's not my feller." Tiffany leaned forward to confide. Aftershave hit her in waves. "And I'm not really sure what's wrong with him."

Dakota kicked up dust as they made their way back to the truck. "Now what?"

She stepped into the truck and waved. The entire parking area waved back. Such a nice group of men.

"We could go for a walk," Thomas said. "The countryside around here is quite spectacular."

"Lame." Dakota switched his attention to his phone.

For a second she was tempted to go with Thomas. And that made the decision for her. "I have things to do."

And those things did not include Thomas Hunter.

Chapter Fifteen

Tiffany dragged the lawn chair outside her room into the shade. The motel might not look like much, but the Wi-Fi was fast and free. Pulling out her iPad, she made notes. She dropped Ryan's mother a quick email about wedding planners. Patti would find the very best person Illinois had to offer.

Dakota disappeared into his room, probably to make wax dolls of her and melt them.

Thomas headed off across the parking lot. The water bottle suggested a walk, as did the trainers and the hat pulled low over his eyes. It wouldn't surprise her if he came back with an alligator in tow, wrestled into submission.

After about two hours, she'd gone through every wedding dress site she could find. Any more ivory and lace and she might lose it and run screaming across the parking lot. Somehow, nothing really appealed to her. She must've gone through pictures of over a thousand dresses. Some were beautiful, but she couldn't really see herself in any of them. The models all had that look on their faces. The one that said they were living the happily-ever-after thing.

Try as she might, she couldn't picture herself with that

face. Maybe because she'd seen love's young dream go up
in flames and gotten singed in the process. Possibility two
was more disturbing. The groom standing beside the glow-
ing bride refused to take Ryan's shape. Even worse, when
he did take shape, she couldn't get the image of Daddy
standing right beside him to separate.

Heat haze shimmered over the scrubby brush on the far
side of the horizon. Thomas had been gone for over two
hours now. Maybe if she'd spent less time scanning the
parking lot for signs of him and more time concentrating
on her wedding, she might have gotten something done. At
least nailed down a dress designer who appealed. She
acted out of concern, nothing more. A quick bit of research
on crime statistics reassured her. And made an excellent
excuse not to look at the table-setting sites Ryan's mother
had sent her. Patti made a determined case for cream and
black, like the royal wedding. Tiffany nearly suggested
orange and green, just to mess with her.

Pamphlets from the Grand Canyon lay in the bottom of
her bag. She hadn't input any of the information yet. Normally, she couldn't wait to start messing with statistics, to
take something and put it into numbers. The blank page
stared back at her. There must be something. She flipped
back a few pages to see what she'd been working on. Her
scribbles ran across the page. She could finish comparing
crime stats across states—that might relax her enough to
stop looking for Thomas.

Dakota tramped past a little while later. Grunted something about going to get a burger and disappeared in the
direction of the diner.

How much longer could Thomas take? God, he could've
hiked back to Chicago by now. Okay, not really, but still, it
was a bit irresponsible to go hiking off into the wilds of
Utah when he didn't know the area. Crime might be low,

but there could be snakes and scorpions and mountain lions out there in the dark smudge of the mountains against the horizon. Definitely mountain lion territory.

An email pinged onto her screen and she opened it. Patti wanted to know about flowers, bridesmaids—who and how many—venue, china, and flatware. Seriously, flatware? How important could that be? The list of questions scrolled right off her screen and she closed the email. Another email followed right on its heels. Patti's planning frenzy, the sequel. God, she couldn't deal with this right now.

A truck chugged to life and snaked its way out of the parking lot.

She shifted her chair back into the shade and out of the moving sun. Damn, the heat wouldn't quit, but it beat sitting in her dingy motel room.

Clutching a takeout bag, Dakota slouched back, looking only a little bit less like a serial killer. He vanished into his motel room without a word.

Her phone vibrated in her lap.

Thomas Hunter: *Nice dress.*

Her heart gave a jaunty little thump. She tried not to smile, but failed. No sign of him in the parking lot or the corridor. He couldn't have gotten past her without her seeing him.

Where are you? She hit Send.

Her phone vibrated. *Watching you.*

That's creepy!!!!

You have a point.

She laughed. She couldn't help it. He was such a dumbass.

Her phone shook again.

Are you still ignoring me?

I'm trying, but you being a stalker is making it difficult.

"Hey." He appeared right beside her.

Tiffany almost dropped her phone she jumped so high. "Where the hell did you come from?"

He propped one shoulder against a supporting pillar. Dust and sweat streaked his face and arms. His T-shirt clung to the angles of his chest and belly.

Trust me, I'm a Jedi, she read.

"I followed a path and it came out behind the motel." He made a vague motion with his hand.

"Okay."

Tiffany fiddled with the hemline of her dress, which had ridden halfway up her thighs. Would he notice? Look at her legs, like he had when she wore her shorts? *Get a grip, Tiffany.*

"About this morning."

Huge warning signs flashed behind her eyes. "There is nothing to say about this morning." She couldn't look at him, so she took out her phone and fiddled.

"You don't want to talk about it, I get it. But I have something to say." He crouched down in front of her, his legs framing hers, his hands on the arms of her chair.

Tiffany was forced to look at him.

"You're right," he said. "You and me, a really bad idea. Especially considering all we have going on." Thigh muscle bulged under his cargo shorts. Coarse hair, slightly golden in the sun, covered the muscle.

A twang that felt suspiciously like disappointment caught behind her breastbone. "There is no you and me."

"Yeah, there kind of is." He ducked his head, meeting her downcast gaze. "I like you, Tiffany, and I'm seriously attracted to you. This morning, you were sweaty and half-naked and you slammed right into me." He shrugged. "I'm a man, I reacted."

It really didn't help when he said shit like that. It crept over her in slow, insistent burn. "I can't be attracted to you."

"I know." Thomas's voice stroked over her and she shivered. "And I can't be attracted to you. When this is over, I'm going to see my family for a bit and then it's back to Zambia."

Gone. No more Thomas Hunter. It shouldn't hurt, but it kind of did. "I know all this."

"You're a forever kind of girl, and I'm a right now kind of guy," he said.

Irrationally, she wanted to punch him as he said that. "Do you have a point?" It came out with a lash of bitch on the end, and she winced.

"Yeah, I do. I'm a man and you're . . ." He shrugged.

What? What am I? What did he see when he looked at her?

"That doesn't mean I'm going to jump you," he said. "So, do you think you could stop ignoring me as well as what happened. It's going to be a long few days if you keep that up."

She didn't want him to be, but he was right. Time to put her schoolgirl back in her box. Along with the purring kitty trying to mentally rub up against him. He'd caught her off balance that morning, but she was better now. Really, she was. They could be mature about this. Just because they had a little bit of a spark between them didn't mean they couldn't handle it. "Okay, but to be clear, nothing is going to happen."

Up went the mouthy eyebrow. "What's that?"

Tiffany followed the direction of his gaze and froze. Her book rested on the seat beside her. "It's my diary."

He titled his head and studied her book. "It's very pink."

"Yes, it is." She picked it up and shoved it into her bag.

He watched her, two lines creasing between his eyes. He was putting things together in his head. She recognized that look. The silence prickled between them.

"You hungry?"

The subject change caught her off guard. Her shoulders drooped from their defensive stance. "A little."

"Let's get something to eat." He held his hand out to her.

Her hand slipped into his like she'd done it a hundred times before. Heat spread over her palm and up her forearm. Part of her brain told her to tug her hand away, but the rest of her was all for leaving it there.

He tightened his grip slightly and pulled her to her feet.

Her forward motion carried her much closer to him than she expected.

He stilled.

Tiffany took in a deep breath of sun, laundry detergent, and man. Oh, boy, this wasn't going to be as easy as she'd hoped.

He squeezed his fingers and then let go. One side of his mouth tilted up. "I guess no hand holding."

"You guessed right." She went for a light tone, but it came off not sounding quite right. She curled her fingers into the palm of her hand, but she could still feel his touch.

"Let's get you some lettuce leaves and a piece of celery."

Corey's lip quivered as they loaded up the Miura.

Thomas wasn't sure what upset the man more, the loss of the vintage Lamborghini or the loss of Tiffany, aka Delilah. Sentiment, however, didn't stop him from presenting Thomas with the invoice.

Tiffany snatched it from his hand and doled out cash from a wad of greenbacks fat enough to make a drug dealer happy. By the light in Corey's eye, she'd left him a little something extra. Thomas had her pegged for a charge card, no-limit credit card kind of girl. "No black American Express card?"

"No." She spun away from him and stalked out of Corey's office to the parking lot.

Okay, it had been a rude question. Still, he got the feeling it was more than that.

Her little group of admirers stood gathered for The Departure.

Hank loaded the Miura up with all the fervor of a born enthusiast. He then spent the next half hour lecturing Thomas on the trick to driving a trailer. Thomas listened patiently and nodded at the appropriate moments. He didn't have the heart to tell Hank he'd towed earth-moving equipment across virgin African bush.

It was late by the time they had everything locked and loaded, and they decided to spend one more night at the motel. They wanted to get going early in the morning. Five hours, a bit longer for the trailer, and they would be in Canyons. He should be elated to be getting this traveling circus moving.

He couldn't get the way Tiffany fit right against him out of his head.

Chapter Sixteen

Tiffany chewed her lip. There must be some way out of this without pissing Thomas off. She'd caught sight of the algebra primer in the convenience store beside the gas station as Thomas paid for gas, and had been standing there wondering how to buy it without letting on when Thomas wandered over and launched into a session of book-buying enthusiasm.

"Fuck, I do not want to be seen looking at this shit." Dakota ducked his head and slunk away, throwing her a look of disgust as he went. He was giving off a lot of attitude for a kid who'd delayed their early departure. First, he overslept and then he insisted on a long breakfast before they left.

"I don't want one." Tiffany stepped away from the book stand. "I have a whole list of books I haven't read on my iPad."

Thomas caught her by the hand and pulled her back. Tingles spread up her arm from the contact. His hands were slightly rough, as if he worked with them a lot. Not like Ryan's perfectly manicured touch. It shouldn't feel this good, for God's sake. Not when she was busy planning a wedding to another man. Tiffany tried to wriggle her fingers free, but his grip tightened.

"This one looks good." He plucked a book from the rack and read the back.

"Seriously, we don't have time for this." The algebra primer hovered in her peripheral vision. The trouble with teaching herself everything was that she was never sure which parts of her education were missing and was too humiliated to ask anyone to fill in the blanks. Maybe she could get it online.

"But you don't want to read any of those." He reached for another. Gleaming male torso captured in blue tones of the kind Piers photographed. "Hey, this guy must work out."

Thomas had gone through the best sellers one by one, trying to narrow down her preference, with the sort of patience that meant he'd keep at it all day until he found something she liked. In the end she'd let him go with romance. When Daddy had a bug up his ass about something, she'd learned to go along to get along. Thomas threw himself into her choice with enthusiasm.

"And he's a Navy SEAL." Thomas flipped the book over and read the back. "You should get this one."

Tiffany took it and concentrated on the description.

"Whoa." Thomas snagged another one. "This guy must be able to bench-press over three hundred." He opened the book. "And he's a cop. Cops are hot, right?"

Tiffany ducked her head and kept reading the back of the first book. The words danced around on the cover in front of her. *Damn.* Her cheeks got hotter and hotter. She mumbled something incoherent.

Tell him, screamed her gut. *Tell him what you really want to read.*

Yeah, right! her brain yelled back. *You'll tell him and he'll get the look all over his gorgeous face.*

But he didn't when he explained pi. Her gut wasn't backing down without a fight.

"Yeah." Thomas breathed softly. "Cops are totally hot. I should've been a cop."

He didn't need a cop's uniform to make him hot.

He nodded and grabbed another book. "What about firemen?"

"Firemen are good." Her stomach clenched. "We really don't have to do this."

"Yeah, we do." He shrugged one big shoulder and grabbed another book. "Reading is great. I know if we get you the right book, you're going to love it as much as I do."

Algebra Made Easy, bold lettering on a bright yellow spine. Her fingers twitched, eager to pluck it from the plastic shelf, but she wrapped them firmly around the books Thomas handed her.

Thomas would rock those overall things firemen wore. Not pulled up to the top, but folded down low over his hips. A sweaty white T-shirt clinging to his chest and abs. Or skip the T-shirt altogether. Her cheeks burned even hotter. She shifted her legs as the hot thing spread a bit lower. This was so not good. And he was being nice. What the hell was a girl supposed to do with that?

Thomas frowned down at the book in his hand. "Why is this guy wearing tights?"

"Those aren't tights." She took the book from him. "Those are breeches, and it's because the book is historical."

"Huh." He opened the book in the middle. A bad-boy grin flipped the corners of his mouth and lit unholy hell in his eyes. "Tights or not, this one you've got to get."

Her answering grin followed right on its heels. "Are you reading the dirty bits?"

"Yup."

"Such a dog." She shook her head, but her heart wasn't really in it. Since they'd had their little talk, things were good between them. Not exactly comfortable, but Thomas was easy company.

The yellow spine winked at her. *For grades ten and up*, it said in small writing below the title. Tiffany hesitated, then turned away. She'd had her shot at school and blown it.

"So." He stacked the books in his hands. "We get the cop, the fireman, and the hung guy in tights?" His voice carried across the quiet of the store.

Tiffany snatched the books from his hands and marched over to the salesclerk. She slapped her books down on the counter.

Thomas ambled after her and added some soft drinks and a few bottles of water.

The clerk ignored her cash and took the card from Thomas.

"I can buy my own books." Her hand fisted around the cash.

"Sure you can." He accepted the bag from the clerk. "But this way, you have to read the good bits out loud to me."

Tiffany wished the ground would open up and eat her alive. She hadn't spent this much time in blushing pink since her debutante ball. "Come on."

The clerk gave Thomas a coy smile as she waited for the card to process.

"How you doing?" Thomas smiled back and got chatty. Not flirty, but warm and friendly, and the clerk lit up like it was her birthday.

God, Tiffany could walk his card all the way to the bank and back in the time it took for the transaction to go through. As soon as it did, she snatched up the bag and slapped open the door to the parking lot.

The Miura had a new batch of fans. The rest of the parking lot was empty. "Where's Dakota?"

Thomas came up behind her. "Bathroom?"

The door to the men's room opened and Dakota wandered out, attention locked on his phone. Miraculously, he didn't walk into something as he wound his way toward Thomas's truck. He jerked his chin at the two of them and climbed into the back of the truck. On went the Beats and shortly thereafter more frenetic, tinny noises.

Thomas quietly maneuvered them back onto the highway.

Tiffany dug in the bag and took out one of the books he'd bought her. She sat with it in her lap, waiting for the comment.

His attention stayed on the road.

The muted beat of Dakota's music was the only sound above the purr of the truck.

Tiffany opened the book. She liked romance, but it wasn't the algebra book. Her chance to fill in some gaps disappeared as the convenience store grew smaller and smaller in the side mirror. She probably couldn't do that math in that book anyhow. *But you could learn*, insisted a stubborn, little voice in her brain.

"I have a question for you." Thomas broke into her thoughts.

"Okay." She could think of any number of questions he might have that she didn't want to answer. Beginning with why she hadn't bothered to get a divorce before.

"We've traveled sixty miles so far."

"Okay."

"We have another, maybe, two hundred and thirty to go."

"Okay."

"At an average speed of fifty-five miles per hour, because of the trailer, how long will it take us?"

"Four hours and eleven minutes, if we don't stop."

He thought about it for a second. "Fucking amazing." He shook his head. "You're a human calculator."

Tiffany's chest warmed. Nobody had ever called her a human calculator before.

"Here's another one for you."

She looked up from her novel.

"How come a smart girl like you is working for that prick of a photographer?"

Tiffany squirmed in her seat. Her face burned as she tried to think of a clever answer for him. She couldn't. And the reason she couldn't. Because with no education worth spit, working for Piers was the only job a girl like her could get. She might be able to do a bit of math, but that was her only item in the smarts department. A bit of modeling had made her some contacts. A friend of a friend had introduced her to Piers.

She didn't like to think about it, so she shrugged and opened the book. After a while, she sensed him look over at her. She braced for more questions, but he started an annoying tuneless whistling beneath his breath. Slapping her book shut, she glared at him. "I'm not smart."

He stopped whistling and snapped his head toward her. "Sure you are."

Was he faking the look of surprise on his face? She wished she'd kept her big mouth shut, because now she'd have to keep talking. She stared at the picture of the fireman in her lap. What she should have done was put her ear buds in and carried on reading. "No." She gritted her teeth together so hard her nerves tingled. "I don't know smart stuff. I never went to college."

"Why not?"

The flash of hurt around the college thing caught her by surprise. She thought she'd made peace with that years ago. Some people had the smarts for college and others didn't. People like Thomas could probably pick and choose which college they went to. He probably had a pile of letters after high school, begging him to come and study with them. Just like Ryan had. She'd seen them one day when Patti had brought every single one out to show her. "Not everyone is college material."

He made a noncommittal sound.

What the hell did that stupid little grunt mean? It was like he didn't believe her. "Not everyone gets good grades in high school."

He raised his eyebrows. "You didn't get good grades?"

"No."

"Why not?"

She waved her hand down and up again to circle her face. "I have this."

He glanced at her out of the corner of his eye.

"I did not get this." She tapped her finger against the side of her head.

"Wow." He shook his head slowly from side to side. "That is so fucked up."

"No, it's not." She crossed her arms over her chest and sat back in her chair. "It's life. Nobody gets everything."

"Not that." She caught the harshness in his voice. *What the hell?* "It's fucked up that you believe that." He thumped the steering wheel with his palm. "Why would you even think that way?"

"Because I didn't pass high school, okay?"

That showed him. His head jerked. He opened his mouth, shut it again, and glanced in her direction. "What?"

"I didn't get through high school." It came out with barbs on it. "Daddy made sure I got my diploma and graduated with the rest of my class, but I didn't pass."

"Jesus," he said so low she nearly didn't catch it. "How did that happen?"

"I missed a lot of school. Most of my junior and senior years." Her stomach twisted. She could count on one hand the number of people who knew that about her. It wasn't the sort of thing you went yelling your head off about. *Shit.* What sort of person couldn't even get their high school diploma? Not many, that's for sure. She bet she was the only one he knew. "People who don't pass high school don't go to college."

He frowned and narrowed his eyes in thought. The silence in the car oozed like mud.

Tiffany opened the novel, but the words kept dancing across the page. Not because she was dyslexic or anything. That would have been an excuse. She couldn't concentrate with all that silent fuming coming from the driver's side of the car.

"Can I ask you something?"

She rolled her eyes. "Can I stop you?"

"What would you have done? If you had made it to college, I mean. What would you have chosen to do?"

Tiffany stared out the window at the endless black tarmac in front of them. Nobody had ever asked her that question. "Economics." The confession left her naked.

"Economics?"

"I like numbers."

"You certainly have a gift for them," he said. "I can see you doing well at something like that."

Her eyes stung and she blinked them rapidly. There he went with the nice thing again. "No, I wouldn't." She wanted to believe him, but she wasn't that dumb. "You have to be smart to be an economist."

"Who told you you weren't smart?"

Tiffany wanted to stamp her foot. She didn't need

anyone to tell her that, her grades said it all. Hadn't he even been listening? "I just know."

"Nobody wakes up in the morning and just knows they're dumb."

Tiffany clenched her fists. "Okay then, people have always told me I'm dumb. And even if they don't say it, I can see them thinking it."

"And you always take what someone says about you as the truth?"

Who was he to be getting all judgy on her? Was judgy even a word? Judgmental, that was a word. This conversation pissed her off. Therefore, she wasn't going to have it.

"Do you?"

"Yes. No. I don't know." *Shit*, did he have to be this persistent? "People see you a certain way and you are that way. That's it."

He snorted. "Do you even like those books we bought?"

Busted. Tiffany swung her head to hide her expression. "What?"

"The books we bought. Do you even like those sorts of books?"

"They're romance novels. Who doesn't like a love story?" Her throat closed up. If she told him she didn't like them, he would be mad for sure. Madder than he already was.

"But I'm asking you." His eyes got deep cold.

"No."

"Then don't read them." His hands tightened on the steering wheel. "Read the books you want to read. And next time someone says you're dumb, kick them in the nuts."

Chapter Seventeen

Tiffany mulled their conversation over in the silence. People didn't decide they were dumb. Thomas called that right. So where had she gotten the idea? And her book? If she was really dumb, would she have the book? Thinking about this made her head ache. "Tell me about Zambia?"

Thomas glanced over. "What do you want to know?"

"What it's like?" Talking about him seemed a better option than digging around in her head.

"It's . . ." Thomas tapped his long finger on the wheel. "It's Africa, and like nowhere else on earth." The quiet passion in his voice hooked her. His strong face softened as if he had gone to his happy place.

"Tell me," she said.

"Zambia has this immediacy. Life and death are right there, so close you can touch them on a daily basis. When I'm there, I feel alive, really alive. The colors are brighter, somehow." He gave a soft, half-shy laugh. "I love it and it drives me crazy at the same time. It gets under your skin."

Tiffany didn't think she'd ever felt that kind of connection to a place. She could picture him there, Big, blond, and tanned, striding through his own *National Geographic* feature. He belonged someplace like that, and she'd like to see it.

"Hey, does anyone want to play a game?" Dakota leaned over the back of her seat.

"Sure." Thomas's gaze flitted to Dakota's reflection in the rearview mirror. "How about I Am Botticelli?"

"Say what?" Dakota blinked back.

"It's really easy," Thomas said. "You pick a famous person and we have twenty questions to guess who it is. Only the answers have to be yes or no, it can't be a long explanation."

"That's called Twenty Questions." Dakota curled his lip.

"Not in my family." Thomas's jaw clenched. "Now, do you want to play or not?"

The familiar knot tightened in Tiffany's stomach. The only person she could name was Britney Spears. Thomas and Dakota would die laughing at her. "You play," she said. "I'm going to read my book."

Thomas shot her a glance.

"I am."

He raised his brow. *Whatever.*

"How can you read that shit?" Dakota spoke from over her shoulder and made kissy noises in her ear. "It's so stupid."

"You know what's stupid?" Thomas cut in before she could say anything. "Stupid is when you put someone else down."

"Yeah, but they're romance novels." Dakota added tongue action to his kissing noises.

Her cheeks burned. Dakota majored in mean sometimes.

"And you play music that shakes your brain cells to death," Thomas said. "But nobody is calling you stupid."

"Jeez." Dakota rolled his eyes. "I was just saying."

"Don't." Thomas didn't raise his voice. He didn't need to.

Dakota dropped his chin onto his chest and shrugged.

"Okay," Thomas said. "I've got someone, ask your questions."

Tiffany kept her focus on the book, but listened to the game.

Dakota fired questions at Thomas. His high-pitched laugh jarred her. She gave up pretending to read her book and watched him surreptitiously. Something was a bit off with him. Then again, how would she know? She had only seen him in bits and pieces since her "divorce," and he'd sneered at her and called her Barbie ever since.

Dirt and stones kicked against the wheel well as Thomas suddenly pulled over to the side of the road.

Tiffany looked up at him in surprise.

A muscle jumped in the rigid line of his jaw. He hopped out of the truck and wrenched open the back door. "Out."

Dakota jolted back and opened his mouth to argue.

"Get. Out."

Tiffany stared. A whole new Thomas stood beside the truck with Dakota locked in his crosshairs. *Uh-oh!* Thomas looked ready to rip Dakota a new one. He was a difficult little shit, but he was still just a kid. "Thomas—"

"Don't." His eyes blazed.

Tiffany shut up. Damn, Thomas got scary when he was mad.

Dakota hopped from the truck.

"Stay there." Thomas nodded at her and stalked off into the brush at the side of the road.

Dakota followed him, dragging his feet in the dust.

Thomas breathed in through his nose and out through his mouth. For all the good that did. He was so pissed off right now he ached to punch something. Tiffany and her dumb thing got him mad enough, but Dakota pushed him right over the edge.

Dakota's feet scuffed the dirt behind him.

When they were far enough away from the truck not to be overheard he turned. "What are you on?"

Dakota's eyes widened and he swallowed. "What are you talking about?"

"Don't bullshit me." Thomas took a step closer. "I know you're on something and I want to know what it is."

"You're crazy." Dakota glanced to the side. He swung around and headed for the truck.

"Don't do it." Thomas didn't know what he would do if the kid took one more fucking step, but it was not going to be pretty. The little shit was high as a kite. His best guess would be cocaine. Whatever it was, he must have taken it in the bathroom before they left the rest stop. Like he'd taken it the other day when he and Tiffany were at the Grand Canyon.

Dakota's eyes bugged out and his dilated pupils almost swallowed any eye color. It would be better to wait until he came down before he attempted another conversation. So be it, but this getting high shit stopped now. Thomas knew Luke well enough to know the other man would freak out if he found out his kid brother was taking drugs.

Dakota stopped. The first smart move he'd shown in days. "I don't know what you're talking about."

"Cocaine?" he asked.

Tiffany peered through the window at them, her forehead puckered in a frown.

"I don't do drugs," Dakota said.

"Bullshit." Thomas almost lost it. "Is there more in your bag?"

"You're losing your mind."

"Wanna come clean before I check your bag, because I got no problem doing it."

"No."

"No, what?" Thomas wasn't going on a ride along with some kid and his fucking idiotic habit.

"There's none in my bag."

"Where did you get the stuff you're on?"

"I had it."

"Go get your bag."

"I told you, I don't have any." Dakota glared up at him, his breath coming hard.

"Get it." Stupid damned kid, maybe if he grabbed him by the ears and drop-kicked him into next week he'd get some sense out of him. *Jesus.* Seventeen and putting shit up his nose like a seasoned junkie.

"You've got no right to check my stuff."

"I've got every right when you're in my car, underage, and doing illegal shit. Now, get your bag, or I will."

"You're fucked in the head."

"No." Thomas got right into his space. "You are, and you're not going to get that way again. Not on my dime and not when I'm the adult that's going to catch shit for it. Get. Your. Bag."

"You're a total douche." Dakota blinked rapidly.

So be it! Thomas spun on his heel and stalked back to the truck. He leaned in through the open door and grabbed Dakota's bag.

"Hey." The kid reached out to snatch it back.

The look Thomas gave him had him backing off, fast. Thomas could feel Tiffany's stare on both of them, but he didn't look up. She didn't deserve this crap. None of them did. Least of all Dakota. He searched the bag thoroughly. The kid was either telling the truth or it was too well hidden.

"I told you there was nothing in there." Dakota snatched his bag and shoved it in the back. "Maybe you get off putting your hands all over my stuff. Is that it? You're like a perv or something? You like touching other men's underpants?"

Thomas strode around to the driver's side.

"What is it?" Tiffany whipped around in her seat, glancing between them. "What's going on?"

Thomas thought about lying to her and then abandoned the idea. "Dakota's high." She might be fragile as all hell, but she still deserved to know. "I was making sure it doesn't happen again."

"Seriously?" She made a soft noise of disbelief beneath her breath. "And he calls me stupid."

Dakota got into the back, slamming the door so hard the entire truck rattled. He retreated immediately behind his Beats.

Thomas got back on the road. "Did his mother tell you what kind of trouble he's in?"

"No." Tiffany shook her head. "She got in the cab so fast, I didn't have the chance to ask questions. Do you think it's drug related?"

"Shit, I hope not." Thomas glared at the dark strip of tarmac stretching out in front of the truck's hood. He hoped like hell he was wrong, but his Spidey sense shrieked at him. Whatever this kid was into, it wasn't going to be good. And where was his mother in all of this? Taking the sun in Africa. *Fuck.* What the hell was wrong with the woman, anyway?

He jerked his head toward Dakota. "His mother do this a lot?" It couldn't be further from his own mother. Donna was always there when someone needed her. Always. "Take off, I mean, and leave him with someone else."

Tiffany shrugged. "I think so. I really haven't had much

to do with them since my di—since Luke left. But I think I'm still some sort of legal guardian or something because they didn't get around to changing it."

"Why is that?" He wanted to know all of a sudden. He didn't get any of this messed-up situation.

"I would guess Lola is too lazy to bother with changing a legal document."

"Not that." Frustration soured his gut. "Why are you still married to Luke?"

She caught her bottom lip between her teeth. "I don't really know."

"You don't know why you're not divorced?" He found that hard to believe.

"I tell myself it's because I couldn't be bothered to track Luke down, but I don't think that's the truth."

Thomas waited. There was more to this story. A hell of a lot more.

"I think the truth is more like I'm scared to see Luke again. But then, that doesn't really wash either because I could have had the papers taken to him and gotten him to sign them like that. Maybe what I'm really scared of is letting go."

Her honesty rocked him a little. He stared out at the road for a while, not knowing what else to do. Man, her party pack full of surprises kept coming. A drop-dead body wrapped around a tender heart. Fragile, like one of those ornamental balls his mother hung on the Christmas tree. So beautiful, perfect to look at, but ridiculously easy to shatter.

That dickhead Ryan didn't deserve someone so beautiful and delicate. He had her all tied up in knots, trying to be something she wasn't. Who gave a shit if she'd never read Tolstoy? He shook his head. Why was he wasting so much mental energy on this shit? He would take her to

Luke, get them all sorted, and get the hell on with his life. Back home, his family waited for him. Babies didn't hang around for their people to be ready. His brother Josh said he was making headway in getting his kick-ass girlfriend to marry him. And he missed it, going round and round the world chasing whatever he fancied. Time to plug into family again and feel their love and warmth. He teetered off center, too big for his own skin. A trip back home would right-size him pretty quickly.

"Are you still in love with Luke?" Was that his mouth that just opened up and asked the question? It must be.

She glanced at him out of the corner of her eye. They were the most incredible green color and surrounded by lashes as thick as a Disney princess's. "No." Her teeth went at that bottom lip again. Perfect white teeth making indents into that lush pillow of a lip. What a crying shame to do such a thing to a mouth like that. "Maybe." She sighed. "I don't know. The thing with Luke and me, it was so intense and it burned so bright. I don't know what that means."

"You and the almost fiancé, you don't burn bright?" There he went again. Exactly what was this crap to him? Nothing. That's what it was. Nothing. Still, he listened for her answer.

"Oh, no." She laughed. "Ryan and I have a mature relationship. It's not all up and down, in and out, and burning hot one day and blowing freezing the next."

Sounded like a snore to him. "No?"

"No." She slashed the air with her hand. "I am done with that shit. I want stable and secure. Ryan is that and more. I want peaceful."

Thomas stopped himself from shaking his head. Peaceful? How could anything be peaceful when you had a woman this amazing in your life? The way he saw it, you had a woman like this in your life, it was passion. All the way passion, burning hot and strong and pretty much all the time. He gripped the steering wheel tighter.

Images of Tiffany lying spent and drowsy in his bed took up room in his brain. He shook them off. He had no business even going there. Her life was one massive hot mess. The best thing he could do was steer clear. Way clear. This time next year, if he got those results, he would be breaking ground in Zambia.

Chapter Eighteen

"Canyons, Utah. Reach for the Sky." Tiffany read off the sign as the afternoon drew to a close. Tiffany breathed a sigh of relief. Stuck in a car with a moody teen and an angry man stretched the last two hours into forever.

The small town of Canyons lay forty minutes south of Salt Lake City. Quiet and baking in the evening sun, it nestled happily at the base of the Wasatch Mountains. The sky behind the peaks bragged the sort of endless blue that made Tiffany's eyes water. It was the exact color of Thomas's eyes.

Canyons looked more like a sprawling residential neighborhood than a small city. Low buildings spread beneath a huge sky. Space. It stretched around them everywhere. They found a motel just off the main road and booked two rooms. The boys would share—Thomas didn't trust Dakota out of his sight, and apparently he had good reason.

Drugs! She'd bet her last dime Lola knew. How the hell could the woman leave when her son was in this kind of trouble? Any kid deserved more than that.

Dakota hadn't spoken a word since the incident with Thomas and the bag. Instead, he kept his attention glued to his phone and the steady beat of his music going constantly.

She let herself into her room. It smelled of disinfectant and that strange musty odor of too many strangers passing through and leaving a piece of themselves behind. Ryan would have a fit. The air-conditioning worked, however, which was a blessing because Canyons was as close to hell as she ever wanted to get. The heat rocketed clear into the high nineties and climbed, even as the long summer evening descended. Nobody was hungry, so they didn't make any plans to meet for dinner.

Tiffany hunted around for something to do. Even her book couldn't hold her attention. The conversation in the car had scratched her up inside. There had been a time when she'd thought about redoing her high school diploma and going back to college. Then she got scared. Scared of having to face her failure, maybe. Marrying Luke had provided a distraction for a while, and after that it seemed easier to just go along with her father's plan for her. After meeting Ryan, there didn't seem any point in going back to school.

She'd never messed with drugs, but the similarities between her and Dakota were clear enough for even her to see. Two lost rich kids, the rebel and the pleaser. One kicking out as hard as he could, and the other doing all she could to keep her father's approval. She'd decided at a young age it was her job to ease her father's pain after her mother died. Luke had been her one jaunt into rebellion, and that hadn't ended well.

Since then, she'd more or less been drifting. Every now and again she got the feeling that she should make a break for it and fight her way clear. But, fight what? A father who adored her and gave her everything she wanted? A life that didn't demand anything of her, merely that she show up and drift along? *Poor princess Tiffany, everything she wants and she's still not happy.* It sucked and she didn't want to be alone with herself anymore.

She changed into a light summer dress and kick-ass strappy sandals and braved the heat. Outside, the warm air rushed to surround her and stuck to her skin. She jammed her sunglasses over her eyes and looked around. It was a pretty standard motel. Except for the tall peaks of the Wasatch Range etched like the backdrop to a spaghetti Western against the sunset. Luke had chosen a beautiful part of the world to disappear.

The bass thump of music drew her toward the end of the long row of motel rooms. A bar. A nice dry martini would take the edge off. She stopped and frowned. She didn't like martinis. Why the hell did she drink martinis when she didn't even like them? Ryan liked martinis and it seemed the right thing to do. She was going from being a daddy pleaser to a husband pleaser. When, in all this pleasing of others, was Tiffany going to get an inch?

The bright, shining Coors sign beckoned. A world of alcoholic possibilities opened up. She pushed open the door to the bar and blinked in the dim after the bright sunlight outside. The smell of beer and old cigarette smoke rushed to meet her. It was surprisingly full for a bar in the middle of nowhere.

Trying not to feel the stares on her, she made her way over to the bar. Bruce Springsteen wailed about lost America from the jukebox. There were other women clustered around, but they were mostly dressed in T-shirts and shorts. At a guesstimate, she would say she was 92 percent out of place. She lifted her chin. It didn't matter. You were only overdressed if you decided you were, and she totally rocked this Michael Kors dress.

She eased onto a bar stool and crossed her legs. Across the bar, a bearded man lifted his chin. Dropping the eye contact, she ordered a shot of tequila.

The barman slid it in front of her with the salt and lime. She went through the ritual and took the shot, sucking in her breath as it seared down her gullet and crashed into her stomach.

"Hey." A shadow fell across her shot glass. Thomas. She knew it was him without looking up. "A girl like you could get into trouble in a bar like this one."

"Where's Dakota?"

"Sleeping." He perched on the stool beside her. "He's crashed off that high. I don't think he'll surface for the rest of the night."

"And if he does?"

"I've got his phone." Thomas showed her. "I don't see him going anywhere without it." He turned toward the bar. "So, what are we drinking?"

"*I'm* drinking tequila." *Ouch*, that came out a bit bitchy. Giving him attitude when she was kind of glad to see him didn't seem the best option when she was outnumbered twelve to one in the bar. It had been a bit of a weird day. Scratch that. It had been a batshit crazy day. Dakota doing drugs? She snorted softly beneath her breath. That was why Lola had taken off so fast. This shit got way too real for Lola.

"Sounds good to me." Thomas tapped the bar top to get the barman's attention.

Tiffany studied him out of the corner of her eye. *God*, he was fine. He had showered and changed. His damp hair clung to his nape and he wore a fresh tee. She had no idea how he managed to fit them all into that one bag of his. She eyed the slogan across his chest.

Have you tried turning it off and on again? Not her favorite, but good for a smile. She spread the salt onto her hand and licked it off. The tequila made her eyes water on the way down, and the lemon had her sucking in her breath.

He watched her do the shot, an unreadable expression on his face.

She opened her mouth to ask what and then shut it again. She didn't feel like caring. She motioned the barman for two more. Beside her, Thomas's arm snapped as he took his shot. No salt and no lemon, just straight up. Thomas Hunter—a straight-up kind of guy. She snickered to herself.

He slammed his shot glass against the bar and sucked in a deep breath. "Damn, that had claws."

Tiffany grinned at him. Of course it had claws. It was tequila. She lined up her next shot and shook the salt out onto her hand.

"Now, that's just no fun." He snagged her hand and raised it to his mouth. His eyes locked on hers—deep liquid blue—as his tongue slid hot against her skin and lapped up the salt.

Her belly tightened beneath her dress. Tiffany fought the desire to look away. As he turned and took the shot, her breath came out in a whoosh. This was certainly not helping the attraction thing. "I think salt licking should be off the agenda as well."

He gave a wry smile. "You're probably right." His smile widened into a grin. "You know, in Africa, animals share salt licks all the time? In a totally nonsexual way."

His brand of goofy eased the tightness in her chest. "Is that so?"

"Honest. It's considered a sign of trust." He shook salt onto his hand and offered it to her. For a crazy moment, she was tempted. Then she shook her head and took her own salt.

His expression mocked her lightly. "What are we drinking to?"

"Me." The next shot went down easier and she ordered another two.

"Sounds good to me." He turned to look at her, a question in his eye. "Anything specific about you?"

"Freedom. As in me getting mine."

"From Luke?"

Funny, she hadn't been thinking about Luke. "Sure. Why not?"

"To your freedom." He raised his glass and clinked it against hers.

"Tell me something?" She got a waft of his Thomas smell as he leaned closer to pour salt over her hand. "Do you ever get the feeling like you want to run hard enough to forget where you came from?"

"Sure." One corner of his mouth lifted. "You're talking to the man with permanently itchy feet." His tongue whipped out and took the salt from her hand.

That tongue had serious talent. His flirting snapped her feel-good synapses. Tiffany let the tingles do their buzzy thing and grinned at him. Hey, she might be having fun here. They took the next shot together.

"Do you dance?" She gestured the small space beside the bar where a couple was shuffling around, more vertical making out than dancing.

"I'm sad to say I don't." He smiled, with a little something behind it she couldn't put her finger on. She liked it anyway. "Why don't you tell me your story instead?"

The tequila created a nice fuzzy warmth in her midsection. She motioned the barman for another two. "I've got a better idea. Why don't you tell me yours?"

"Me?" He looked taken aback. "I don't have much of a story. Pretty much, what you see is what you get."

"Tell me anyway."

"Okay." He took a breath. "I'm the youngest of three brothers. My family lives in Willow Park, north of Chicago. Older brother is a doctor, middle brother a financial whiz kid, and I'm an engineer."

"Hmm." Not what she had been hoping for, but it was a start. "Married? Girlfriend?"

"Neither." His smile did those great crinkle things to the corner of his eyes. "I move around a lot, so I don't really have time for that sort of thing."

"Commitment phobe?"

"Maybe." There went that killer smile again and the tingles crackled beneath her skin. "Or maybe I haven't met the girl to make me want to stay in one place."

She missed her hand with the salt and squinted down as it wavered a bit. Finally, she got enough to lick. She glanced at Thomas as she did it. His hot gaze tracked the movement of her tongue like a starving man. A surge of power warmed her up inside. "So you've worked in Zambia, where else?"

"Chile. Gaspé—"

"Where?" He didn't seem to mind that she didn't know stuff, and it made asking so much easier.

"It's in Canada, eastern Quebec. Very cold and tons of snow."

"Not like Zambia?"

"Not at all, and if I have a choice I'd much rather be hot than cold."

She nodded and drank. "And that's where you ran into Luke."

"Yup."

"What do you think he's doing in Utah?"

"Dakota says he's working in some sort of bike shop here. Works during the weeks and goes mountain biking on the weekends."

"Ah." Now it made perfect sense. Thinking about Luke made her happy buzz waver around the edges. She hadn't clapped eyes on him in seven years. Had he changed? Of course he'd changed, and she had, too. Luke would have loved this dress. Tiffany looked down at her dress and sighed. White and curve hugging, it clung in all the right places and ended short enough for her legs to do the talking. "He would have liked this dress."

"Any man with a pulse likes that dress."

"You say a lot of stuff like that. It's making the ignoring part difficult to . . . um . . . ignore." The tequila disintegrated her erase button. His shot sat on the bar and she snagged it. And then his wrist, and poured salt all over it. Salt scattered over the bar top and onto his pants. She didn't care.

Up went one of his eyebrows in a silent challenge.

With a grin, she bent and lapped the salt from his wrist. He tasted yummy, salty, with a tang of warm skin. Warm man-skin on her tongue. "So, why do you say them, the dog things?"

His eyes screamed danger, but the tequila laughed in its face. "I'm a man, we all think things like that. I say them."

"I noticed." There it came again, the smile, the warning and the tequila smoothing away the edges.

"And I think you're hot."

"Yeah." The pit of her stomach dropped. What a total disappointment. She wrinkled up her nose at him. Not to sound ungrateful or anything. She was glad she'd been born with her fair share of natural assets, but she liked it better when he called her smart, or a human calculator. She especially liked that one. "Yeah, but it's not real."

"Say what?" His gaze roamed her from top to toe. "It looks pretty real to me."

"Nuh-uh." She shook her head and signaled the barman. If she was going to have this conversation, she definitely needed more hooligan juice. "I mean, some of it's natural, but not the rest."

His eyes sparkled down at her, his interest snagged. "Which bits?"

"Botox." She tapped her forehead.

He frowned at her. "How old are you?"

"Twenty-six, but it's never too early to start." She leaned forward. *Oops*, her balance seemed a bit iffy.

He steadied her with one of his huge hands. He could get her whole breast in a hand that size. Which reminded her. She pointed at her chest. "Sweet sixteen present."

"No." He eyed her breasts.

"Great job, but fakes." Sitting back a little, she let him get a proper look.

"What else?"

She tapped her nose.

His eyes widened.

"And that's it." She rapped the counter. The barman must be asleep. She needed him here with that next shot.

The barman's gaze drifted over to Thomas.

"Don't you think you've had enough?" Thomas cocked his head.

"No." She slapped her hand on the bar. "Another one."

He grinned and shook his head. "Okay."

"I don't like being told what to do. Ryan does it all the time, and it's okay when he does it because he loves me and he's my fiancé."

His beautiful blue eyes chilled. "Almost fiancé."

"Tomahto, tomato." She waved her hand at him. He seemed pissed and she had no idea why. The barman put down another two shots and she beamed her thanks at him. "Wanna do a body shot off me?"

Thomas looked kind of primitive for a moment. She thought he might grab her and drag her off to his cave. The weird part being how on board she was with the idea.

"No."

"Aw, come on." She slung her arm around his shoulders and tugged him closer. He had such pretty eyes. And his mouth. His lips were kind of stern and sexy all at once. His bottom lip was full and biteable, his top lip clearly drawn in strong lines. "I thought you were a model."

"I know."

"You're very good-looking." She tightened her grip around his neck and his face got closer. Maybe he wanted to kiss her. She wouldn't mind that. He was always telling her she was hot and stuff. He probably wanted to kiss her. That would be great. No. She sat up suddenly and released him. That would not be good at all. That would be very, very bad. "I'm engaged."

"Almost engaged." He touched the end of her nose. "And you're a sloppy drunk."

She almost took offense. Maybe if he had looked like it bothered him even the teeniest bit, she might have. Instead, he looked like he thought the whole thing was a hoot. "No." She held up her index finger. Then she cupped the end of his lovely, strong chin. With a chin like that, she bet he made up his mind in a big way. "I am a horny drunk."

"Good to know." He grinned. "Let's get you to bed."

"Oh, no, no, no, no, no." She reeled back. Unfortunately she misjudged her momentum and went too far back.

He caught her around the waist. He had those biceps that looked like they wanted to bust free of the arms of his T-shirt. *Nice.* She blinked at his totally hot arms. Were they as strong as they looked? She gave them a squeeze.

Oh, boy, a girl could sink her teeth into those. Maybe she shouldn't. Of course she shouldn't, which brought her back to where she was before he made her look at his arms. "I'm not going to bed with you."

"I'm heartbroken." His arms tightened around her waist as he pulled some cash from his pocket and dropped it on the counter. "And I didn't ask you to go to bed with me. I said we should get you to bed."

He edged her off her bar stool.

She wavered on her feet for a moment. It was the Manolos. Great shoes, but they didn't go well with tequila. "What exerts more pressure per square inch when walking, a one-hundred-pound woman in heels, or a six-thousand-pound elephant?"

His eyebrow shot up as he steadied her against his wide chest. "Is the elephant wearing heels?"

"No." She snorted a laugh and his expression softened.

"Damn, you even make that sexy."

"Do you know?" She patted the rigid line of his chest.

"Pressure is defined as force over area," he said. "Pressure being directly proportional to the force and inversely proportional to the area. So, given that the area of the tip of a high heel shoe is so small, and an elephant's foot is so much larger and it walks with two feet on the ground at once, I would say the woman in the kick-ass shoes wins hands down."

He got it right. Tiffany beamed at him and stroked his chest. His mind was as sexy as the rest of him. *Nice.* Her feet didn't want to stay under her. "You don't want to sleep with me?"

"I never said that." He took her weight and half carried her to the door.

"So, you do want to sleep with me."

"Tiffany." He stopped suddenly and turned her toward him. Her Manolos tried to run away again and he tightened his grip. "You're loaded right now, so you probably won't remember this. I would give my left nut to sleep with you, but you would have to be sober at the time."

"Oh." That made her feel a lot better. She took deep breaths of the sticky night air as he propelled her down the walk to her room. The crappy motel looked a lot nicer at night, warm and welcoming.

He propped her up against the wall while he opened her door. "Here we go."

"Thomas?"

"Yup."

"If you gave your left nut, would you still be able to sleep with me?"

He gave a short bark of laughter.

She might not be smart, but he thought she was sexy and funny and he knew numbers like she did. It made her feel like one of those people in the movie *Cocoon*, all glowy and stuff.

He pushed her gently into the room. "I'll see you in the morning."

"I might need help getting into bed." She leaned toward him and giggled.

He caught her and steered her back into her room. "I think that's a horrible idea."

The door started to close. Grabbing the edge, she tugged it out of his grasp. She leaned toward him, but lost her balance. "Thomas."

He caught her against his chest. That, too, was a whole lot of lovely. His head seemed a very long way up, so she grabbed his T-shirt and tugged until he brought it down to her level. She plastered her mouth over his. His lips were soft and firm at the same time. She pushed him away before her tongue gave way to the impulse and went for it.

He looked a little mussed and a lot frustrated.

Good. I am woman, hear me roar. She'd read that somewhere and she thought it sounded rather good. "Thanks for a lovely evening."

She shut the door and leaned her weight against it. Her nipples tingled against the stretch of her dress, standing up and waiting to be noticed. Except there was nobody to notice them. Nobody but her. She brought her hands up to cup her breasts.

Thomas had noticed her breasts. She looked at the door again. *Nope.* She shook her head and stumbled over the edge of the carpet. Going out there again was a bad idea. She ran her hands down her torso to the apex of her thighs. Heat pulsed through the thin fabric of the dress. Her breath caught in a soft gasp as she pushed her fingers against her mound. She could give herself relief, but she didn't want that.

Irritably she yanked off her sandals and tossed them across the room. Well, she had a fiancé, right? Almost. Screw that. Tiffany dug her phone out of her bag and hit Dial. "Hello, baby," she purred as Ryan answered.

"Tiffany?"

"How you doing, babe?" Delilah came out to play.

Silence met her for a moment. "Are you all right?"

"Ryan." She sprawled across one of the two beds in her room and arched her spine like a cat. She ached and she wanted to make it feel good. "You know what we've never done?"

"Tiffany, have you been drinking?"

"Yup, I have. We've never had phone sex. I think we should change that right now."

"You know I don't like it when you drink."

"You'll like it just fine in a minute, baby. Ask me what I'm wearing?"

"No, Tiffany, I am not asking you what you're wearing, because I'm not playing this ridiculous game. Sleep it off. I have work to do."

The phone went dead in her ear.

"Ryan?"

Silence.

"Fuck."

Chapter Nineteen

Tiffany cracked open an eyelid and moaned. Tequila waited until the next morning to make you suffer. The sneaky bitch. Pounding reverberated through her head. Not her head, the door.

"What?" She worked her tongue off the roof of her mouth to get some moisture going. *Yuck.* Her teeth had fur on them.

"Rise and shine, princess," Thomas called. "We're burning daylight here."

"Okay."

Sweet baby Jesus. She'd planted a drunk, sloppy kiss on Thomas last night. Shit, and she hadn't stopped there. Bloody tequila—there was a reason she didn't drink the stuff. She'd told him about her boob job and nose job and the Botox. She dropped back onto the bed with a groan. Maybe she could stay here for the next sixty years of her life and he'd get tired of waiting.

"Don't go back to sleep." He almost hammered the door right off its hinges.

"Okay." Face him she must.

Here came another day of staring at Dakota's sullen face and angry eyes. Dakota used to follow her and Luke around, his little face alive with curiosity, chatting as fast as his mouth could move. He'd adored his older brother to the point of hero worship.

Luke loved Dakota right back. Nothing was ever too important for him to drop it and deal with Dakota. And Dakota needed a lot of dealing. She'd been jealous as hell at the time. But Luke had been gone for seven years. So who had been listening to Dakota chatter in those years? Not Lola, that was for certain.

Lola. Tiffany snorted. Debbie Wilson from Iowa had a lot of explaining to do. After Luke's father was jailed for embezzlement, Daddy had advised her—very strongly— to keep her distance from Lola. With her own money intact, Lola got on with her life, single in all the ways she needed. Luke left, Tiffany drifted, and Lola launched into her life as a socialite. So what had happened to Dakota? He'd gotten lost in the shuffle.

"Are you up?" Thomas went at the door again, dragging her out of her misery. "Don't make me come in there after you."

He'd do it, too. She'd made enough of a dick of herself. Having him come in there and see her would be the final insult. If she felt this bad, it stood to reason she wouldn't be an oil painting this morning.

"I'm coming." She fell out of bed and staggered into the bathroom.

Her reflection greeted her and she shrieked. Her sexy sundress hung around her like a rumpled dishrag. Michael Kors would slit his wrists if he saw what she'd done to his dress. Leftover mascara gummed her lashes together and made track marks under her eyes and down her cheeks. She laughed. That was no princess blinking back at her. Ryan would need a clinic to recover. Ryan. *Shit.* He'd have plenty to say.

She ran warm water and did some damage repair. Her phone pinged. She didn't need to check caller display to guess who that was. Best get it over with. After washing and drying her face, she went to find her phone. It was halfway under the bed, lighting up like a Christmas tree with the calls from Ryan.

She hit his number and waited.

"Tiffany," he greeted her.

"Hi there." She tried to keep it light. A threatening silence loomed back at her. "So, um, last night." Time to get this out in the open. "I had a bit too much to drink."

"You know how I feel about drinking." Ryan sighed. The weight of his disapproval settled across her shoulders and she sat on the edge of the bed. "Last night took me by surprise. I have never known you to get drunk like that."

"I was just a bit buzzed," she said.

"I think the more important question here is where you are, Tiffany." Ryan continued as if she hadn't spoken.

"What?" Her mouth dried up. Ryan had that *I know something* tone.

"After last night, I was concerned about you. I did a bit of checking around. Your father said you were at a spa, but I called and you're not at any spa you normally frequent."

Frequent? Tiffany took her phone away from her ear and glared at it. Who spoke like that? He sounded like a banking commercial. "No, I'm not," she said. "I needed some time to think, so I went somewhere different." She glanced around her expressionless hotel room. Way, way different, in fact.

Silence stretched between them as Ryan waited for her to tell him more. No way was she doing that. His clipped tone could've cut glass. "Are you going to tell me where?"

"No." Her stomach tightened. He wasn't going to like

that, but telling him the truth was so not an option. "I wanted to be alone to think, and I went somewhere nobody knew me."

"Is this still about the other night?" Ryan sighed, bending the phone lines with his heavy exhalation. "Your father said you were upset. Is that what getting drunk and behaving out of character is about? I thought we'd settled this, Tiffany."

"No, it's not, we have, I'm okay about that. I just had too much to drink." She was babbling and she shut her mouth.

"The issue isn't how much you drank, it's why you felt the need to do it. The call, I put down to the drinking. We're not going to even talk about that. It was a symptom and now I want to hear the cause."

"Tequila?" She giggled.

"Don't be flippant, Tiffany."

Oops. She dug her toes into the rough pile of the carpet. Ryan would turn this into a big deal. He wasn't one to let things roll. Her bright red nail polish stood out against the beige carpet. She'd drunk dialed and tried to get her almost fiancé to have phone sex with her. Ryan acted like she'd run naked down the Magnificent Mile. "It was just a stupid call."

"Don't trivialize this, please," he said, frost tightening his clipped vowels. "You upset me with that so-called stupid call, and I believe I'm entitled to an explanation."

Ryan never yelled or got mad. He got meaner and sharper. She scrunched her toes together, yanking back on the urge to shout back like a thirteen-year-old. Ryan made her feel like a child, and it was bullshit. He was mad because she wanted to have phone sex. How dumb was that? Most men she knew would've liked a call like that.

Thomas would've played. She shoved that thought away. Facing him and that sloppy kiss still loomed in her future. "You know what, Ryan," she said, done with this conversation and squirming, "you've got your explanation. I got drunk, I get horny when I'm drunk, and I called you. End of story. Done."

"This conversation is not done."

"Ah-ah." So deliciously and childishly satisfying. "This conversation *is* done."

"Tiffany." His composure sounded a little frayed around the edges. "Do not hang up this phone. We have to talk about this. I need to—"

"You know what, Ryan? You do a lot of talking. I've really had enough of your talking." This beat the crap out of phone sex. Almost.

"Tiffany." His voice rose. "I don't like this side of you at all."

"I'm not a polygon, Ryan."

"What?"

"A polygon." She took a note from Dakota's book and drew out each sound with a silent "idiot" hanging on the end. "A plane figure with at least three straight sides and angles, and typically five or more."

"I know what—"

"Well, I'm not one of those. I don't have sides. I'm all one big piece, and some of those pieces are wonderful and others are messy. Deal with it."

"This isn't the girl I'm going to marry speaking," Ryan said.

Hot anger jabbed through her gut. "You aren't going to marry me because you never asked." She relished how her voice bounced off the walls. "You assumed I would say yes. Well, what if I don't say yes? Did that even occur to you? No, it didn't. Well, Ryan, think about this. I might not want to marry someone who thinks a drunken call is a federal offense. Think about that."

She hung up before he could speak again. Her phone rang almost immediately. Her hand hovered over it. She should pick it up. Her heart pounded so fast, she thought she might throw up. She didn't want to pick up. Not picking up, though, was only going to make him madder.

"Are you coming?" Thomas yelled through the door.

"Just wait." She shoved her phone deep into her bag. It stopped ringing and she breathed a sigh of relief. Her phone started up again. She kicked the bag under the bed and ran for the shower.

Tiffany inched out of her room and into the hideously bright day.

Thomas greeted her with another of his big smiles. "You okay?"

Dakota pretended she didn't exist, which, given her state that morning, was fine by Tiffany.

"No." She avoided Thomas's knowing look and jammed her sunglasses on.

"Hey." Thomas snagged her arm and tugged her in front of him. Blue eyes, kind, warm, and caring, soothed the jangled edges of her nerves.

"I think I might have sort of broken up with my boyfriend."

"What?" Thomas jerked his head back. "I was asking about your hangover, but this is a lot more serious. How do you sort of break up with your boyfriend?"

A small huddle of men surrounded the trailer with the Miura. Legs akimbo, arms across their chests as they discussed the car loudly. A couple of small boys stood beside the men, miniature versions of their bigger counterparts.

"What year is she?" a man called out.

"Seventy-two," she said.

"Back to the boyfriend." Thomas turned her face back to him. His hand pressed warm against her chin. "Either you broke up with him or you didn't."

She shivered under the intensity of his blue-eyed gaze. "I got mad at him. He said I had sides, I said I didn't, I had bits and some of them were messy, so he could deal."

Thomas's grip on her arm tightened a bit. "That's it?"

"I've never spoken to him like that." Tiffany's head reeled a bit. Might have been the hangover, but probably more the conversation with Ryan. "I told him I might not want to marry him anyway."

"And he said?"

"I don't know. I hung up." Her phone started ringing again.

Thomas looked down at her bag. "You going to get that?"

"Nope."

"What kind of torque does this baby have?" a voice called out from the fan club.

"Almost three hundred pounds," she called back.

The fan club clucked that over in their huddle.

Thomas tugged her a step closer. "That doesn't sound like a breakup to me."

"I said I wasn't sure if I wanted to marry him."

"And how much of that is the tequila talking?"

"None of it." He stood there, looking all self-righteous, just like Ryan. "None of it was the tequila talking. Last night, okay, tequila all the way, but this morning, I was sober." Suddenly, Tiffany had a gut load of men and their crap. All of them. "You're all the same, all of you." Dropping her chin to her chest, she deepened her voice. "I'll tell you what to think, Tiffany. Don't you worry your pretty little head about that because you're not so good at thinking, anyway. Let me do that . . ." Tears crept up on her. Damn, stupid things.

Big arms wrapped around her and pulled her closer. "Whoa."

The fight bled right out of her and she leaned her cheek against the hard expanse of his chest. He smelled of man and laundry detergent, his tee soft against her skin. "Too much?"

"Maybe a little."

She sighed into the warm comfort he offered.

"What happened last night?" His voice rumbled through his chest. "I left you and you went to bed."

"Nothing." Swift heat rushed up her neck and over her face. "I called him and he got mad."

"What about?" Broad hands swept the skin of her back and took the tension away with them.

"Why do you want to know?"

His nose brushed against her ear. "Tell me."

"Why?" She squirmed inside. This could get so humiliating, but tucked up against the strength and heat of him, she ached to confess all her secrets.

His laughter vibrated against her. "Because I like you, Tiffany."

That thrilled her right to the toes of her Jimmys.

"And because there's a little something going on between us. If you're engaged and ready to marry this guy, then I'm not going to step on anybody's toes. But if this guy is the jerk I think he is, then you deserve better."

A small sound squeaked out of her throat. The blood roared through her ears. "You're hitting on me."

"Not right now." His arms tightened. "So tell me."

He scared the crap right out of her. The words were one thing, but there was no denying how much she liked hearing them. And she really shouldn't because things were way, way messy enough. She wrenched out of his dangerous hold and stalked over to the men surrounding the Miura. "I'm not talking about this anymore. Or ever."

Tiffany spent the next fifteen minutes discussing specifications with a rapt audience. She tried to ignore Thomas, but he didn't make it easy by standing there watching her. He also didn't move too far away from Dakota the entire time. That situation wasn't getting any easier either.

They got on the road a short while later. Dakota gave them the address of the shop where Luke worked.

Tiffany wished she could swap places with Dakota and hide out in the back. The bellowing bass coming off Dakota's headphones made short work of that idea.

She sipped the coffee Thomas had bought her and ate tiny pieces of her muffin (also procured by Thomas). Her belly roiled and her head pounded with a combination of anxiety and hangover. The muffin was the wrong side of fresh and tasted like it had been pounded out with another ten million just like it, but she ate the entire thing anyway. And enjoyed it.

"How's your hangover?" Thomas broke the silence between them. A smug smile curled around his mouth.

Tiffany cursed the heat creeping into her cheeks. She'd hoped they could go the entire day without having to discuss any of this. At least this way, she wasn't obsessing about seeing Luke. Or Thomas's latest confession. She threw a surreptitious glance over her shoulder to make sure Dakota wasn't listening. "Not so good."

Dakota glanced up and gave her the death stare.

"My head is fine." Thomas's smile grew bigger.

"Okay." She sighed. Smug so didn't suit him. "Get it over with."

"What?" He looked genuinely confused.

Tiffany glared at him. "Don't be a dickhead."

"What?" Surprise morphed into injured.

"You know what I'm talking about. Me going on and on about my stuff." She waved her hand over herself. "Making a complete ass of myself, getting tanked on tequila and throwing myself at you."

"That was you throwing yourself at me?" He made a noise of disbelief in the back of his throat. "And here I thought you were just a friendly drunk. If I'd known you were throwing yourself at me, I definitely would've paid closer attention."

"Seriously?" Tiffany shook her head. He was going to compound her humiliation by making fun of her. She took a huge gulp of coffee and scalded the back of her throat.

"Come on," he said with a laugh. "You had too much tequila, Tiffany. Nobody got hurt, nothing stupid happened. Lighten up a little."

Easy for him to say. She folded her arms across her breasts. Lighten up? Was he kidding her? She'd gone and made a total idiot of herself. She'd like to see how he'd feel if he had done the same. Actually, try as she might, she couldn't see him making a big deal about it. What she could see was him flashing that big, beautiful grin and making a joke out of the whole thing. Maybe, and at the very most, looking a bit sheepish. "I feel stupid."

"Sure you do." He shrugged one big shoulder. "But it's over now."

"Really?"

He made a face. "Hey, if it makes you feel any better, remember I was the one that said I'd give my left nut to sleep with you."

Actually, it made her feel a lot better. "We were drunk," she said. "I think we should agree to discount anything the other one said."

"No." He shook his head. "You were drunk. I was lightly buzzed and I still want to sleep with you. I think I made that clear earlier."

Her mouth dropped open and she had to shut it fast. "You can't say things like that."

Dakota's head was down, his music still going as he tapped into his phone.

"Sure I can. And when you quit ducking and diving, you'll admit you feel the same way. It doesn't mean it's going to happen or anything, just like to put these things out there." Thomas shrugged. "Anyway, how do you want to go about looking for Luke?"

"I don't know." Her brain cycled to catch up with the subject change. Clearly, Thomas thought the other part of their conversation was over, and she sure as hell wasn't going back there.

"I think we should go straight to the store. If we get lucky, we'll run into Luke. If not, we might find someone who knows him." He went silent for a moment. "You guys going to be okay?"

"Luke and me?"

"Yup. Last I heard, you couldn't be in the same room without making the walls shake."

"I've grown up since then." Sort of. He had a point, though. Those last months with Luke had been one battle after another, both of them drawing as much blood as they could. Luke had a vicious mouth on him. She did a mental flinch. She hadn't exactly done herself proud with her comebacks. The demolition job on the Miura being number one on that list. "I'm going to calmly explain what I want and get him to come back with me. Then I'm going to give him back the Miura and we can be on our way. It sounds like your business with him is going to be a hell of a lot more serious."

"Yeah." Thomas grimaced at the windshield. "I have a whole lot that needs saying when I see Luke, and he's not going to like any of it." He paused. "How do you think Luke is going to react to his brother?"

Tiffany dared another glance at Dakota.

His fingers whirred across his screen. From this angle, it was the only sign of life.

"Dakota adored Luke when he was a kid. He really looked up to him."

"And Luke?"

"Luke took care of him," Tiffany said. "He didn't have a lot going for him. I know it's hard to see now, but he was the cutest kid." She kept her tone low in case Dakota could hear anything through the raucous pounding his ears were taking. "Lola never had a lot of time for him, and their dad . . ." She didn't know how much Luke had told Thomas.

"He's in jail, right?"

"Right." She breathed a sigh of relief. This would all be easier if Thomas knew everything. "Embezzlement. Lola had her own money tied up, so it didn't touch her. But even before that, their dad was not really the kind of dad who noticed his children much. When Luke was a kid, their father used to keep filling up his bank account, and other than staying out of his hair, that was all their father did for them. Luke's parents were divorced, but his mother was great."

An old sadness gripped her. It wasn't long after the death of his mother that things with Luke had changed. "After his mom died, Luke seemed to want to spend more and more time with Dakota. Like he was all that Luke had."

And that was what had just about killed her. She had
wanted, no, needed Luke to turn to her for comfort. Instead,
he had virtually cut her out, spending as much time with
his brother as he could. Always polite to her, but cold and
distant. That was when she learned how to push his buttons.
And push them she did.

Looking back now, it was hard to believe that was her.
She'd pushed and Luke had struck back. In the beginning
they had used sex to keep the connection alive, but soon
the verbal skirmishes grew too awful for even that. Then
Luke had turned to other women to ease his pain. She
couldn't say any of this out loud. It burned enough to even
think about it.

"How do you want to handle the drug thing?" Thomas
turned off the main road onto a quieter street.

Tiffany blew out her breath. "It's not like either of us
really has any say in how Dakota lives his life and what he
does," she said. "And he sure doesn't want to know what
I think about his life."

"You have a point." Thomas gave a wry smile. "But I
can't leave it at that. I'll try talking to him."

"Good luck with that." Traffic slid around them.
Normal people having a normal day, with no idea of the
time bomb ticking down in Thomas's truck.

"Whatever happens, we'll have to tell Luke," Thomas
said.

Tiffany shook her head slowly. Luke's day was about to
slide into the toilet.

Chapter Twenty

Tiffany kept her gaze on the streets as they wound between strip malls and quiet suburbs. They stopped at a pedestrian crossing for a family on bicycles. Mom, Dad, and their two kids happily pedaled down the road.

"Are we there yet?" Dakota took off his headphones. He straightened in his seat and looked around him. His mouth tightened in a grim line.

"Almost," said Thomas.

Almost there. Almost at the store where Luke worked. Almost *with* Luke. Tiffany's belly twisted inside out. Best case scenario, Luke wouldn't be too pissed to see her. They all got worse from there, so she stopped thinking about his reaction and looked at the small dot that was them moving across the GPS map.

They arrived at the store that screamed "boys and their toys." Massive TV screens rolled image after image of men throwing themselves over cliffs, under towering walls of water, down ravines, and up fortresses of rock. All of the men wore neon and little more than a cool headband.

"Help you?" A young guy shuffled toward them, long hair and tattoos, with the sort of stringy shape you got from hours spent sweating up and down mountains under the Utah sun. A chin lift in Thomas's direction said she'd obviously been identified as the least likely buyer.

"Yeah." Thomas looked up from the mountain bike he was admiring. He'd look at some lucky girl the same way some day. "Cool bike," he said. Then he seemed to remember what they were doing there. "Actually, we're looking for Luke."

"Luke?" The shaggy-haired salesman shoved his hands into the pockets of his cargo shorts. Those shorts would hit the ground if he kept putting pressure on the pockets like that. They seemed to be barely saying hello to his hip bones. "He's not here right now. Can I help you with anything?"

Her head spun for a moment. Momentary reprieve. She got a mental hold of herself. There would be no wussing out now, when she'd come all this way.

"Is this a hardtail?" Thomas wanted to talk bikes? Tiffany stared at the side of his head.

Dakota slouched over and ran reverent fingers over the bike's handles.

"No, dude." The salesman's scraggly beard parted to show perfectly white teeth. "This is way, way more than that. Check this out." As one, they crouched to stare at the frame of the bike. "This is a new feature Specialized are putting on their bikes. Totally righteous, man. This little baby is going to give you the sweetest ride."

And they were off.

Toward the back of the store, another bike stretched over a sort of rack thingy as another long-haired outdoors type spun the wheels. She studied the other salesman. She really didn't get the "pants on the ground" thing. What was the point in having half your underwear hanging out? In her opinion, one of the best parts of man watching was butts and thighs, and those hanging pants gave you nothing.

Thomas wore his faded jeans low on the hip, but curved to the butt. Not tight, but not too loose and hiding his prime ass. His T-shirt of the day left her clueless—*There's no place like 127.0.0.1*—but it rode up as he crouched and showed a strip of tanned waist. His thighs pulled the faded denim to straining point.

It would've been better if he'd never said that thing about wanting to sleep with her. Her head kept going back there. It must be her low-level hangover still making white noise in her head. She forced her gaze to some snowboarder on the screen carving up a vertical rock face with his board.

"So, he'll be here tomorrow?" Thomas asked.

"Should be." The salesman shrugged. "Today is riding day. So unless he lands his ass in hospital, Luke will be here tomorrow."

"Cool." Thomas nodded, casting another loving glance at the bike.

"You wanna take her for a sling?" The salesclerk recognized a brother when he saw one.

Thomas's entire being lit up. "Can I?"

"Sure." The guy unracked the bike with a practiced flick of the wrist. "Just give me your car keys and some ID."

They all looked at her, Thomas with open pleading in his blue gaze. Would any woman be able to resist that look? "Go ahead."

They hit the front of the store. Thomas threw his leg over the bike. The huge parking lot stretched behind the building. When they'd arrived, Tiffany had been glad they could get the trailer in without hassles. Now she saw the full reason for the large parking lot as Thomas stood on the pedals and shot across the empty space.

The salesman sidled up beside her. "That is not a Miura?"

And they thought their bicycles were cool. Tiffany turned to look at the salesman with a smile. "It sure is."

"Righteous." He breathed and headed for the car.

Thomas pulled tight turns at the other end of the parking lot.

Beats back in place, Dakota propped himself up on a cement bollard.

"Luke said he had one of these." The salesman stared at the Miura like he'd had an epiphany.

"He did and he still does," Tiffany said. It was going to be hard saying good-bye to her baby. Maybe Ryan was a little bit right about all of that after all. Her lip curled back from her teeth. Except she was mad at Ryan and didn't want to think fair. What the hell kind of man turned down phone sex? And then went on to make such a big, stinking deal about it?

The salesman's eyes grew wide as he turned back to her. "This is Luke's?"

"Uh-huh." Tiffany nodded. "I've been . . . looking after it for him for a little while. Now I'm bringing his best girl home."

Luke had always called the Miura his best girl. He used to joke Tiffany was his second best girl. Her eyesight misted suddenly. They used to laugh a lot, she and Luke. She didn't seem to laugh like that anymore. Until recently.

With a whir of wheels, Thomas cycled back to them. He looked like a kid, all ruffled hair and shining eyes as he slid his leg over the bike. Thomas could make her laugh, too.

"Hey," the clerk called. "Cool shirt."

Tiffany rolled her eyes. Everyone seemed to get it but her.

"I don't get it." Dakota sniffed. She wanted to cheer, but could guess how that would go down.

Thomas looked down at his shirt. "127.0.0.1 is the address of your home computer."

Okay, she got it.

He grinned at her, boyish and endearing.

Tiffany really tried not to smile. The T-shirt was amusing, but his grin would get anyone smiling.

"So, like, if that's Luke's car," the salesman said, "I don't know where he lives, but a lot of bikers end up at Prospectors bar after they ride. You could try to catch him there. He loved that car, man."

"Yes, he did." Tiffany blinked back the moisture. If Luke had loved that car only a tiny bit less, she might not have done what she did. She gave the Miura an apologetic pat on the door panel.

The salesman gave Thomas directions to the bar.

"Hey." A strong hand curled around her waist. She leaned in as she looked up. Thomas's eyes were kind, but not smiling anymore. "You okay?"

"Sure." She managed a smile. His hand around her waist felt nice, like it fit there. She moved out of his light clasp. "So, what's the plan?"

"I'm hungry," Dakota said. As far as she could tell, it was the only time Dakota's Beats came off.

"Sure you are," Thomas said. "Why don't we go back to the motel? We can off-load the trailer and head out and find something to eat."

"Will it be safe?" Tiffany wasn't sure about letting her girl out of her sight.

"Sure." Thomas shrugged. "A car like that is way too easily traceable for anyone to risk stealing it. Besides, we'll put it somewhere safe. Trust me."

Chapter Twenty-One

Tiffany handed the car keys to the motel owner, who clutched them to his chest, eyes gleaming with scary fervor. He'd probably spend the afternoon babysitting the Miura in person. "It would be my honor."

The car sat like the empress she was amongst some dusty boxes, a garden hose, and a row of trash cans.

Thomas and Dakota had disappeared into their room earlier. They were all going to meet up later and try to find Luke. The evening got even hotter, and she wanted nothing more than a shower and a change. Her feet ached from hours in heels, and she was seriously considering buying more flats. She strolled down the corridor to her room. And stopped.

The door to her room hung ajar. Hadn't she locked it? Sure she had. She toed the motel room door with the edge of her shoe.

It swung open with a creak.

She leaped back. Her blood pounded in her neck, reminding her this was a massively stupid idea. This was what happened to girls in movies. They always went into the scary room or house. And everyone knew how that ended. Not her. She trotted over to the next room and rapped on the door. Nothing.

The shadowy inside of her room gaped at her through the crack in the door. Tiffany banged even harder. Maybe she should find the motel owner?

Footsteps came from the other side of the door and it was yanked open.

"Hey, sorry." Thomas stood in the doorway wearing a scattering of water droplets and a bath towel. "I was in the shower and Dakota is listening to music."

Tiffany swallowed. She spent most of her working day around men in various states of undress. There was no need to stare like a tourist. "My door is open."

"What?" Thomas glared at Dakota. "Didn't you hear the door?" Wasted effort, as Dakota kept his focus on his phone.

"The door to my room is open."

Thomas turned back to her with a frown. "Your door is open?"

"Yes, and it was locked when I left." God, she wished he would go and put on one of his geeky tees before she gave in to the urge and leaned forward to lick water droplets off him.

He stepped into the open corridor. The back view was as distracting as the front. Lots of muscle and ripply things happening all the way down to his trim waist and tight ass. "Shouldn't you get dressed first?"

He approached the open door. Tucking his towel more firmly around his waist, he stepped into the room. Yeah, right. Men could do that. It wasn't them that got whacked in all those movies. Why was that exactly? She stood at the door and peeked into the interior.

"Fuck," Thomas said from within. "Get the owner."

"What is it?" Tiffany took a careful step into the room

and froze. This couldn't be her room. There was some
mistake. She never flung her clothes around like this. Oh,
God, her new D&G dress looked like someone had stamped
it into the ground. With a cry, she leaped for it.

Thomas stepped in front of her.

Tiffany found herself mashed up against his chest. For
once, she didn't give a crap how hot he was. Her Manolos,
one heel broken off, lay wedged under the bureau. Someone needed to pay for doing that, with their life.

Thomas held her arms, keeping her from moving.

She struggled against the hold. She'd been violated.
Someone had put their hands on her stuff. Even her makeup.
A strangled scream stuck in her throat. That was her com-
pact, broken and crumbling all over her ivory La Perla set.
"Let go of me."

"Tiffany, sweetheart," he said.

She wasn't anyone's sweetheart. "Oh, God, did you see
what they've done to my Kate Spade?"

"No, babe, I didn't, but you can't come in here. Go and
get the owner and tell him to call the police."

"Why?"

"Because it looks like someone broke in and trashed
your hotel room."

"I meant, why would anyone do this."

He steadily backed her toward the door and she didn't
like that. She dragged her stare over the destruction. Even
the mattress had been shoved aside from the bed. It was
like a giant hand had come into her room and smashed. It
was worse than if they'd stolen everything. This felt a
whole lot more personal.

"Tiffany." Thomas shook her slightly. "Stay with me.
I'm going to wait here and make sure nothing gets dis-
turbed. You need to go and get the owner and tell him to
call the police."

"Jesus." Dakota stood in the doorway. "What the fuck happened here?"

"That's what we both want to know," Thomas said. "Tiffany's in shock. Can you go and get the owner? Tell him to call the cops."

Dakota sprinted off toward the reception area.

"Babe," Thomas said. "I need to put some pants on before the cops get here. Can you promise not to touch anything?"

"Why would you destroy a pair of Manolos? Do you know how much they cost? And they're this season's."

Thomas's jaw tightened. "Right." He tugged on her arm. "I think that answers my question. Come with me."

And then she saw her book lying in a bright pink tatter, facedown. Oh, God, no. She wrenched out of Thomas's grasp and flew across the room. They'd ripped open the lock. Tiffany picked it up. Pages fluttered onto the floor at her feet. Her vision swam. She reached out blindly for physical support and found warm skin.

"What is it?" Thomas's voice came from right beside her.

"My book." The spine was cracked, and it fell open like a bird with its wings broken. Truncated edges of ripped-out pages stared at her accusingly. The one thing that was totally hers, and they'd broken it. Tears leaked down her face to drop onto the damaged pages. She tried to wipe them away, but the tears smudged the ink, so she stopped.

"Sweetheart?" Thomas's big hand reached for the book.

She yanked it back and cradled it against her chest. "No."

"Was it important?"

"It's everything." Tiffany gave a ragged little laugh. "It's my book, my thoughts, my everything."

"I don't understand." His face shadowed with concern

as he stooped a little to look at her. "Is it some kind of diary?"

"They broke it." It came out on a soft sob.

"Let me look, maybe I can fix it." He bent and gathered up all the scattered pages at her feet. Slowly, almost reverently, he smoothed them between his palms. He went still, his head tilted as he read them.

Tiffany wanted to snatch them back, but it was too late.

"Babe?" He glanced up at her, his eyes full of questions. "What is this?"

"It's my thoughts." She grabbed the pages from him and tried to tuck them back into her book.

"But these are equations." He gave her the remaining pages. "Most of this is mathematical equations and statistics and stuff like that."

He didn't understand. She could see it on his face. "It's mine."

"Oh, my God." The motel manager, a compact man with a large beard, stood in the entrance and stared.

"The cops are on their way." Dakota toed her Kate Spade out of his way. "Fuck."

"Can you stay and wait for them?" Gently, Thomas encircled her arm with his hand and tugged. "Come on, sweetheart. Bring your book with you."

She let him pull her out of the room and into his room next door. She stood as he hauled on a pair of jeans. She wished she could appreciate the fact he went commando. He tugged a tee over his head and grabbed a pair of sneakers.

Her knees hit the bed. Obediently, she bent them under his gentle backward pressure. She tucked her book safely in her arms. The velvet on the cover was torn and the ragged edges fluttered against her fingertips. Too late. They'd broken it.

Thomas sat down opposite her. "I've seen you with that before. Tell me about the book."

"I write stuff in it," she said in a numb, small voice. "Stuff I want to know about and stuff I need to work out."

"Like equations?"

She nodded. Small sobs caught in her throat and she let out a shuddery breath. Her book was her secret, her piece of sanity in her life. "It's mine."

"Can I ask why you write them in there?"

"Because of school, I don't know stuff that I should know," she said. "I told you before. I didn't pass high school, and there is so much I don't know."

"You write the stuff you don't know in your book?"

"Yes."

He leaned forward and wiped the tears from her cheeks with his fingers. "And then you ask somebody? Or do you work it out for yourself?"

It seemed important to him. She didn't know why, but she didn't have any excuses handy. The truth was so much easier. "I don't ask because this is stuff everybody knows. I look it up or I work it out."

He went silent for a long time. More tears welled over her bottom lid and he wiped them away again. "That's incredible."

"No, it's not." She shook her head. Unclasping her arms slightly, she let the book fall away from her chest. Everybody knew stuff that she didn't. Her life had been that way since preschool. Ryan and his friends read *The New York Times* and *The Wall Street Journal* and all those books on her iPad. Other kids learned this at school. Princess Pearly Perfect smiled and looked pretty instead.

Thomas took the book from her. His head bent as he sifted through the pages. He stopped on the one with pi and studied it. "Jesus, sweetheart." He moved more pages to see them. "Look at this mind on you." He examined a graph she'd drawn. "And you worked all this out with no help?"

She nodded and tapped the edge of a page. "That's Newton."

"Yeah, I know." He nodded.

Of course he knew. She sat back again. Her hands shook and she threaded her fingers together and put them in her lap.

His big fingers soothed the truncated edges where they'd ripped out the pages. "You have this incredible brain and you hide it away in a *Legally Blonde* diary?"

"I got the idea from the movie," she said. "You know, Elle carries that book. Nobody ever asked me what was in it. They wouldn't believe me anyway."

"Here's the good news." He glanced up at her. "Knowledge doesn't stay in a book. It sticks in your head and then you get to keep it."

"But it was mine." Saying the words opened the wound again and more tears welled up. She had a whole crate of her books at home. Some were pink, others silver, some purple—whatever. She wanted the stuff in them, her fix of *everything's okay*.

"And the knowledge still is." He cupped her cheek in his palm. "The bad news is that I have just realized you're a fucking genius. Look at this shit, sweetheart. People spend years in college and don't get this. And you . . ." He shook his head. "You look it up and work it out yourself."

"Is she okay?" Dakota's voice made her jump.

"She will be." Thomas tucked her book into a drawer beside the bed. He lifted her hand and kissed it. "All this and she's a geek, too? I must have died and gone to heaven."

Chapter Twenty-Two

Tiffany picked shit up and dropped it again, her best effort as far as tidying went. Whatever the cops did in her room took forever. They jotted down her statement, but there wasn't a lot she could tell them. Nothing appeared to be missing, just a whole mess of damage. The police took a few things away with them, but left the rest of the room for her to tidy. She barely had the heart to do it. It would be easier to toss a match and move on.

Thomas dove right in, sifting through her stuff with a huge black garbage bag in one hand. Even Dakota helped, taking the stuff Thomas handed him and piling it to go to a dry cleaner. He did a great job of sorting through her shoes.

Any embarrassment she might have felt about the two of them handling her underwear vanished beneath a big layer of numb. The entire thing was so random. As she halfheartedly sifted through her things, it pissed her off more and more. She felt grubby knowing someone had their hands all over her stuff.

It took most of the afternoon to get the room sorted.

The manager found her another room, two doors down, because she sure as hell wasn't sleeping in this one tonight.

Her handful of wearable stuff sat in a crumpled heap on her bed. She had to find something to wear in that, because these assholes were not stopping her from going to find Luke tonight.

Her phone rang and she checked it. Ryan again, that made it call number six, and she hit Ignore. Ryan could damn well wait until she was ready to speak to him. What would she say to him anyway? She'd pretty much said it all that morning.

And Ryan might be a dickhead, but he was a sharp dickhead, and she couldn't take the chance he'd pick up that something other than their fight that morning was wrong. The questions would start and go on and on until he dug out the truth.

Dakota's voice came through the paper-thin motel wall from their room next door. The kid kept arguing and arguing until all of them were ready to scream. She didn't know where Thomas found the patience to deal.

They'd hit a bit of a snag with Dakota and the plan for tonight. They couldn't take an underage kid to a bar, and leaving him alone at the motel didn't look like a great option, either. In the end, they had to trust him, because time was running out and if Luke found out who was looking for him, Tiffany didn't put it past him to pull another disappearing act. God, Tiffany wanted to rip every hair from Lola's pampered head. Dakota needed help and he needed the people around him to give him that help. Luke also had some stepping up to do.

She poked through the clothes the assholes hadn't touched. They'd whittled her four suitcases down to barely enough to fill one. Slim pickings for a girl wanting to look her best. She settled on a new pair of skinny jeans, a knockout pair of heels, and a flirty little blouse that left her shoulders bare and showed a hint of cleavage. She took extra care with her hair and makeup. It took a bit longer to achieve effortless.

A knock on the door interrupted her as she finished up. She opened the door to find Thomas outside. He'd replaced his tee with a white button-down. Holy shit, he cleaned up nice.

"Here." He handed her a bag.

"What's this?"

He shrugged and shifted uncomfortably. "Just something I picked up at the store down the road."

In the bag was a book like the one she'd lost, but this one had huge multicolored polka dots all over it. Her belly flopped and she got a bit squishy inside. It was the best gift ever. Tears prickled under her lids and she blinked rapidly. If she cried now, she'd totally ruin her makeup.

"There wasn't much to choose from," he said.

"It's perfect." And it was. Tiffany tucked the plastic around the book and hugged it to her chest. Turning back into her room, she laid it carefully on her bed. She ran her fingers over one of the dots. Later.

Thomas waited by the door. Raising herself onto the very tips of her toes, she kissed his cheek. He smelled like slightly spicy cologne, and the touch of his cheek tingled against her lips. She may have lingered there a moment more than strictly necessary. "Thank you."

He curled his hand around her hip and kept her close to him. "You're welcome." His voice deepened. "But there's a catch with this one." His beautiful eyes grew solemn and the look on his face implacable. "You can't keep hiding all the stuff away and pretending it's a dirty secret. You want to know something, you ask me. Deal?"

"Deal," she said. "But you're not allowed to laugh at me when I say something dumb."

"Babe." His face softened.

She got it. He didn't think she was dumb. Could he get any more perfect? She probably looked like a total idiot grinning up at him right now, but who gave a shit.

His leer swept her from head to toe and a bad-boy grin spread over his face. "You look smoking."

Good, because she needed all the help she could get.

Tiffany paused outside the bar and eyed it dubiously. So not her sort of place. A number of dusty, mud-spattered SUVs filled the parking lot of the wood-clad structure. A hand-painted sign of a man panning gold announced its name as *Prospectors.*

The door opened and a man and woman tumbled out. The man was tall and dark, just like Luke.

"Relax," Thomas said. "It isn't him."

And thank God for that. She wasn't ready. Would she ever be ready for this?

The couple stumbled to their car, arms locked around each other's waists. They didn't even glance away from each other. She and Luke had been like that, in the beginning.

Tiffany stopped at the door, her feet stuck to the ground. She rubbed her sweaty palms on the sides of her jeans. "Do you think he'll be here?"

"Maybe." Thomas watched her. Not pushing her to go forward or back, just waiting to see what she did.

Tiffany took a shaky breath. Five years and she was about to come face-to-face with a man she never wanted to see again. Her heart hammered so loudly, it almost drowned out the bass thump coming from the other side of the door.

Thomas leaned forward and wrapped his large fingers around hers. "Hey, I'll be right there with you. And if all else fails, you can call up Delilah."

How did he manage to make her smile at a time like this? Tiffany curled her hand around the warm comfort of his grip, her lifeline. "The last time we saw each other, it didn't go well."

His smile warmed his features and reached out to her. "But this is a whole new day."

"I have to do this." She stared at the closed door.

"Yeah, you do."

"I need to get my divorce and then I can get on with the rest of my life."

"That's up to you to decide." He shrugged one large shoulder. "But you can't do anything or make any decisions by staying in the same place."

"You're right."

"You ready?"

"Nope."

He grinned and gave her hand a squeeze. "At the very least, you won't have to put up with Dakota anymore."

A hysterical squeak of laughter came out of her. Man, she needed to get a grip. "I feel bad for him."

"Yeah. He doesn't make it easy on himself, poor kid. Come on." Thomas tugged her hand and took a step forward. He pressed open the door and Tiffany let him lead the way.

The bar was—a bar. A wooden counter with glasses and bottles on display behind it made it pretty much like any normal bar. Tables filled the wooden floor between them and the bar. Talk about an anticlimax. What had she expected? Maybe something like the Rabbit in Red Lounge. One or two people turned to see who had entered, but for the most part people seemed intent on their conversations. A classic rock ballad thumped, but set low enough for conversation. Most people wore cargo shorts or long pants like they were dressed for the outdoors. One or two men wore cycling gear. Thank God she hadn't worn a dress.

Thomas moved toward the counter, propelling her along with him. Tiffany ticked off the tables one by one. Thirty-two tables, ten of them high-topped; eighteen bar stools. Not all the seats filled, so she'd guess 83 percent occupancy. The numbers stilled her mind enough to concentrate on the faces. No Luke. Then again, if he wasn't there now, she'd only have to get all geared up another time. Well, shit.

"I'll ask at the bar," Thomas said.

Tiffany pulled her shoulders down from around her earlobes. They'd expected to get there earlier, so perhaps he'd been and gone. Or maybe he hadn't even come in tonight. She took a deep breath. If Luke wasn't there, then she'd been granted another reprieve for the night. The bar looked like a nice enough place. Perhaps they could relax and have a drink. No tequila, but a relaxed drink or two.

"What will you have?" Thomas turned to ask her.

"Martini?"

Thomas turned to place the order.

"No." Tiffany stopped him. "Actually, I don't like martinis. Could I have a beer?"

"A beer?"

"Yes, a beer." She hadn't had a beer in years.

His eyes twinkled. "Did you count the calories?"

"Nope." She shook her head. "I'm living wild tonight."

He gave her a big grin that made her feel much, much better and turned to place their order. He pulled out a bar stool for her, and Tiffany sat. Now that the danger was over, she really looked at the bar. It was a nice place. Nothing fancy, but clean and well ordered. Pictures of extreme sports hung on the walls, interspersed with the normal mirrors and signs advertising various alcoholic beverages. Huge picture windows framed a beautiful view of the mountains behind.

Imagine Ryan sitting here in one of those loud cycling outfits drinking a beer. That was if she could get past imagining Ryan somewhere like this at all. She and Ryan didn't go to bars, as such. They preferred clubs or restaurants. The sort of upscale places where people went for a drink after work. Or to check out who else was out and about, who they were with, what they were wearing, that sort of thing.

The barman slid two beers and two frosted glasses across the polished wood counter in front of her.

Thomas took a beer and poured it, then slid it in front of her.

"You always act the gentleman," she said.

He shrugged off the compliment. "My dad raised us that way."

"It's nice."

A comfortable silence settled between them. Propping his hand on the bar, Thomas turned sideways to her. "We probably shouldn't be gone too long." He surveyed the bar as he sipped his beer. "I don't trust Dakota on his own."

That was another thing about him she'd noticed. He had this way of taking care of the people with him. And he didn't do it in a bossy or pushy way that made her feel managed. He quietly and competently took charge. Of course, Dakota probably didn't feel the same right about now.

Tiffany sipped her cold, sharp beer. She savored the bitter bite of hops on her tongue. She didn't drink beer because Ryan thought it was uncouth. Thomas would have lots to say about that. He would tell her to make up her own mind what she wanted to drink. He was right. She should make up her own mind. And if that meant she never had to drink another martini, all the better.

"Fuck, no." Luke's voice cut through all the noise around her, deep, rough, and a tiny bit husky. She would know it anywhere. All the blood left her head as she gripped the edge of the bar. Her knuckles whitened as she dug her fingers into the wood.

One of Thomas's big hands covered hers. He gave it a warm squeeze as he turned and said calmly, "Hey, Luke."

"What the fuck is she doing here?"

Slowly, she edged around on the bar stool. Thomas still had her hand in his and she gripped it tightly.

Shit, Luke looked good. He had let his hair grow. It hung over his ears and around his neck in a dark tangle. He'd lost weight and looked lean and tanned. The clean lines of his face were carved into predatory angles that were very, very sexy. Luke had always been good-looking, but now he'd added a whole new level of animal hotness. And he still had those dark toffee eyes that could draw you in and hold you. A rush of heat swept her nerve endings. Luke still had it, whatever it was. "Hello, Luke."

He glared at her and folded his arms over his chest. The muscles in his jaw worked in the silent expression of fury she'd seen facing her for most of their marriage.

"Have a seat," Thomas said, not quite an invitation.

Luke glanced between the two of them. "What is this? Some kind of lynch mob?"

A woman stepped closer to Luke and put her hand on his arm. "What is it, baby?"

"My worst nightmare." Luke growled.

The woman swung her gaze to Tiffany. "Who is she?"

"My fucking ex-wife." Luke spoke to the woman but kept his glare locked on her. Cold as ice, stripping her bare and leaving her raw.

"Actually, that's why I'm here."

Luke jerked his chin toward Thomas. "With him?"

"We came looking for you." How the hell did Thomas manage to sound so calm and relaxed while the air around the three of them flickered and snapped with tension?

Tiffany straightened her spine and took a deep breath. She could do this. She'd left the girl who married Luke in the past and grown up. And after this, she would never have to see him again. "I need to talk to you."

"We have nothing to say to each other."

"Actually, we do." Her voice came out a bit shaky and she cleared her throat.

"Fuck." Luke dragged his hands through his hair. "I'm looking right at you and I can't believe you're sitting there. Just how far do I have to go to get away from you?"

Shit that hurt and it shouldn't because she knew he felt that way. "I need some of your time and then we're done forever."

Luke took a deliberate step toward her.

Thomas shifted his weight, putting the solid comfort of his presence beside her.

"I don't have any time for you. I have nothing for you, and as far as I am concerned, we are done," Luke said.

"Hey." Thomas stepped forward. "Why don't you hear her out? You need to hear what she has to say."

"Don't give me that shit." Luke turned on Thomas with a snarl. "I know exactly why you're here, and it's got nothing to do with her."

"Then if you know that, you can give me those survey results." An edge of steel encased Thomas's voice.

"No way." Luke curled his lip, almost exactly like Dakota. He spun on his heel and stalked toward the exit. "I'm done here."

Tiffany sat, frozen to her bar stool, as Luke stalked out.

"Wait here." Thomas disappeared after Luke.

Luke's friends stood there staring at her. The woman's eyes were openly hostile. "Why don't you just leave him alone?"

"I'd like to." And boy, would she like to, but she'd come all this way to see this done. Now or never. She dropped some money on the bar and chased after Luke and Thomas. "But right now, I need him."

Chapter Twenty-Three

Tiffany followed the men, her legs shaking so much she nearly tripped over the gravel in the parking lot. Thomas had never looked that pissed off. Not even with Dakota's shit. And Luke—well, Luke hadn't changed much.

Twilight hung thick around the parking lot, and it took a moment to pick them out in the shadows. They'd moved to the left of the door, out of earshot. Thomas stood with his arms crossed. Luke seemed to be doing most of the talking, waving his arms around as he spoke.

Tiffany stepped closer.

"I had to do what I thought was right," Luke said.

"You stabbed me in the back." Thomas narrowed his eyes to slits.

Luke grimaced and dropped his gaze, briefly. "Yeah, I know, man. And it was a dick move because you totally saved my life in Zambia." He glanced up at Thomas. "But you know how I feel about big international business coming into these places and raping the resources."

"That's not how it's going to be, Luke," Thomas said.

Luke jabbed his finger at Thomas. "That's a lie and you know it."

"No, it's not." Playing it calm, but a new edge of impatience entered Thomas's voice. "I started this company because I believe in progress, but not at the expense of everything else."

"Progress?" Luke gave a bitter laugh. "Why don't you ask those Zambians what they think of your progress?"

"I did." Thomas stuck his chin out. "And they told me they'd like to be able to feed their families." Thomas caught sight of her and turned to face her.

Luke glanced up, too. He muttered something beneath his breath and looked away again.

"You need to hear her out," Thomas said.

Tiffany took her cue and stepped up beside Thomas. "We need to get a divorce. And I need you to come back to Willow Park with me to make it go quickly."

Luke gaped and his head jerked up. "No way am I going to Willow Park."

"It won't take long. We file together and it happens quickly. You can be there and gone in a day or two."

"Forget it."

Tiffany faltered. She glanced at Thomas. He gave her a reassuring nod to continue.

"Look, if you come with me, it'll be fast. We don't have any kids, all the money was either your dad's or mine, and we've been living apart for more than two years. I won't contest it. Done," she said.

"Why now?" Luke sneered down his nose at her.

She didn't have a good answer for that one. "I don't know. It just didn't seem important before. I was out of your life, you were—wherever the hell you were, and it didn't matter."

Luke's expression grew even harder.

"All I need is a day or two of your time and then I'll be out of your life forever."

"You were already out of my life." He shook his head. "And here you are again, fucking it up."

"Hey." Thomas's deep voice rumbled a clear warning. "I don't care how mad you are, you don't speak to her like that."

"What do you know about it?" Luke turned his anger that way. "She totally fucked up my life. I can talk to her any way I damn well please."

Shit, Luke had nerve saying that. "I didn't fuck up your life. You did that yourself. You were the one who decided to sleep around."

"I wouldn't have slept around if I had a wife to come home to and not some spoiled princess. And you had no right to do what you did to my Miura."

He had her there, so she stuck with the one part she could deal with. "And that's your justification?" Tiffany had heard it all before. She wasn't buying it now any more than she had back then. "You tell yourself it was okay to sleep around because I wasn't a good enough wife? You never let me be your wife. You shut me out."

"Bullshit. Daddy's little princess never had time for anyone. You were too busy getting your fucking nails done."

"That's not true."

"Which part?"

"I—"

"This isn't getting anyone anywhere." Thomas cut off her hot reply.

Tiffany took a deep breath. Thank God he had, because this had drifted into sickeningly familiar territory so fast it made her head spin. "I need to get our divorce. You don't want me in your life anymore. There doesn't seem to be much to fight about," she said.

"So why did you have to drive all the way to Utah to find me? Couldn't find your way to the post office? Send the sheriff after me?"

Tiffany ignored the last jibe. It wasn't easy, but she managed. Something about Luke made her want to bite back. Like old times. "I didn't have the time to wait."

"Why? Daddy find out you were still married to me?" Luke threw back his head and laughed. The ugly, harsh sound scraped against her raw nerves. "Man, that would have gone down well. I'm only sorry I wasn't there to see it."

"My father has nothing to do with this."

"Really?" Luke sneered. "I find that hard to believe. Your father is so up in your business, it would take an act of God to get him out of there." Luke and her father had butted heads from day one. Another strike against her screwed-up marriage.

"Let's leave my father out of this." Her teeth clenched together so hard, it made her jaw ache. No way Luke was dragging her back into a stupid argument.

Luke stared at her for a long moment. Comprehension dawned on his face, followed by a huge, smug grin. "You're getting married again. That's it, isn't it? You're getting married again, only you have to get unmarried first."

"Yes. No. Maybe."

"Jesus." Luke sucked in a deep breath. "Who would be that fucking stupid? Do they even know you?"

Tiffany gasped. It hit her like a punch to the gut. For a second she had no comeback; she stood there and blinked at Luke.

"That was an asshole thing to say." Thomas came to her defense, his face tight with anger. She'd seen him angry about Dakota and the drugs, but this was a new level of frightening. He took a step closer to Luke and got right in his face. "You're being an asshat."

"You don't know what she put me through." Luke stepped into him.

"Yeah, I do," Thomas said. "And I also know what you put her through. You owe the lady an apology."

"Fuck that."

Thomas grew deathly still beside her. He clenched his fists, the muscles in his arms and chest swelling.

Holy shit! It was like the eye of the hurricane. She didn't want this. Quickly she inserted herself between the two men. Waves of anger battered against her back from Thomas. "It doesn't matter. I just want the divorce and then we are done with each other."

"Move out of the way, Tiffany." Thomas's voice sent chills chasing up and down her spine.

"No," she said to Thomas, but kept her gaze on Luke.

"Why should I do anything for you?" Luke glared at Thomas over her head.

"There's more." She got the words out quickly. "Dakota is with us. He is waiting for you back at the hotel."

Luke glanced at her. "Dakota?"

"Yes. Lola is out of town and she left him with me. He doesn't want to be with me, he wants to be with you."

Luke's jaw worked again. "Not my problem."

Tiffany sucked in a shocked breath.

Thomas's hands fastened around her arms as he lifted her and set her out of the way. And then he was on Luke, hauling him up by a fistful of his shirt. "That's your brother, you dickhead."

"I walked away from that." Luke ripped free of Thomas. "And I am not going back."

Thomas growled low in his throat and lunged for Luke.

Tiffany got in the way again. Thomas's forward momentum carried him straight into her. It was like being hit by a truck, and she went over. He caught her seconds before she hit the ground and jammed her up against his chest.

"Leave it." Her heart beat so fast it almost jumped out her chest.

Luke glowered from Thomas to her and back again. He curled his lip up in disdain and stalked away. "Stay away from me."

Thomas sprang, grabbing Luke by the shirt and turning him. His fist shot out and connected.

Luke's head snapped back. He staggered a few steps and hit the car parked behind him.

"No." Tiffany grabbed the back of Thomas's shirt. She hung on for dear life as he dragged her forward with him. Fabric ripped and she lost her grip on Thomas.

Luke stood, braced and ready for Thomas.

"Stop it," someone yelled from behind her. Luke's three friends sprinted across the parking lot. The woman reached Luke first. The two men came on slowly, eyeing Thomas warily.

"Leave him alone." The woman latched onto Luke and fussed with his face. "Can't you just leave him alone?"

With a growl, Luke jerked his head away from her.

Scalding glare locked on the men flanking Luke, Thomas breathed hard.

"Come on." Tiffany grabbed his arm and tugged on it before he decided to take them all on. Her money was on Thomas, but she still didn't like the odds. His shirt hung in two strips, ripped nearly in half down his back.

This time, he allowed her to pull him away. "You need to man up," he said to Luke.

"Come on, Thomas. Leave it. For now."

"You have responsibilities," Thomas said. "And a man

doesn't spend his life running away from the people who need him."

Luke raised his head and glared at Thomas.

Tiffany pulled, hauled, and coaxed Thomas back to his SUV. Her nape prickled as any minute she expected Luke or one of his friends to start up again. Her hand shook so badly she fumbled the driver's door open and shoved Thomas behind the wheel. He let her, because no way would she be able to move this much bulk unless it was willing.

He started the SUV in silence and peeled out of the parking lot. He didn't drive fast or say anything, but stared straight ahead in a deafening silence.

Tiffany risked a peek at him. An angry Thomas was a scary Thomas.

"Fuck," he whispered.

That about covered it, and Tiffany sighed. "Yeah."

"Did I hurt you?"

"No." Tiffany shook her head.

"You have really shitty taste in men."

Tiffany blinked at him. Where the hell had that come from? And ouch! "Are you trying to say this is all my fault?"

"No." He cut a glance at her. He took a deep breath and seemed to release a tiny bit of tension. "What I mean is, for a beautiful woman, you sure don't pick the men who will value you as you deserve."

"Ryan is nothing like Luke." Her hands shook so badly she tucked them under her thighs. "Ryan is kind and considerate, and he never yells at me or tells me what a bad person I am."

"No," Thomas said, his jaw locked tight. "He just tells you how to be all the time, which in my book amounts to the same thing. Only Ryan's more polite about it."

"That's bullshit." Her voice shook and she cleared her throat hastily. "That is such bullshit."

But it wasn't bullshit, it cut so close to the truth it hurt more than any of the insults Luke had hurled her way. And now that she had admitted it, what the hell was she going to do?

Chapter Twenty-Four

Tiffany's heart fisted in her chest as they drew into the motel parking lot.

Dakota sat on a bench outside his room, his packed bag at his feet. The Beats lay around his neck. He'd even washed all the makeup off and, for once, didn't look like the living dead.

Oh, man, the poor kid. The hits kept coming for Dakota. How the hell could she tell him Luke didn't think his kid brother was his problem?

"Fuck," Thomas said.

It was the first word either of them had spoken since the conversation about Ryan. Tiffany pushed her anger to the back of her mind. She had no idea what to tell Dakota. The possibility that Luke would say no had never even occurred to her. And it should have. But, damn, Dakota was vulnerable right now. The two people who should have been looking out for him, Lola and Luke, had skipped out on him. The poor guy was stuck with her and Thomas.

Dakota stood as Thomas parked the car and they climbed out. He glanced from Thomas to Tiffany and behind them. "Where's my brother?"

The hope on his face killed her. Tiffany wanted to lie, to tell him that they hadn't found Luke.

"He's not coming," Thomas said. He didn't say it unkindly or with any emotion. Just the truth, plain and unvarnished.

Dakota frowned at them. "What do you mean?"

"Thomas means we think it's better if you stay with me." Tiffany tried to soften the blow a bit.

Dakota squinted at her viciously. "You don't get to say what happens to me. You're nothing to me. I'm going to my brother. Did you even find him?"

"We found him, kid." Thomas stepped in front of Dakota. "And Tiffany is not the one who said you should stay with her."

"Who, then?" Dakota paled as the truth occurred to him. The piercings stood out in sharp relief on his narrow face. "You're talking shit. Luke would never leave me with this bitch."

"Don't," Thomas said.

Dakota rounded on her. "What the fuck did you say to him?"

She had nothing. Tiffany opened and closed her mouth.

"This is because of you." Dakota's face tensed into a vicious pinch. "He saw you and freaked out. He hates you because of what you did to him. And when he needed you, too. He hates you."

"You're angry with the wrong person," Thomas said.

"Fuck you." Dakota clenched his fists.

"If you say so." Thomas shrugged. "Come on." He picked up Dakota's bag and walked into the room they shared.

"This is your fault." Dakota got right in her face and spat the words at her.

Tiffany closed her eyes. Dakota wasn't all wrong, and

she ached for the kid. Luke did hate her. "Not all my fault," she said. "But I really am sorry for my part."

"Like hell."

She wanted to bathe. The residue of Luke's anger and hatred seemed to settle in a thick layer on her skin. She'd been stupid to think she could walk up to Luke and get his agreement. The scar tissue between them ran way, way too deep. Her crappy little motel room seemed like a safe haven.

"I'm sorry," she said to Dakota.

He threw her an evil look and stomped after Thomas.

Her shoulders dropped as the door slammed. She was sorry. Sorry for all of this and sorry as hell Dakota was going to pay the price. Again. But this was not all her fault. Luke had been right there with her, screwing up their relationship as much as she had. Back in her room, she ran the water for a bath and then sat on her bed. A faded poster of Moab stared back at her.

"I'm a mess," she told the poster. Her eyes stung and she blinked back the tears. Seven years, and the Luke wound still smarted as much as it had when it was fresh. She'd been so sure she was past all of that, but one look at Luke and she felt like that girl.

Dragging her ass into the bathroom, she checked the water. She'd pushed Luke and her marriage to a dusty corner of her mind and ignored it. That didn't mean it had gone away. A tear trickled down her cheek. Mascara smears covered her fingertips. Cheap, damn mascara making a panda out of her. She didn't even have a decent makeup remover to take it all off.

How could two people so in love go so wrong? God, how she'd loved Luke. Luke had been her everything. From the moment he picked her up in a coffee shop, they'd been inseparable. She couldn't remember the coffee shop, but she remembered Luke. Younger, wearing jeans and an R.E.M. T-shirt, he'd sat opposite her and started talking.

She stripped out of her shirt and kicked her jeans off. They slithered across the bathroom. She and Luke had been wild and out of control. They couldn't keep their hands off each other or have enough time together. They'd spend all day together and then stay up half the night talking on the phone. The sex had been explosive. Nothing in her life up until that point had prepared her for the roller coaster of wild and wanton that was her and Luke. Luke had wanted her to move in with him. She'd held out for marriage. Her father had fought her every step of the way, but in the end five hundred people had watched her marry Luke and, nearly to a person, they said what a beautiful couple they were. What a joke.

She shucked her underwear and stepped into the bath. Warm water soothed the tight bunch of muscles in her back and shoulders. Luke's mom had died, and right after, his dad was busted for embezzlement. In good times and in bad, that's what they'd promised each other. Did anybody really know when they said those words how bad the bad times could get? She certainly hadn't.

More mascara turned the water gray on her hands as she scrubbed away fresh tears. When the trouble started, the fights got out of hand so fast she'd been reeling in their aftermath. Ugly words hurled at each other. Hurtful actions aimed to wound. Neither of them had been prepared for what happened when all that passion went in the wrong direction. Tonight, Luke's anger brought it all back. The old hurt and rage on his face, the frustration as she had tried and failed to reach him. Nothing worked—every word they had said ripped the chasm wider and wider. She lay back in the water and tried to find that peaceful place inside. Fail.

It was over. The thought rippled through her with such force it dragged a small noise out of the back of her throat. Not until right that moment had she really gotten her head around that. The fairy tale wasn't hers anymore. As long as she was married to Luke, she could still hold on to that tiny fragment of Wild Tiffany. She'd lost it, or thrown it away. Whatever.

A knock on the door dragged her out of her head. She hauled herself out of the bath and snagged a towel. The bath hadn't really been working anyway.

Thomas stood in the doorway. He'd changed back into a T-shirt. *Back up! I'm going to try science.* It got a weak smile out of her.

"Hey," he said.

"Hey."

His gaze gently traced her face. "You've been crying." He didn't wait for her invitation, but crowded her back into her room.

"How's Dakota?" She didn't want to talk about it, especially when she was naked under the towel.

"He's okay. He wanted to make a phone call, so I thought I would come and apologize."

Tiffany stared at him. "Apologize?"

"For losing my temper," he said. "At the bar, with Luke. I know better than that, but he got under my skin."

Oh, boy. That makes two of us.

He moved closer and cupped her chin in one warm palm. His thumb swiped at the moisture on her cheeks and came away smudged. "Then after, I got shitty with you, and I'm sorry. I was pissed at myself for losing my cool. Now I'm thinking I should have hit him again."

Her voice came out all wobbly and thin. "It's not Luke."

"No?"

His gentle tone made her want to cry even more. His

big chest was right in front of her, with its stupid T-shirt. She gave in to the temptation and pressed her forehead against it. His arms came around her and tucked her tightly against him. His cheek settled on the top of her head. Safe. Wholly and completely safe. And like the complete girl she was, she burst into tears.

Thomas didn't do girl talk or soothing noises, he tightened his arms and held firm. He kept her tucked into him, surrounded her with his strength. It felt wonderful. It felt so wonderful, she cried even harder.

"I should definitely have hit him again," he said.

Some girl was going to get so lucky one day with this man. She lifted her head from his chest. "I'm feeling sorry for myself."

He drew back enough to meet her eyes. "Why's that?"

"Because I made such a mess of things with Luke, and now I am making an even bigger mess with Ryan. Dakota hates me, and I think I might agree with him."

"Well, I like you," he said.

"You do?"

"Sure."

"You don't think I'm horrible?"

"Hell, no." And she believed him. "You've got about two men too many in your life right now, but I don't think you're horrible. You might have the merest hint of an issue with closure, however."

"You think?"

"Just a theory."

She chuckled and laid her cheek back against his chest. He smelled like soap and warm skin. The beat of his heart pumped steady and sure beneath her ear.

"You okay?"

"I am now." Tiffany let herself relax and just be, right

here, right now. Something he'd said bugged her, though, and she lifted her head. "Two men too many?"

He shrugged. "Three, if you count Dakota."

Tiffany counted them off with her fingers against his pectoral muscle. "Ryan, Luke, Dakota and . . ."

"Me."

Her heart did a crazy nosedive before crashing through her gut. "You?"

"Come on." He put her gently away from him. "I'm going to do something stupid if we stand here like this for much longer. Finish your bath and put some clothes on. I'm going to check on Dakota and then we can order a pizza or something."

"Two hundred and eighty-five calories per slice," she said.

"That so?"

"If it's regular crust and just cheese pizza."

He made a noise and nodded. "Want to load up on some calories with Dakota and me?"

"Sure." She didn't even have to think about it. "And afterward we can have chocolate."

"How many calories?"

"What type of chocolate?"

Chapter Twenty-Five

Apparently Tiffany in a little black dress and a pair of Jimmys could move mountains. The barman gave up Luke's home address without a fight. Of course, the trip outside to admire the Miura hadn't hurt either. The crowd swelled around the car world's Pied Piper rather quickly. It had taken her a good half an hour to get away from the Miura's fan club. It made a nice send-off.

She'd left a text for Thomas and Dakota, their door still shut tight. Probably still sleeping after a night of movies and pizza that ran well past midnight. This was her mess to sort out, hers and Luke's. After she got divorced, she didn't know how her life would play out anymore. But the weight of the past had gotten too heavy to haul around with her.

It wasn't hard to find the house. Sitting halfway up South Mountain, it nestled comfortably amongst others like it in a quiet neighborhood. The modest front only added to the spectacular view from the back. Below her spread the entire Salt Lake Valley, drowsy in the piercing sunlight.

No time like the present. She wiped her hands on the front of her dress and unfolded from the car. Getting out of an Italian sports car in a short skirt and heels took practice. She'd had plenty of that while she babysat Luke's baby. It was time to give her back to her rightful owner. Tiffany ran her hand over the gleaming metal of the roof. She sure was a beauty. She let her fingers linger for one more heartbeat. "I'm going to miss you."

Straightening her shoulders, she picked her way up the stone walkway to the door. The woman from the bar answered the doorbell. It took her a moment shy of a second to recognize Tiffany. Her face went rigid with displeasure. "What do you want?"

Tiffany took a deep breath. She needed to stay calm for this. Her battle was with Luke, not this woman. Whoever she was. "Is Luke here?"

"No." The woman crossed her arms over her chest.

Tiffany bet she would have said that whether Luke was home or not. Bitch or not, this woman stood between her and her mission. She'd put money Luke was skulking in the house somewhere.

The woman moved to block her view of the interior of the house. "He's not here."

"Babe?"

The woman started.

Tiffany's gaze met hers. *Liar, liar*. That was Luke.

"Tell him I have something to show him," Tiffany said.

"There is nothing of yours he wants to see." Man, this woman was tough. Not tough enough, though.

"I think Luke will disagree with you." Tiffany stepped aside and revealed the car.

The woman sucked in a breath. She glowered at Tiffany accusingly. If her face wasn't so twisted in anger she might have been pretty. Luke had sure chosen differently this time. This woman was blond and tanned, with the sort of figure that said she spent a lot of time outside being healthy. "He told me what you did."

"I'm sure he did," Tiffany said. She had only so much humility in her, and none of it for Nature Girl. "I'll wait by the car."

Thank God, she made it back down the walkway without tripping. Her legs shook so hard she didn't trust her balance. The Jimmys might have been a mistake.

"Tiffany?" She hadn't even made it all the way back to the Miura when Luke's voice stopped her. "What the hell?"

"I don't want to fight." Holding up her hands, she spun to face him.

His face was a closed mask, but he didn't look quite as furious as he had at the bar. "What are you doing here?"

"I came to return something." The words got caught in her throat and she cleared it rapidly. "Something of yours."

He jerked to a stop. Like a junkie jonesing for a fix, his gaze ate up the Miura. He took a step outside and then another one. "Is that her?"

"Yes." She curled her fingers into her sweaty palms. The Miura belonged to Luke, not her. "After you left, I had her repaired."

Luke frowned and took another few steps toward the car.

"It took a while to find all the original parts. And, of course, to find someone certified to work on her." Her mouth kept running, laughing at her half-assed effort to get a grip. "I only got her all fixed about two years ago. She's barely been driven. Only enough to keep her running smoothly, and as you know, she's not the easiest car—"

"Why?"

"I owed you."

He looked up sharply. "You owed me?"

"After what I did to her." Tiffany nodded. "After what I did to us."

Luke's dark gaze searched her face. What did he see when he looked at her? The urge to fidget rode her hard, and the silence built like a scream in her chest. "I didn't come here to pick the scabs off," she said.

"Then why?"

Tiffany shrugged. She didn't have all the answers. "It seems like there's a lot I didn't say and I should have. I did a lot of things wrong. And if you think this is easy to say, then you're nuts, but it needs to be said."

He frowned a bit, as if he were thinking about it.

"We . . . I didn't do so well with the marriage thing." *Way to go with the euphemism, Tiffany.*

He dropped his gaze and gave a harsh laugh. "You had some help with that."

"Yes."

"What happened that night?"

Tiffany blinked at him. That's right, they'd never spoken about it, because Luke had packed his bags and left. Well, here she stood and there he stood, and for once they weren't screaming. "I saw you at a club that night." This bit still had claws. "And you were with another girl."

He frowned. "What girl?"

"I don't know what girl, Luke. Does it really matter?"

He closed the distance between himself and the Miura and stood there gazing at her. "I suppose not. So you saw me with the girl and trashed the car?"

There was a bit more to it than that. "I was driving home, crying my eyes out." Crying so hard she could barely see the road. "And that Carrie Underwood song came on the radio. The one about the guy being a cheater."

Luke shook his head. "I don't know it."

Luke was more of an alternative rock guy, but it didn't

matter. "It's about this girl that trashes her boyfriend's car when she catches him cheating."

"So you trashed my best girl?" Luke rubbed the back of his neck. "I can't believe you did that."

"I couldn't believe you had your hands up some girl's skirt."

His eyes flashed fire for a second, then he grimaced. "Fair enough. We were young."

"And stupid." Stupid enough to act without thinking, and stupid enough to both run away without talking about it.

Luke shoved his hands in his pockets and stared at the car.

"The keys are inside." Tiffany couldn't figure out what he was thinking. "I'm going to have to ask you to drive me home, though. Or I could call Thomas to come and get me."

"I don't know what to say," he said.

Tiffany gave a half cough, half laugh. "That's a first."

"Yeah." Shaking his head, he trailed his fingertips reverently across the seam of the door, down toward the handle. "I loved this car."

"I know. It's why I did what I did."

"I know." His caressing hand reached the handle and he popped it open. The door swung open on a soft hiss. Horns of the bull. Luke bent to peer inside. It took a while and then his head popped out again. "You fixed it all."

"Yes." Tiffany took a careful step forward. "Even the busted fuel gauge, and I had nothing to do with that."

"It must have cost a bomb." He shook his head.

"It did," Tiffany said. "I got a job."

He raised his eyebrow. Okay, she'd give him the skepticism. "Not much of a job. Working with a photographer as his assistant. I paid it off bit by bit."

"Why didn't you just ask Daddy?" His lip curled up in a faint sneer.

She couldn't let him drag her into another insult fest. She'd had enough of those, too. "It didn't seem right."

The shutters closed over his expression and his face went so cold it made her shiver. *Back the fuck up*, screamed her instinct. She took a step closer to him anyway. "I don't want to fight."

"So you said before. What do you want?"

"I want to give her back to you. Call it a bribe if you want. I want you to come back to Willow Park and get our divorce. Then we never have to see each other again."

"And if I don't want her back?"

Tiffany stopped and stared. She almost started laughing. The Miura had been Luke's passion. He had loved that car almost as much, in fact more, than he'd loved her. "I don't know."

"I'm being a dick." He dropped his chin onto his chest and folded his arms. "Of course I want her back."

Tiffany's head reeled with relief. The thought of the Miura going to someone else made her stomach knot and her chest ache. She loved that car. Really loved it.

"But I don't know if I want to keep her." He stared at her as if trying to see right down to her heart. "Why did you do it? Fix her."

The question she really didn't want to answer. Like peeling off her skin and leaving her nerve endings exposed. "I owed you."

"That's bullshit." No anger. The truth. His eyes silently asked her for the truth.

Tiffany took a deep breath. Luke was probably the only person who stood a chance of understanding because he'd been right there with her through their crazy ride together.

"She was us." Tiffany let the words come. "She was everything that we were to me, all the passion and the excitement. All the incredible craziness. Most of it bad, but some of it so good." She was utterly alone as she met his gaze, like something hanging out in the desert to die. Tiffany shivered and crossed her arms over herself. But the cold came from inside and it didn't help. "You, me, her, we were free."

Luke moved suddenly. He came toward her and stopped. A slow burn seeped into his expression. "Who's this guy you're going to marry?"

"Actually, I'm not so sure I'm going to marry him now." She and Luke, they'd seen each other at their worst. She didn't have to pretend to be anything with him.

"You love him?" Luke cocked his head.

"My father thinks he hung the moon."

"Ah." Luke stepped closer and tucked a strand of hair behind her ear. It was such a familiar gesture it twisted her heart. "Don't do it, Tiff. We imploded, but the girl you were with me—in the Miura, hair streaming in the wind, laughing like the world was ours to bend—that girl was special. The kind of girl a man wants to keep forever."

Her heart kicked up an uneasy rhythm. She drew in a shaky breath. Citrus, leather, and man hit her in a familiar sensory tsunami. The smell of him used to drive her crazy. She used to bury her head into the place where his neck met his shoulder and draw it inside her in great gulps. It was the smell of wild, crazy, off-the-charts sex that left both of them wrung out.

"Tiff." His voice grew husky. He knew how it affected her. His voice said he still knew and he felt it, too. "Don't bury all that passion. It's one of the best parts of you."

She couldn't meet his gaze. Wild Tiffany stirred inside, responding to the want in Luke's voice like she always had.

"Babe." Warm hands on her arms.

Tiffany closed her eyes. One touch from Luke and her knees grew weak. Luke, touching her, drawing her closer until his chest pressed against her breasts, reminding her of how it felt to be truly alive. Beneath all the anger had always been this. Hot and needy. She tipped her head back and he took her mouth. She braced for the onslaught of blistering heat.

His tongue slipped into her mouth and she tasted Luke. The taste of freedom and desire, coursing through her like a runaway train.

Except—not so much.

It was a great kiss. Luke could kiss any girl out of her panties, and there'd been a little interest from the girl bits. But no raging flood. More of a fitful trickle.

Luke lifted his head. A small frown creased the skin between his eyes. "Tiff?"

"Yes."

He closed the distance between their mouths again.

Huh! Same thing. Luke's kiss was loaded with memories, sweet, breathless memories, but still—memories. She pulled away from him and looked up.

"That was . . ." He frowned down at her.

"Different."

"Yeah." He laughed softly. "Not what I was expecting."

"Nope, me neither." She stepped away from him and his arms dropped. "You still give one hell of a kiss."

"Thanks. You got a little something going there, too." He snorted and shoved his hands into his pockets. "This is weird."

"Not really." The relief nearly made her giddy. A weight

lifted off her chest and she breathed free and clear. She finally got the closure thing. "It's over."

Luke's head whipped up and his expression went speculative and finally, softened. He got it, too. They were both free. "Yeah."

"Great." Thomas's voice dashed across her in an icy wave. Both she and Luke jumped and turned. He stood between them and his truck. "Is he coming back to Willow Park?"

Tiffany looked at Luke. "It's time."

"It's time." Luke nodded.

Thomas glared at Luke like he wanted to rip him to pieces. He yanked his stare away and stalked over to her. "Great. You done here?"

"Yes."

"Let's go."

Luke lifted an eyebrow. Tiffany's cheeks burned. No man had ever used that tone on her, and she wasn't about to let one start now. She walked over to where Luke stood.

Thomas and his bulk were suddenly between them.

Tiffany threw him another look and neatly stepped around him. "Thank you, Luke."

"We both know we should have done this years ago, Princess." His use of his old pet name caused a sweet pang in her chest, and she smiled at him. He had picked it up from Daddy, but Luke used it differently, like a silent joke between them.

Luke raised his hand and touched her face. He leaned in toward her.

"No more kissing." Thomas honest to God growled the words.

The look Luke shot her made her laugh. Then he raised her hand and kissed her knuckles. "Some of it was fun,

Princess," he said. "Most of it was a pain in the ass, but there was some fun in there, too."

"Truck." Thomas stalked over to the truck and threw himself behind the wheel.

Tiffany gave Luke a hug. Thomas could bark all he wanted, she was leaving when she was done.

"I'll come around and see what to do about Dakota tomorrow," Luke said. "I think we've all had enough for one day. The big guy included."

Chapter Twenty-Six

Tiffany was ready to rip Thomas a new one by the time they arrived back at the motel.

Thomas's jaw looked fused in place. Unlike Luke, he was a silent fumer—anger simmering below his skin. Ryan had another take on anger. Ryan looked disappointed and then calmly and rationally pointed out why he was right and she should have known better. Screw Ryan. And screw Thomas Hunter, too.

All of his moody, silent fuming scratched her raw. With him, you couldn't tell what he was thinking. And she needed to get inside his head and understand what the hell was happening. She could do with a touch of Luke here— let it rip and the consequences be damned. She knew how to handle that.

Thomas turned the truck engine off.

Sitting here in a shivering puddle wasn't her thing. "You going to tell me what has your panties in a knot?"

His jaw actually got tighter. "I saw you kissing Luke."

Well, she'd guessed that much. She might not have read as many books as him, but she wasn't entirely clueless. "And?"

"I didn't like it."

Him admitting his jealousy was kind of cute, so she gave a tiny bit. "It was a good-bye kiss."

"I heard that."

Okay. She sat for a moment more. Now she really didn't get it. If he knew it was the end, shouldn't he be feeling okay about this? "So?"

"I'm jealous." He forced the words through his gritted teeth. "I'm jealous and I have no right to be and it's not making me feel any less jealous."

"Oh?" Thomas of the Zen outlook and maddening calm having a childish, green-eyed fit. There was no end to today's surprises.

"I have never been jealous," he said to the windshield. "Okay, maybe when I was a kid when Dominique Frazer had a crush on my brother, Josh, and I wanted her to have a crush on me instead. But that was the ninth grade." He turned to look at her as if she could shed some light on the matter and winced. "No, that's not entirely true. There were a couple of girls after who had crushes on Josh." With a shrug, he went back to staring out the windshield. "You had to get used to it when you were Josh Hunter's brother." Tiffany sat and waited for more. So, his brother was hot stuff and the girls went for him big-time. There had to be something more.

"We should talk," he said.

"Okay."

"But not here." He nodded as if they'd settled it and reached for his door handle. He stopped and turned to her. "Are you okay? With giving the car back, I mean."

"I'm going to miss her," Tiffany said.

He totally disarmed her with the genuine concern on his face. Tension still came off him in waves, but the question was real. He took her hand and placed a soft kiss against her fingers. "You did well. That took a lot of doing."

Her fingers tingled from his mouth and her insides tingled from the compliment. When Thomas gave a compliment, he really gave a compliment. The man was 100 percent genuine. He didn't use a pat on the head as a launching point for his next foray into what she needed to change. "Thanks."

"Come on." He jerked his head toward the motel. "Let's go and see what our juvenile delinquent is up to."

"Are we good?" Tiffany stepped out of the truck.

"I guess." He stopped and turned toward her. "I'm being a jerk."

"Oh."

He stalked away from her toward his motel room. The door shut behind him while she stood next to the truck like a fool. Now that was being a dick, right there. Tossing out half bits of explanation that added up to a big, fat zero. And did his goddamned ass have to look so fine in those jeans? She still didn't get the jealous thing. That is, she got it, but she didn't *get* it. Thomas liked her. He'd told her often enough that he did. But he didn't do anything about it. Even that time she was wasted, he let her kiss him and put her to bed. Alone.

In her experience, men didn't do shit like that. If they liked you, they made a move. Thomas got jealous of her kissing Luke. Still nothing. He'd had a little minor shit fit and gone in to see Dakota.

Now, there was another crappy talk session on her day's agenda. Sure, he was a pain in the ass, but she couldn't dump Dakota there and leave him to fend for himself. She rapped on their door.

Thomas answered her knock. Behind him, Dakota stretched out on the bed.

"We need to talk," she said.

Thomas raised an eyebrow. "Wasn't that my line?"

"About Dakota." Actually they had a lot of talking to do, but one snarl at a time.

His eyes gleamed down at her. "You want to talk about Dakota?"

"And then we can go and have a talk about the other thing," she said.

He grinned his challenge at her. "Other thing?"

"You know what other thing." She called his bluff.

"Yeah." He rubbed the back of his neck. "I think I owe you an explanation."

"You do."

His smile broadened into an appreciative grin. "Finding your inner ballbuster?"

"A little." *A lot.* Time for a girl to jump off the emotional roller coaster.

Dakota glanced up at her and went back to watching the television. She didn't know how Thomas could stand it that loud. She was pretty sure Dakota's eardrums were so deadened by his music he could barely hear anything anyway.

"Hi." She edged closer to Dakota. He kept his stare glued on the television. "So, I took the car back to Luke." Dakota actually flicked his gaze in her direction. The honor almost went to her head. "And he's agreed to get a divorce."

"He should have got rid of you years ago," Dakota said.

She bit back any snappy comeback. Dakota was like a mad dog; if he sensed fear, he would attack. "Yes, he should have. Luke said he would come around tomorrow and we could talk about what to do with you."

"Yay."

Tiffany took a deep breath and sat on the other bed. Thomas's bed, some part of her brain registered. "Before

Luke gets here, though, I wanted to ask you what you wanted to do."

Dakota actually took his attention off the television to glare at her. His eyes glinted behind the heavy black eyeliner. "Why?"

"Why what?"

"Why would you ask me? You don't give a fuck what I think anyway." And there it came, all the hurt and the confusion.

"Dude." The bed dipped beneath his weight as Thomas settled beside her.

She stayed pressed close to Thomas's side. Things always felt more manageable when he was near.

"What *dude*?" Dakota snarled.

Thomas opened his mouth and Tiffany pressed his knee with hers. "I do care. That's why I'm asking."

"Whatever." Dakota shrugged and turned back to his television program. Not surprisingly, there seemed to be a lot of dismembering happening on the screen. Tiffany winced as somebody lost an arm and jets of blood squirted all over the wall.

She snagged the remote and turned the TV off. "You know, if you want some say in what happens to you, it helps if you actually say something."

"Really?" Dakota glared back at her, venom arcing out of his brown eyes, eyes so like Luke's it was uncanny. "Because I did before, and I'm still fucking stuck with you two."

"Only until tomorrow," Tiffany said. "Then Luke is coming and you can go where you want."

"You're so full of shit." Dakota knifed into a sitting position.

Tiffany recoiled physically. "You're going to have to explain that one. Maybe without calling me names," she said.

"Okay." Dakota swung his legs around and sat up. He sat and glared, eyeball to eyeball with her. "I said I wanted to go and live with my brother, and what did my mother do? She off-loaded me on his fucking ex-wife." He glared at Tiffany as if it were her doing. "Now, it turns out my brother is a total douche who doesn't want me. So maybe my mother is not as much of a dumb bitch as I thought. And I'm still stuck with the fucking ex-wife, who would rather stick her head in a bucket of bleach than keep me around. So I say again, what the fuck does it matter what I want?"

Scattered in amongst the liberal insults was enough hurt to deaden Tiffany's mad. She'd been there to see how much Dakota loved his big brother. This would leave huge claw marks right through Dakota's heart. "You know, I don't mind having you around. I really don't like being called *Barbie* and *the fucking ex-wife*, but you never once asked me how I felt about having you around. You just assumed I hated it."

He sneered at her and flung himself back on his bed.

"I mean it. You're a total pain in the ass, but we were friends when you were a kid, and if you stopped being mad at me, maybe we could be friends again."

Dakota glared at the blank screen.

"I have plenty of space at the condo, and a summer in downtown Chicago could be some fun." Nothing. "You know, I understand," she said.

Dakota rolled his eyes.

At least it showed he was listening. "No, I do. I understand what it feels like to not have any control over your life. I thought you might want some."

Nothing.

"Think about it." Tiffany got to her feet.

Thomas stood with her. "I'm going to take Tiffany for a drink. You going to be okay here?"

"Sure." Dakota grabbed the remote back and turned the TV on. "Maybe if you get her drunk enough, she might actually let you fuck her."

Tiffany sucked in a breath. Wow, Dakota lined her up and took his shot every time. It made it so hard to remember he was still a kid, a hurting kid.

Thomas surprised the hell out of her when he laughed. "You think?"

"Shit." Tiffany breathed deep as Thomas closed the door behind them.

"He's hurt and angry," Thomas said.

"He's good at it."

Thomas whistled between his teeth. "Damn good."

Heat baked off the blacktop in shimmering waves that crept beneath her clothing and stuck to her skin. So far, this day had lasted almost a lifetime.

They both slowed their pace as they made their way toward the small motel bar. One or two trucks outside said they weren't the only ones in need of a drink.

"He adored Luke as a boy," she said.

Thomas took her hand, threading his fingers through hers. "He still does."

Lola as a mother was a bad enough draw; combine that with a father in prison and a brother like Luke, and he was zero for three. No wonder he'd found his way into a crowd that did drugs. Dakota's reality pretty much blew.

"I think Luke will come around," she said and wished she could believe it more. The truth was, she didn't really know this Luke. She hadn't known the old one all that well, either, or they wouldn't have screwed up their marriage like they did.

"Yes, he will."

She looked up at Thomas as he said it. It sounded more like a promise than a statement. The thing with Luke and her was over. Chapter closed. Suddenly, she needed to celebrate a bit. Maybe a lot.

He pushed open the door to the bar. "Let's get to the other elephant in the room."

"I think I may need to be drunk for this one," Tiffany said.

He tugged her over to the bar. "You and me both."

Today she ordered a vodka and soda. It sounded cool and refreshing. The barman slid their drinks in front of them.

"So, here's the thing." Thomas turned to her. "I like you, more than I should, all things considered." He took a sip of his beer, glancing around the bar at the other patrons.

There had to be more coming. He took another sip of beer. Hardly worth ordering a drink to hear. "That's it?"

"Yup."

She stared at the drink in front of her where bubbles clustered happily around the ice cubes. Some country singer wailed the loss of his love over the sound system. No way she could bring the subject back without coming across all needy and desperate. If he told her how much he liked her, or added all the detail she'd been secretly wishing for, how would she respond? Only an hour earlier she'd disentangled her life from her ex. An angry teenage boy waited for her in his motel room. Her life was plenty messy enough.

"Define like," she said. *Fuck it*, she should put nail glue on her mouth sometimes.

The corners of his mouth turned up as he slid a look her way. "Really?"

"Maybe not." She wrinkled up her nose and took a sip of

her drink. Gross. It tasted like penicillin. "Could I get some 7Up in here?" She motioned to the barman. "Not diet."

Thomas spun her to face him, then turned on his bar stool, putting his feet on her footrest and caging her knees between his. "What the hell," he said. "Let's go there."

Her girl bits perked up. "You first."

He cupped her face between his big palms. "I really like you, Tiffany. The timing couldn't be worse and your life is a serious mess—and so is mine. I should be concentrating on getting my company out of the shit Luke landed us in. Instead, I'm fixating on how much I want to get close to you."

All the breath left her in a rush. "Wow."

"That's it?" A smile danced in his eyes. She nodded and he dropped his hands from her face. "Luke always said you were beautiful, but I had no idea until I met you."

"Luke tends to stretch the truth." Her cheeks heated.

"Not in this case." He shook his head. "Let's forget about it and drink." It was the best idea.

He grabbed his beer, but kept her caged with his knees. The denim pulled taut over the muscles of his thighs. They really were great thighs. The sort you could dig your fingers into and there would be no give. Her fingers twitched, but she kept them to herself. Her gaze strayed to the front of his T-shirt. *May the F = ma be with you.*

"I think you're beautiful, too." Oops. She hadn't really meant to say that. Okay, maybe a little.

His glass clunked back on the bar. "Beautiful?"

"In a totally manly way."

"Of course."

Her bad, bad fingers moved up, hovered over a thigh, and then traced the lettering over his chest. Hard all the way. Hard and hot to the touch. "What does it mean?"

"May the mass times acceleration be with you. Mass times acceleration is force. So, may the Force be with you."

"Oh." She got it. "Newton."

"Yup."

"You're such a geek."

"I really want to kiss you."

"Oh."

"Ever been kissed by a geek?"

"No, but I really want to." Her gaze flew up to his. She'd like to blame the drink—*but not this time, sister*. Her pulse kicked up and pounded in her neck.

His gaze got hotter and dropped to her mouth. He was going to kiss her. Hallelujah! She stopped breathing as he dipped his head toward her.

He paused within a heartbeat of her mouth. The choice was hers. His breath huffed warm against her mouth. The pull between them tugged harder, insistent. *YOLO.*

Tiffany hopped off her bar stool. She grabbed a fistful of his geek shirt, tugged, and docked her mouth to his. So good. The touch of his mouth shot right through her, and her toes curled.

He pulled back slightly, keeping the contact light.

She tightened her fingers in his shirt to stop him. She wanted it all. Tongues, teeth, and temptation.

He fastened his hands around her hips, tugging her into the cradle of his thighs. Shit, he was hard already. Thank you, God.

The touch of his tongue lit her up from inside. She moaned softly and pressed closer into the kiss. He tasted slightly of beer, but under that was the heady musk of man. It was addictive. And oh, Lord, could the man kiss. It short-circuited her brain and roared through her girl parts. Her breasts pressed, heavy and achy, into his hard chest. She wanted to crawl into him and burrow deep. She poured her building frustration into the kiss. He took it all and handed out more, until the bar faded into the background. Nothing existed but this man and his incredible mouth. He broke the kiss long before she was ready.

She swayed toward him.

He dropped his forehead against hers. "Whoa." His breath came fast and harsh. His lips were wet from hers and his tongue lapped up the taste.

"More." She gave his shirt a tug.

"Any more and we're going to have to get a room." His soft, husky laugh stroked across the bits of her already clamoring for attention.

"Yes," she said.

He drew back slightly so their eyes could meet. His color was high and the strain showed in the tight line of his jaw. "Tiffany, I'm trying really hard not to be the ass-hole that takes advantage of the vulnerable girl here."

Enough with the chitchat. "So stop."

She fastened her mouth on his. He caught on quick, her hot geek.

Chapter Twenty-Seven

Tiffany wanted to crawl up inside the man and live there. Electricity sparked and crackled through her nerve endings.

Thomas dropped some money on the bar, grabbed her hand, and headed for the door.

Tiffany tottered on behind him, almost running to keep up with his long strides. Somewhere, way, way, way down deep inside, a warning muttered. She stamped it right out. Today, she didn't care. She wanted Thomas Hunter, from about two seconds after she'd seen him. Having him now, best idea ever.

The bar door slammed shut behind them.

Thomas spun and jerked her against his chest. Hard flesh met her breasts and drove the air out of her chest. God, he felt so good. Her head snapped back, but he snagged it in his big hand, tangling his fingers in her hair and dragging her mouth to his. Wet. Wild. Wonderful. Damn this man could kiss.

He was strong, beautiful against her, and she curved to the defined planes of him, soft where he was hard, giving where he demanded. So thrilling it shot straight to her crotch.

He lifted her right off her feet, hands cupping her ass. She slanted her head to increase the contact between their mouths. *More, please. All of it.*

A car started in the distance. She wrapped her legs around his waist, tight, gripping him and holding him between her thighs. He felt so good, so right. The husky taste of him, the thrust of his tongue, his hands spanning her entire ass as he carried her down the passage.

Someone shouted; she didn't give a crap who saw them. The door pressed hard against her back.

Breathing hard, Thomas lifted his head. "Key?"

She slid her shaking legs to the ground. With scrabbling fingers, she dug out the key and handed it to him. Oh, God, they were really doing this. She was wet already, throbbing between her legs and desperate for more.

Thomas grabbed for her in the cool dimness of the room. Their breathing rasped hard. The heat came off him and she had to touch. Had to. She burrowed her hands under his T-shirt. Warm, smooth skin under her palms as she slid them up his back. Under the skin, hard-packed muscle that jerked and tightened under her touch.

He brought her pelvis into contact with his. He was so hard against her, as ready as her. Needing to get inside her as much as she needed him there. Her mouth opened under his. She couldn't get enough of the taste of him. She pushed against him impatiently. His shirt had to go. She shoved it up.

He pulled his mouth from hers and reached behind him to grab a fistful and tug.

So fucking beautiful, and all hers. Hard slabs of muscle, browned in the sun with a light scattering of hair over his nipples and marching in a straight line beneath his pants. She had to taste, and she put her mouth against the column of his neck. She breathed the musk of him in as she opened her lips and lapped his skin. Salty sweat, man and skin.

He groaned. The sound rippled through her. He liked her mouth on him and, shit, she liked putting it there. She nipped at his chest, wanting to suck all that hard into her. Down over the corrugated ridges of his stomach. Lower to what she wanted so badly her mouth watered.

He sucked in a breath.

She whimpered her protest as he gripped her nape, pulling her mouth back to his. Hard, hot gaze on her. "I want to taste you."

Her knees almost folded. Her zipper rippled open, and his fingers slid over her spine, pushing her dress down to her waist. Cool air hit her heated skin.

His breath caught, his gaze eating up the sight of her bare breasts. Big, rough hands cupped her breasts, almost reverently, the fullness fitting into his palms and swelling over his fingers. Too gentle—she wanted hard and dirty and fast. All the heat building between them. Hours in that truck, wanting him just where she had him now. She arched her back, pushing her nipples deeper into his touch.

"Beautiful." His thumbs caressed her nipples. "Everywhere."

Heat shot straight between her legs and she swayed toward him.

He dropped his hands to her waist, spanning the curve as he pulled her into contact with him. Naked skin against naked skin, burning, slick with sweat, needy. She could come just from the feel of his skin.

He slid her dress all the way off.

Good decision on the thong today, as his hands took

advantage of her bare cheeks, grabbing and squeezing, pulling her against his erection.

He walked her back, and when her legs hit the bed, she dropped onto the mattress. He stopped, poised above her.

Denim rasped against her bare legs. She had to get under those clothes, see him, touch him, taste. Drive him batshit crazy, just like he was doing to her. She grabbed hold of his belt and slid the buckle open.

He braced his weight on his forearms, his face intent and still.

Clumsy and frantic, her fingers trembled on the buttons of his fly. His erection pressed against the back of her hand. She caressed his hot length. Sweet mercy, she was in for a treat.

"Oh, yeah." Thomas groaned and slanted his mouth over hers again. He pushed his jeans down and kicked them off. Naked flesh scorched through the insubstantial barrier of her thong.

Shit, right there. He pressed his cock where she throbbed, rotating his hips to increase the friction. He reared up to look at her beneath him, his eyes dark and stormy as he catalogued her.

She writhed for him, sensual and powerful, loving the way his hungry gaze took it all in, drank her all in and demanded more.

His head dipped and hot breath seared her nipple. She needed his mouth there. Arching her back, she whimpered under the hot, wet suck of his mouth. Deeper he pulled at her nipple, pushing the barrier of pain and pleasure.

"More. Now." Her breath came in incoherent pants. *Just more of everything.*

Impatient fingers nudged aside her thong to slide over her wet heat. His thumb found her clitoris and pressed.

Yes. Oh, God, she was close. Her hips bucked against his fingers.

Finding her slick opening, he slid his finger around and in, filling her.

She clenched around him. More of that would push her right over the edge. "Yes."

He slid another finger deep inside her, his thumb working her clit. "Fuck, babe, you feel so good."

He had no idea how good she felt right now.

He moved his mouth down and pressed open-mouthed kisses across her ribs and onto her flat belly as he stripped her thong down her legs. He pressed her legs open and slid down off the bed. His hot gaze raked her, harsh breath panting through his parted lips.

His cock stood rampant between his thighs, thick and swollen. For her. She writhed her hips. He lowered his head, settling between her thighs.

She raised her hips impatiently, wanting his mouth on her. And then it was, and she flung her head back as need raked through her.

He took his time, tasting her, exploring her with his tongue and his lips.

Tiffany sank her fingers into his hair—selfish maybe, but damn, the way he used his mouth was a beautiful thing. He didn't rush as if it were some kind of obligation. He licked across her clit slowly and then faster, sucking the bud into his mouth.

Oh. My. God. Her grip tightened on his silky hair; if he stopped now, she'd die for sure.

Her orgasm pushed closer. He slowed down, prolonging her pleasure until she nearly screamed at him to let her come. When she did, it was on a low keen of his name that lifted her off the bed.

Tiffany drifted down again, her bones melting into the bed beneath her.

He crawled up over her. A satisfied smile turned the corners of his mouth up. "You're beautiful when you come."

He grabbed his jeans. Finding a condom in his wallet, he rolled it over his length.

She wanted that. All of it inside her. "Now, Thomas."

He grinned and settled between her thighs. He fisted his cock and guided it into her. Her soaked tissues stretched around his girth. He filled her completely and then more. She lifted her hips to take all of him, and he slid home with a soft curse.

Perfect.

Raising himself on his arms, pleasure, raw and primal, stamped over his features. It made her crazy just watching him.

He thrust slow, deep and sure. Pushing all the way in, as much as she could take before drawing out again. His abdominals bunched and flexed with each push of his hips, sweat glistening on his stomach.

Tiffany wrapped her legs around his hips and pushed up, desperate to take all of him.

He responded and quickened his pace, keeping his focus on her face, watching her pleasure and reflecting it back at her.

She didn't hold back, urging him with soft cries to go faster, deeper.

He fucked like they'd been doing this for years. The pressure in her core built as he stroked her higher. He lowered his hand between them and found her aching clit.

She came so hard the room dipped and swirled. She shut her eyes and let it take her over the edge.

He gave a guttural shout as he joined her, pushing right

into her as far as she could take him. Squeezing him tight, milking his orgasm, she clenched around him.

As he lowered his weight onto her, their sweat-slickened skin pressed together.

She kept him there with her thighs, bringing her arms around his torso to hold him in place. A series of small aftershocks rippled through her. And, finally, she lay quiet.

He kissed her, her head tenderly clasped between his hands.

Tiffany opened her eyes.

He smiled. A beautiful, satisfied beam of happy that warmed her. "Hey."

"Hey, yourself." Laughter bubbled up inside her.

He kissed her quickly and rolled onto his back, tugging her into his side, pressing her cooling skin close to his. He smelled of sweat and sex, and she burrowed her face against him.

"Incredible," he said.

She couldn't have said it better, so she didn't. She snuggled closer to him, the slow thump of his heart steady against her ear.

Chapter Twenty-Eight

The unwelcome chimes of her ringtone wrenched Tiffany out of sleep and into the dim light of her motel room. She thrust a hand out the covers and grabbed it.

Thomas stirred, his arms and legs sliding between the sheets, hogging most of the bed in the process.

Tiffany stared blearily at the screen. "Hello?"

"It's Luke." Typical. Right to the point and no pleasantries. "I can be there in half an hour."

Shit, shit, shit. Luke on his way over. And her still lying there, naked and smelling of sex, with Thomas. "Okay." Tiffany named the small restaurant close to their motel.

She tossed the phone onto the nightstand and rolled over, straight into Thomas, awake and watching her with his head propped on one hand. All sleep rumpled, big and contented, with a glimmer in his eyes that said he would be looking for more of the same. "Good morning."

"Hi." A kind of dorky squeak came out of her mouth. Ah damn, still drop-dead gorgeous and sexy as hell. "Luke's on his way." She gripped the sheet tightly over her breasts. Way, way too late, but better than sitting there naked under the exposure of that raunchy gaze. "He'll be here in about thirty minutes. I need to get dressed."

She bolted for the bathroom. The door clicked shut behind her and she locked it. Only then did she release the breath she'd been holding. Oh, my God. She'd had sex with Thomas Hunter. Off-the-charts, hot and steamy sex. All through the afternoon and then the night. She ached, and she'd done things that were probably illegal in Utah. Her reflection blinked back at her. Yup. Incontrovertible evidence starting with bed head and ending in razor burn. Freshly fucked. That's what she looked like. Now what? Her reflection didn't answer. She closed the toilet seat and sat on it. Stupid. She needed to get dressed, and she really needed to get Thomas up and dressed and way the hell out of her room.

"Tiffany?" Thomas knocked gently on the door.

"I'm just getting in the shower," she called, and flipped on the water.

There was a pause and then a careful "Okay. I guess I'll grab a shower next door."

"Good idea." Way too loud. She took a deep breath, but it didn't help. She was totally panicking. What the hell had she been thinking? Sure he was hot and nice and she felt like she could take on the world with him at her back. Still, having sex with him had not been her best idea.

Ryan. Her skin got suddenly too tight. She couldn't think about Ryan now. Thomas had rocked her tiny world. Her nipples tightened as a wash of memories flushed over her. The shower water had warmed enough and she hopped beneath the spray. Luke was coming over to discuss Dakota, and Dakota needed her attention now, not Thomas. She'd meant what she said yesterday. If it came to it, he would come home with her and stay in Chicago until his mother got back. *Shit,* her father wasn't going to like that, but he'd have to deal because she didn't see any options. Not with the drugs and whatever else. Forcing herself to breathe, she dipped her head beneath the spray.

Hot water drummed against her scalp and ran in warm rivulets down her back. What did she know about teenagers? A trip to the water park wasn't going to cut it. Piers expected her back at work in a few days. Maybe Dakota could go along with her. Except there was a lot of sitting around involved, and Dakota would be bored. God, her job bored *her* most of the time . . . except when Thomas had walked in.

She grabbed the shampoo and lathered up her hair. Daddy had never been a big fan of her job. As far as he was concerned, he paid most of her bills, and one day soon, her husband would take that over.

The shampoo ran over her face and she closed her eyes and rinsed.

It had been one of her father's greatest disappointments that she wouldn't run for Miss America. Once he got over that, it became all about finding the right sort of son-in-law.

Tiffany worked the conditioner through to her ends. She had always known she was a Daddy's girl. *Daddy's princess.* Except maybe she was less of Daddy's princess and more of Daddy's puppet.

"Everybody has a gift, Princess. In your case, it's right there for the whole world to enjoy."

Enough. She rinsed out the conditioner and snapped off the water. She didn't have time for big reveals right now. Luke was on his way and she had to get ready. The mirror had fogged and she swiped it with her forearm. Her makeup lay spread out on the vanity in front of her. Tiffany stared at it and then stared at her reflection. To hell with it. No war paint this morning, and no hair styling either. *YOLO.* Yo—fucking—lo. Well . . . maybe some mascara and a bit of lip gloss. Old habits died hard. All right, the five-minute face, but that was it.

"Shit." She lost years off her life as she opened the bathroom door and found Thomas lounging on the bed. "What the hell?"

"I thought we should talk." He'd managed to shower and change. His gaze stroked every inch of her skin not covered by the skimpy towel.

Her girly bits fluttered and she clenched her thighs. "Great. I get stuck with the only man in the world who wants to talk."

"So, last night was something else," he said.

Tiffany's traitorous face heated and she dug for some clothes to hide it. The silence twanged like an elastic band between them. "It was great."

"Look at me, babe." It wasn't quite a request. He waited until she looked up. "That's what I thought, you're choking on regret this morning." His smug tone stung.

"Well, it shouldn't have happened."

"Because of the asshole?"

He meant Ryan, maybe. Hard to be sure. She was gathering assholes by the boatload lately. "Because of Ryan. Because of Luke. Everything." She tossed her hands into the air. "My life is incredibly messy right now, and last night made it a whole lot messier."

He stared at her. Blue eyes, direct and straight up. Damn, the honesty stung. She yanked out her underwear. "I need to get dressed."

He appeared right in front of her, caught her around the waist, and yanked her into him. Not hard enough to hurt, but forceful enough to get her attention. He kept her there for a moment, thigh to thigh, breast to chest. Every ridge and swell of him pressed through her thin towel. He dipped to kiss her. *Evasive maneuver needed, duck to the side. Move. Do something.* Instead, she tipped her chin upward and made it easier for him to claim her mouth.

And claim it he did. His kiss branded her, not allowing her to hold back. Who was she kidding anyway? Tiffany clamped her arms around his neck. His kiss ripped right through her, hotter than hell, and she loved it. He swept her along in his kind of magic and left her panting when he stepped back. "Last night wasn't a mistake. It was an inevitability."

He turned and sauntered his perfect, geek ass out of the door. The latch snicked shut behind him.

Tiffany released a relieved breath when Luke pulled up in a battered SUV that looked like it had gone up, down, and all around the mountain a time or two. She'd steeled herself for the Miura, and seeing the beat-up truck was a huge relief.

They met at a nearby breakfast place. Talking Dakota into coming took some work, but at least he'd left the Beats in the motel. Unfortunately, he'd worn more makeup than her, and his hair strayed even lower over his face than normal.

Luke stared at him, a slightly mystified look on his face. "So, Lola's in South Africa?"

Dakota glared at his fingers, tapping out a complicated drumming rhythm on the tabletop.

"Yes," she said. Somebody had to get this conversation going.

Luke's jaw got tight. "And she just left Dakota?"

"Jesus." Dakota rolled his eyes. "I'm seventeen, not four."

"I know that, bud." Luke's tone got more placating. "But you still can't be left on your own for weeks."

"I'm not on my own. I'm with Barbie."

Tiffany sucked in her breath. They were right back to that.

"Barbie?" Luke raised his eyebrow at her.

"That would be me," she said.

Luke laughed softly under his breath.

Dakota glanced up, a smug little smile across his mouth.

"Seriously?" Thomas said from beside her, across from Luke and Dakota.

"Dakota would rather stay with you," Tiffany said.

"You would?" Luke looked at his brother.

An uneasy prickle crept up Tiffany's spine. She knew that expression on Luke's face, all too well. The kind that said Luke was about ready to wriggle his way out of this situation.

Luke shifted in his seat.

The waitress saved him by arriving with their order.

"You may as well know, there's some trouble with school." She brought the conversation right back on track.

"It's bullshit." Dakota's fingers drummed faster. He had to stop for the waitress to put his plate down.

"What sort of trouble?" Luke kept it casual, but tension tightened around his jaw.

"They say I'm dealing at the school," Dakota said.

Tiffany stiffened and held her breath. This was so not good. Talk about whipping the lid off a whole can of ugly.

Luke's eyes narrowed. "Are you?"

"It's bullshit." Dakota shrugged and turned his attention to his loaded plate.

"He's on summer break until August," she said.

Luke looked at her and then Thomas. He slid a quick glance at Dakota. "That's cool."

"I could stay here until I have to go back to school." Dakota glanced at Luke.

Shit, it was painful to watch. Dakota had a good game face, but the longing was there all the same.

Luke kept his stare fixed on his plate.

Tiffany pressed her knee against Thomas's. He was there, a solid pressure.

"Bud, that's great." Luke got a kiss-ass smile all over his face. Here it came. Just this once she wanted to be wrong about Luke. "But my life here is complicated. I work all the time, and when I'm not working, I'm riding. I'm in training for this two-week ride across Moab. Unsupported." Luke paused as if they should all remark on the fact.

Tiffany had a few choice remarks for him. Beginning with a bitch slap across his head.

Dakota shoveled eggs into his mouth.

"You're saying Dakota can't stay with you?" Thomas broke the silence.

"Normally, I'd love to have the little dude with me, but now is not a good time. We would have no time together. He would end up just sitting around the house."

"I'm not a little dude," Dakota said.

"No, you're not." Luke rushed the words out. "But you have to see that I can't spend time with you right now."

"Sure." Dakota went back to shoveling.

"I don't see that." Tiffany laid her knife and fork neatly side by side on her plate. What she did see was Luke running for cover. "All I see is you making this somebody else's responsibility. Your brother needs you, and the best you can manage is that you're training for a ride?"

"I've been training for over a year," Luke said. The miserable, whining coward wouldn't even meet her eyes. "As soon as this is over, dude, I'll call you and you can come and stay with me. How about Christmas? There's no riding in the winter. We could go snowboarding and shit. It'll be cool."

"How about you stop being such a selfish dick?" This from Thomas.

"What the fuck has this got to do with you anyway?" Luke flushed and dropped his fork. "What are you, like screwing my ex-wife and now you think that gives you the balls to get up and in her shit?"

Thomas went so still it was creepy. The hair on the back of her neck stood straight up.

"It's fine." Tiffany rushed into the mounting anger. They had enough crap on their plates without adding a fight with Luke to the mix. "Dakota can stay in Chicago with me. The company will be nice."

"Hey, Chi Town." Luke bumped shoulders with his brother. "Parties, hot chicks, all on your doorstep. That's gotta beat hanging around my house, watching the trees grow."

"It's not—"

"It's cool," Dakota said before Tiffany could finish. His gaze met hers over the table.

They finished breakfast in a tight silence. Tiffany only managed a few bites of her pancakes. She looked at them mournfully as the waitress took her plate away. Her one total food rebellion and she couldn't eat.

Luke didn't hang around. With the look on Thomas's face, she might have made a run for it, too.

"You got Luke's number?" Thomas asked her as Dakota said good-bye to his brother.

"Yes."

"Give it to me," Thomas said.

"Why?"

"I want to tell your ex a few things, explain them to him

in a way he'll understand and I don't think Dakota needs to hear it."

Thomas had been longer getting back to Tiffany and Dakota than he would have liked. His conversation with Luke still had his blood spitting like hot fat. Jesus, this kid was in trouble, and nobody who should be taking notice was taking notice. "Hey."

Dakota glanced up as he entered the room.

Luke stuck with the party line that this was not his problem. He was also still resisting giving the survey results back. Thomas didn't want to get the cops involved, but Luke had stolen from him and he needed that information. The Zambian meeting was a couple of days away, and his calls from his partners were getting slightly more desperate. He was all out of reassurances.

Dakota flipped through channels.

Thomas sat on the opposite bed. "Can I ask you something?"

"Can I stop you?"

It was what Tiffany would have said, and it almost made him smile. Christ, he didn't know what he was going to do about that, either. In a day or two, she would be back in Chicago and he would be out of reasons to hang around. He pushed Tiffany into a different mental compartment and forced the door shut. "Why the dealing?"

Dakota looked up at him and went a bit red around the jawline. He turned the volume up on the TV.

Thomas grabbed the remote and snapped the TV off. "From what you say, money is not the problem."

"I told you that was bullshit." Dakota's voice rose.

Yeah, kid, yell all you like, but we both know you're lying.

"What the fuck is it with you, anyway? I tell you something and you automatically believe I'm lying."

Hot, impotent rage took Thomas's words away. His hands were tied here. He barely even knew the kid. He was in no position to do anything about the fuckup Dakota made of his life. Luke was. Except Luke had decided to bury his head in the sand. *Fuck*. He had to get out of the room before he started hitting walls.

A man didn't walk away from his responsibilities, his father and his older brother had taught him that. Except . . . hadn't he been kind of doing exactly the same thing? Luke had flung the statement at him during their angry call. The challenge had gone unanswered because it had stopped Thomas cold.

Richard as the oldest had stepped up when their father died. He and Josh had let him, happy to do what they wanted knowing Richard had their backs. Thomas got to travel the world, do projects in places most people had never even heard of, while Richard stayed in Willow Park and kept an eye on their mother. Richard had dealt with their father's estate. Still dealt with it, for all Thomas knew.

That thought bugged him most of all, because he didn't know the answer. Hadn't even asked the question. He found himself standing outside Tiffany's door before the conscious thought had even risen to the surface of his brain.

"Hey," she greeted him as she opened the door. "Did you talk to Luke?"

"I spoke to him." He brushed past, the need to be near her pushing him deeper into the room.

Tiffany followed. "He's not going to do anything, is

he?" She looked at him as if she expected him to come up with some reason for being there. He had nothing, other than the burn to be with her. "So," she said. "I'll take Dakota back to Chicago with me. Lola will get back at some point."

"You don't have to do that," he said.

"Yes, I do."

Tiffany wasn't going to dump the kid. From the start, and despite what crap the little shit handed out, Tiffany had Dakota's back. For all his strutting around feeling like the man in charge, whose back did Thomas Hunter have, other than his own?

"When do you want to leave?"

Her question pissed him off so badly, he saw red for a moment. Leave. Go home.

"I have to get my survey results." He sucked in his breath and made himself get a grip. "That's the only reason I'm still hanging around."

She paled and dropped her eyes. Shit, that had been a dick thing to say. And nowhere near the truth. "That's crap," he said. "It's the reason I started this, but not the only reason I'm here. I'll try Luke again a bit later. Who knows, he might decide to man up. Otherwise I'm going to have to get the cops on it. I can't leave here without those results."

"Okay," she said. "We can wait a day or two more."

"And then what?" The question came out of nowhere and surprised the hell out of him as it hit the air between them.

She looked up, her beautiful face guarded. "What do you mean?" She knew what he meant, because she had one of those faces that was painfully easy to read. He waited her out. "I go home." She shrugged. "I go home and pick up my life. What else?"

"What about your book?" he asked. "What about all that?"

Her eyes opened wide in surprise. "What about it?"

The anger rushed back. He jammed his fists into his pockets to keep from shaking her. "You have this incredible brain and you're just going to go back to writing it all out in secret again. What the hell is the point of that?"

"What else would I do with it?" She was getting defensive, but he couldn't back off on this.

"The waste of a brain is a tragedy," he said. "You can't keep pretending that you don't have one. I know you do."

"And what would I do with my so-called brain?" She crossed her arms over her chest. Her breasts swelled under the fabric of her tank.

Keep your eyes on her face, you horny prick. "You could do anything. Anything you wanted."

She made a rude noise and turned her back on him. "That's easy for you to say. You have a college degree behind you."

"I have two," he said. "But you could get as many as you wanted."

Her shoulders tensed and she ducked her head. And up came her barriers.

"Fuck it, Tiffany." He took a step closer and turned her to look at him. If he did nothing else, he had to make her see this. He couldn't leave her, go back to Zambia and let her marry the asshole and disappear again behind that brittle shell she'd built around herself. "You want to learn. Do something with that. It's a rare and precious gift, and you're jamming it behind your beautiful face and pretending to yourself and the world it doesn't exist."

"You don't understand." Her voice rose close to an outright yell.

"You're right. I don't get it." He waved his hand from

her feet to the top of her head. "You think that all you are is this, but you're so much more than that. You fixed Luke's car because it was the right thing to do. Your life was running off track, so you jumped right in and put it right." How did she not get this about herself? She let her father and that dickhead, Ryan, convince her she was worth shit. "You didn't want to do all of this and see Luke again, but you did. Dakota is in such deep shit, it would take a backhoe to dig him out, and you're in that hole with him. He takes your head off, but you stick with him. On your own, you work out shit that takes the rest of us years of study to get a handle on. How can you not see that?"

Tiffany stared at him. The words made sense to her, and yet her gut tossed them out as ridiculous. She'd created all of this mess. It would be the height of hypocrisy to turn around and take credit for the way she'd handled it. As for the stuff about her brain, she didn't believe any of it. She had to stop him from talking. She did the only thing that came to mind and mashed her mouth against his.

His arms came around her like manacles. He took charge of the kiss, pushing his tongue into her mouth and demanding her response. It was crazy how quickly he could make her want him. And she did want him. She knew she shouldn't and couldn't, but the taste and feel of him were imprinted on her.

"I was planning to marry Ryan." She yanked her mouth away from his.

"Why?" His expression got even stormier. "You keep saying you're going to marry this guy, that you have to marry this guy. Why, Tiffany? Do you even want to marry him?"

He shifted closer. His chest brushed against her nipples. The heat in his gaze turned her knees to spaghetti. One hand drifted down the column of her neck to grasp the back of her head. Heat oozed over her skin, tightening her nipples and moving lower. She pressed her thighs together. It didn't help.

He wanted her. She could see it in his face. And, dammit, she wanted the same thing.

"You're sure you want to marry this guy?"

She opened her mouth to say yes. He looked at her and the words wouldn't come. "No, but I must." Her voice grew hoarse. "I've wanted this for so long."

"Not the same thing," he said.

"It has to be."

"Why?"

There was no answer to that.

"And yet, here you are with me," he said.

"No." Her eyelids got too heavy to stay open. She tried to force her gaze away from his mouth as it came closer.

"No?" Thomas's breath caressed her face. His fingers stroked her nape. His other hand dropped lightly to her hip. It stayed there, branding her through her jeans.

She'd pictured her future with Ryan a thousand times. It would be everything she wanted, but it wouldn't be this. This thing she had with Thomas—compelling, hypnotic, hot as hell and dangerous to touch. Like Luke. Except not like Luke at all. With Thomas she was more herself than she was with anyone. She didn't need to pretend or be something he wanted her to be. He looked right at her, saw her for what she was, and still here he stayed. "Please?"

"Please what?" His fingers tightened on her hip. "Please let me go, Thomas, or please fuck me, Thomas?"

His coarse words combusted inside her. Her hand twisted into his T-shirt and hauled him closer. "Fuck me. Please."

Their mouths slammed together in a tangle of tongues, teeth, and lips.

She ached for this. Tiffany grabbed his head and speared her fingers into his hair. The taste and smell of him surrounded her. God, she needed more. The all of him kind of more.

Her back hit the wall.

His hands cupped her ass and brought their crotches into alignment. Heat seared through the connection. Tiffany wrapped her legs around his hips and ground down. A rip of fabric, the ping of buttons, and his hands were on the bare skin of her waist. Her bra disappeared and his hands latched on her breasts.

Plumping them up, he dipped his mouth and sucked her nipple.

Damn, too good. Tiffany pushed her head back against the wall. She lost the connection with his mouth as she hauled off his T-shirt. Then it was back again and she moaned. Sensation shot straight from her nipple to her core. And just like that she was wet and hot and ready for him again. Her skin was hypersensitized. It was almost too much and not nearly enough. She wriggled free.

He let her slide down the wall. His mouth suckled first one breast and then the other.

She needed him inside her. Now. Tiffany reached between them and grabbed the buttons to his jeans. With shaking hands she got them loose. Finally, she cupped his cock in her hand. It jerked under her touch. Tiffany fisted him and stroked.

Thomas growled and reared back to kick off his pants. He pushed her pants roughly down her legs with her panties and lifted her again.

Bare skin slid against bare skin as she wrapped herself around him. His cock was right against her wet slit, silently demanding entry. Thomas braced her back against the wall. He guided himself inside her, slamming all the way home. The wall rattled as he thrust.

Somewhere, something crashed onto the ground. Tiffany didn't care as she bore down on him.

His breathing rasped in her ear. Harsh catches as he thrust into her again and again.

She clung to his shoulders, using him and the wall to create counterpressure against his upward motion, rubbing herself against him. She came with a shout.

He was right with her, slamming hard into her as he spilled.

Their breathing mingled, panting, as they stayed where they were, her back pressed against the wall, him leaning into her as he recovered.

"Shit," he whispered right beside her ear.

Tiffany released her legs from his waist.

He lowered her to the ground, still holding her tightly against him. Her legs wouldn't hold her and she let him support her weight.

"Damn," he said. "That was hot." His hand spread over her ass to hold her tight against the cradle of his thighs. "Baby?" His breath stirred wisps of her hair. "We didn't use a condom."

Tiffany's eyes whipped open. She never had unprotected sex. Protection had not even occurred to her. She wanted to stay there, wrapped around him like that forever. "I'm on the pill."

"I'm clean." He feathered a light kiss on her temple. "They test me before I go on assignment."

"And I'm clean."

"So, no harm done, then?"

"No harm." Except she'd abandoned one of the most

ingrained habits of her adult life. And she was having earth-shattering sex with the wrong man.

A phone rang. Thomas let her go to reach for it. "It's Luke," he said before he answered the call. "Yeah?"

She slipped into the bathroom to clean up. A brief glance in the mirror told her she had that look again. The one that screamed she had just got it and got it good. She closed her eyes. She had to stop doing this.

Thomas ended the call when she slipped back into her room.

"Babe." He looked at her. "We have to settle this, but not now. Luke is on his way."

"Luke?" That gave her enough distraction not to have to deal with what was going on between them. "What does he want?"

"He says he's been thinking," Thomas said. "He wants to talk to me alone first."

Thomas went next door to clean up. A human-shaped lump in the second bed meant Dakota was sleeping. Poor kid. This shit was a lot to handle.

With shaking hands, he splashed water on his face. He had no idea what had just happened with him and Tiffany. Never in his adult life had he lost control with a woman like that.

She'd said she would go home after this was all done, and he'd flipped. Lost it. Home meant without him. It shouldn't have mattered, because that's how he rolled. Moved out and on, off to the next assignment. Out of sight and out of mind. He washed and slipped into a clean pair of jeans.

He loved his life on site. Stuck in the African bush, living out of a huge military-grade tent and a few trailers.

Communication with the world limited to the sat phone. An ice-cold beer at the end of the blisteringly hot day out of the huge generator-powered fridge. Sitting back in his camp chair watching the incredible pyrotechnics of the African sun sinking below the horizon, catching the dust raised by animals as it went.

In three weeks, that would be his life again. Except now it felt empty as hell without a black-haired, green-eyed math geek in it. Sometimes those sunsets made him feel like the only man in the world. For the first time ever, it felt lonely. His mother not there to get on him about something or other. No Richard or Josh. His brothers were settling down, finding women who made them happy, having kids. And no Tiffany.

Just one man, sitting at the edge of civilization watching the day end.

Chapter Twenty-Nine

Tiffany banged on the door to the room next door. Dakota couldn't hear a damn thing when he had that music going. She gave the door another hefty pound, putting a little foot action in there for power. She waited, but the door didn't so much as squeak.

Thomas had texted her a few minutes ago, asking her to bring Dakota and meet them in the same place as their abortive breakfast with Luke. *Screw this.* If Luke and Thomas wanted Dakota, then they could use Thomas's key.

She found them in the regular coffee shop. At least it was becoming regular, as one day dribbled into another. She really had spent more time in Utah than she ever would have imagined.

Thomas's expression gave nothing away as Tiffany sat down.

For once, Thomas and Luke weren't looking like they were a few breaths away from tearing into each other. "What's going on?"

"Dakota?" Luke raised an eyebrow at her.

"I banged on the door," she said. "I couldn't get him to answer."

"How loud did you bang?" Luke inserted his unwelcome drawl of derision into the conversation.

Okay, if Luke tried a little more not to light her fuse every time, this whole simmering-down thing would be a lot easier. "Any harder and I would have brought the management down on my head."

Thomas frowned and looked thoughtful for a moment. "I thought I left him sleeping."

"Either you did or you didn't," Luke said.

Tiffany glared at him. Did he really think that tone was helpful? Clearly he did, because he looked unbearably smug.

"I saw a lump in the bed." She admired Thomas's patience, she really did, but Thomas hadn't been married to Captain Charisma for two very long years.

"You didn't check?" Luke's eyes widened. "It's the middle of the day."

Thomas sat back and folded his arms. "No, Luke, I didn't check. He's seventeen and the last thing he wants is some dude hanging over him while he sleeps." Even Thomas had his limits.

Dakota, all on his own, so not good. "Should we go and check now?"

"I'll go." Thomas got to his feet. He turned to Luke before he left. "Why don't you tell Tiffany what you told me?"

A couple of the female patrons watched him go. She had the insane urge to leap up and shout "mine." She glanced back at Luke instead.

He shifted uncomfortably in his seat.

"Well?" She had to admit making Luke squirm felt all kinds of good.

"I was a dick," he said.

"When?"

"Come on, Tiff." He glared at her. "Let me get this out and then you can take all the shots you like."

"Okay." She took a deep, deep breath.

"I should never have let Dakota think I didn't want him with me. I should've said that it would be great to have him with me."

"So why didn't you?"

"I was shocked." Luke fidgeted with the handle of his coffee mug. "I've spent the last few years of my life running from my family and all the shit around them. You arrived with Dakota and I panicked. I felt like it was all there again, waiting to suck me in."

Tiffany got it. After he'd disappeared, she would have done anything to put some distance between herself and her screwed-up marriage. She envied him his escape across the world. Why hadn't she run? Because she'd been busy trying to make it up to her father that she'd made such a colossal mistake in her marriage.

The waitress arrived and gave her a brief reprieve from her thoughts. She ordered a cup of coffee and the pancakes, determined to eat them this time.

"You were there, Tiff. You know how fucked up it all got, with my dad going to jail and Lola swearing blind she knew nothing about it. Then you and I imploded. I looked at what you did to the Miura and I wanted out. It wasn't only you, though. It was all of it. Looking at that wrecked car was like looking at myself. What I had become, what my life had become, and I wanted to get as far away from it as I could."

"Yeah."

"You'll probably find this hard to believe, but I'm not the sort of man who screws around. And yet, I was exactly that with you. It was like I was hell-bent on destroying anything that had value in my life." Luke took a deep breath. "I needed to get away. I needed to find who I was. And I did find him. I was even starting to like that man. Then you arrived and nightmare Luke came back. One look at you and I'm stuffed full of all this rage and self-destruction."

"I can understand that." He'd the same impact on her. "What now?"

"Now I find Dakota and apologize. Not just about this summer and him staying with me, but about all of it. I should have stayed in contact with him." He made a face. "I knew how things would be in that house, with Lola. He was a kid. He relied on the adults around him to take care of him."

"Did Thomas tell you all of it?"

Luke's face got tight. "You mean about the drugs? Yes, he did. Dakota and me are going to make that a priority." He shook his head and his anger blurred into a different expression. He looked almost guilty. "I fucked up, Tiff. I should have been there for him. This shit is partly on me. But I'm going to make it right."

"Just what did Thomas say to you?" Man, she'd loved to have heard that conversation.

Luke stuck his chin out. "That's between him and me. The important part is that it got through to me. I was halfway there on my own, he just gave me a shove." Tiffany was less sure of that. Her expression must have said so, because Luke looked indignant. "It's true."

"Okay." She shrugged. So not worth fighting about.

Thomas entered the diner. Alone.

"Did you find him?" Luke frowned.

"No." Thomas slid into the booth beside her. Two creases wrinkled the skin between his eyes. "The bed was rumpled, but he wasn't in it. It felt cold as well, so he hasn't been in it for a while."

"Then where is he?" Luke's eyes narrowed.

"I think that's what we'd all like to know," Thomas said.

"You must have seen him earlier," Luke said.

"That was a while ago."

"What were you two doing without him?"

Tiffany's face got so hot it might explode.

Thomas stilled beside her and dropped his gaze.

Luke stopped with his mouth half-open. He glanced from her to Thomas and back again. "You are fucking kidding me." Luke threw himself back in the booth. "You two are fucking each other?"

Who the hell was Luke to judge her? "Not the point."

Thomas tapped his knuckles on the table. "He could have gone anytime after that. Like I said, I saw the bed, but I didn't check."

Luke glared at her. "And where does your so-called fiancé fit into you doing Thomas?"

"Drop it," Tiffany said, a little desperately.

"No way. You wrecked my car because I screwed around on you. You just lost the moral high ground, Tiffany."

Tiffany's jaw dropped open and she snapped it shut again. "What has one thing got to do with another?"

"You were all outraged—"

"Nothing," Thomas said. "The two have nothing to do with each other. And nothing to do with where Dakota went and where he is now."

Luke opened his mouth like he might argue further, but sat back in his chair with a growl.

"He could be at the mall." Tiffany pointed to a strip mall across the road.

"What would he be doing at a mall?" Luke's eyes narrowed. "Thomas already made sure he had something to eat."

"He was upset," Tiffany said. "After you left this morning, he was very upset."

"I tried to talk to him, but he nearly took my head off," Thomas said.

The waitress slid the plate of pancakes in front of her. Tiffany eyed them and sighed. "We'll have the check, please. We need to split up and look for him." Tiffany took a quick gulp of her coffee. "He doesn't know that many places, so he can't have got far."

"True." Thomas smiled at her. "Luke, you try the shop where you work. I'll look around here."

"I'll try Luke's house." Dakota so owed her for risking another round with Luke's nature girl.

"Good." Thomas got to his feet. "We'll keep in contact by cell."

Dakota was not at Luke's house. Nature Girl was, however. She looked plenty ready to have her say as she answered the door. Tiffany cut her off. "Dakota's missing. Is he here?"

The woman blinked and then recovered. "Why the hell would he be here?"

"Maybe he came looking for Luke?" The woman needed to check her attitude.

"Weren't you and the big guy supposed to be looking after him?" The woman glared at Tiffany.

"Yes." She and Thomas were supposed to be looking after him. They'd fucked that bit up royally. "If you see him, could you give Luke a call?"

The woman nodded and slammed the door.

"Nice knowing you," Tiffany said to the closed door. She walked back down the pathway. The Miura wasn't parked on the curb where she'd left it. Luke must have put it in his garage or something. Tiffany stopped. Slowly she retraced her steps to the door. It was a long shot, but it made a weird sort of sense.

The woman must have been watching from the window, because she yanked the door open before Tiffany could get there. "You can't come in and check."

"The car." Tiffany glanced around for some sort of garage. "Where does Luke keep the Miura?"

"You can't have it back."

"I know that and I don't want it." Tiffany took a deep breath. "But I thought maybe Dakota would be there."

"Why?"

"Because of me." The more she thought it out, the more sense it made. When she had been angry with Luke, she'd taken her rage out on the car. It had certainly gotten Luke's attention. Dakota was more than angry enough to give it a try, as well. "I think Dakota is doing the same thing to the Miura I did."

"You mean key it up?"

"Yes."

"And carve your name into the seats?"

"Maybe."

"Slash the tires? Break the headlights?"

A recitation of past sins was never the best fun, especially from someone who'd made up their mind to hate your guts. "Where does Luke keep it?"

"Garage down the end of the road." The woman jerked her head to the left. "It's locked."

"Do you have the key?"

"Yes."

"Can I have it?"

"Not sure."

Tiffany dug her nails into her palms. "I'll bring it right back. As soon as I've seen whether Dakota is there or not."

"You don't need the key. He couldn't get in anyway, because it's locked."

"He could have broken in," Tiffany said.

The woman went all squinty eyed. "I don't trust you."

Ditto. "You don't have to, but if Dakota is there, then I might be able to stop him. You can call Luke and tell him where I am."

The woman glowered at her. Her expression grew almost comical as she weighed her options.

"What the hell have you got against me, anyway?" Tiffany didn't have time for her to decide.

"You broke Luke." The woman snarled at her. "Before you, he could have loved. He could have had a good relationship, but you broke that in him."

Tiffany stepped back at the woman's vehemence. "I think you give me far too much credit."

The woman's mouth tightened. Tiffany braced for another helping of grief, but Nature Girl stepped into the hall and grabbed a key from a hook on the wall. She held it out to Tiffany. "I'm calling Luke and telling him where you are. If anything happens to that car again, he'll blame it on you. I'll make sure of it."

"Fine." Tiffany snatched the key. She trotted down the walk toward Thomas's truck. Then she stopped and turned again. "You know, I think you're the one who should forget about me. Luke already has."

"Go fuck yourself." Slam went the door.

Tiffany jumped into the truck and followed the road to a dead end lined with small garages. As it turned out, she didn't need the key. The wooden barn-like door to the second one on the right was open and there was the Miura. Tiffany parked and got out of the truck. Her heels clacked loudly on the sidewalk as she approached.

From the front, the car looked okay. So, headlights not

bashed in and tires not slashed. So far, if Dakota intended doing a Tiffany on the car, he was way behind. The light in the garage was on and she stepped inside. "Dakota?"

Her heels got louder on the smooth cement floor of the enclosed space. The Miura's paintwork gleamed in the glow from the overhead light. "Hello, baby." She couldn't resist giving the car a stroke. The paintwork was fine. Tiffany peered through the window. The seats were fine as well. Disappointment clenched in her gut. She must have been wrong.

"What are you doing here?" Dakota appeared so suddenly she jumped. For once, her first feeling on seeing him was delight. She'd found him.

"Looking for you." She might actually have beamed at him, she was so glad to see him.

"Why?"

"I thought you might be thinking of doing a Tiffany on the car."

Dakota blinked at her, his eyes so heavy with eyeliner it was hard to read his expression. His mouth, though, turned down at the edges. He looked young and defeated. "I couldn't." He shrugged and opened his hand to show her a small pocketknife. "I was going to mess up his car, but I got here, and I couldn't." He stared down at the car.

"She's a beauty, isn't she?" Tiffany ran her hand over the curved lines of the roof. "Believe it or not, I cried for three days after I hurt her."

"Lame."

"Yes, I know, but I did. It took me most of this time to put her back together again. I'm glad I did."

Dakota shifted around the side of the car. There wasn't a lot of room and he had to turn sideways. "So, now what?"

"Now I call your brother. We've all been looking for you."

"Please, he doesn't give a shit about me." Dakota's top lip curled. He shifted the pocketknife in his grasp.

"Yes, he does." Tiffany kept her eye on the knife. It didn't have to be big to leave a huge mark. "He came around this afternoon to tell you what a dick he's been. He would love to have you stay for the summer." Okay, Luke hadn't said that, exactly, but she was pretty sure that was what he meant.

"I'm thinking Chicago would be better than this place. And his girlfriend's a bitch."

"At least she's not a Barbie."

Dakota's lips actually twitched. Then his expression grew guarded again. "Does he know?"

Tiffany nodded and he swore beneath his breath. "We had to tell him," she said. "You can't expect us to care about you and not do anything about this."

He made a rude noise and pursed his lips.

"It's up to you," Tiffany said. "You can decide who you want to stay with. All I'm telling you is that you have options. Luke wants you. And I . . ."

He glanced up at her suddenly, alert and keen.

"I can put up with you," she said. This time, there was an actual smile at one corner of his mouth. It was nowhere near a grin, but it was a start.

Dakota sauntered around the car to where she stood. "Are we going or what?"

"We're going." Tiffany barely stopped herself from putting her arm around him as they turned for the door.

Two men blocked the exit.

Chapter Thirty

Tiffany had seen these men before, but where? Both wore jeans, one with a burgundy polo and the other a dark green T-shirt. They looked like regular guys, both dark haired and in good shape. Tiffany would never have glanced twice at either of them—except T-Shirt carried a gun. Not pointed at them—*thank you, God*—but resting in his hand, enough of a threat to dry her mouth right up.

Dakota went pale enough to faint. "Fuck."

"Do you know them?" Tiffany stared at the gun. She caught Dakota's nod out of the corner of her eye.

The penny dropped. It was the two men from Youngtown. The ones Thomas had pointed out from across the street. The men must have followed them. A quick glance at the street behind them confirmed it was empty.

"Good morning." Polo Shirt stepped forward. "How are you, Dakota?"

Dakota took a small step closer to her. "Fine."

"You look well." He grinned a flash of perfect white teeth.

That gun looked huge to her, gray and nasty.

"Who's that?" T-Shirt jerked his head in her direction.

Tiffany tried to focus on his face, but the gun kept making her look at it.

"She's nobody." Dakota got his shoulder in front of her, as if to shield her from the men.

"She's hot," said T-Shirt, his leer doing a slow, creepy inventory.

"Really, Sid?" Polo Shirt glanced at his companion. "You're making the lady uncomfortable. My apologies." More white teeth flashed in his attractive, clean-cut face.

Tiffany gave a weak nod. The gun made her way more uncomfortable than the comment, but what the hell. She was not going to argue the point.

"You are, however, rather lovely," said Polo Shirt. "My maladroit friend here is quite right about that."

"Thank you?" What the hell did *maladroit* mean? Thomas would know. Except Thomas wasn't there. It was just her and Dakota and two men with a gun. Sweat broke out over her.

Polo Shirt gave her a polite nod. His glance cut back to Dakota. "You have been difficult to track down, my young friend. Sid was becoming rather difficult to manage." He turned back to her with a shrug. "You see, Sid likes cities. Sid doesn't like the desert, although he did concede to a fondness for the mountains this morning."

"I wasn't running." Dakota's breath rasped harsh and hard.

Dakota was scared shitless. That made two of them. She took his hand. He twined his fingers with hers and pressed hard.

"No?" Polo Shirt raised his eyebrows. "Because it certainly looked that way to us." The corners of his mouth turned down in regret. "And if it looked that way to us, then it looked that way to Ronnie."

"I was coming back." Dakota stepped forward.

The gun moved an inch. Tiffany tugged back on his hand and he obeyed the silent command. She increased the pressure between their fingers, a silent warning. "He was," she said to Polo Shirt. She couldn't bring herself to look at Sid. "He was coming back with me."

"I believe you, ma'am," Polo Shirt said. "Unfortunately, our young friend here, I do not believe. I would say that you were as much a victim of his creative relationship with the truth as me and Sid."

Tiffany didn't have much she could say to that, so she snapped her mouth shut.

Sid scratched at his forearm with the blunt, ugly barrel of the gun. A large tattoo of a dragon curled around and disappeared behind his elbow.

"Ronnie wants his money, Dakota." Polo Shirt stopped with friendly. His expression went hard enough to cut diamonds.

"I'll get it to him," Dakota said, a silent plea in his voice.

Tiffany squeezed his hand. He returned the pressure.

"I don't believe you."

"It's true, Patrick, I swear it." Dakota's hand slid sweaty against hers.

Polo Shirt was called Patrick. Tiffany tucked that away. She'd read somewhere that it helped if you had a name. It was a way to make them see you as human. No, they needed your name. That was it. "I'm Tiffany," she said. Both stares swung in her direction. "Dakota is traveling with me."

"Great to meet you, Tiffany," Patrick said with a smile. "Sorry about the circumstances."

Sid ogled the car. "Is this a Miura?"

"Yes." Great, a car lover, she could use that.

He gave a long whistle of appreciation. "Sweet."

All right then, if he wanted to do a little bonding over

the car, she could manage that. "It's an SV," she said. "All the parts are original."

"Seriously?"

"Well, authentic, anyway. It met with a bit of trouble and needed some repair. But I made sure to track down the genuine replacement parts."

"I bet she's a sweet ride."

"The sweetest." Tiffany winced as her voice came out overly enthusiastic.

"I'm not much of a car man," said Patrick. "Sid is. I am more of a money man. As in, I am here to collect."

"We could take the Miura," Sid said with a hopeful gleam in his eye.

"No." Dakota stepped forward as if he would guard the car.

Up came the gun and Dakota stopped. Tiffany froze. If they wanted the car, let them take the damn car.

"Dakota is quite right," Patrick said. "A car like this would be child's play to trace. No, we'll take our money. Now."

"I don't have the money." Dakota slumped back at her side. Tiffany stepped closer to him, trying to reassure him with her presence.

Patrick heaved a sigh and shook his head. "That is regrettable, Dakota. We have a serious problem in that case. Because I am not leaving without the money."

"I'll get it." Dakota openly pleaded with him. "As soon as I get home, I can get it."

Patrick shook his head. "No deal, Dakota."

A car appeared in the road behind Patrick and Sid. Luke's battered SUV. *Thank you, Jesus*. A rescuer—or a witness. She dragged her gaze away. Perhaps if Luke could sneak up behind them? A door slammed and then another, and Patrick swung around. A gun appeared in his hand as well.

"If you would." He gestured to her with the gun. "Quickly, Tiffany. I do not wish to face your large friend without a little insurance."

"Take me." Dakota stepped forward.

Bless his heart. Dakota had balls. Damn, but she couldn't let him do it. "No." Tiffany moved quickly closer to Patrick. "It's fine."

He snagged her arm and dragged her in front of him. "I apologize for the necessity of this," he said, his voice a purr in her ear. "But your friend is rather big and looking somewhat murderous."

Thomas stepped from the car. He stopped in his tracks, his glare locked on them. Patrick was right. He did look like he could rip someone apart.

"Get Dakota." Patrick jerked his head.

Sid grabbed Dakota by the shoulder.

Tiffany flinched as Dakota got slammed into the wall. "Don't hurt him."

Sid shoved Dakota's head against the garage wall, his gun resting against his temple. Dakota's eyes went so wide they nearly swallowed his face. Shit, she had to do something. Why wouldn't her brain work?

"You didn't think you could take Ronnie's product and not pay up, did you?" Sid snarled in Dakota's ear. "You little rich punks. You always think you can take what you want and not pay."

Sweat beaded Dakota's forehead as he gabbled a denial.

Oh, fuck. The drugs he'd taken on the road, the accusation of dealing from school, even her trashed room started to make a gut-churning sort of sense. "Please?" She spoke to Patrick because she didn't like her chances of reasoning with Sid. And his gun. "He's just a boy. We'll get you your money. Just don't hurt him."

"Tiffany?" Thomas spoke, his muscles locked in a rigid line. He looked ready to spring into action.

"Don't." She shook her head at him. If he did that, somebody was getting shot for sure. "They have Dakota."

"And we have these. Don't be a hero." Patrick brought the gun up so Thomas could see it. He pressed it against the side of her neck, cold and hard.

Luke's gaze took in everything. He seemed to be mentally assessing his chances.

"What is this about?" Thomas held his hands to the side, in clear sight.

Thank God for Thomas and his calm.

Luke edged a step closer. A whimper got away from Tiffany. If stupid, numb-nuts Luke tried anything, she or Dakota would be target practice for sure. She glared at him not to come any closer, giving it everything she had.

"Dakota owes an associate of mine some money," Patrick said. His calm, polite tone scared the crap out of her. This man had no fear.

"Little fucker." Sid shoved Dakota against the wall. Dakota's head thunked on the unforgiving cement.

"How much?" Thomas asked.

"Five thousand dollars, and a little more for interest," Patrick said. "Not a huge amount, by any means, but Ronnie has the need to send a signal to Dakota and his friends. They haven't been behaving well and Ronnie has run out of patience."

"I'll get you the money," Thomas said. "Let Tiffany and the kid go and I'll get you the money. Hell, I'll even come with you and you can keep me until I get the money."

"That is a very generous offer." Patrick sounded impressed. "You are a good man, I can tell. However, our issue is not with you. The police tend to take a dim light of getting civilians involved in our dealings."

"How about children?" Thomas kept going with the same reasonable tone.

Patrick chuckled. "Children who deal drugs are given special treatment by the authorities."

"Not such a big man, are you?" Sid slammed Dakota's head again.

Sid was going to brain him if that carried on. "Please?" Tiffany whispered to Patrick. "Stop him."

"If you take another step, I will have no hesitation in shooting your brother," Patrick said. It took her a moment to realize he wasn't talking to her. Fucking Luke had edged even closer.

"I won't kill him," Patrick said. "That would be self-defeating. No, but I can make it hurt. I can also make sure he has a reminder to last him the rest of his life."

Luke stilled and raised his arms like Thomas.

"Good," Patrick said. "Step back, please."

Luke did as he was told. His gaze drifted to Dakota. God, she hoped good sense won, because one of them could end up dead otherwise. She clenched her fists by her side.

Thomas stared at her, sending reassurance with his look.

Tiffany appreciated the effort. Sweat dripped down her sides. Her nails bit into her palms. Her gaze drifted over to her purse. She must have dropped it when Patrick grabbed her. Her purse. She almost laughed out loud. "I have your money." All heads swung in her direction. "At least, most of it."

"Tiffany." Thomas's voice held a heavy warning.

"No." She shook her head at him. Over her shoulder she kept her words directed at Patrick. "I have a little under four thousand dollars in my purse, right now. You could take it and leave."

"That would leave me a whole thousand short," Patrick said, but he sounded a little intrigued. "Minus the interest, of course."

"It would leave you one thousand and twenty-five dollars short," she said. "That's seventy-nine percent of your five thousand."

"You forget, Tiffany, that I have you and Dakota, and that guarantees me one hundred percent of my total."

Numbers. It all came down to numbers. Her brain slowed from panic mode and started to cypher. "I have some other numbers for you. Did you know the average crime rate in the US last year was two hundred and fourteen point zero one per hundred thousand people?"

Silence greeted her. Patrick went still at her back. "No, I did not."

"There are no figures yet for this year, or I would have them," she said.

"You have crime rates in your head?" Patrick grunted.

All of them, including Dakota, looked at her as if she's just lost the plot. "No," she said to Patrick. "I have a head full of all sorts of numbers, because I like numbers and I'm always looking up statistics."

"Jesus." Sid shoved Dakota and made him wince. "Let's get the fuck out of here."

"You could do that." Tiffany leaped in before Patrick could answer. "But before you do, you should know that Chicago has a crime rate of almost six hundred crimes per hundred thousand people, and Canyons is below two hundred. Compare that to national average of around three hundred."

Luke shook his head, as if to clear it.

Thomas gave her a tiny nod. He got it.

She rushed on before she could get scared and back out. "Combine that with the fact that the FBI reports a five point four percent decrease in violent crime for the first quarter of this year . . . Okay, those statistics are preliminary, but I think you get the picture."

"I don't," Sid said. "I haven't a clue what the fuck she's talking about."

"She's telling you that you screw with her and you're fucked," said Thomas.

"I don't think so," Patrick responded with a smile in his voice. "I hate to sound obvious, but I have the gun."

"And the police force of two cities on your ass if you use it. One with very little else to do but hunt you down, and the other with the manpower and knowledge to help them do it well." Thomas slammed the point home.

"That's bullshit." Sid loosened his grip on Dakota slightly.

"I'm with Sid," Patrick said. "None of this adds up." He laughed softly at his own joke.

"You clearly know Dakota." She stared at Thomas. He sent her silent encouragement. "You trashed my motel room, so you also know, if not who I am, what I am."

"A princess?" Luke looked confused, but still trying to play along.

"Exactly." Tiffany swallowed as the pressure from Patrick's gun increased. "A rich, spoiled, pampered, and adored princess whose daddy will rip this country upside down and inside out if anything happens to her. A daddy with the kind of clout to make me a number one priority of not just those two police forces but the FBI as well."

"Yeah." Sid broke the silence. "But we've still got the fucking guns."

"And if you use them, you'll make a mess for yourselves that there will be no getting out of," Thomas said.

"It would mean murder. Quadruple murder—three of us and a princess."

"Murder is such an ugly word," murmured Luke.

Patrick moved the gun and jammed it into her ribs so hard Tiffany whimpered.

Thomas lurched forward.

"Don't." Patrick's voice got ugly.

Thomas bunched his hands into fists. "How many of those violent crimes were murders?"

"Five hundred in Chicago," she said. "One in Canyons."

"Really?" Thomas nodded as if they were discussing the weather.

"We don't need to kill anyone," Patrick said, but the confidence in his tone faltered. "We will take Dakota with us, and that will give us enough insurance for your numbers to be meaningless."

"Kidnappings?" Thomas asked her.

"Hard to say," she answered immediately. "The FBI deals with those, but they say it's on the rise."

Sid sneered. "You see, you don't know everything."

Thomas nodded his head slowly. "Who was it in the FBI that your daddy knows?"

"James Comey," Tiffany said. "Some people call him the director. I call him Uncle Jimmy. Kidnapping is a serious federal offense and a felony, and on average prison sentences are around twenty years, depending on prior convictions and case specifics."

Sid glanced from her to Thomas and back to Patrick. "What the fuck are they talking about?"

"So, here's the deal." Tiffany got in quick before they could sort out the bullshit from the facts. "I give you the money in my purse and forget I even saw you. That puts the odds in your favor."

"Don't listen to her." Sid shoved the gun at Dakota's

head. "As soon as our backs are turned, the bitch will go to the police."

"I have another two hundred with me," Thomas said.

"That takes you to eighty three point five percent," she said.

"Hey." Luke finally got with the program. "I can add another four to that."

"Ninety one and a half percent," she said to Patrick. "With the odds in your favor of getting away free and clear."

"I just want Ronnie's five thousand dollars." Sid looked a little sick.

"There is a risk factor that we will call the police immediately." Tiffany rushed in again. "But consider that the average police response time to a nine-one-one call is ten minutes, with a best of four minutes and a worst of one hour. The average interaction time with a criminal being just ninety seconds. It means we have to wait another two and a half minutes for the police to arrive."

"What the fuck is she saying?" Sid got a bit whiny.

"She's saying we've got twelve minutes to get away." Patrick's grip on her tightened painfully.

"And I'm going to sweeten the deal and give you all of our cell phones," Tiffany said. "That should give you a little longer, given that the nearest house is a little way down the road and, being the middle of the day, there might be nobody at home." She held out her phone, and Patrick snatched it and hurled it against the wall. It shattered on impact, making them all jump.

The silence stretched out until it made her want to scream.

"Give me the fucking money," Patrick said.

"It's over there." Tiffany motioned her purse.

Patrick prodded her toward the purse.

"Get their money," he said to Sid. "Break their phones, make sure you get the kid's at the same time."

"I have sixty." Dakota hauled the twenties out of his pocket.

Sid snatched them. He made Dakota collect the money from Luke and Thomas and then returned to Patrick's side.

Tiffany used the time to pull out her cash and count. "I have a little more than three thousand nine hundred and seventy-five," she said. "With Dakota's sixty and my extra forty-five, you now have four thousand six hundred and eighty, that's ninety-three point six percent, and over twelve minutes to disappear. If you lock us in, you stretch that window."

Luke made a noise of protest, his eyes huge in his face.

Thomas looked at her calmly. He trusted her, and Tiffany's confidence grew.

"I like how you think," Patrick said. "Get in here." He motioned to Luke and Thomas. "Over there by the wall." The two men shuffled into place. He gave her a shove with his gun. "Now you, Princess."

Tiffany had trouble walking on her rubber legs. She reached the wall and sagged against it. Dakota's hand found hers and squeezed. She returned the pressure.

"Nice going," Luke whispered. "Lock us in?"

"Shut up," Thomas muttered back.

Sid moved to stand by Patrick. Both of them kept their guns trained on the group.

"I hate fucking rich people," Sid said.

Luke muttered beneath his breath and Tiffany gave him a hard pinch. He jumped a little, but shut up.

The two men backed away from them, guns still raised.

"I will return if Ronnie is not satisfied," Patrick said.

"Make sure he is," Thomas said. "Because this is a one-off deal. Next time I see you, I'm calling the police."

Patrick looked wounded and shook his head. "So unpleasant."

Nobody moved as Patrick and Sid slid the garage door closed. The lock clanked into place and the garage closed hot and dark around them. Car doors opened and closed outside. An engine coughed into life. Tires squealed in protest as Sid and Patrick wasted no time in taking advantage of their twelve minutes.

Luke broke the silence. "Now what?"

"Now we open the door." Tiffany's throat closed and her voice came out in a hoarse whisper.

"We're locked in." Luke slammed his fist against the wall.

"But I have the key." Her hand shook so badly she almost dropped it as she handed it over. "And that lock opens from both sides."

"Babe?" Thomas's voice broke her trance.

Tiffany turned, pushed past Luke, and walked straight into his arms. Only when she had her cheek against the solid bulk of Thomas's chest did she relax. She sucked in a lungful of that unique Thomas scent. Her arms locked around his waist and she let him support her weight.

"You okay, baby?"

"No."

"You will be." He tightened his hold on her.

Tiffany nodded. She would be. If he held her for another few minutes, she would be fine.

His lips pressed the top of her head. "A fucking genius."

Chapter Thirty-One

Tiffany stumbled through the next couple of hours in a haze of Luke, Dakota, the police, and even Luke's angry girlfriend. Tiffany still hadn't caught her name, and right now, she didn't give a shit.

Thomas stayed glued to her side the entire time. His hand—on her back, around her shoulders, or just holding hers—anchored her as the world dipped and swirled around her. It was late into the night when she and Thomas finally climbed into his truck. Dakota and Luke followed them back to the motel to pick up Dakota's stuff.

"Fuck," Thomas said as they started driving.

Tiffany nodded. *Fuck indeed.*

The motel looked strangely normal as they drew up and parked. The rest of the world had a perfectly normal day, while she got held up at gunpoint.

"Get your stuff," Luke said to his brother. They would spend a couple of days in Utah, let Luke get himself organized, and then go to Chicago together.

Dakota went straight to his room.

She and Thomas stood clustered with Luke around his car. There must be something to say, after what they'd been through, but Tiffany had nothing.

"The drug thing." Luke cleared his throat. "I'll take care of it."

"Good," Thomas said. "Because next time, Tiffany won't be here to save your asses."

"There won't be a next time." Luke stiffened and shut up for a moment—not nearly long enough—then turned to her. "How long have you been like a walking calculator?"

She shrugged. "Pretty much always, but you know my father."

"Yeah." Luke snorted. "He still writing those books?"

"No." Tiffany folded her arms. She'd almost forgotten about the books.

"What books?" Thomas glanced at her.

Luke gave a short bark of laughter and shook his head. "Do yourself a favor, read one some time. I think it will explain a lot."

"Books?" Thomas turned to her.

She wanted to duck the question, but Thomas didn't judge and they were way past the point of her giving a shit. "When I was little, my dad wrote a series of books. Sort of princess type things. He had a publisher friend and they were out there for a while."

"Books about you?"

"Sort of." Why had Luke brought up those awful books? "They were called *The Pretty Princess Pearly Perfect.*"

Luke shook his head. "Read one."

Dakota reappeared with his backpack in hand, Beats dangling around his neck. He slouched over to Luke. "Take care." Dakota jerked his chin at her. "That thing you did, way cool."

Tiffany's eyes pricked with tears. Coming from Dakota, it was the equivalent of a heartfelt hug and a bunch of roses. "Pay me back by not making me do it again."

"You got it." A shy grin tilted his mouth up. He looked exactly like Luke when he smiled. "So long . . . Barbie."

"Bye, Tiff." Luke bent and kissed her on the cheek.

She folded her arms around him. It hadn't been all bad. And it was over now.

"When are you going to stop being Daddy's Princess?" Luke said against her ear.

Good question. She pulled out of Luke's arms. "Take care of Dakota."

"Sure." He followed his brother to his SUV and climbed inside.

"So long, big guy," Dakota called to Thomas.

Thomas wrapped his arms around her from behind. Tiffany leaned into his weight and let the sheer awfulness of the day melt away. Her senses reacted to his nearness. Not a flash-fire reaction like before, but a slow burn of need that made her press into him.

His breathing hitched in her ear, and his erection hardened against her bottom.

They stood there as the red taillights of Luke's SUV vanished down the road.

"Come." He took her hand and led her into her room.

They touched each other with hands and mouths. Reverently and slowly he loved her, and Tiffany let herself flow with it. It wasn't just about passion, but something deeper, an affirmation that they were together, and a celebration of life.

When they were done, Thomas tucked her into his front, his heavy arm over her waist.

Tiffany snuggled into his warmth and fell asleep. The last thing she remembered was feeling perfectly at peace.

They woke up late, made love again, and got ready for their day. By tacit agreement they didn't talk about time running out, or going back to Chicago. First stop was breakfast. Tiffany went straight for the pancakes. Thomas lifted an eyebrow, but that was it. She ate the entire thing and then had to loosen the top button of her shorts and pull her top over it.

Next, the mall and new phones. Tiffany's phone lit up with missed calls: Ryan, about ten, and her father, a few more. She carefully and thoroughly deleted every one. They could wait until she was ready to deal with them.

Thomas didn't bring up leaving, and Tiffany drifted along in their stolen moment of pretend. For once, they had nothing better to do than hang out, and she sucked up each moment and tucked it away. They went to a movie—the latest geek show, Thomas assured her it would be great—had a late lunch, and drove back to the motel.

"We should talk," Thomas said.

The bubble in Tiffany's belly burst. They couldn't not talk about this much longer, no matter how much she wished it so. "Yeah, we should."

"We can't stay in Utah forever." Thomas sounded wistful. "So, now what?"

"We go home." The words hurt coming out. Tears stung and she blinked them away. Home. Such an alien word, meaning an empty condo and a job she hated.

"You could come with me." Thomas broke into her thoughts.

"To Willow Park?"

"Wherever." He shrugged. "I want to be with you, babe. I don't give a crap where that is."

"And when you go back to Africa, or wherever else you go? What then?"

Pushing his fingers through his hair, he stared at the ground. "I don't know. I don't have all the answers. This thing between us, it happened so fast. I'm not even sure where we go from here. I just know that wherever I go, I don't want it to be without you."

Until he said those words, she had no idea how much she wanted to hear them. And oh, God, she did want that. To go with Thomas. He made it sound so simple. Could it be that simple?

"Babe, I'm not leaving for another couple of weeks. Once I get the results back to my partners, I'm taking some time off. Being with my family. We could spend that time together, see where this thing leads."

"I want to be with you, too." But Ryan was back home, and Daddy. She didn't know what she wanted to do about Ryan, but he did deserve an explanation. "I just don't know . . ."

Thomas pulled into the motel parking lot beside an imported sedan.

"Fuck!" She wasn't ready. Not like this.

Thomas glanced at her. "What?"

"Daddy."

A silver-haired man waited inside the sedan. He caught sight of her and his face split into a beautiful smile. When she'd been a little girl, she'd thought her daddy was a movie star.

"What?" Thomas peered at her father.

She was too much of a coward to look at Thomas. "That's my father."

Carter Desjardins unfolded his tall, lean form from the sedan and raised his hand in greeting. Tiffany waved back.

"What's he doing here?"

"Looking for me." Reality pressed against her chest, and Tiffany barely got the words out. She opened the truck and slid to the ground like there were lead weights attached to her ankles.

Her father held out his arms to her. "Princess."

"Daddy." Tiffany did as he knew she would and walked straight into his embrace. The familiar smell of her father surrounded her, leather, fine wool, and spicy aftershave. The smell of comfort, only . . . not so much anymore.

Daddy pressed his lips to the top of her head. Putting her at arm's length, he studied her.

Tiffany was suddenly conscious of her cheap jeans and the hair she hadn't styled that morning, of her face bare of makeup.

"Princess, I know everything." Her father had a voice like a movie star, too. Rich and smooth, "Trust me," it said, "trust me to make the bad thing go away."

"You do?" This had been the thing that sent her running in the first place. Her greatest fear came true, right here and right now and—nothing. No guilt, no fear, just nothing.

"Yes." He nodded, his hair gray catching the light. "And you are a very silly girl to think you had to lie about your divorce. If you'd come to me, I would have had it all fixed by now."

Tiffany blinked up at her father. He wore his disappointed face. The familiar knot tightened low in her belly. She hated that face. "I know, Daddy, but I was ashamed that I hadn't done anything about it. I wanted to sort this out on my own."

"Princess, why would you do a thing like that? That's my job." He smiled and tugged her back into his arms. "Anyway, I'm here now and everything is going to be all right."

She wanted to tell him that she would get it done herself. She thought she might explain about Luke and her trouble with letting go. Tiffany opened her mouth and shut it again. Daddy wouldn't understand about Luke. He didn't hang on to past regrets. Onward and upward, that was how her father rolled.

"I'm Thomas Hunter."

And Thomas? How could she explain about Thomas when she didn't even have the answers for herself?

Her father stiffened, and she stepped out of his embrace.

Daddy looked at Thomas with a speculative gleam, the questions building and building in his gaze.

"Thomas helped me find Luke," she said. "He was also looking for Luke, so we decided to team up. Thomas has been with me the whole time." And so much, much more. Somehow Thomas had become . . .

"Carter Desjardins." Her father's expression softened marginally, and he took the hand Thomas offered. "You're a brave man to take on the role of protector to my Princess. She has an unerring ability to get herself into trouble if you don't watch her."

Thomas glanced from her father to her. "Actually, I find she takes care of herself, and sometimes me while she's at it."

Her father stilled. "Do you?" His voice went silky. Holy shit, she knew that voice, and Tiffany stiffened. "How long have you known Tiffany, exactly?"

That found its mark, and Thomas's face tightened.

Her father took his silence as agreement and nodded. Point made. He turned back to her. "It would be best if we could get Luke to Chicago for the divorce."

Wow, her father really did know everything. "I know, he's already agreed to do it."

"Then you're done here," Daddy said. "And I can take my Princess home."

Thomas watched her like a hawk, catching every nuance, assessing every word. Daddy's words sank in. He had come to take her home. That meant her time with Thomas was over. She swung her head to look at him. The question lurked in his beautiful blue eyes. Everything.

He silently asked her for everything. His look searched and seared inside her mind. She dropped her head quickly. God, the wanting to be the woman Thomas saw clawed inside her chest.

"All right." Her father broke into the moment. "Let's get going." He held out his hand to Thomas. "Thank you, Mr. Hunter, I am most grateful for the good care you took of my Princess." Daddy turned to her, brow raised in a silent question. Only it wasn't a question at all. "Go and pack your bits and pieces, Princess. Call me and I'll carry your bags."

And here it was, go with Daddy or stay with Thomas. To go ahead with her engagement or not? These were not the sort of decisions you made standing in a parking lot. A parking lot she stood in because she'd just extricated herself from her last impulsive decision.

"I'll do it," Thomas said.

"Great." Her father beamed at him, sure in the knowledge she would do as he asked. "I'll wait in the car, Princess."

She nodded obediently. "Okay."

She opened the door to her room. It wouldn't take long to pack her things. Replacement makeup lay scattered on the vanity top. None of it she'd ever use again. She swept it all into the garbage. It lay in the bottom of the bin like downed pins. She liked that lip gloss. That she would use again. Tiffany reached into the bin and pulled it out. And the mascara wasn't all that bad. Next, she examined the clothes she had left. So much had happened since that day Thomas walked into the studio.

The door opened and she half turned. Thomas blocked out the light as he stepped through and closed the door behind him. Tiffany busied herself folding her clothes.

Silently, he folded the clothes on the bed.

"You don't have to do that." Her voice came out in a breathy whisper.

He shrugged. "I know." He stood right beside her folding her jeans, but he could've been a thousand miles away. His face gave her nothing.

"It's been fun." What a lame thing to say. Fun. God, it had been so much more than that.

"Fun?" He sneered the word as if it were dirty.

"I didn't mean it like that. I just said it because I couldn't think of anything else to say."

He gave her a hard look. He shoved the jeans into the plastic bag so hard his fist came out the other side. "Fun it is, then."

"What do you want from me?"

"More than 'thanks, it was fun.'"

"I told you, I didn't mean it."

"I don't care about that." He came as close to yelling as she'd ever heard him.

She couldn't breathe, and dropped on the edge of the bed. "What, then?"

"I want to hear you say that this was just sex for you. That you are happy to walk away and go back to Ryan and Daddy and that asshole you work for."

Tiffany blinked at him. His words brought up a flood of feelings. Outside, her father waited. Waited to take her back to her life. And in this room with her, Thomas. "I need to go home," she said. "He needs me to go home." She made a jerky motion with her arm to the car outside. It was getting hard to breathe and the room swam in front of her. "I can't drop everything, everyone, and disappear with you. As much as I might want to."

He didn't speak for so long she risked a look at him. He seemed to be tossing something over in his mind. "Look," he said. "We haven't known each other that long."

"A week," she said. "Just a little more than that."

"Right." He blew out a long breath. "That's not long at all, but I want you to think about something for me. Can you do that?" Like she would be doing anything but thinking. She nodded. "This thing between us." He motioned her and him. "I think we both know it's more than sex. I think it could be a lot more. If you gave it a chance."

"But you're not sure." Tiffany's heart pounded in her ears. "You can't say for sure, can you?" And she needed sure, needed to know this wouldn't turn out to be another Luke. And that meant time away from Thomas. Time to find out who Tiffany was.

"Nothing is for sure," he said. "But what we have feels good. More than good. It feels right. Not just the sex, but all of it. You could give us a chance."

"My father needs me. I can't leave him like this." Splinters of glass pressed against her lungs, tearing into her. "He's always needed me. My mom died and—"

"Nobody's asking you to leave your father. But I am asking you to think about what you want. What do you need, babe? Not your father and certainly not that pompous prick you were almost engaged to. Not even me, but you, Tiffany. What do you want?"

Him, she needed him, but she couldn't get the words out of her mouth. It wouldn't be fair to him, because more than that, she needed her. All the disparate parts of her fighting it out for space were exhausting. Somewhere between Wild Tiffany, Daddy's Tiffany, and the woman Thomas saw was the real Tiffany.

His stare bored into her, stripping her right down to basics, and she couldn't lie. "I need some time," she said. "I need some time to sort this out in my head."

He dropped his head forward, shielding his face from her. "Fuck."

"Please, Thomas." What was she asking for exactly here? Don't give up on me? Don't walk away? More time? All of that and more. "I know this is not just sex. I know things are great between us, but this has all happened so fast. Go back to your family. They're waiting for you. Let me have some time."

"Okay." His stormy glare tore right through her. His jaw worked as he clenched it together. "Take your time, but do me a favor. While you're thinking about us, and what we have, think about yourself and what you want. Find out what you want to do about that incredible brain of yours. Think about what makes you happy, babe. And don't get married before you know. Can you do that for me?"

"Yes."

Chapter Thirty-Two

Thomas sat in his truck as the Mercedes taillights disappeared around the corner. Even now, he kept hoping the brake lights would suddenly light up, the door would open, and she would come back. Fuck, what a stupid shit. She was a Gold Coast princess and her daddy, the king, had swept in to take her back to their palace.

It had been pitifully easy to forget, lulled by funny, sweet, and so sexy it made his gut clench Tiffany. It all happened so fast. It didn't make any sense. How could he be sitting there wanting to cry like a baby over a woman he barely knew?

But he did know her, his gut argued. He knew the things about her that mattered. He understood her in a way that her dickhead of an almost fiancé never would. Or her father.

Carter Desjardins had waited only long enough for Tiffany to finish packing, and reluctantly agreed to a last meal before he hustled Tiffany into his car. Luke had arrived with the survey results, and in time to get into a joint sneer-off with Tiffany's father.

Thomas thumbed through the small picture book on his lap. Luke had found an old copy and given it to him. The thing made his hair stand on end. He pictured Tiffany sitting beside him on the way back from the Grand Canyon, the utter hopelessness on her face. Princess Pearly Perfect choked her like a toxic skin her father kept shoving on her. Inside it, Tiffany shriveled and died. But not with him. She had come out of her princess shell, so fast his head had spun.

She made him feel things he'd never been aware of. For the first time ever, he wanted to be there for someone. Not drift in and out of their life. Watch them grow, watch them live their potential. Know that this incredible woman felt the same way about him. He wanted to share their lives together. None of this made any fucking sense. He scraped his fingers across his scalp.

She needed time and he'd agreed to give it to her. What the fuck had he done that for?

Time to go home, but he made no attempt to get the truck started. Beside him on the passenger seat nestled the reason he'd come here. Luke had finally handed over the survey results. One tiny little thumb drive that had so much power over his life. He'd tracked Tiffany down to find Luke. All he'd wanted was this little piece of hardware and to get on with building his company. There'd been no thought in his head other than sort this out, spend some time in Willow Park and then jump on the next plane back to Africa. Then he'd walked into that studio. She'd flipped her mane of dark hair and turned those eyes on him, and it was like *what survey*?

The road trip had settled her deep into his being. He didn't want to be free-as-a-bird, I'm-outta-here Thomas anymore. He had the chance here for something special, someone special. The sort of girl a man showed up for and stayed.

The smell of her perfume lingered in his truck, making

him want to bury his face in the scent and pull it deep inside him. His partners were thrilled. He'd texted them the good news as soon as Luke had handed it over. He'd already uploaded the survey results and emailed them to Lusaka. They still had a good chance of getting those mineral rights they were after. Everything sorted. He still wanted to fucking bawl.

He picked up his iPhone and thumbed through the contacts. Where the fuck was Yoda when you needed him? A name caught his eye and he hit Dial. Not Yoda, but the next best thing.

"Thomas?" said a sleepy voice. "How the hell are you? You coming home soon?"

"Yes." Maybe this was a stupid idea.

"So, what's up?" his brother asked.

He dragged in a breath. Josh was cool. His older brother, Richard, was all ruthless logic and linear thinking. Josh, on the other hand, got most shit and didn't judge the shit he didn't.

"How's Holly?" He played for time.

"She's good, man." Thomas could hear the smile in Josh's voice. "She still won't marry me, but I'll get her in the end."

Thomas chuckled. He had no doubt Holly would be wearing white and marching down the aisle in the near future. The thought of Holly gave him the kick in the ass he needed. "Can I ask you something?"

"Is this like the time you asked me if oral sex was talking dirty?"

A smile creaked across his face. Josh would never let him live that one down. Josh had teased. Richard had gotten a book out and explained in relentless detail. So much more detail than a twelve-year-old kid ever wanted. Which was why he hadn't called Richard on this one.

"Kind of." He laughed. "How did you know, Josh? About Holly, I mean. How did you know?"

Josh went silent for a minute. "You've met someone?"

"Could you answer the fucking question?"

"I knew when I was a kid, but I was just too stupid to realize it," Josh said. Well, that was about as helpful as a mustard enema. "But this time, when Holly came back into my life . . ." Josh sighed. "This is going to sound totally lame, but I knew within seconds."

"Just like that?"

"What more do you want?"

Some of the load lifted off Thomas's chest. "What if it makes no sense?"

"Are you kidding me?" Josh laughed. "Have you met Holly? And her sisters? How much sense did that make?"

"Right." Josh had a point. Thomas liked Holly a lot, but he was relieved she wasn't his bundle of feistiness to deal with. Her sisters plain creeped him out. Except Grace, she was okay, but the twins? Thomas's nape prickled just thinking about the Partridge twins.

"Who is she?" Josh asked.

"Someone I just met." A cleaning lady pushed a cart down the corridor, stopping in front of Tiffany's room to use the skeleton key. "She's totally wrong for me."

"Why?"

"She's all like girly and *Legally Blonde* and I'm—" He shrugged. "I'm me."

"Is she hot?"

"Smoking."

The cleaner got the door open and disappeared inside. In the room cleaning away any traces of Tiffany.

"Does she make you smile?"

"All the time. Except for now, because I watched her drive out of my life with her father."

A muted voice came from Josh's end. It made him smile despite the ache in his gut. Holly. Demanding to know the whos, whys, and whats of the call. Josh replied with something smooth that shut her up. Damn, but his brother had a way with women. What a pity it didn't run in the genes.

"What about your job? The traveling?" Josh came back on the line.

"It's geography." As he said it, he got how true that was. "I can work anywhere I want to. Once my company is established, I could even stay in Willow Park and run that end of the business."

"Would that make you happy?"

"It would if it meant I could have her." And they could travel. He'd like to take Tiffany and see all the places he'd been through her eyes. God, he'd give his soul to see the pink glow of an African sunrise kiss Tiffany awake.

"You know what I think?" Josh took a breath. "I think you're talking to the wrong person."

"What if she says no?" What sort of chickenshit lightweight even asked that question? It was like being thirteen again and asking Tyler Lewis to ask his sister if her friend, Sydney, would say yes if he asked her to Homecoming. Fucking pitiful, and Thomas braced for all-out scorn.

Josh must be mellowing because he said, "Would that be worse than never knowing if she might have said yes?"

Fuck it. He should have known Josh would say something like that. God, he hated it when his brothers were right. "Don't tell Mom."

"Of course I'm telling Mom," Josh said. "She lives for this shit. Then I'm going to tell Lucy, who will tell Richard. So if you wuss out, you're going to have a whole hell of a lot of explaining to do."

"I never wuss out. One word, brother: Ironman."

"Right," Josh said with a little edge behind it. It still bit both his brothers on the ass that he'd killed their times. "But be sure, man. Be sure this girl is for you."

"I'm sure."

"So why are you sitting there instead of going after her?"

The sigh came right up from his boots and made static over the line. "I agreed to give her time."

"Then give her time," Josh said. "Come home, kiss the babies, and give your lady time. You know that thing about if you love something, set it free."

"Really? You're going to talk to me like a Hallmark card?"

Josh chuckled. "I was going to say, if it comes back to you, great. If it doesn't, hunt it down and drag it back."

Daddy drove her straight to a private airfield. Of course he had a friend who had a plane, and they were soon in the air. Tiffany looked out the window to see the Wasatch Range disappear beneath her. She was going home. She had done what she set out to do and she should be feeling relieved. She wasn't feeling anything.

"Princess?" Her father watched her. "Is everything okay?"

"Sure, why?"

"You look sad."

Sad? As good a word as any for the dead feeling in the middle of her chest. Sad was such a tiny word it didn't even begin to cover the ache. Love. Another of those small words that carried a massive punch. She looked at her father. How could a man with such a discerning brain only see what he wanted to see? "I don't want to marry Ryan."

He sat back in his seat abruptly. A slight frown marred his brow as he stared. "You don't want to marry Ryan?"

"No."

"Can I ask why not?"

Excellent question. How to make sense of what whirred through her mind? The real answer was one she wasn't ready to give. "I don't love him."

"Okay," he said on a deep breath. "I thought you did. I thought you and Ryan were perfect together."

Tiffany gave a small little laugh, but nothing about this felt funny. They were perfect. She and Ryan would make the perfect couple. If she were still Perfect Tiffany. She must be all kinds of nuts with the amount of people she had shuffling for space inside her: Wild Tiffany, Daddy's Tiffany, Delilah, Princess Pearly Perfect. Which one was she really? Somewhere between Chicago and Canyons she'd started to find out. She'd wanted to marry Ryan because he was the total opposite of Luke. Ryan was sensible, considerate, deliberate, and reliable. On the other hand, you had Luke—all fire, passion, and snarling emotion. Two totally different men offering two entirely different futures, and a different Tiffany for each of them. Then you had Thomas, all of the above and a bit extra. The best of Luke and the best of Ryan, rolled into one gorgeous package. And the only man to see all of Tiffany and come back asking for more.

"Why don't we get you home," her father said. "Then you can think about all of this."

"No," she said. Her father looked taken aback. She didn't blame him. She'd surprised the hell out of herself with that one. "I don't need to think about this."

"No? You are suddenly sure you don't want to marry the man who, less than a week ago, you were sure you did want to marry."

"I'm sure."

"Don't be ridiculous." He adjusted the perfect crease in

his trouser leg. "A week ago, you were upset because Ryan didn't propose. Now you're determined that he won't do. I am not going to say anything to Ryan until you have given it some thought. And neither are you. You will look like a complete airhead."

Ouch—first blood to her father. She would look like an airhead, and a feckless one. She'd found that word in one of the books Thomas had bought for her. Feckless. It was a good word. "I am an airhead, Dad," she said. "I drift along and let other people do my thinking for me. I don't want to be that way anymore."

"Princess." He shook his head and looked pained.

He didn't come right out and say it wasn't true, though. "It's true, Daddy. Marrying Ryan would be a mistake."

"And who is going to tell Ryan this?" He pursed his lips. "Ryan and I are in business together, this will complicate matters."

"I'll tell him," she said. "I will simply tell him the truth and see what happens. He'll be mad and he has every right to be, but that isn't a good enough reason to lie to him."

"Oh, for God's sake." Her father groaned. "Listen to that crap you're spouting. If you want to demonstrate how mature you are, pick another time. This is not the time to make your play for independence."

"When, then?" A big part of her wanted to buckle under her father's displeasure and let him take control. It was so tempting to have him make this all go away. But she had this nagging sense that even if she let him, this wasn't going away. There would be another time and another, until she stopped it.

"I don't know when, but I do know the right time will come." Daddy so nearly echoed her thoughts, she almost laughed. Her father looked angrier than he had in years and she swallowed her nervous giggle.

"Then," she said, slowly and carefully as it crystallized in her mind, "I will step up that time as well. I need to make decisions that work for me."

His expression softened a little. "Princess, I see what you're trying to do, and I applaud it, but trust me on this. Okay?" It would be so easy to open her mouth and say "okay." Habit had the words on her tongue, but her lips refused to form them.

"No, Daddy." Her throat felt so tight it was a miracle the words came out.

"This is ridiculous." His expression grew hard again. "Is that idiot you married behind this? Has he been saying things to you again? Telling you stuff and turning your head?"

"This has nothing to do with Luke."

"Then it has to be that other one, the big guy. I am an excellent judge of character, and there is something about that one that got up my nose."

"Thomas." Just saying his name made the ache throb. "His name is Thomas and he's a really good man."

Her father's eyes narrowed. Tiffany wished she'd kept her mouth shut. She could see the wheels grinding in his mind. "Are you involved with him?"

"No." *Throb*, went her chest. *Throb, throb, throb*.

Her father looked doubtful. "Listen to me, Princess, and listen well. Men like Ryan don't grow on trees. If you let this one go, there isn't another one like him waiting in the wings. You screw this up with Ryan and you will regret it for the rest of your life."

"Yes." Tiffany understood that only too well. She swallowed hard and looked down at her hand. The hand without the ring she'd wanted so badly. Tears blurred her vision and she tried to blink them away before he saw them.

"Men like your Thomas, on the other hand, are a dime a dozen. You can pick them up at any football stadium or bar."

It wasn't true. Oh, God, she couldn't seem to stop the tears. The harder she blinked, the faster they came. There was only one Thomas with that smile that could light up the darkest parts of her. The way he touched her so reverently, the way he never looked at her as if she was an airhead. The way he saw *her*. The ache sharpened into hard edges. Her breath caught on one of the jagged corners and snagged.

"Princess?" Her father leaned forward in his chair. "Oh, sweetheart, don't cry." He put one finger under her chin and lifted her face to his. "Don't worry about a thing. That man is behind you now." He didn't mean it to wound, but that hurt so badly her breath stopped altogether. "Ryan will never find out because you and I will forget this and everything that happened." He squeezed her hands. "Come on, Princess."

The tears poured down her cheeks. She freed one hand and swiped at them.

Her father tugged her forward and held her. For the first time, Tiffany didn't want to be there. The smell of him caught in her throat. The feel of his arms about her were like restraints. She sucked in a large breath and tried to get the crying under control. Gently, she wriggled out of her father's embrace.

"There, now," he said. "Why don't you have a little sleep? You can't have gotten much rest in that awful motel. You have a little sleep and before you know it, we'll be home."

"Okay." She sat back in her chair. She could speak about

this all the way back to Chicago and he still wouldn't hear her. "Daddy?"

"Yes, Princess?"

"I thought I might get my high school diploma."

"What?" He looked thunderstruck. "You have one."

"No," she said. "I mean, like, get a real one. I thought I might try to get into a college."

Her father's mouth dropped open and he looked totally floored. Then he cocked his head and the sides of his mouth turned up. "This is a joke, right? You're joking?"

"No, I—"

"You don't need to go to college, Princess. You do fine with what you have."

"That's not the point. I want to get it."

His mouth tightened as he looked at her. "For God's sake, you've been gone one week and now you want to turn your whole life inside out."

"It's important to me." She held on to his hard gaze with everything she had. "I'm going to get my high school diploma."

He threw himself back in his chair. "You don't need to get your high school diploma," he said. "You have one already."

"I mean a proper one."

"I know what you mean, I am not stupid." Her father fiddled with his trouser crease. When he looked up again, his eyes were hard as gemstones. "And. You. Have. One."

Maybe he really didn't get what she meant, because it sounded like—"What?"

He growled at her impatiently. "I had it all organized. You would have passed anyway because I would have made it so. I didn't need to in the end. You passed on your own, Tiffany."

Chapter Thirty-Three

Tiffany glared at the girl in the mirror in the exquisite dress. A masterpiece of draped chiffon over silk, drifting fairy-like from a sequined collar. Nope, the trouble didn't lie with the dress. Or the beautiful crystal-studded heeled sandals. The problem was inside all of that. She looked like a modern-day princess, and it bothered the crap out of her.

She'd filed her college application a week ago. The first thing she'd done all on her own. It gave her a unique sense of achievement. A feeling she hugged close to her. She didn't share it with Ryan, or even Daddy. Somehow, she sensed this was not what they wanted for her.

Ryan took the news she wasn't going to marry him in rather typical fashion. He'd gone very quiet, a small frown puckering his brow, and then he'd started talking. He started by telling her to think about it. Why did all the men in her life assume if she thought about it, she'd see it their way?

And then Ryan had talked some more. All about how it was so typical of her and he didn't really blame her, he blamed her upbringing. Then he went on about how the mark of a person's worth was in how they overcome the hardships life offered them. And all the time he

spoke, she'd obediently nodded and wondered how Ryan
came by this information.

Sitting in front of her in his custom suit and handmade
shoes, spilling about hardship and suffering and strength
of character, she got the earthy waft of bullshit. It had
been so unexpected, she'd been struck dumb. Ryan took
her silence for acquiescence and warmed to his theme. All
through their four-hundred-dollar bottle of wine, he'd kept
telling her how much he'd had to overcome to be the man
he was today.

She'd thought about what sort of man he really was.
Ryan grew up in the same neighborhood as her. He'd gone
to the same schools and enjoyed the same advantages.
Hell, his mother hadn't even handed him over to "the help"
to raise. She'd done the playgroups, been right there for
toddler gym and Clamber Time. This did not make him
an ass. He'd just been born with a silver spoon in his
mouth. No, what made him an ass was the way he believed
his own press. He took unashamed credit for things that
had been handed to him. What made him a jerk was the
way he looked down on everyone else around him.

She frowned at the girl in the Armani dress about to go
to a jerk's birthday party. Three weeks she'd been back and
it felt like a life sentence—the only bright light her divorce
decree, uncontested and greased along by her father. So
many times she'd had her phone out and in her hand, ready
to call Thomas and give him the good news. The corners
of his eyes would crinkle into his beautiful smile and he'd
probably hug her. Thomas was big on hugging, and she
missed that more than she could say.

Resisting had been frighteningly hard. *"Be sure of what
you want,"* Thomas had said, and that's what she was
doing; thinking this through, feeling it out. Three weeks of
doing little else but thinking, and keeping Ryan at arm's

length. He was getting impatient with her, but she stayed firm. She couldn't think when her life resembled a revolving door of men.

Tonight her father was sending a car to whisk her to Ryan's birthday celebration. It would be an event worthy of a Gold Coast prince. A family barbecue, he called it. Tiffany snorted loudly. Only if you considered the work of one of Chicago's biggest chefs manning an open flame to be a family barbecue.

She stared hard at her reflection. How did a student dress for a family barbecue?

The party was in full swing when she got there.

"Jeans, darling?" Ryan's mother enveloped her in a cloud of Chanel. "How very modern of you."

"Hi, Patti," she greeted the other woman, kissing first one cheek and then another.

"Ryan is outside, pressing the flesh." Patti tucked her arm through Tiffany's and towed her through the house toward their huge, manicured garden. A woman of Patti's age came down the hall toward them.

"Val, darling." Patti pulled her to a stop. "I don't believe you've met Ryan's Tiffany." She made a graceful motion as Tiffany and Val greeted each other politely. Tiffany wasn't Ryan's anything, but Patti and her father both suffered from the same strain of deafness. "Val is one of Ryan's work associates. She's been with the company for years. The place wouldn't run without her."

Val inclined her head and made small noises of denial. Nobody, including Val, was convinced she meant it.

"Isn't darling Tiffany daring, Val?" Patti tittered. "She is making us all look overdressed in her jeans."

Val's gaze swept her from head to toe. "Of course, Patti,

if we had that body, we would also be wearing jeans. Whose are they, Tiffany?"

"Walmart's."

Val and Patti froze and then broke into laughter.

"Such a sense of humor." Val chuckled. "I can see right away why Ryan adores you as he does. He talks about you all day in the office. Tiffany this and Tiffany that until we are all quite terrified to meet you." Oh, God, she might puke, any second now. Thomas would be laughing his ass off.

They moved through the vast living room, tastefully decorated in earth tones. A flower arrangement blocked the view of the garden, but the rise and fall of conversation drifted through the open bank of glass doors. Fantastic smells floated in with the sound of glasses and laughter. Spare ribs. Tiffany took a deep breath. Thank God, her jeans had a bit of give in them.

Through the glass doors onto a patio spanning the entire length of the house they went. People flitted like exotic birds amongst the lush greens and vivacious flora of the garden. The smell of money hung heavy in the air, brought to her on the back of expensive colognes and perfumes. Val and Patti kept up a polite flow of small talk, barely noticing, or needing, her contribution. Sedately dressed wait staff slid through the crowd like ghosts.

Tiffany snagged a glass of champagne from the tray extended to her and followed the other women deeper into the throng. Patti stopped constantly, making introductions and drawing people into her orbit for a few moments before drifting on again. "Ryan has been waiting for you," Patti whispered in her ear.

"Where is he?" She needed to wish him happy birthday.

"Over there." Patti waved. "Holding court, as he does."

"Excuse me." She drifted around Patti and swapped her glass for a full one.

"Call me, Tiffany," a voice called. "I would love to hear all about the wedding plans." That would be the shortest conversation on earth. Her father had kept the news of their broken almost engagement strictly on the down-low. And she'd let him. After their plane ride, she'd stopped fighting him. Out loud, at least. This was her thinking to do, and she needed to do it on her own.

Tiffany approached Ryan, who stood beneath a white awning beside the pool, in the center of at least a dozen people his age. A table behind him peeped out from under the weight of an immense amount of ribbon and wrapping. Shit, she hadn't brought a gift. Well, it wasn't his actual birthday. That was still a few days away, and she would do something then.

"Tiffany." Ryan's voice cut across the general noise, and she looked up. He strode toward her, smiling like the happy prince that he was. "I wondered when you were going to get here." Leaning forward, he kissed her on the mouth, tugging her close to him. "I missed you."

Gently she disengaged from his grip. "You saw me yesterday."

"Yesterday was days ago. I have a surprise for you."

Tiffany drained her glass. Another tray appeared by magic and she placed her empty on it and snagged another.

"Nice jeans," Ryan murmured.

"Thanks." The champagne soothed the words down her throat.

"I thought you were going to wear the Armani," he said, his gaze drifting over her outfit.

There must be a hole in the bottom of her glass, because this one emptied faster than the last. "Nope, changed my mind."

"Is everything all right?" Ryan drifted closer and kept his voice pitched only for her.

She took a leaf out of Thomas's book and answered a question with a question. "Why do you ask?"

"I don't know." The skin puckered between Ryan's brows. "Your outfit, the way you're acting. You don't seem yourself." Which struck her as very funny because she'd never felt more like herself. "Do we need to talk?" Ryan gave her the therapist voice, along with the grave expression.

She almost stuck her tongue out at him. "No."

What would she say anyway? *I think I may be in love with someone else. I'm just waiting until I'm sure.* Was that what she was doing? Waiting? Her heels caught in the grass and she stopped.

Ryan slipped his arm around her waist and guided her into a group of people. Most of them she knew, but a few of the faces were strange. Ryan performed the introductions.

Her face contracted into a polite smile as required. Her mouth opened and closed and made the appropriate responses. This must be one of those out-of-body experiences. Like she sat at the top of the awning and looked down at herself.

"Princess." Her father's voice dragged her back to the present. He leaned forward to kiss her. His gaze drifted over her hair and down, taking in everything. He was too well aware of the interest around them to frown, but his censure rose like a wall between them. "Really, darling, you could have made an effort."

"It's a barbecue," she said. And she was so tired of playing dress-up.

He merely lifted one brow. "I taught you better than that," he said. "Ryan has a surprise planned for you."

Tiffany didn't like the sound of that. "What?"

Her father shook his head, but gave her left hand a heavy stare.

Across the lawn, Patti caught her eye and gave her a wink.

Ah, hell no. She had better be reading this wrong.

"Tiffany?"

"Princess?"

She hadn't realized she'd moved physically until she looked up and saw her father and Ryan watching her, wearing identical quizzical expressions. Her feet took over and put another step between them and her. "I need to go."

"What are you talking about?" Her father took a step nearer. She took two more back. Twenty minutes down the highway. After three weeks of racking her brain, the answer beamed down at her.

"You're kidding, right?" Ryan frowned in confusion.

"No." She shook her head. "I need to go."

"You can't go." Ryan glanced between her and the people around them.

Sensing blood in the water, several conversations stopped and heads turned to them.

"I can." And she could. The car her father had sent would be waiting to take her home or wherever she wanted to go. "And I am."

Ryan turned to her father. "Carter?"

Her father closed the distance between them. His smile didn't move but his expression went glacial. "Don't be silly, Princess. You're making a scene and embarrassing Ryan and me. Pull yourself together."

She was together, more together than she'd ever been: a little bit princess, a little bit Delilah, a touch of Wild Tiffany, and a large helping of geek. She didn't have to be one or the other. Didn't need to carve herself into pie pieces and judge one as suitable and the rest not good enough.

Ryan glanced from her to her father, his expression clouded. She felt genuinely bad for him. Her father was right. She was making a scene and embarrassing Ryan. "I'll speak to you later," she said to Ryan. "There is something I have to do."

"Ryan?" Patti appeared beside her son. "What's going on? Where is Tiffany going?"

"I'm sorry," Tiffany said to Ryan. She was doing a shitty thing to him. But it was him or her when it came right down to it. "I'll call you later."

The I-90 and then the 94, and twenty minutes later, she'd be there.

"Tiffany." Her father's voice followed her across the lawn. Her heels clacked loudly over the marble of the patio. People made way for her as she hurried past.

"Tiffany." Her father chased her into the ornate living room. He caught her arm and brought her to a halt. Tightening his grip, he tugged her through the nearest door. As soon as the library door shut, his urbane expression morphed into fury. "What the hell do you think you're doing? Ryan has it all planned—the ring, the band, everything. You are not leaving."

Yup, that's pretty much what she'd thought. "I'm sorry about that, but you should have spoken to me about this first."

"It's a surprise. He's going to ask you to marry him," her father said.

Tiffany stared at him before she found the right words. "I'm not going to marry Ryan."

"Of course you are." Her father adjusted the cuffs on his shirt with a snap. "You are going to stay here, get your ring, smile prettily, and behave."

It wasn't really his fault. Her father had been getting his way for so many years. It would never occur to him that this had changed, because her father had selective hearing to go along with that selective vision. All her life, he'd been carefully whittling away the bits of her that he didn't want until she was left a two-dimensional dress-up doll who always felt like she belonged nowhere.

"Dad," Tiffany said. "I'm twenty-six. I don't think anyone needs to tell me how to behave."

He reeled back as if she'd hit him. Tiffany's heart squeezed. She didn't want to hurt him. She didn't want to hurt anyone.

"That's just the problem, Tiffany." Her father's mouth tightened into a nasty line. "You don't think, and when you do, you fuck everything up." It hurt so much she gasped. Tears stung the back of her eyelids. Her father's expression went immediately contrite. "Princess." He took a step toward her. "Now look what you made me say. You made me so angry, I went and said something awful to you."

"No." Tiffany evaded his outstretched hand. "You don't get a free pass on that one, Daddy. You also don't get to think for me. Not anymore."

For one glorious week she'd been gathering her parts into a whole. And she'd liked that whole Tiffany. Her legs wobbled as she walked toward the door. "I don't want to fight with you," she said over her shoulder. "I love you, Dad, but I can't be your princess anymore."

"What does that mean?" Her father's brows thundered down. "I don't even understand what that means. I don't understand any of this."

"I'll explain it all." Tiffany pulled open the door. Her hands were sweating so badly, the handle almost slipped out of her grip. Now whole Tiffany wanted something, not to complete her picture or fix her together, but to have all she wanted, all she deserved. Thomas Hunter was first on the list. "After I do what I need to do."

The problem with being a princess was that they spent a lot of time waiting for their princes. Rapunzel in her tower. Sleeping Beauty behind her forest of thorns. Even Cinderella waited for the prince to come to her.

Fuck that.

Chapter Thirty-Four

A man answered Tiffany's knock.

Hello! Tall, dark, handsome, linebacker shoulders and filling out a pair of faded jeans like a cover model. Blue, blue eyes registered, beautiful eyes just like Thomas. This must be Josh. She was so nervous she couldn't hear a word past the roaring in her ears. She stared at his mouth, trying to make sense of what he said.

"Can I help you?"

Relief made her head spin. She could handle that question. "Josh?"

The corner of his severe mouth twitched slightly. "No, I'm Richard. Josh is inside."

Oh. My. God. This was not even the hot brother? Mind blown. "I'm Tiffany." The strap of her overnight bag slipped against her sweaty palm, so she didn't offer her hand to him. "I'm a friend of Thomas's."

"Ah," said Richard, in a tone that made her think this was not exactly news to him. The slight tilt around one corner of his mouth widened into a *holy hell* smile that hit her straight in the male appreciation department of her girl brain. "He's inside." He stepped aside to allow her to enter. "Can I take your bag?"

"Yes. No. I'm not sure." She had to give him points for not laughing in her face. He merely looked grave, polite, and patient. This one was the doctor. Maybe he was used to crazy people in his work. "What I mean is, I don't know how long I'm staying."

"Yes." He nodded sagely. "But you're probably staying long enough to give your arm a rest. Perhaps even long enough to have a glass of water or—dare we hope—a glass of wine."

She stared at him. Shit, he was joking. Tiffany broke into an agonizingly high-pitched titter of laughter. "I'm a little nervous." Because, at this point, what else was she going to say? She stood in Thomas's family home making a complete dork of herself. Confessing to nerves could only be an improvement.

"I would recognize a pair of Jimmys anywhere," said a second male voice.

Tiffany turned and forgot to breathe.

"I'm Josh," said the Man God. "And you must be Tiffany. Man, are we glad to see you." She clearly must have tripped into a parallel dimension because Man God grabbed her and engulfed her in a hug that was all muscle and incredible-smelling male.

"Jesus," said Richard. "It's a conditioned response, like Pavlov's dog."

Tiffany blinked away the daze over Josh's shoulder.

Richard shook his head and glared at his brother. "Any woman breathing and he flirts."

"I'm just friendly," Josh said, pulling away from her. He kept his hands on her shoulders and surveyed her from head to toe. "He said you were beautiful."

"Who?" Blue was such a mundane description for that particular blend of sky and velvet midnight of Josh's eyes.

Any time her brain decided to check back in would be good with her.

"Thomas."

"He did?" Again with the squeak. As far as first impressions went, she'd pretty much blown this one.

Josh looked at his brother. "Does he know?"

"Not yet." Richard grinned.

"I'll get the camera," Josh said. "You take Tiffany to run the gauntlet."

"Um . . . can I just talk to Thomas?" She had totally lost control of the situation.

Richard shook his head with an apologetic look on his face. "Unfortunately, the whole family is here, and they'd have my guts if I let you go without meeting them."

"Really?"

"Yeah." He shrugged. "You picked a good day to show up."

Tiffany didn't think she could have picked a worse one. She needed to talk to Thomas, alone and quietly. The only thing she knew for sure was what she was doing there. How Thomas would react remained to be seen.

She was going to barf. Not even in the swimsuit section of her beauty pageant days had she been this nervous. She wanted her book so badly her fingers curled around an invisible pen.

Richard used the opportunity to guide her through the entrance hall and into a large kitchen. Home. The kitchen breathed home. On one side of a huge central table, a blond woman sat with an infant in her arms. Another woman of about the same age but shorter and with the most outrageous head of hair leaned with her hips against the counter. An older woman sat feeding a toddler. As one they turned to stare at her.

Run, screamed her brain. One foot moved to get started,

but Richard's hand pressed firmly into the small of her back. "This is Tiffany."

All the women perked up and their scrutiny got even keener.

"Tiffany." Richard tugged her farther into the room. "This is my mother, Donna."

"Pleased to meet you."

"Over there is Josh's wife, Holly."

"I'm not anyone's wife," said Holly.

Donna threw Holly an evil grin. "Not yet."

"Pleased to meet you," Tiffany whispered into the building silence.

"And that's Lucy," Richard said with all the pride of a man unveiling his lifetime's achievement.

"Pleased to meet you," Tiffany whispered for the third time. God, how much lamer was she going to get before this was over?

"Hey, Tiffany." Holly smiled at her. "Has Josh seen your shoes yet?"

"Yes."

"He's going to love you."

She had no idea what to say, so she gave a weak sort of smile.

"And don't let Donna intimidate you, she does that to all the new women in her son's lives." Holly shot a mischievous grin at Donna, who raised her eyebrows serenely.

"Welcome, Tiffany." Donna got to her feet. Instead of taking her outstretched hand, Tiffany found herself tugged into a warm embrace of lemon and vanilla. The older woman released her and stepped back, cupping Tiffany's face in her palms. "I know somebody who is going to be very glad to see you."

Tiffany blinked away the tears. "Really?"

"Really," Donna said.

"Tiffany?"

She froze. Her legs refused to move. Her gaze sought Donna's again. Reassurance filled the other woman's eyes. Tiffany looked past her at the blond woman at the table. Lucy gave her a smile and a small wink. Holly managed a wide grin.

Thomas stood behind her, like a force of nature. Finally, she turned.

AH! The element of surprise, she read across his chest. A smile started deep inside her and oozed into her chest, over her throat, and onto her mouth. "You're such a geek."

"Hey, Barbie." He grinned back at her.

She threw back her head and laughed. This was Thomas. Thomas with his dumb T-shirts and his huge smile. Thomas who bought her books and wanted her to read the naughty parts out loud. Thomas who always saw her and not what he wanted to see. Her Thomas.

And then his arms were around her and her feet left the ground. Her Jimmy Choos dangled somewhere about halfway between his feet and his knees as he pulled her tight against him.

For the first time in three weeks, Tiffany breathed. She clung to the solid width of his shoulders and let herself feel happy.

He tilted his head, his mouth finding hers.

"Thomas," she said against the warm, press of his lips. "Your family."

"They all know how this is done." He kissed her and she didn't care anymore. It all melted away in the taste of warm man and spice. She wrapped her arms around his head and pressed into his kiss.

"I guess this means she's staying for dinner," a man said. It could have been Richard or Josh, she had no idea.

Tiffany broke the kiss, laughing. Her face went hot, but she kept her gaze on Thomas. "Am I?"

Thomas's huge smile curled around the corners of his mouth. "Damn straight, you are. And for a lot longer than that."

"I only brought a small bag," she said.

"We have stores." He cupped her face in his big palms. "Josh can even take you to the sort you like."

"Okay."

He stared at her as if he couldn't get enough of the sight of her. "Stay forever."

"Let's start with today and see what happens." It was all so new, she didn't want to jinx it or rush it and make it all go shitty. What they had was new and shiny and beautiful.

"Okay," he said. "But just so you know, I'm going for forever."

"Okay."

Epilogue

Tiffany stared out the passenger window as Thomas parked the truck and looked over at her. "You all set?"

"Yup." The quadrangle in front of a set of wide stone steps was awash in people. Young people marching about like they knew where they were going and what they were doing there. She swallowed and rubbed her palms on the legs of her jeans.

"You got your lunch?" Thomas asked.

She held up her Louis Vuitton mini tote. "Yup."

"You know, you could buy something on campus."

"I could." She dredged up a weak smile. "But that would be over five dollars every day, and you know I'm on a budget now."

"I know, baby." He leaned over and took her hand. He gave it a warm squeeze that she felt all the way to her churning tummy. A pretty blond girl laughed and chatted over her shoulder at another pretty blonde. So young and eager and full of life.

Who was she kidding? She must be mad. "Remind me why I'm doing this."

"You know why you're doing this." Thomas lifted

her limp hand and gave it a kiss. "Want me to walk you to class?"

Very tempting, but no. She shook her head. "I'm going to do this on my own."

"Yes, you are."

"Right." She blew out a long breath and reached for the door handle. She stopped and turned back to him. "How do I look?"

"Beautiful," he said. "Always."

God, she loved this man. Tiffany launched herself at him.

Thomas caught her against his chest, his hand coming up to grip the back of her head.

The rush of heat took her by surprise every time. Tiffany gave herself a small moment and let the taste and feel of him wash over her. She broke the kiss and brushed her fingers over the pillow of his bottom lip. "Save that thought for later."

"You know it." He gave her the bedroom eyes that shot straight into her pants. "Your place or mine tonight?"

"Mine," she said. "I'll probably have homework."

"I'll bring dinner."

"You're on," she said. "But no more pizza. I'm heading toward bigger jeans at a scary rate."

"Looks good on you."

Such a dog. Tiffany rolled her eyes and opened the door.

"Love you, babe," he called.

"Love you, too." And she stepped out of the truck.

Thomas watched her walk away. She looked about eighteen in her jeans and T-shirt, her backpack thrown over one shoulder. His chest grew tight. He was so fucking proud of her it hurt.

Even her stubborn insistence she keep her own place made him want to glow with pride. She wanted her own place. She wanted to experience what it was like to be independent. As much as he wanted her under his roof, tucked in next to him all day, he understood. Tiffany had tackled some major changes in the last year. They spent every night together anyway. That would be enough for now. But he had plans and she knew about them, and she was totally on board. Another of his partners was working out of Zambia while Thomas managed the business side from Chicago. As soon as Tiffany got her degree, they would head that way together. She wanted to focus on those countries that had been receiving assistance from the former Soviet Union.

After that, who knew? Wherever life took them next, and whatever new adventure was waiting. As long as they went together.

His gaze tracked the sexy swish of her ass as she climbed the steps. He had no idea how he'd gotten so damn lucky. A group of young dickheads lounged around the base of the steps. And they had their leers on his girl's ass. He rolled down the window. Time to make his presence felt.

"Oh, my God." The pretty blond girl who was talking to her friend dashed up the steps after Tiffany. "Excuse me?"

Tiffany stopped and turned.

Thomas leaned forward to hear what happened next.

"I, like, love your shoes," said the girl.

A smile spread across his face.

Tiffany tossed back her mane of glossy black hair and smiled back. "Thank you, but they're so last season."

"Yeah, but they're Jimmys, so that totally doesn't count."

His smile widened into a great goofy grin.

"Are you new?" the blonde asked.

"It's my first day." Tiffany smiled, looking so adorable and unsure of herself, he nearly sprinted out of the truck and tucked her into his arms. He was learning to control this desire to pick her up and bundle her in silk every day of her life. It had taken her this long to get away from her father's suffocating brand of love, the last thing she needed was Thomas taking up where he'd left off. Her dad was coming around. He'd sulked for a few months, and that had been hell on Tiffany. But she'd held to her line, and when Carter finally got around to calling, she'd given him love and understanding. She also held firm on not taking any money from her father.

"Oh, don't worry about it," the blonde said. "You're going to love it here." She turned and yelled to the group of boys, "Hey, guys, come and meet"—she stopped and turned back to Tiffany—

"Tiffany."

The horny little shits got up those steps so fast they could get altitude sickness. Thomas suppressed the desire to bang their heads together.

"Is that, like, your boyfriend?" Blond girl motioned over to him, and Thomas waved one hand.

His lady turned and looked at him. Her beautiful face split into a smile that, honest to God, made his chest hurt.

"Yes," she said. "That's my man."

Keep reading for an excerpt from

POSITIVELY PIPPA,

the first in a new series from
Sarah Hegger!
Available in Summer, 2017
from Zebra Books.

"Aren't you—?"

"No." Not anymore she wasn't. Pippa snatched her boarding pass from the check-in attendant and tugged her baseball cap lower over her eyes. Couldn't Kim Kardashian help a girl out and release another sex tape or something? Anything to get Pippa away from the social media lynch mob. She kept her head down until she found her gate, and chose the seat furthest away from the other passengers waiting to board the flight to Salt Lake City. Latest copy of *Vogue* blocking her face, she flipped through the glossy pages. At least she wasn't on *Vogue*'s shit list yet and they still sent her an early copy. Probably not for much longer.

She peeped over the top of her magazine and straight into the narrowed gaze of a woman three rows over. Pippa dropped the woman's gaze and went back to Vivienne Westwood bucking the trend.

The woman's eyes beamed into the top of her head across the airport lounge like those laser tracking things you saw on spy movies. Pippa buckled under the burn and slouched lower into her seat.

Look at that, Fendi was doing fabulous separates this season. And, really, Ralph Lauren, that's your idea of a plus size model? Stuff like this made her job so much harder. Her former job. Losing her show still clawed at her. Losing? Like she'd left the damn thing at Starbucks as she picked up her morning latte. More like her jackass ex with zero conscience had knocked it out of her hand. Framed, stitched up, wrongfully accused—judged, found guilty, and sentenced to months of public loathing wiping out all the years spent building her career. Burning sense of injustice aside, she was stuck in this thing until it went away.

Angry Woman lurked in her peripheral vision. Pippa risked another glance. Sweat slid down her sides and she tucked her elbows in tight.

Under an iron-gray row of rigidly permed bangs, the woman's eyes gathered heat. A housewife on a rampage.

Back to *Vogue*. The knot in her stomach twisted tighter, and she checked her cap. What the hell? A baseball cap and shades always worked for other celebrities. Why not her?

Angry Woman kept right on glaring.

This could go one of two ways. Either Angry Woman would come over and give her a piece of her mind on behalf of women everywhere, or she'd confine her anger to vicious staring and muttering. Maybe some head shaking. Please don't be a crusader for women. *Please, please, please.* After two weeks of glares, stares and condemnation, Pippa had gotten the message:

Pippa St. Amor, the woman America loves to hate.

Right now all she wanted was to sneak home and stay there until someone else topped her scandal. God, didn't *Vogue* have anything fresh? She'd make a list. Lists were good. Soothing. *Item one, run away from Angry Woman and hide in the bathroom. Item two, get your career back.* She moved *Item two* up to first place, where it had been since she left home at eighteen.

The woman lifted a phone and snapped a shot of Pippa.

Damn, she'd forgotten that option, this one by *far* the worst. She was no longer trawling the Internet for mentions of her name at this point. God, she hated Twitter. And

Facebook. And Instagram, and Vine, and whatever-the-hell new social torment site some asshat was thinking up right this minute. The ongoing public derision chipped off bits of her until she felt like an open nerve ending.

A friend huddled next to Angry Woman, long hair that was totally the wrong shade of brown and aged her by ten years at least. A cute, hip cut would do so much more for her face.

Pippa was getting it with double barrels now. Lips tight, matching twin spots of outraged color staining their cheeks as they whispered over the first woman's phone. They both wore mom jeans. Up until two weeks ago it had been her mission to deliver moms everywhere from jeans like that. Along with those nasty, out-of-shape T-shirts they sold in three-packs of "meh" colors that had no business existing on the color spectrum. Angry and Long Hair were so her demographic. They'd probably seen the original episode live and watched it over and over again on demand or something. Maybe even watching it right this minute on YouTube.

YouTube! She hated YouTube, too.

Why didn't they call her flight already and get her the hell out of here?

You didn't sleep with the boss, and especially not in television. For four years. Ray had always been a bit sneaky, but to annihilate her career to boost his own? She hadn't seen it coming. How stupid could you get?

Three minutes until boarding.

"Excuse me?"

Shit. So close. Two minutes and fifty-five seconds. Smile and look friendly. "Yes."

Try not to look like you.

"You're that woman, aren't you?" Angry Woman narrowed

her eyes viciously, and Pippa leaned back in her chair, out of striking range.

"Hmm?"

"It is you." Long Hair got into the eye action with some lip pursing. "I watched every single one of your shows. I can't believe you said those things, and I—"

Two minutes, thirty seconds.

"—should be ashamed of yourself. What you said is a crime against women everywhere. You made that poor woman cry."

Of course they cried. They were supposed to cry. The shows were edited to make them cry even more, but not the time to point it out.

"Shocking. And cruel. You're just a . . . a nasty bitch." Angry Woman got the last word in. She'd been called worse. Recently, too, and it still stung.

A man in the row opposite turned to watch the action. The three teens beside him openly stared.

I didn't say it, people. Okay, she'd said it, but not like that. Editing, people. Creative editing—the scourge and savior of television celebrities worldwide. She could shout it across LAX and it still wouldn't do any good. Until the next scandal broke and hers was forgotten.

"This is a boarding call . . ."

Thank you, Jesus!

"I'm sorry, that's my flight." Pippa creaked a smile and gathered her things. Handbag, iPad, and coat. Her hands shook under the combined weight of several sets of eyes and she nearly dropped her phone.

No cabin baggage, not on this flight. Nope this flight she'd packed just about everything she owned into the two heaviest suitcases on the planet. Paid extra weight without an argument. Anything to get the hell out of LA and home to Philomene.

Phi would know what to do.

"Isaac, if the plumber needs quarter-inch pipe, get him quarter-inch pipe." Matt threw open the door to his truck as he half listened to another lame excuse. He could recite them by heart at this point anyway.

"No, I can't get the pipe. I'm at Phi's house now." He sighed as Isaac went with the predictable. "Yes, again, and I can't come now. You're going to have to fix this yourself."

He slammed his door and keyed off his phone. Damn, he missed the days of being able to slam a receiver down. Jabbing your finger at those little icons didn't have the same effect.

When God handed out brains to the Evans clan, he must have realized he was running low for the family allotment and been stingier with the youngest members. Between Isaac and their sister, Jo, there could only be a couple of functioning neurons left. And their performance, like a faulty electrical circuit, flickered in and out.

He grabbed his toolbox from the back of the truck. This had to be the ugliest house in history. As if Hogwarts and the Addams family mansion had a midair collision and vomited up Phi's Folly.

His chest swelled with pride as he stared at it. He'd built every ugly, over the top, theatrical inch of this heap of stone. He'd bet he was the only man alive who could find real, honest to God, stone gargoyles for downspouts. Not the plaster molding kind. Not for Diva Philomene St. Amour. Nope, she wanted them carved out of stone and mounted across the eaves like the front row of a freak show.

"Hey, Matt," a voice called from the stables forming one side of the semi-circular kitchen yard.

"Hey yourself." He couldn't remember the name of Phi's latest rescue kid doing time in her kitchen yard. Kitchen yard! In this century. Diva Philomene wanted a kitchen yard, so a kitchen yard she got, along with her stables.

"I want a building to capture the nobility of their Arabian ancestors thundering across the desert." She'd got it. Heated floors, vaulted ceilings, and pure cedar stalls—now housing every ratty, mismatched, swaybacked nag the local humane society couldn't house and didn't want to waste a bullet on. A smile crept onto his face. You had to love the crazy old broad.

He skirted the circular herb garden eating up the center of the kitchen yard. A fountain in the shape of a stone horse trough trickled happily. He'd have to remind her to drain it and blow the pipes before winter. He didn't want to replace the piping again next spring.

The top half of the kitchen door stood open and he unlatched the bottom half before stepping into the kitchen. The AGA range gave off enough heat to have sweat sliding down his sides before he took two steps. He opened the baize door to the rest of the house and yelled, "Phi!"

He hadn't even known what a baize door was at nineteen, but the Diva had educated him because she wanted one and it became his headache to get her one.

"Mathieu!" The Frenchifying of his name was all the warming he got before Philomene appeared at the top of her grand, curving walnut staircase. Thirty-two rises, each six foot in length and two feet wide leading from the marble entrance hall to the gallery above.

The soft pink of the sun bled through the stained glass windows and bathed the old broad in magic. Her purple muumuu made a swishing noise as she descended, hands out-stretched, rings glittering in the bejeweled light. "Darling."

Hell, she made his teeth ache. "Hold onto the railing, Phi, before you break your neck." It had taken a crew of eight men to put that railing in, and nearly killed the car-penter to carve a dragon into every inch of it.

She pressed a kiss on both his cheeks with a waft of the same heavy, musky perfume she'd always worn. She smelled like home. "You came."

"Of course, I came." He bent and returned her embrace. "That's how this works. You call, I drop everything and come."

A wicked light danced in her grass green eyes, still bright and brilliant beneath the layers and layers of purple goo and glitter. She'd been a knockout in her youth, still had some of that beautiful woman voodoo clinging to her like sun motes all around her. If you doubted that for an instant, there were eight portraits and four times that many photos in this house to set you right. Or you could just take a look at Pippa. If you could catch a quick glance as she flew through town. He made it his business to grab an eyeful when he could.

"I am overset, Mathieu, darling." She pressed her hand to her gem-encrusted bosom.

"Of course you are." The Diva never had a bad day or a problem. Nope, she was overset, dismayed, perturbed, discomposed and on the occasion her dishwasher broke down, discombobulated.

"It is that thing in the kitchen." She narrowly missed taking his eye out with her talons as she threw her hand at the baize door.

Her kitchen might look like medieval reenactment, but it was loaded for bear with every toy and time saving device money could buy—all top of the line. "What thing, Phi?"

"The water thingy."

"The faucet?"

She swept in front of him, leading the way into the kitchen like Caesar entering Rome in triumph. "See." He dodged her hand just in time. "It drips incessantly and disturbs my beauty rest."

He clenched his teeth together so hard his jaw ached. He ran a construction company big enough to put together four separate crews and she called him for a dripping faucet. "I could have sent one of my men around to fix that. A plumber."

"But I don't want one of your men, darling." She beamed her megawatt smile at him. "I want you."

There you had it. She wanted him and he came. Why? Because he owed this crazy, demanding, amazing woman everything, and the manipulative witch knew it. He shrugged out of his button down shirt and pulled his undershirt out of his jeans. He was going to get wet and he'd be damned if he got faucet grunge all over his smart shirt.

Phi took the shirt from him and laid it tenderly over the back of one of her kitchen chairs. "This is a very beautiful shirt, Matt."

"I'm a busy and important man now, Phi. A man with lots of smart shirts."

She grinned at him, and stroked the shirt. "I am very proud of you, Matt."

Damn it all to hell, if that didn't make him want to stick out his chest like the barnyard rooster strutting across

Phi's kitchen yard. He turned the faucet on and then off again. No drip. "Phi?"

"It's underneath." She wiggled her fingers at the cabinet.

He got to his knees and opened the doors. Sure enough, a small puddle of water gathered on the stone flags beneath the down pipe. Good thing Phi had insisted on no bottoms to her kitchen cabinets. It had made it a bitch to get the doors to close without jamming on the stone floor, but right now it meant he wouldn't be replacing cabinets in his spare time.

"You should be out on a date," Phi said from behind him.

"If I was out on a date, Phi, I wouldn't be here fixing your sink."

"Yes, you would."

Yeah, he would. He turned off the water to the sink. "Have you got some towels or something?"

She bustled into the attached laundry and reappeared with an armload of fluffy pink towels.

Wheels crunched on the gravel outside the kitchen and Phi dropped the towels on the floor next to him. She tottered over to the window to stare. A huge smile lit her face and she gave off one of those ear-splitting trills that had made her the world's greatest dramatic soprano. Everyone, from the mailman to a visiting conductor got the same happy reception.

He leaned closer to get a better look at the pipes beneath the sink. Were those scratch marks on the elbow joint? Neat furrows all lined up like someone had done that on purpose. He crawled into the cabinet and wriggled onto his back. They didn't make these spaces for men his size.

"Mathieu?" Phi craned down until her face entered his field of vision. Her painted on eyebrows arched across her parchment pale face. "I have a visitor."

"Is that so?" What the hell, he always played along.

"Indeed." Her grin was evil enough to have him stop his tinkering with the wrench in midair. "I thought you might like to know about this visitor."

The kitchen door opened. A pair of black heels tapped into view. The sort of shoes a man wanted to see wrapped around his head, and at the end of a set of legs he hadn't seen since the day they tripped out of Ghost Falls and left the town poorer for their loss. His day bloomed into one of those eye-aching blue sky and bright sunlight trips into happy.

Welcome home, Pippa Turner.